S0-BYN-510

Refined

at

Rock Bottom

Kristen Brown

Refined at Rock Bottom

Copyright © 2013 by Kristen Brown

All Rights Reserved. No part of this document may be reproduced or transmitted in any form or by any means, electronic, mechanical, photocopying, recording, or otherwise, without prior written permission of the author.

Cover background by Lora liu via Shutterstock.com

Cover image by Louella938 via Shutterstock.com

When I thought, "My foot slips,"
your steadfast love, O LORD, held me up.
When the cares of my heart are many,
your consolations cheer my soul.

Psalm 94:18-19

Prologue

Jeb watched the solitary female figure walking down the beach silhouetted against the dusky sky. He had missed seeing her during the winter months but now the mystery woman was back just as the hint of spring was on this cold, clear March evening. He never spoke to her; he didn't think she even noticed him. She was too far away for Jeb to see her face clearly but he suspected she was as lovely as she was lonely. The slow, heavy-hearted footsteps she took revealed her pensive mood as she stopped occasionally to gaze out over the water seemingly lost in thought.

Something about her made him want to go speak with her. But Jeb was afraid if he did that she wouldn't come to his beach any more. And he'd become fond of her in an odd way. Each time that he saw her out here on the sandy frontage he called his backyard he prayed for her, believing that somehow his prayers were touching her heart in a way he might never know. He wanted to know. But sometimes God worked in quietly mysterious ways and he decided this was one of those times.

Leaning forward on the driftwood log he was perched upon, Jeb bowed his head and prayed silently for the sad, auburn haired-woman that roamed his beach and had somehow, unbeknownst to her, touched his heart.

Chapter 1

The sun was making a rare appearance this late April morning after weeks of cold and rain. Great gusts blew in off the Atlantic, bringing with them pungent ocean smells and a salty sea spray that Kitty Appleton knew well. She had lived here in Rock Bottom, Maine her entire forty-nine years and never tired of the gentle tides that crept in when the ocean was calm, or the angry tirade of crashing waves when it wasn't. Just like life, they ebbed and flowed constantly and reminded Kitty that even at Rock Bottom there was always hope that tomorrow would bring in the new tide.

For the past two years, Kitty's life seemed to be at low tide. Bill, her husband of nearly twenty-eight years, walked out on her for a younger woman without warning. At least there hadn't been any sign that she noticed at the time; Kitty could admit her numerous shortcomings easily enough and naivety was at the top of the list. The entire community of fifteen hundred residents would surely concur since most had known about Bill's affair with Leslie long before he announced he wanted out of their marriage. No amount of pleas or tears had any effect on her husband and she realized very quickly that her whole world changed in just a few short moments.

But Kitty wasn't one to hold a grudge. In a daze, she helped Bill pack up his things and then drove him to his new home. An ugly ranch house with no curb appeal. No flower beds lovingly tended by a woman's gentle touch or whimsical garden gnomes to brighten up the depressed brown lawn. What it lacked in appeal on the outside she guessed was compensated by what awaited him inside. Leslie was thirty-one, well-endowed and always up for a good time. Who could hold a candle to that, Kitty had wondered sadly as Bill slammed the car door on their life together.

She'd wallowed in self-pity for months with only Ben and Jerry for company. Then she'd decided to give happiness another chance when her lifetime hobby showed the potential to be a full-fledged career. Now she was a successful artist with her seascapes selling off faster than she could paint during tourist season and in demand in galleries as far away as Boston. It made being single bearable, knowing she was supporting herself for the first time in decades. Other than that, she couldn't find many pluses to her newfound single-dom. It was lonely; she hated eating and sleeping alone. There were of course her two cats that her oldest son Charlie had surprised her with right after Bill walked out. Charlie knew she needed company and the kittens had been his solution. Now her girls were her dear companions and snuggled with her most nights. But it wasn't quite the same as having Bill's warm body and soft snores next to her. Sometimes she woke up without her husband beside her and the sorrow would squeeze her heart so tightly she felt like she was surely suffocating. But time dulled the pain and those sad days were fewer and farther between. She had her work and her friends and family to keep her life full. God was still in control and she just needed to accept that this was what He wanted for her. If not, surely Bill would have been home by now instead of with Leslie.

"Afternoon Kitty," old Abel Howard called as he hobbled down the beach toward her. Today she was set up at one of her favorite spots to paint: the long, lonely stretch of Rockland Beach with a distant view of Rock Bottom Bay and all of its boat traffic to the right and miles of beach and jagged rock to the left. It was quiet this time of year with only locals venturing out this far. Kitty enjoyed the solitude it offered as she escaped into her work. With a brush in her hand and the unsurpassed beauty of the ocean all around her she easily became so absorbed in her work that time drifted by unnoticed. "Nice day for painting."

"Ayup. How's your missus?" Kitty asked, pausing with her brush mid-stroke.

"Still recovering and tired of being in bed. Insists I keep up my morning constitutional though I feel like I should stay with her."

"Tell her I'll stop by with some chicken soup this afternoon." The wind kicked up and Kitty tucked the errant strands of auburn hair back behind her ear.

"Thanks Kitty. You're a sweet girl," Abel told her. "Don't know how Bill could have left you and your wonderful cooking."

Kitty plastered a polite smile on her face. It's what she always did when Bill's name came up. "I still have my wonderful cooking at least."

Abel chuckled and patted Kitty on the shoulder before resuming his morning walk down the beach. "You'll be okay in time, love. Don't pay any mind to what folks say."

Kitty's heart sank as Abel resumed his morning walk down the beach. It was hard not to pay attention to what people said. In a town this size, she knew nearly everyone which in turn meant they knew her and all that she had been through. Most were supportive and sympathetic to her plight though the pitying glances sometimes made her feel worse. She oftentimes had to turn away before they saw how their well-intentioned pity was in fact hurtful. Deep down she knew they didn't mean to hurt her so she kept up a brave front and a silent demeanor lest she say anything to make it worse.

In time, they'd see that she was getting by, Kitty thought as she resumed the brisk strokes she used to capture the fluid movement of the waves. Everyone would see that she had moved on just as Bill had with Leslie. It was quite a shock when Bill had actually married Leslie as soon as the divorce was finalized. Kitty had held on to some ridiculous hope that eventually he would get over his mid-life crisis and come home to her where he belonged. Instead he married his business partner and now they ran the Bottom's Up Pub together. Their life was picture-perfect, just like the beautiful paintings Kitty did of Rock Bottom. She was doing her best to show the world that her life was fine, that she was over Bill, but it just wasn't enough based on Abel Howard's words.

Even she wasn't fooled.

"It's not fair," Kitty told the universe, pausing to stare up at the gulls squawking above her. The feelings of despair tried to take over but she shoved them back into the darkness from where they came; she was getting better at that. Best not to dwell on the past, Kitty reminded herself for the hundredth time. *Not my will but Thy will be done*, she prayed over and over and forced herself back to her artwork.

•

Kitty pulled up to the white cottage she called home just after four. She'd always loved this house. It belonged to her grandparents and when she and Bill bought it from them a year after getting married it came with happy memories of childhood days spent here. It was odd-shaped because of add-ons over generations and weather-worn from harsh Maine winters and the salty sea air but she loved it dearly. Maybe it was a little too big for just her now; Kitty didn't really need four chopped up bedrooms upstairs and an odd-shaped dining room built on the backside of the house years ago that she never used. But it was home and she would never leave.

She opened the gate and entered the large front yard that had taken decades to cultivate. Her grandmother had poured her heart into it for most of her life and when Kitty and Bill bought the house she continued her grandmother's work. It was still early yet but by summer the entire yard would be a mass of colorful blooms. Foxglove, asters, catmint and coneflowers were just a few of Kitty's favorites. There would be yards of cascading verbena covering the porch and the evergreen and lilac bushes encircling the house would be a splash of vibrant color against the white clapboard. A small maple tree leaned over the picket fence while a stone walkway led visitors through the lush landscape to the front door. It was a myriad of colors and textures and Kitty loved every single flower that had been lovingly planted over the years.

When she walked through the front door the phone was ringing and she hurried to answer it. "Hello?"

"Kitty dear, where have you been? I've tried calling you for hours," her mother's soft voice greeted her.

"I just walked in the door. I've been painting down at Rockland Beach."

"Oh. I was worried. But I suppose that was a good idea. Keeping busy is the best thing for you," her mother advised gently.

"I'm fine really." Her mother called every week and it was always the same worried tone. It didn't matter that Bill had been gone for two years. "Everything is great up here Mom, I promise. Jenny and Brad are all settled into their new house. Charlie and Bridget and the kids are doing wonderfully. Becca has a three point eight average this semester. And Teddy is Teddy I guess."

"I didn't call for an update on my grandchildren Kitty. I know they're all doing well because they all check in regularly. Well, except Teddy. I called to see how you are. I know it's your wedding anniversary this weekend and how hard it's going to be for you. Do you want your father and me to fly up for a visit?" Her parents lived the golden life in Florida. After sixty-five years of New England weather they had up and moved lock, stock and barrel to Boca Raton eight years ago. Now their days were filled with golf dates and playing pinochle at the club house in their senior community and Kitty was happy for them even though she missed them terribly. They visited every June for a month but it wasn't quite the same.

"No, mom. That isn't necessary. But it's terribly thoughtful of you."

"If you change your mind let us know. It's only Wednesday. We could catch a flight Friday morning. I'm just so worried about you Kitty. I know how hard this Saturday is going to be for you."

Bill left her the day before their twenty-eighth wedding anniversary. This Saturday would have marked their thirtieth anniversary. Instead of a day of celebration it was now the date on the calendar she dreaded the most. But she survived last year and she would do the same this time around. "Thank you Mom. I appreciate the offer. But I have plans."

"Oh? What will you be doing? Do you have a date?" her mother asked hopefully.

"No. It's the annual town rummage sale this weekend."

"Of course! I'd forgotten all about that. That should keep you busy. You'll have Liza Jane with you?"

"You know I don't do anything without Liza," Kitty said with forced cheer. "She'll get me though. Don't worry about me. And tell Dad not to worry either."

Before her mother could answer her father's voice appeared on the line and her mother's garbled words faded away. "Let me have the phone Ellen. Let me talk to my little girl. Kitty Cat, are you there?" her father asked in his booming voice.

"Hi Dad."

"You okay Kitty Cat?" He'd always called her that and the nickname still made her feel loved and special.

"I'm fine Dad, I promise."

"Don't you let that bum hurt you anymore. He's out of your life. Just forget him and move on. He never deserved you anyway."

Kitty knew her father meant well and swallowed the lump in her throat. "Thank you for saying that."

"I still wish you'd let me come up back then and knock some Christian love and humility in his backside with my size twelve *Holy Soles*." Her father continued his rant with a string of colorful phrases to describe Bill.

"Dad!" Kitty cringed.

"Joe!" She heard her mother's intake of breath and a strangled yelp from her father as the phone must have been yanked away. Her mother's scolding tone carried across the line. "I ought to wash your mouth out with soap and then do the same to my own ears."

Kitty heard her father grumbling good-naturedly in the background and could imagine her sweet and patient mother shaking her head in despair. "Pray for your father," her mother said sadly into the phone. "He thinks God actually allows fathers to say such things in these circumstances. Your ex-husband may be a donkey's behind but we aren't supposed to judge others."

"You're right of course Mom. And Bill wasn't all bad you know," Kitty said automatically. "I still wonder if I should have done more to save our marriage. Twenty-eight years is a lot to throw away."

"Oh Kitty," her mother sighed softly. "You've got to let go."

•

It was a cool and rainy Thursday morning and Kitty was happy her commute to work was so short. Just steps out her back door and across the lawn was her studio. Kitty flipped on the overhead light and then pushed the heat up. Her workshop was a twelve by fifteen barn that she had added all the necessary bells and whistles to make into a dream space. It was energy efficient and comfortable to work in year-round when inclement spring weather and harsh Maine winters kept her away from her beloved beach. It was also cheerful to be in thanks to the seaside mural of Rock Bottom she had done this past winter that encompassed three walls. It was so lifelike she almost felt like she was out on the sand when she sat here working for hours.

Kitty worked contentedly to the steady sound of rain pelting the roof, pausing for a brief lunch at noon comprised of a tuna sandwich which was shared with Petunia and Miss Tulip. They accompanied her back to the studio during a brief lull in the rain and watched her paint the reminder of the afternoon perched on the bench by the window. At five she put her paints and brushes away and darted through the raindrops with the girls back to the house to get cleaned up for her night out.

Every Thursday at seven o'clock the Rock Bottom Mystery Book Club met in the town library. Kitty started attending years ago and after Bill left she found it therapeutic to meet with the women who had become such an integral part of her life. It was the only social setting she really felt comfortable in now that she was single and she looked forward to it each week.

Kitty stood in front of the open closet doors in her bedroom determined to spruce herself up. The closet was still half-empty after all this time. She couldn't bring herself to take up Bill's half. Every room in the house had gone through a transformation after he left in an effort to embrace the changes in her life. But all the anger and tears couldn't compel her to take this last step. So she stared at the left half of the closet and considered her options while ignoring the empty right half.

Her wardrobe was plain and dreary, just like her. Lots of navy and beige as far as the eye could see. Kitty cringed. She hated beige. On impulse she yanked everything beige out of her closet and threw it in a pile on the chair while her two faithful felines watched in silence. Satisfied with the purge she turned back to her side of the closet. There wasn't much left. There was a nice soft pink cashmere sweater that made her feel feminine or her old blue tweed jacket that screamed *practical*. The pink sweater would emphasize the shapely figure she came by naturally, while the tweed always looked nice with her dark blue eyes. Both looked passable with the auburn hair she'd kept at shoulder length with soft feathery layers for years. Neither would be appreciated by anyone worthwhile.

Kitty sighed. Miss Tulip twinked and Petunia started washing herself. "I don't know why I even bother." She yanked out the tweed and shut the doors.

•

The weekly meeting of the Rock Bottom Mystery Book Club took place at the Rock Bottom Public Library, the smallest library in the county. The club was open to women of all ages but somehow had developed into a gathering of single women who hashed out book plots as fervently as they hashed over the local pickings of the male variety in Rock Bottom. There was a limited supply of the latter and most had been passed around the single women's circuit as often as the books they were discussing.

The library was within walking distance like nearly everything in The Bottom, as the locals affectionately called it. Kitty closed the gate with a click and started down the street towards town. The house was only a few blocks from the center of town and Kitty walked whenever weather permitted. She had always been an out-door person. When her kids were little they spent countless hours outside scouring the beaches for treasure. How many times had Charles and Teddy come running to her with seashells they had discovered washed up on the sand? Every find was exciting and new for them. She missed those days but didn't pine for them anymore. She had grandchildren to do those same things with now and that was just as good. When she took little Callie and Sam to the beach it was always a fun time for her. It made her feel young and alive chasing after them and sharing their joy.

There weren't sidewalks in Rock Bottom but there were worn paths along the narrow streets and dirt roads that Kitty knew by heart. She knew every inch of the town she'd been born in and never left. The furthest she'd been from Rock Bottom was to Bar Harbor for Teddy's college graduation three years ago. She hadn't left since. She was perfectly content to stay here and live each day as simply as the last.

That was one of the reasons Bill left her, she supposed. Because she was dull. Predictable.

Boring.

"I'm not dull," she argued with herself as she approached old Morgan and Myrtle Mason's place and waved to the couple sitting on the front porch. "I'm practical. What is wrong with that?"

"Evening Kitty," Morgan greeted her politely as he always did. "Fine weather for a walk now, isn't it?"

"Ayup," Kitty agreed. "Looks like we'll be having some warm weather for the rummage sale this weekend."

"Ayup," Morgan agreed. "Summer will be here 'afore we know it and those flatlanders will be underfoot."

"But the tourists sure help the local businesses," Kitty said as she kept walking. "And it's only for a few weeks anyway." Summer was fleeting here in southern Maine and while most locals didn't care for the outsiders, Kitty always thought it was nice having new people visit Rock Bottom. It was like showing off her home to company.

"Ever the optimist, aren't you Kitty?" Myrtle smiled, her face wrinkling. "I just love that about you dear."

"Most everyone does," Morgan agreed with his wife, watching a puff of smoke uncurl and disappear from his pipe. "Except that ex of hers. Poor little thing. She's still waiting on him, isn't she?"

"Hush Morgan!"

"True ain't it? Pining for the ex, aren't you Kitty? Wasting away walking on the beach all the time. It ain't healthy."

"I love the beach Morgan. You know that," Kitty said, plastering her polite smile on.

"The man ain't coming back. You got to know that now."

Myrtle's eyes sympathized with the woman outside her fence. "Sorry Kitty. He doesn't mean nothing by that."

"It's all right Myrtle," Kitty said as she picked up her pace. "No harm done."

"If it helps we think Bill was a fool for leaving ya!" Morgan called after her and she flashed a quick wave in his general direction as she scurried down the lane and out of sight behind a row of overgrown junipers.

•

In the library Kitty spotted local librarian and good friend of many years Annie Goodwin putting some books away in the small non-fiction row. Together they had survived book drives and fund-raisers and walk-a-thons for the community over the last two decades. Annie was the one who started the book club and led the discussions. "Hi Annie."

The tall woman turned and acknowledged the greeting with a nod. She wasn't a woman who wasted words when they weren't needed. Annie was a plain woman in her mid-forties with long brown hair that was always neatly pinned to the top of her head. Her big brown eyes hid behind retro-shaped eyeglasses, the only thing of interest on her face in her opinion. She devoted her life to maintaining and expanding the tiny Rock Bottom Public Library and her greatest passion was working with the Historical Society to preserve old buildings throughout the county. Annie never married and had a black pug named Arnold who came to work with her every day. Arnold, in turn, enjoyed all the attention he got during the children's story hour on Friday mornings, books on tape and napping in the back room on one of the couches during the day.

The five other ladies that completed the book club were already settled in the cheery reading room in the back of the old library. It was painted a faded yellow and the wood plank floors were crooked. There were two red flowery sofas and white wicker tables and chairs circling the room. A large window let the fading light stream through unhindered by the lacey curtains Annie had hung there a dozen years ago at least. Kitty sank onto the red sofa closest to the door and settled herself next to her best friend in the world, Liza Jane Holbrook.

Kitty and Liza Jane had been best friends since kindergarten. They knew everything there was to know about each other, including each other's actual weight. Liza was taller than Kitty by two inches with an athletic build, hazel eyes and more energy than two twenty-year-olds. Kitty trusted Liza Jane implicitly in all matters and knew her dearest friend would always be there for her. Liza was as much a part of her life as the sun rising in the morning and setting each night and for the gift of such a deep, abiding friendship Kitty was truly grateful.

Liza leaned over to Kitty now. "Hangover Hazel told me that Bill and Leslie were snapping at each other at the Bottom's Up last night." Liza nodded to show Kitty she was serious and her ample bottle-blond curls bounced with the motion. "Probably about selling the Bottom's Up again but you never know. Maybe there's trouble in paradise," she said gleefully.

Everyone knew that local developer Lionel Trescott had been trying to buy the Bottom's Up Pub for years. Bill's family owned half and the Abbott family owned the other half; neither side had ever shown any interest in selling the family business. Until Leslie inherited her family's half and appeared to be tempted by the dollar signs Trescott was flashing in front of her, which put Bill in an uncomfortable position: stand firm on keeping the business that should be passed on to his own sons or give into the pressure his new young wife was placing on him to take the money and run. Rumor had it that Kitty's ex had recently and reluctantly agreed to go along with Leslie's plan to sell but that was unconfirmed speculation in Kitty's opinion.

"Well." Kitty had to think carefully before speaking. She didn't want the ladies at the book club to think poorly of her so the right response was imperative. "It's really none of my business Liza Jane. But if that's what they want and they end up selling then maybe I should just be happy for him."

"Happy for him?" Liza Jane sputtered. "He's a lying cheating reptile who ripped your heart out and stomped on it after three decades of you catering to his every whim. Don't you dare be happy for him!"

"It's not going to do me any good to be petty, Liza Jane. They seem happy and so am I." She tried to sound convincing.

"But what about the town?" Annie wanted to know. "What will happen if they sell it?"

"Supposedly Trescott wants to take the Bottom's Up and renovate it. It's a piece of history that ought to be restored to its former glory," Martha Stimple said brightly. She was a portly woman in her late fifties with grey fluffy hair, twinkly blue eyes and an annoyingly cheerful disposition at all times. She worked at the local market and knew every person in town and nearly everything that happened in their lives because she loved to chat with people who came through her check-out lane. Arnold was curled up in her lap and she began to pet him automatically while she spoke. "At least that's what Lionel said at the last town meeting. He thinks if he restores it then it will be a tourist magnet."

Charlotte Perry tsked sadly. The self-appointed matriarch of the group, Charlotte used her considerable years on this earth - eighty-eight of them to be precise – to draw wisdom from and pass on to her girls, as she referred to them. Age was a relative matter and she barely felt seventy-three most days nor did she look it; her hair was snow white and thick, her eyes grey and intelligent, her face only nominally wrinkled and her manner impatient. It irritated Charlotte to no end that she required a cane to get around because her feeble legs couldn't seem to keep up with the rest of her. "Progress can't be stopped once it sets its course," she said wisely.

"Then The Bottom will become like all the other towns up and down the coast," Annie grumbled. "We'll just become another tourist stop and be overrun with outsiders. What happens when they want to stay? Will we see houses being slapped up and chain stores moving in?" She cringed. "What kind of life will that be?"

"A better one for some of us," Lydia Myers said. Shapely and scatter-brained, Lydia had naturally dark curls piled on top of her head, a pretty oval face and an off-beat taste in fashion. She worked for the local real estate office and saw potential growth as a very good thing. Lydia didn't necessarily want The Bottom to boom overnight into a multi-million dollar resort city any more than Annie did. But a little bit of business would certainly be welcome. As it was now there was barely enough turn-over here to justify her position working for Margie Bingham Realty. It was hard to keep up the rigid beauty regime she implemented last year after turning forty on such a tight budget. An influx of fresh families buying new homes would allow for an upgrade at Leticia's Beauty Salon that up till now had only been a dream. Color treatments and pedicures and organic facial masks danced before her pretty blue eyes and Lydia nearly swooned.

"Everyone knows the pub is sitting on a prime piece of real estate. If Bill and Leslie sell, maybe that will help the rest of the town with property values and bring in new people," Regina Long pointed out. Regina was the youngest member of the group at thirty. Her skin was the same color as a cup of mocha latte and her hair was a mass of curls the color of a shiny new penny. She rarely held back her opinion on any given subject and could reluctantly admit that might be the very reason she was still single. And the last thing Regina wanted was to be single. Both her brothers and her sister were married and had moved on. She was the only one left in Rock Bottom with her mother Leticia the hairdresser and her father Martin the bank manager. Working part-time for her mother and going to school nights kept her busy and fueled the dream of being a lawyer, but she already knew the career wasn't going to be enough. Deep down, Regina was a romantic at heart and wanted it all. She was still hoping her Mr. Right was going to ride in on his Ferrari and take her back to his penthouse in New York where they'd have exactly two children who would be looked after by the nanny while she and her husband discussed world politics and her latest case over martinis.

Or possibly she'd consider settling down with a local fisherman if he asked nicely enough. In the meantime, she was stuck here at The Bottom with her parents monitoring every breath she took. Regina sighed. "Something needs to happen here soon."

"I agree," Liza Jane said. "If Lionel's vision brings in tourists just think of how it will help all the local businesses. And most of the investors are of the male persuasion. Rich and handsome I'd wager too. That can only help our cause."

"And by 'cause' you mean catch a husband," Charlotte clarified, nodding in approval. "I could see how rich investors flocking around town could tip the scale in your favor. Good Lord above knows you need all the help you can get. Just hope it's not at the expense of The Bottom."

"Perhaps you could say something to Bill and Leslie," Annie suggested, speaking directly to Kitty.

They all looked at Kitty expectantly, some with cautious hope and others with blatant glares. She spread her hands wide. "I have no say over what Bill and Leslie do with the pub. It's theirs to do with as they please." In the divorce settlement, Bill got the business his family started and she got her grandparent's cottage. It was a deal Kitty was more than satisfied with.

"But our town will never be the same again. The quiet lanes and fresh salty sea air will be tainted with the stench of city people vying for a little piece of our heaven. We'll be overrun with them and it will all be Leslie's fault," Annie wailed. Her purist heart broke at the mere thought.

"She's an outsider now and nothing good ever comes from them," Charlotte pronounced. "Just look at what she did to poor Kitty." She realized that technically Leslie wasn't an outsider. But when one leaves for an extended period of time one gives up the right to be called a native. Since Leslie had been gone for more than ten years her status had slipped several notches to somewhere below local but above foreigner. The general rule of thumb was that Leslie would have to remain here twenty more years to regain full stature. That's just how it was at The Bottom. "And now she's going to destroy our town. It's an outrage."

"We've got to do something," Annie said stubbornly. "I think we should picket the pub."

"How is that going to help?"

"We could make signs demanding that Bill and Leslie don't sell. Or get a petition going and hand out literature on the history of the Bottom's Up and what it means to our town. We can get people to boycott it and pressure them to keep it just as it is." Annie was convinced if people were reminded of the old building's historical significance it could be saved. There weren't a lot of original warehouses from the late nineteenth century left in the area and the Appleton's and Abbott's had done a marvelous job of maintaining its integrity over the years. She was fairly certain a developer had much different ideas for such a building.

"Wouldn't boycotting it just make them want to sell it even more?" Lydia asked, frowning. "Or am I just confused?"

"It could work," Annie insisted. "I'll get started on the 'Save the Pub' campaign immediately."

"I don't think making a few improvements will hurt it honestly," Martha confessed. "A little paint and some freshening up would certainly brighten it up a bit, don't you think?"

"Trescott will change everything about it. Have you seen some of the projects he's completed in other towns? They're stripped of their historical purity and transformed into some modern marvel of horror just to make a buck. It's shameful."

"Let's talk about something else," Martha Stimple quickly interjected. "This is obviously a touchy subject." She cleared her throat. "Let's talk about my date with Sheriff Carpenter."

"What about the book we were supposed to read this past week?" Kitty inquired. She didn't really want to hear about dates. She didn't want to hear about men in general.

"We'll get to it," Regina said. "First we get the dish on the Sheriff. I heard he's a doll."

"Oh, he is," Martha said. "He's a dream."

"He was nice on our one date as well," Lydia fondly reminisced. "I remember it quite clearly even though it was months ago."

"So where'd you go?" Regina asked Martha.

"We went to a coffee shop in Pebble Creek. We had a wonderful time but we won't be going out again."

"Why not?"

"I guess I had a more wonderful time than he did," Martha said, still smiling. "We talked about movies and food and his moving from a big town to a little town like Rock Bottom. He was a perfect gentlemen and easy to talk to and so very handsome. I think he just isn't ready to settle down again. Although he's been divorced for quite some time."

"He's fifty if he's a day. How much more time does he need?" Charlotte snapped.

"A little more," Martha said. "He's still settling into The Bottom anyway."

"Sheriff Carpenter has been here coming up on a year this summer," Liza Jane pointed out. "One of us ought to be able to snag him by now."

"But he's an outsider," Charlotte insisted. "And an indecisive one at that if he's dated half of you and still can't find a relationship. You ladies are about as good as it gets in The Bottom."

"He is a Mainer though. That counts for something," Liza Jane argued.

"The sheriff hasn't dated all of us," Regina pointed out. "I flirted with him at church but got no response. And he hasn't taken Kitty out yet either."

"You're much too young for him," Lydia told Regina, tossing her curls in indignation. "And Kitty had a perfectly good husband but lost him so she shouldn't get a chance with the sheriff. Now, can we get to the book?"

Kitty was hurt by Lydia's careless words. "I didn't *lose* Bill. He left me for a younger woman. It happens all the time. Why is it my fault?" She didn't usually speak up for herself but the image of her doing something wrong, of not being good enough, or smart enough, or sexy enough made her angry on behalf of women everywhere who were blamed for their husband's stupidity and lack of commitment.

"I'm sorry Kitty. I didn't mean to sound judgmental," Lydia quickly assured her. "I meant that you had more than twenty-five years with a handsome man who was good to you most of those years and you had four children. Some of us haven't even gotten that much. I believe someone like me or Regina should have a chance at love before you get another go 'round."

Liza Jane snorted. "If you haven't found someone by now you need to realize that ship has sailed. Or move to another town and start over with a new crop to pick from."

"Love isn't about taking turns," Charlotte said. "But at this point I'd like to see a couple of you married off before I die so I think maybe Lydia has a point. Kitty, I believe you're up."

"Up for what?" Kitty asked warily.

"It's your turn to date the sheriff."

"No." Kitty shook her head adamantly. "I'm done with men. I had one. I don't want another. I have cats now."

"I'll take her turn," Annie offered half-heartedly. She couldn't remember the last time she'd been out with a decent, hard-working man.

"Or I could," Lydia offered.

"You already went out with him when he first got to town," Liza Jane reminded everybody in the room. "And it didn't stick."

"So did you," Lydia said defensively. "Maybe he didn't like going out with a woman who works with dead people."

"I like dead people. They don't argue or judge." Liza Jane was the beautician for the county morgue and liked to point out that both she and Kitty had gone into the world of art. Kitty captured the beauty of life all around them while she got to bestow beauty on to the dearly decrepit and departed. Liza Jane secretly felt that her task was the more challenging of the two but she would never point that out to Kitty.

"You're so morbid," Regina said with a shake of her head. "It's weird. Men must be freaked by it."

"Who here has been married three times?" Liza Jane shot back. "Oh that's right. *Me.* How many times have you tied the knot Miss Fancypants? None? I rest my case."

"Isn't one of your ex's back on the market?" Annie asked abruptly.

"Yes. Husband number one. Harry the medical examiner."

"The silver-haired fox," Lydia swooned. "Harry really is a handsome fellow."

"But a coroner," Annie said, frowning. "Never mind."

"I saw that his wife died a few months back," Regina recalled. "How long do we have to wait before he's officially dateable?"

"After fifty the time is cut significantly," Charlotte informed them. "He's fair game now."

"I could overlook the dead people thing in a man," Martha said, although truth be told she wasn't looking for a husband. She had married the love of her life thirty-five years ago and had barely three years with him before he drowned in a boating accident. She didn't have any desire to remarry but she did enjoy some company and a nice evening out once in a while. "I overlook it in you," she pointed out, nodding at Liza Jane.

"I think I prefer the Sheriff," Lydia decided thoughtfully. "Nice buns."

"I agree," Charlotte said curtly. "I've always enjoyed a fine tushy on a man."

"Someone should get to take a crack at him again."

"Why don't you put your names in a hat and draw one?" Martha suggested brightly.

"It's Kitty's turn and that's final," Charlotte announced.

"Why do you get the final say?"

"Because I am old and prickly and insist on getting my way. Now let's get to this book already." When Charlotte saw an argument brewing she resorted to her fallback plan. She feigned chest pains and moaned softly. She threw in some trembling for good measure and that was enough to get all her girls attention as they immediately began fussing over her.

"Look, you've gone and overdone it," Martha twittered. "You've got to be more careful Charlotte dear."

"I know. You're right. I just get so upset when I think about you girls. I just want to see some of you happy and settled down. None of you are getting any younger."

"Don't you worry about us," Lydia told her, squeezing the older lady's hand. "We're all fine. And you were right. Kitty should take a crack at the Sheriff."

Charlotte wanted to sit up then and get back to business but she instead offered a wobbly smile. "That's very sweet of you to say. Maybe If I had a nice pillow to lean against and some tea I'd feel better."

Annie hurried off to get some tea from the small break room while Kitty, Martha and Lydia tried to make the older woman comfortable. Liza grabbed some pillows from the other chairs and they all arranged them to Charlotte's specifications. Regina watched the entire scene with disbelief and kept her suspicions to herself.

•

On Wednesday Kitty and Liza Jane met for lunch at the local café. Kitty ordered a salad with light dressing while Liza Jane ordered a Rueben and fries. That seemed backwards to Kitty since she was the one who had sworn off men and Liza was always open to the possibility. When Beth the waitress brought their meals, Kitty swiped Liza Jane's sandwich and fries and handed her the salad.

Liza Jane quirked a brow but said nothing. Instead she doused the salad in Thousand Island dressing and helped herself to some fries.

That seemed fair to Kitty so she bit into the Rueben and sighed in happiness.

"So what are you going to do about Bill?" Liza Jane asked, stealing another fry.

"What do you mean?'

"I mean what are you going to do when he comes crawling back to you?"

Her sandwich poised in mid-air, Kitty just stared at Liza. "What are you talking about?"

Liza Jane groaned. "Kitty, you know Bill. He can't *not* have a woman in his life to take care of him. When it falls apart with Leslie, which we all know it will, who do you think he's going to come running back to?"

Kitty finished chewing and swallowed. "Bill isn't going to leave Leslie. He loves her."

"He loved you once too. But then he fell out of love. Men do that sometimes. It sounds like it's happening again with your ex."

"Just because they had a disagreement in public doesn't mean they're getting a divorce. You had fights all the time with your last husband and yet you two were married for six years."

"But we finally got divorced. That's my point." Liza Jane cut her cucumber in quarters. "Look, Kitty. I love you. You're my best friend in the whole world. I just want to make sure you aren't going to take the jerk back."

Kitty was uncomfortable with this discussion. She believed marriage was forever. It was probably ludicrous but she still viewed Bill as her one and only partner in life, even after all the pain and humiliation he caused. There had been some good times together in all their married years. And they had four children together. Surely that must count for something. She didn't believe he was seriously considering leaving Leslie but if he did want her back, wasn't it God's plan for her to forgive him and take him back? Wasn't reconciling a marriage more important than hanging on to her pride? "Liza Jane I know you mean well. But I just can't think about that right now. I don't think Bill will ever leave Leslie. And even if he ever does leave her that doesn't mean he'll run back into my arms."

"All I want to know is if your arms are open for him to come back to."

"Honestly I'm not sure." At this Liza Jane made a choking sound. "Stop it. I know you hate him. I don't like him very much some days either. But I'm not sure what I should do in that situation. I made a vow, till death do us part. It seems like I should honor that vow."

"You are a wimp. A marshmallow. A doormat. And I say this with love. But you make me want to scream." Liza Jean took another bite. "Let me just set you straight. Your ex-husband was a decent man for a while. But then he turned into a schmuck and dumped you – *You*, the nicest, sweetest woman in The Bottom – for Leslie, the two timing tramp who dumped her own husband to steal yours. You are not taking his sorry behind back. Say it."

"I probably won't."

"No, sweetie. Say it with conviction. Say it with purpose."

"I won't take my ex-husband back."

"Okay. That was a little better. I don't think there was a lot of heart in it though. Let's remember how he told you he was leaving you. He drained your bank account the day before your anniversary and when your debit card got rejected at the market you asked him why when he got home from work. And he told you he was leaving you for what? How did he describe his girlfriend?"

"Fun and unpredictable," Kitty said miserably. "She made him feel alive and virile again."

"That's right. Fun, unpredictable Leslie. A woman you've known most of your life. He told you he was leaving you for her and then you helped him pack his things - things *you* bought for him over the years – and drove him over to Leslie's because his car battery was dead. And then he borrowed your car for a week." Liza Jane leveled her hazel eyes at Kitty. "If that man comes near you again you will kick him to the curb."

"Yes," Kitty agreed.

"Say it."

"I will kick him to the curb."

"Oh, I felt it that time. Once more just because that gave me goose-bumps hearing you stand up for yourself."

"If my lying, cheating, good-for-nothing ex-husband comes crawling back to me I am going to let him know exactly what I think of him," Kitty said fiercely, and the patrons in the cafe all stopped eating to send curious glances her way.

"Right on," Beth said, filling their water glasses for them. "I heard about him and Leslie not getting along lately. He's too needy," she explained with a wisdom that far exceeded her eighteen years. "Girls like Leslie get tired of that crap after a while. He'll probably be back on the market by the end of the year."

"See?" Liza Jane said smugly. "I told you."

Chapter 2

On Friday Kitty babysat Callie and Sam. They were the two bright spots in her life and she enjoyed every moment with her darling grandbabies. They were precious above all else to her and having the time in her schedule to spend with them was a huge blessing. Oftentimes they came in her studio and she set up small easels for their little hands to paint and they had a grand, if not extremely messy, time. But Kitty didn't mind at all. They were colorful memories she would be able to cherish for years.

There were moments when she looked at Sam and Callie and mourned the fact that she and Bill wouldn't get to do all the 'grandparent' things together that they had talked about doing. In fact, Bill barely acknowledged Callie and Sam at all, which wounded not only her but their son Charlie and daughter-in-law Bridget. Charlie was already angry at his father on her behalf and while the sentiment and loyalty were sweet it was only detrimental to his children's relationship with Bill. Kitty had gently encouraged Charlie to try to make amends with Bill and he grudgingly made a half-hearted attempt. Her son had managed to establish a polite rapport with his father to appease her but it extended no further than that. And Bill seemed unaffected by his son's animosity and the lack of intimacy with his own grandchildren.

Kitty took the children to the beach in the afternoon for a brief visit while the sun was out and the three walked along the surf bare-footed, letting the chilly water play with their toes as it slid in and out. Two year old Callie screamed with delight each time the water made contact while four year old Sam was his more usual cautious self as he veered away from the water each time it came too close. He much preferred hunting for treasure and today he was greatly rewarded. They found a starfish and Kitty examined his wondrous find with him, sharing in his awe as he pointed out its size and shape and texture to her.

She brought them home for their favorite lunch of home baked beans and hot dogs. When Callie couldn't keep her eyes open a moment longer Kitty tucked her into the daybed in one of the spare rooms and kissed the rosy little cheeks. Callie didn't even fuss and she was out before Kitty closed the door behind her.

In the cozy living room she sat with Sam and watched super hero cartoons and worked on the daily crossword in between his leaping and jumping on the floor like his favorite super hero character. He asked her excitedly if she could make him a cape and because grandmothers weren't allowed to say 'no' she kindly agreed. She wasn't a remarkably gifted seamstress but sewing was a favorite hobby and she knew she could whip up a practical cape for her young man. Sam rewarded her with a wet sloppy kiss and she smiled as he resumed his superhero antics.

By the time Charlie and Bridget picked the kids up at five she was exhausted. Kitty happily waved them off until they were completely out of sight. When she returned to the living room to straighten the mess left by her active grandchildren Petunia and Miss Tulip came creeping down the stairs, looking anxiously about.

"They're gone, girls. You can come out now," she told them fondly. "Mother will fix you a bowl of tuna for your suffering."

They followed Kitty expectantly into the kitchen, having long ago realized what the word 'tuna' meant in their limited feline understanding. Kitty opened a can and divided it into two bowls, which she set on the counter. Petunia and Miss Tulip jumped up and graciously accepted the peace offering.

Kitty pet them both before returning to the living room to finish straightening it. Then she fixed herself a bowl of leftover soup and watched the news. After tidying the kitchen she retired to her small craft room that had once been Bill's office. There were baskets all over filled with yards of fabric and scraps of material and skeins of yarn. During the long cold winter she spent much of her free time in here making various creations for the church bazaar, the children's home or family and friends.

She found some suitable material for a heavy cape and set to work. It didn't take her long to shape and hem the dark material. Kitty thought it was a bit drab so she decided to make a bright colorful 'S' on the back of it out of some of the scraps in her basket. Miss Tulip assisted in the selection as Kitty went through the pieces and decided she had enough for a pink cape for Callie. By nine she had the perfect capes for the children folded neatly on the hall bench that she would give to them Sunday after church. Kitty took care of the litter box and filled two bowls with fresh cat crunchies and water for the girls before heading upstairs for the night.

The next morning Kitty walked to town to help at the rummage sale. The hub of Rock Bottom was comprised of one main street with a dozen small buildings on each side. They were old and battered from being so close to the ocean but still stood proudly against time and the elements. To some it might look like a dilapidated row of buildings but Kitty just saw it as home. She headed for the library on the edge of town that had a large green to the right of it and housed the rummage sale each year. Rock Bottom had one tiny claim to fame and this was it. Every year more and more donations came in from the country and now the rummage sale spilled over into the neighboring parking lots and the municipal building. There was already a crowd of people milling around and Kitty expected by mid-day there would be throngs of people searching for hidden treasure amidst the piles of riffraff.

The parking lot and green were roped off in such a fashion that people had to enter at one area and exit on the opposite end where the tables were set up to pay for their finds. Kitty had volunteered for two decades and always stood at the front where people came through so she could greet people with her warm smile, offer one of the dozens of baskets they provided for shoppers to carry all their treasures in and answer any questions shoppers might have. The last several years it had been mentioned in the Maine tourism magazine as a great stop for visitors to find lovely vintage New England rarities which brought more and more tourists to Rock Bottom each year.

Kitty spotted her daughter Jenny and waved. Jenny was twenty-five and nearly a mirror image of her mother at that age. She taught first grade at the elementary school and had married her high school sweetheart Brad last spring. Several months ago they had discovered they were expecting and Kitty couldn't wait to have another grandbaby in the family to spoil.

Jenny made her way over to Kitty and they hugged. "You look wonderful," Kitty told her oldest daughter. They lived barely a mile apart yet Kitty still loved running into her daughter around town. She had to remind herself not to smother them though. Jenny and Brad had their own life to lead and Kitty tried to respect that by giving them their privacy.

Jenny rubbed her rounding abdomen and beamed. "I feel terrific. So far this pregnancy is a breeze other than eating so much. I guess I'm very lucky. How are you doing Mom?"

"I'm fine honey. I've been looking forward to the rummage sale all week."

"Are you sure?" Jenny asked, reaching out to take her mother's hand. "Brad and I are worried about you. I know today has to be hard. Why don't you come over and have dinner with us tonight?"

"After working here all day? No, love. I'm fine. Being here with visitors to talk to and friends to catch up with is the best thing in the world for me. And then I'll go home and crash."

"All right. If you're sure. But if you change your mind..."

"I won't. Now scoot."

Jenny smiled. "I guess I better hurry before all the good stuff is gone."

Kitty patted her daughter's cheek affectionately. "You go shop, little mother. Maybe you'll find some baby items."

"That would be great. We still need so much stuff."

"I still have some of your baby furniture if you want it. You know you're welcome to it."

"Thanks mom. We may end up taking you up on that offer. But I know you use most of it when Sam and Callie are over."

"Then maybe I just need to buy some things for you. A crib or bassinet. A high chair or a changing table perhaps?"

"Mom," Jenny laughed, "it's okay. You don't need to buy everything for us. We'll manage fine."

"It's a grandmother's prerogative to buy baby stuff. Pick something out that you desperately want and I am going to buy it for you. That's final."

Jenny kissed her mother's cheek. "Fine. I'll go home and look through the baby catalogs again. But we'll need two of anything I pick out."

"Two?" Kitty gaped at her daughter. "Twins?"

Jenny nodded, grinning hugely. "Found out yesterday. We were going to wait to tell you together but I can't keep it from you a moment longer."

"Oh sweetheart!" was all Kitty could say before hugging her baby girl. Twins!

After Jenny wandered away Kitty worked the table in the back where people brought their treasures to pay. Jenny came through a short time later with some baby blankets, sheets and curtains that would match the nursery. They spoke for a few moments about decorating ideas before Jenny happily hurried home to wash all her purchases. It was only a short time later that Kitty spotted Bill and Leslie meandering through the crowd in her direction. Living in a small town meant running into each other wasn't uncommon. But today she didn't feel like dealing with them. Bill and Leslie had a way of stealing the joy out of whatever moment she happened upon them and she didn't want to see them while still on a high from Jenny's news.

Kitty looked around in search of an escape route.

Some volunteers were pulling out boxes of more items that could be put out for sale as space was made on the tables. Kitty immediately offered to assist and handed over the cashier position to Charlotte who was more than willing to relieve her for a little while.

She followed the other volunteer toward the far right side of the rummage sale and he pointed out some boxes hiding under a table behind a draped sheet. Per his instructions she set to work pulling out already marked merchandise to place on the slowly emptying tables.

The first box was heavy and Kitty bent over to tug it out far enough to see what was in it. Glasses, plates, a small lamp, candlesticks, knickknacks and such. Kitty stopped shuffling the items around in the box and focused on the candlesticks. She pulled one out and stared at it in disbelief. These were *her* candlesticks. Antique silver candlesticks that had been her great-grandmother's and passed down for generations until they finally landed in her own possession. They were a wedding gift from her mother and it had meant the world to Kitty. She remembered seeing them at her dear grandmother's cottage - now her home – growing up. She had placed them in the same spot on the mantle that grandmother had. They were one of those things she associated with her childhood memories since they were always displayed prominently in whichever house they resided.

Before the divorce was being finalized, Kitty had sadly packed them away and put them in the garage in the hope that not seeing them for a while would erase the wedding memories associated with them. It was always her intention to bring the precious gift from her mother back into her home so she could look upon them with fondness and pride once again.

How on earth had they ended up in the rummage sale? Kitty wondered.

Bill. It had to have been Bill. He went through the house and cleaned it out after moving in with Leslie. Then he'd moved on to the garage and took nearly everything that wasn't nailed down. Lawn chairs, every tool they ever owned, boxes of college memories, Christmas decorations. He'd even taken the lawnmower.

And apparently her great-grandmother's silver.

It wasn't like Kitty to get steaming mad. She always tried to be positive and forgiving. If someone offended her she tried to brush it off. If Jesus could forgive her transgressions than it was the least she could do to follow His example. She didn't harbor anger or resentment in the face of unpleasantness. Everyone knew that about Kitty.

But this was different.

Bill had known, had always known, how she treasured these simple gifts that were a part of her family and its roots. And yet he took them along with everything else that she had willingly conceded to him in an effort to be agreeable in the face of adversity.

Until now.

Kitty stood up with a candlestick in each hand. She spotted Bill across the green and began a purposeful march directly toward him. Her heart was racing and her blood was pumping furiously as she parted the people in her way as easily as Moses had parted the Red Sea.

She stopped directly in front of Bill and Leslie, mindless of the throngs of familiar people surrounding them.

"Hey Kitty," Bill said without any enthusiasm.

"How dare you!" Kitty choked out.

"What's the matter with you?"

Kitty held up the candlesticks. "You took these. These were *mine*. My family's. But you took them. How low could you possibly be so low, Bill?"

Leslie crossed her arms over her large chest and frowned. "They're just ugly old candlesticks Kitty. Get over it."

Kitty felt a surge of feistiness overwhelm her. Kitty had never felt feisty in her entire life but she decided in this one moment she would give it a try. "You stay out of this Leslie."

Bill frowned. "Don't take that tone with Leslie."

Kitty frowned right back at him. Funny. She'd always thought him such a handsome man. Light brown hair, still thick and wavy, and eyes as blue as her own. Masculine features that weren't anywhere near perfect but when put together made for a very pleasing male countenance. He was a bit over six feet, broad shouldered, barrel-chested and strong as an ox. Kitty always felt safe with Bill, secure when his arms were around her. She supposed he could still be considered attractive but the once comforting face and arms and voice just made her angry. Really angry.

Since the day Bill told her he was leaving her for the woman he'd been unfaithful with Kitty had been passive and unobtrusive save the small tearful pleas for counseling. She didn't want to make waves. She didn't want Bill to think she was petty and difficult in the face of a divorce. Somewhere deep down inside she had hoped Bill would see she was the bigger woman in this and come to his senses.

Well today Kitty had finally come to her senses.

"I will take whatever tone I darn well please," Kitty said recklessly. "And right now my tone is angry. Very angry, Bill. I tried to make the divorce easy for you. I did everything you asked of me. And yet you took something that you knew had such sentimental value to me in order to hurt me."

"Oh for goodness sake Kitty," Bill grumbled. "If you just noticed they were missing now after all this time than they couldn't have had that much 'sentimental value' to you after all."

"That's not the point. Your vindictiveness is."

"I didn't take those to hurt you," Bill insisted. "Leslie liked them. That's why I took them."

Kitty turned her focus to the other woman. "You wanted my *ugly* candlesticks?"

Leslie shrugged. "I thought they would look nice on the dining room table. Turns out I was wrong. They're old fashioned and dreary. A lot like you."

Normally that would have made Kitty cry. She was overly sensitive and careless words touched her heart deeply. Today the feistiness was like a shield over her heart. The words did no damage to the intended target. "I am a mature, considerate woman Leslie. I don't say hurtful things to people. I'm not crude or promiscuous. And I certainly don't steal other people's husbands. If that makes me old-fashioned then you can say that about me as much as you want."

"Maybe if you'd made a little effort to improve yourself Bill wouldn't have had to come looking for me. No man wants the same drab thing on his menu day after day, night after night."

"And maybe you should have worked on saving your own marriage to Randy instead of ruining mine."

"If your marriage had been solid nothing I did would have mattered. The truth is you two were running on empty for years. Just like me and Randy. We're all much happier now."

Kitty was appalled. "How dare you say that to me, as if you did me a favor by taking Bill off my hands! We made promises, Leslie. Those vows actually mean something to decent, honest people. You ought to hang your head in shame for what you did."

Bill's mouth dropped open in shock. Kitty was so pleased with the effect she wanted to say more but couldn't readily think of anything to add. "Kitty, what has gotten into you? You're acting crazy!"

That got the fire going again. "I'll tell you what's gotten into me. Common sense. I was good to you Bill. We had a nice life, great kids and good friends. I stood by you through all the ups and downs that come with any marriage and then you left me the day before our anniversary for this," she said, pointing to the curvy woman at his side. There was no doubt Leslie was attractive. She was much heftier than Kitty but all her pounds were in the right places. Leslie had waves of thick hair the color of wheat, large green bedroom eyes and a knowing smile. The woman radiated sex appeal and obviously Bill had been too weak to resist her. Kitty knew she could never compare to that and it tweaked her pride even now that she had been unable to hold on to her husband. "What kind of man does that? An unprincipled one. That's who."

Leslie whistled. "She's really got her dander up Bill. Now you've got both of us mad at you." Leslie tilted her head. "I suppose you heard about the disagreement at the pub? Everyone else seems to have."

"It's none of my business. And that's another difference in us. I never went around yelling about our private life."

"We have a passion for life and each other. Sometimes we get carried away," Leslie said, sliding her arm through Bill's. Kitty noticed the movement and didn't think they looked like they were angry at each other at all. "We work through things differently than some. At least we have emotions and feelings that move on the scale. Yours never seem to leave 'dull'."

"I am not dull," Kitty said, but the conviction in her voice was seeping away now.

"Not at the moment," Leslie agreed. "But this is the first time I've ever seen you even slightly riled up and it's over a family heirloom. You didn't get this upset when I took your husband from right under your nose."

This was a bad idea, Kitty realized. It was only making the situation worse. She should have just bought the silly candlesticks and left it at that. Now it was too late to save face.

"You do realize I saw those candlesticks when I went over to your house to be with your husband, don't you? I was eating breakfast in your bathrobe and saw them sitting on the mantle and thought how nice they would look in my house. I made a mental note for the future. That was months before Bill told you about us."

Kitty was utterly and completely horrified at the thought of Leslie wearing her bathrobe and the fact that her husband had been intimate with another woman in their bed. The knowledge that Leslie had been plotting and scheming for months to take her husband and family heirloom bolstered the feisty spirit enough for one last round. "You two deserve one another. I wouldn't take you back if you were the last Mainer in Maine Bill Appleton. And as for these," Kitty added, holding up her precious candlesticks, "they are never leaving my house again."

Leslie's eyes were dancing. "Good grief Bill, she's going to explode if she gets anymore worked up than she is. Maybe we should buy the silly things for her as a peace offering."

"Sure," Bill said, still in awe of his first wife's sudden temper. In all the years they'd been married she never raised her voice or even an eyebrow. This was a remarkable display from a woman he thought he knew completely.

Leslie reached for the candlesticks and tried to take them from Kitty. Kitty yanked them out of her grasp. "You keep your hands off my candlesticks!"

At that Leslie hooted with laughter. "Kitty dear, you really do remind me of a little wet kitten when you're mad. You're puffed up and spitting mad and still completely harmless. It's just so cute."

Kitty felt her righteous anger was completely justified and long overdue. She didn't care that locals and tourists alike were gawking and listening to every word. "Don't you mock me Leslie. I have every right to be upset about what you did. I held it in all this time but this is the last straw. From now on I refuse to be pitied or looked down upon because Bill walked away from his commitment for a woman of little principles and absolutely no morals. I didn't do anything wrong and I am not going to apologize for it anymore."

"Good for you." Leslie nodded approvingly. "You shouldn't have to."

Kitty was further emboldened. "And I am going to make some changes in my life. Do things I've always wanted to do and go places I've never been."

"That's the spirit." Leslie was probably laughing at her but Kitty didn't care.

"I'm moving on with my life. Starting right now."

Bill watched in amazement as his ex-wife stomped off in a huff.

Chapter 3

"I can't tell you how proud I am of you," Liza Jane said as they ate lunch. Liza Jane had shown up at noon with containers of stew and baked bread from the café. Now they were sitting on the library steps eating while the crowd of people poked through the tables of donations.

"Of making a fool of myself?" Kitty asked weakly. The bravado she felt earlier had long deserted her and now all she felt was mortified by her own outburst.

"For standing up for yourself," Liza corrected her with some annoyance. "You've been a doormat your whole life Kitty. This was long overdue. I just wish I had been here to see it. I've waited decades for the big moment and you do it the one time I'm not around. I should be angry at you really."

"I'm sorry Liza."

Liza Jane threw her arms out dramatically. "Stop apologizing!"

Kitty started to apologize again but stopped herself in time. "It did feel good," she finally admitted. "In a decidedly terrifying way."

"Oh how I wish I could have seen Bill's face," Liza Jane chortled. "And Leslie's too!"

"Leslie was surprised but not really upset or offended. She seemed more amused than anything."

"That is very disappointing."

Kitty smiled ruefully. "Bill's face was priceless. But it was wicked of me to feel so satisfied."

Liza Jane shook her head. "You aren't that petty. I think you're just pleased as punch you finally stood up for yourself. You should have done it years ago instead of throwing your life away on that man."

"I hadn't thought about it like that." Kitty considered her friend's words. "Do you really think I threw my life away on Bill? We did have four great kids from that marriage. I don't think that was a waste at all. I'd do it all again for them."

"They did turn out fairly well despite Bill's genes," Liza Jane agreed. "And what I think doesn't really matter in the end, does it?"

"You're my best friend in the world; of course it matters. Do you think I can do what I said? Try new things? Stretch myself?"

To her horror Liza Jane looked supremely uncomfortable at this question and shoveled another spoonful of stew into her mouth.

"You don't," Kitty said, wilting. "My own best friend doesn't believe in me. No wonder Leslie was so amused. They didn't think I would do anything either."

"I believe you meant it when you said it," Liza Jane quantified. "But sweetie let's face it. You haven't left Rock Bottom in years. And the only reason you left it three years ago was for Teddy's graduation from college in Bar Harbor."

"Everything I really need is right here in The Bottom," Kitty said with her usual quiet logic. "That's why I never leave. I could if I really wanted to."

Liza Jane looked pointedly at her friend. "Rock bottom shouldn't even qualify as a real town. It should be dubbed a village. We have the basics and a few nice beaches and shops to visit. And great seafood. But it's not enough for most people. They have to get out and experience things. Shows, concerts, real shopping malls."

"I do all my shopping online from Bean's," Kitty argued.

"You are completely missing the point. It's not normal to never leave this town Kitty. It's not healthy."

"I'm normal."

"You don't do anything but paint and walk along the beach at night. It's like you're only half living. What kind of life is that Kitty? I'll tell you. A sad one. And everyone knows it. No wonder people treat you the way they do."

"They're being polite and kindhearted."

"They're snickering behind your back because you're pining for a man who's moved on. You need to forget the past and go forward."

Kitty was heartbroken. This community was her home and it was all she had now that Bill was gone. She loved the town and the people dearly. They were an extension of her family. She'd known they felt bad for her, even pitied her, but to know how truly little they thought of her was like a knife through her heart

The realization left her suddenly ill. Her stomach rumbled and the stew she was enjoying moments ago threatened to reappear.

"I've got to go," Kitty said, standing abruptly and moving down the steps. This overwhelming humiliation that swept over her was too much to bear in public.

"Kitty wait!" Liza Jane called after her but Kitty kept moving through the crowd.

She didn't stop until she was walking along the beach. The salty spray always soothed her spirit and she counted on it now to work its magic. There was a chill that crept up the beach on days like this when it was mild but just fell a few degrees short of warm. The wind coming in off the ocean made the temperature feel much colder, even when the sun was shining. Kitty didn't mind; she was already cold and empty inside.

She sat on the beach for a long time. Hours or minutes she wasn't sure. It didn't matter. She had nothing to go home to. Well, there was Petunia and Miss Tulip of course, and she loved her girls dearly. But it wasn't quite the same as having a husband waiting for you.

"I've got to do something," Kitty told the vast ocean as the she watched the water roll in and out again and again. "I just don't know what." Her life was just as vast and open as the ocean in front of her, stretching as far as the eye could see and with just as many possibilities. What did she want to do with her life? What had she always dreamed of doing? What was her secret heart's desire? Kitty delved deep into her inner being and carefully considered the things she found there. All she'd wanted was her husband and family, a comfortable life in the community she adored and to grow old and happy here. Could she truly grow old and happy without someone to share it with? Without Bill?

Hadn't she secretly thought he would come back to her someday? Was it only now that she realized that Bill wasn't coming back?

"I am a ninny," she said out loud.

She thought about the confrontation with Bill. It was painful but it was also eye-opening. Bill was no longer the man she married thirty years ago. Back then they both attended church and she thought because he grew up surrounded by faith that he possessed some of his own. But over the course of their marriage she saw evidence that he did not in fact have a relationship with Christ. Her own feelings had blinded her to the truth, or perhaps she was so young in her own faith that she had stupidly thought they would grow stronger together. Either way it had ended badly. Bill was not a man after God's heart or even hers.

And the truth revealed itself to her then.

Kitty didn't need Bill to be happy.

"It's true," Kitty breathed. "I just didn't want him to be happy without me since I thought I couldn't be happy without him."

She didn't think that made sense exactly but it did explain her feelings and clarify some things. What did she have without Bill? A lot! She had her children for starters. Two of them anyway. Teddy was the only one of her brood who hadn't stayed close to home. He chose to stay in Bar Harbor after college. He was a bit of a rebel and still searching for himself and that was fine with her. Charlie of course was settled happily in The Bottom and would never leave. He was a fisherman and loved the ocean almost as much as he loved his wife and kids. Kitty knew she would always have him close by. And Jenny and Brad were happily settled now with a little house of their own and starting a family. They too, would be lifers. Her youngest child Rebecca was twenty and working at a gardening center just twenty miles from Rock Bottom while going to school at the local college for agricultural studies. She had inherited Kitty's love of plants and was going to take it to the next level. Kitty was immensely proud of her daughter and loved seeing Becca whenever she could slip back to The Bottom for a visit in between her work and classes. She just wasn't sure where Becca was going to end up when it was all said and done.

Still, two out of four close to the nest wasn't bad, Kitty decided. Not bad at all. And of course she had Liza Jane and the ladies of the book club. Then there was her painting. It was a dream come true being able to come down here with her paints and her canvas any time she wanted and paint God's beautiful world. The fact that she was making a living doing what she loved was more than she thought possible.

It occurred to Kitty that her life story may not be perfect but that was okay. She was satisfied with the beginning, most of the middle, and even quite possibly the direction her ending was headed. So what if she was alone? Did that mean she couldn't be happy? No of course not! She had love and joy and peace in her life. God had blessed her with everything she'd ever wanted. That was enough wasn't it? Of course it was. It shouldn't matter what everyone else thought about her. After all, the only thing missing was a man.

Kitty was learning to be happy. She was content with her lot. Her life had meaning and purpose with or without a husband. Why didn't anyone think that was possible? Why did the opinion of others have to matter anyway?

"If I had a man in my life people would think everything was fine," she said out loud. "They don't think I can move on without one. Like I'm just sitting here waiting on Bill."

Well. She *had* been waiting for a very long while, Kitty realized. But not anymore. She just needed to convince her friends and family but the only way to do that would be to find another one.

Kitty drew in a quick breath.

Was that the answer to this? If her friends saw her out laughing with another man then they would stop feeling sorry for her. Why, they'd say *'Well look at that! Kitty has a new fella. 'Bout time!'* and everything would be fine. She wouldn't even have to keep said man. Just a few dates down around The Bottom with her having a marvelous time would do it.

And wouldn't it be something if Bill and Leslie saw her out on a date? She was giddy at the very thought!

There was only one hitch in her plan. Where would she find an eligible man? Kitty chewed her lip thoughtfully. The Book Club gals were always talking about the single men in The Bottom and if memory served her correctly, pickings were slim right now. At the last meeting Martha had mentioned her date with the sheriff. She did say he was a nice man. Perhaps she should take Charlotte's words to heart and claim her turn. The man was obviously open to dating a wide assortment of women.

"And since he is being stalked by every eligible woman in The Bottom, maybe he might like a reprieve," she told the water creeping up to her bare toes as a plan formulated itself. "Perhaps this could be mutually advantageous."

It was a crazy idea really. Asking a man out on a fake date to make everyone think she had a social life was a pathetic attempt by any standard. But Kitty couldn't help but think the idea had merit. It could change the scope of her life. She could be free of the stigma she was living under and enjoy life as she had only recently decided to live it.

Before she could change her mind Kitty pulled her practical brown shoes on and hurried back to town to implement the most impractical plan Rock Bottom had ever seen.

•

Kitty marched into the sheriff's office like she'd been there a hundred times. The truth was she'd never set foot in the door. It was small and messy and Kitty thought it needed a woman's touch but that was neither here nor there. The walls were light paneling and the trim was faded white. There were four faded burgundy chairs along the wall as she entered but she ignored them and kept her feet moving purposefully to the front counter and only stopped when she couldn't continue forward. About ten feet across from the counter was an office with a glass front and inside there was a man sitting at a desk engrossed in paperwork. After an appropriate amount of time of being ignored Kitty reached over and rang the small bell sitting in front of her with vigor.

The man looked up and the surprise that registered on his face threw her momentarily. Did he recognize her? Had her reputation reached even a stranger's ears? Did he too know Bill had found her wanting and left her for a younger woman? It stung the little bit of pride she had left. For a moment Kitty started to lose her nerve but then she remembered that was exactly what everyone in town would expect from her. She searched desperately for some resolve, found a smidgeon long buried from years of non-use and she latched on to like a lifeline, refusing to let go of it till this was done. Her back straightened and she met the intense eyes watching her curiously as he rose and slowly approached.

The sheriff was rather handsome in an unconventional way. Neatly trimmed salt-and-pepper hair, eyes the color of melted chocolate, a strong, square jaw line and a faded scar on his right cheek. Very masculine and appealing, though he was by no means the most handsome man Kitty had ever seen. Certainly not compared to Bill. Still, she could understand why the ladies of The Bottom were all drawing numbers in the lottery for this man. "Are you the sheriff?" she asked, just to make sure.

He nodded. "Sheriff Carpenter. What can I help you with?" His voice was gravelly and deep.

Kitty swallowed. "My name is Kitty Appleton and I have a proposition for you."

The sheriff's face flickered with surprise again. "What kind of proposition are you going to make, Kitty Appleton? Nothing illegal I hope. Since I am the sheriff." He pointed to the badge that clearly displayed his title.

"Yes I see that. And it's nothing illegal," she assured him. "I happen to belong to the Rock Bottom Mystery Book Club," she started.

"Not interested," he said quickly. Then added more politely, "But thank you for the invitation."

Kitty blinked. "I wasn't finished. We don't want you in our club. You're not allowed anyway. It's a women's book club."

He quirked a brow. "That sounds like discrimination."

"No. It's a *requirement*. Anyway, it appears you have dated most of the women in our little club over the last few months. Most recently there was Martha Stimple. Before that was my best friend Liza Jane. And Lydia Myers. I also know Regina Long has been trying to get you to ask her out. If Charlotte were younger she'd no doubt be seeking your company as well."

He nodded and frowned. "I know those names. They've been hounding me, along with several others in town. I'll admit it was flattering at first but now it's downright irritating."

This was exactly what Kitty needed to hear to press on. "There aren't many single men in The Bottom. Especially decent, hard-working men over a certain age. You are one of the last of a nearly extinct species and every woman in town wants to be able to claim you."

"I came to that very same conclusion not too long ago. And I try to avoid dating but honestly when they corner you in the dairy aisle at the market there's just no escape. That's how Martha finally weaseled a date from me."

"And with Liza Jane it was on the road one night when her car broke down. Yes, I know all the details."

"Then you know there was nothing wrong with her car," the sheriff said in annoyance. "She was probably waiting for me for an hour."

"Two actually," Kitty said with a small smile.

"So the women of your book club have repeatedly set traps for me and caught me a couple times. But I always manage to get away. How does this affect you?"

"Well according to Charlotte Perry, the matriarch of our little group, it's my turn."

"Your turn?"

"Yes. To date you."

"I see." Jeb Carpenter was more than a little a little startled to see *her* standing in his station. He knew it was her, this mysterious woman from the beach. And he was right about several things. She was very pretty. Maybe not magazine pretty but she had eyes the color of sapphires and dimples that peeped out when she smiled the softest, sweetest smile he'd ever seen on a woman trying to bag him like a deer. But Jeb was good at reading people, at seeing things they didn't want others to see. And what he saw in this woman was a sadness that touched his own heart. It didn't bother him overly much that she was trying to wheedle a date out of him and that he was actually quite willing to succumb. Still, he decided not to make it *too* easy for her. "So you simply have a more direct approach than your friends to snag and bag me?"

Kitty looked appalled at his words. "I don't want to snag and bag you at all."

"If you aren't here to ask me out then why exactly are you here?"

"It just dawned on me recently that you and I both have a problem. And I think I have a solution."

This was really making an otherwise dull day considerably brighter. Getting to meet her up close was worth almost any price, even if she was just trying to reel him in like a fish. Because he was pretty sure that's what she was doing. He just hadn't figured her motive out exactly. "What are our mutual problems and this solution you've come up with?"

"Do you mind if we sit down? I've just come from the beach and I have sand and pebbles in my shoes. It's making me crazy."

"Of course." Jeb moved over and swung the gate open for Kitty to come through. She hesitated only a moment before stepping around to his side. When she glided past him he caught the faint smell of ocean and fresh air and the tiniest hint of Jasmine.

When they were both seated and Kitty had emptied her shoe of the offensive debris, she sat back and met Jeb's curious eyes across the desk. "Sheriff Carpenter, I have just recently discovered that I am the town joke. The one everyone feels sorry for. I feel like a leper in my own home and I can't abide it a moment longer."

Jeb's warm brown eyes were sympathetic. "I'm sorry to hear that Ms. Appleton."

"My husband up and walked out on me for a younger woman." She waved her hand dismissively. "I'm sure you've heard it all before. It happens everywhere to lots of women and they get over it. The problem is that no one here in The Bottom believes I am over my ex."

"But you are?"

"Yes. I don't care if I ever see him again. Same thing with Leslie."

"Leslie?"

"The new Mrs. Appleton. She's everything I'm not. Brave, fun, exciting, sexy, young. Men apparently don't want a dowdy, old-fashioned, God-fearing woman with principles." She looked down at the hands clenched in her lap. "At least Bill didn't."

"Excuse me for saying this but you don't seem like you're completely over him."

"I am," she reaffirmed, meeting his eyes. "But everyone thinks I am miserable without Bill. I intend to show them that I am perfectly fine without him by getting myself a new man."

Jeb swallowed. "I see." Maybe this was a little more than he bargained for, Jeb thought. Perhaps he was a little too hasty in his opinion of Kitty Appleton.

Kitty was finding it easier to talk to this perfect stranger than she first thought it would be. Probably because his eyes were so warm and sympathetic. And scared to death now. It made Kitty laugh. "I don't think you do. I just want everyone to think I have a man in my life so they'll see I've moved on. It would just be a farce. And after a short time, I would get to dump him because I just wasn't looking for a serious relationship. I would tell everyone I just want to be carefree and single now."

Jeb scratched his head, troubled now by the whole premise. "I think I see where you're going with this and I can't say I'm feeling inclined to participate."

"But if you agreed to do this if would be just as beneficial to you."

"I'm not seeing that part of the plan very clearly then."

"If you were in a serious relationship the women in this town would leave you alone. You could grocery shop in peace. No one would call you in the middle of the night to come rescue their cat or lie in wait on a deserted road for your assistance. You could have a normal, stalker-free life again."

Jeb really liked the sound of that. Single women seemed to abound in this town and he appeared to be the top prize in the hunt. "Keep talking."

"All you'd have to do is pop around to my house for a nice home-cooked dinner a few times. A few casual but highly public dates. If you came to church with me that would be wonderful."

Jeb hadn't had home cooked meals in a really long time. Most nights he ate something microwavable out of a box, either here at work or alone in front of the TV at home. "Are you a good cook?"

Kitty beamed. "I don't want to brag but I have won the Rock Bottom Baptist Church Chili Contest three years in a row. I can also cook a lobster that will melt in your mouth and a meatloaf with all the trimmings you would sell you own mother for. You can ask my kids for references when it comes to my baking."

"Then I would want home cooked meals several nights a week," Jeb said, envisioning meatloaf slathered in gravy and heaps of mashed potatoes, warms rolls and apple pie for desert. Craziness aside, the food aspect was definitely an excellent selling point to this plan.

Kitty was greatly encouraged by the dreamy look in the sheriff's eyes. "Done. I love to cook; I just don't have anyone to cook for anymore. It's not fun cooking for one."

Jeb drummed his fingers on the desk, allowing her to think he was weighing the merits of her plan very carefully. She had long since captured his attention walking on the beach each night. He'd wondered about her, prayed for her, even dreamed about her. Now here she was in the flesh and he was both overwhelmed and utterly intrigued. He didn't think it was a stretch at all to think he could fall for someone like Kitty. In fact, he suspected he was well on his way into infatuation, which of course was not what God wanted at all. But perhaps this was simply a first step. If God was opening this door he had contemplated for so long, should he even be hesitating about going through it?

But Jeb didn't like deception and it would be on her end of this arrangement. On his part spending time with her wouldn't be deceitful at all because he honestly wanted to get to know her. If he told her the truth though he suspected she'd run for the hills. Still, he couldn't stop himself from asking a simple question. "Have you considered the idea of actually finding someone you like to spend time with instead of this pretense?"

Kitty shook her head vehemently. "No. I can't go through that again. No relationship, no dating, no emotions. Just a straightforward arrangement up front without the mess."

"Letting someone into your life doesn't have to be a mess."

"In my limited experience it is. So I've come up with the solution to my problem. And yours too by the way. It's win/win."

He wanted to but his sense of right and wrong was really unhappy with this situation. "I don't like lying to people, Ms. Appleton. And this would be deceiving a lot of people."

"Well." She was close, she could tell. He was perfect if she could just convince him. "What if we called it a business arrangement? We both get out of this what we want. It's not hurting anyone. And really it's not our fault if people misconstrue it as a relationship after all."

"You're really stretching it now."

"Are you interested or do I need to go find another potential boyfriend?" Kitty asked in desperation.

Picturing her propositioning some other fool sealed the deal. She could end up involved with a much less honorable man and that could become unpleasant all around. No, for her own safety he would go along with this ridiculous plan. That was what he told his conscience anyway. "You've made a very compelling case, Ms. Appleton," Jeb finally said and when her face lit up his heart did a tiny flip flop. "But I have one more question. What happens when this farce is over? Won't I be back in the same boat I'm in now with women hunting me down?" And possibly nursing a broken heart to boot, he thought.

Kitty shook her head. "I don't think so. You see, when I break up with you in...what's a fair amount of time to fall hard for someone?"

Jeb wanted to say 'two seconds' but he opted for "Two months."

"Okay. In two months when I break it off with you, gently of course," she said with a sweet, apologetic smile, "then you will be so heartbroken that you will need time to heal your wounds. Women love that, and respect it. You could feasibly use that for years. You'll have a heart that never mended and you just can't even consider dating another woman until you're good and ready. It's perfect."

"Whereas you come out as the woman who turned down the prize bachelor of Rock Bottom."

"Exactly. Oh!"

"What?"

Kitty had another idea that could only add to the drama and excitement of the whole plan. "If you were to propose to me and I turned you down that would be even better!"

"It would certainly improve your image," Jeb conceded. "But it leaves much to be desired for mine."

"That's true," Kitty said, sinking back in her chair.

"Basically we'll be trading places. I'll be the one everyone pities and you'll be the most eligible bachelorette for miles."

Kitty hadn't viewed it from that angle. She certainly didn't want him to have to bear the cross she carried. Nobody should, she realized sadly. "Oh, you're right. I'm so sorry. I hadn't thought it through from your side entirely."

"It is kind of a flaw in the plan, isn't it? It could all go wrong at that point. I might have women bringing me soggy casseroles and trying for the sympathy angle."

"I suppose so."

Kitty could never intentionally hurt another person like that. Especially such a respectable man as this one. She couldn't live with herself knowing she had caused someone any degree of pain or shame. No, the whole idea was terrible, Kitty realized. Completely stupid. She stood up abruptly, embarrassed and ashamed that she had acted so impulsively. "What a goose I am. Bill always said I was. I suppose I am at times." She held out her hand as a gesture of good will. "I'm sorry Sheriff for taking up your time with this. Please just forget I was ever here."

Jeb stood up as well. "I happen to like geese. And I really want some of that meat loaf. Just be gentle when you stomp on my heart in two months." Jeb grasped her hand in his large one.

Kitty felt the warmth of his touch tingle all the way up her arm. She was overwhelmed he was willing to do this for her. "Are you sure?"

"My stomach is adamant."

"Thank you, Sheriff."

He didn't want to let go of her hand. "You're welcome, Ms. Appleton."

Kitty finally pulled her hand away. "When should we start?"

Jeb thought they should begin seeing each other immediately but that was rash and totally out of character for him. "I suppose it would help if we were to bump into each other somewhere rather public and ease into this thing."

It came to her instantly. "Monday night is the fire station's annual clam chowder dinner. Everybody in town goes."

Jeb nodded. "Then we should meet there."

Kitty smiled and her brilliant sapphire eyes lit up. "I'll see you there at six."

Chapter 4

Kitty left the Sheriff's office with a spring in her step. She couldn't believe she had just done that! It was so unlike her in every possible way. She'd been cool, calm, decisive and bold. She was quite sure he hadn't seen how nervous she was at all. With the sheriff's help she could overcome this stigma and once again hold her head up high when she walked through town. She wouldn't be referred to as "Bill's ex" or "Poor abandoned Kitty" anymore. No, people would see her and say, *"There goes Kitty Appleton. She turned down the sheriff you know, the most eligible bachelor in the county"* and she would smile and keep walking.

What a marvelous plan, Kitty thought. If only she could share it with someone. She would love to tell Liza Jane about it. Her best friend would be so pleased and impressed. But as much as it pained her to not share this one thing with Liza she felt it was imperative that nobody know the truth. If a single word got out the whole plan would unravel and then she would be an even bigger laughingstock than she already was. No, this needed to remain need-to-know-only, and nobody else needed to know.

It was barely three and Kitty felt guilty for running out of the rummage sale the way she had. She veered down the footpath that took her to the library and emerged just yards from the swarms of people still buzzing around the tables. She spotted Liza Jane bagging purchases in the back and made a beeline for her.

Liza was visibly relieved when she saw Kitty approaching. "Kitten!" Liza said, calling her the pet name she'd given her best friend back in kindergarten. "Sweetie, don't run off like that again. You scared me!"

Kitty refrained from pointing out that she was nearly fifty and could leave the premises if she desired. "I'm fine. I just needed to think. I am sorry for leaving everyone in a lurch though."

"Not at all. We've been fine. I shouldn't have said what I did. I'm sorry Kitty."

"I just over-reacted. You know what a goose I can be."

Though she wanted desperately to share her exciting news with Liza, Kitty remained quiet and resumed her duties greeting and assisting the people coming through the line over the rest of the afternoon. She spoke with many friends and neighbors and greeted new faces that were getting a head start on the up-coming tourist season. Eileen Abbott, Leslie's mother, stopped by and they spoke for several minutes about the Fourth of July picnic which they would co-chair together. Kitty was very fond of sweet Mrs. Abbott. Their families had been intertwined for generations and she couldn't ignore that fact, nor could she possibly hold a grudge against the woman just because her daughter was a home-wrecker. She even waved to Leslie's brother Connor when she saw him across the parking lot because he was a decent sort and worked on the wharf with Charlie.

When it was finally time to go Liza waited to walk home with her. "I just need to find my candlesticks. I left them under the table where you're standing," Kitty said, hurrying behind the tables where the ladies taking money sat in lawn chairs. She looked under the table but didn't readily see her bag, though there was one about the same size holding a lamp. "They aren't here!"

Liza Jane came around and peeked under the table too. "I saw them here earlier." She rifled through the bags and then popped back up. "I don't see them though."

"Someone must have stolen them." After all the fuss she was going to end up losing her family heirloom anyway!

"Now don't panic," Liza Jane said matter-of-factly. "I'm sure there's a logical explanation. At least two of us have been back here the whole time. No one could have stolen them."

"Miss Charlotte worked here this morning and had a bag of stuff underneath as well," Maggie Swanson said as she continued helping customers while listening to the conversation. "She just left a little while ago with a bag. Maybe she grabbed yours by mistake."

Liza Jane patted Kitty's shoulder and smiled. "There. You see? Logical explanation. Charlotte took it by accident."

Kitty breathed a sigh of relief. Of course that's what must have happened. Charlotte was well into her eighties and could easily have gotten confused. Kitty would see her tomorrow at church and get her candlesticks back then. "You're right. I'll talk to her tomorrow. Let's go then."

By the time she got home that evening she was exhausted. She showered and slipped into her favorite turquoise blue leisure pants and shirt before checking on the chicken and dumplings simmering in the crock pot. It was nearly done and Kitty decided a short power nap would be just the thing while she waited for it to finish cooking. The girls were happy she was home and demanded some attention before she finally sank into her favorite chair and closed her eyes. Time slipped by and she dozed with Miss Tulip in her lap until the doorbell woke her up.

The last thing Kitty expected was Bill to be standing on her step. She was so shocked to see him she just stood there with her mouth open for several moments before snapping her jaw shut.

"Evening Kitty."

She nodded a formal greeting. "Bill. What are you doing here?"

He found her tone less than gracious. But he supposed she had a reason to be a little upset with him. He was big enough to see that. "Can I come in?"

Kitty hesitated. She really didn't want to talk to Bill right now. He had a way of making her feel bad about herself whenever he had anything to say, regardless of what it may be. If it was going to be this morning's words she certainly didn't need to be reminded of the scene she made. It may have been liberating at the time but now she was a little embarrassed by her own behavior. "No. I don't think so."

Bill raised an eyebrow in surprise. "Why not? I just want to talk."

"You mean you want to scold me for the way I talked to your wife. But I won't apologize. Anything I said was long overdue."

Bill shook his head. "That isn't why I came over."

Kitty was the one surprised now. "Really? Then why?"

"Let me come in and I'll tell you."

Against her better judgment Kitty stepped aside and let him inside. Perhaps what he had to say was about one of the kids, in which case she very much wanted to hear what he had to say.

She watched Bill take in all the changes as he made his way to the couch. Her couch. The one she'd bought after he moved out. It was aqua blue and she made throw pillows out of bright floral material for a splash of color. She'd also painted the walls a pale green and hung bright yellow curtains in the windows. Bill swiveled to see everything. "It's so bright in here now."

"Yes." Kitty sat down on the matching aqua wingback chair. "I like bright now."

"You used to like tan."

"I did like neutral colors. We both did. When you left I wanted something completely different." She looked around the room. "I didn't realize how much color my life was missing."

Bill cleared his throat. "Look Kitty. I'm sorry for the way I walked out on you. It was wrong of me."

An apology out of the blue was almost more than her sleepy brain could process. She swallowed and awkwardly nodded. "All right. I accept your apology. Was there anything else?"

"Actually I was wondering if you could give me your opinion on something."

"Why?" She couldn't imagine why he would seek her out for any reason at all.

"Because I..." He paused and awkwardly sought the words he needed. "Because you still matter. You could always see things for what they really are. And I know as much as you must hate me you'll still give me an honest answer."

His words and tone easily breached the thin wall she had around her heart where he was concerned. "Of course I will Bill."

He smiled sadly. "You were always able to be completely honest with me without being mean."

"I always tried to give you the best counsel I could when you asked for it."

"I see that now. You were a good wife," he said softly. "And I messed it up. I don't want to do that with Leslie." To her utter shock Bill dropped his head in his hands and sat there silently brooding.

"Bill. What is wrong?"

After a moment he looked up. His blue eyes were desperate. "Leslie wants to have a baby."

"Oh," Kitty breathed. She hadn't seen that one coming.

Nor had Bill apparently. "She hit me with it a couple months ago and now it's just a constant argument between us. It's what we were fighting about at the pub this week."

Kitty let the news settle in her mind and heart. It was shocking to be sure. She tried to picture Bill as the father of a newborn at the age of fifty, spending sleepless nights with a crying baby and fun, unpredictable Leslie for support. She waited for the pain to come but it didn't. Instead she wanted to laugh. Laugh! What a sight the pair of them would make walking through town with a baby. She could almost visualize Bill fumbling with baby gear and wiping spit-up off his clothes.

It also occurred to her that Jenny's babies could grow up with their aunt or uncle!

Wait until Liza Jane heard this one, Kitty thought.

"Am I too old for a baby?" Bill asked her roughly. "Because I think I'm too old for a baby."

"You're a grandfather Bill. Does that answer your question?"

He flinched. "But I'll lose her. This is really important to her."

This time Kitty was absolutely floored and had to look away. When had Bill ever – in all their years together – uttered anything even vaguely close to those words about her? Never. Not once. Bill had never considered her wants or needs above his own. He was so used to her sacrificing and not complaining he didn't even know what her wants and desires were.

The truth smacked her right in the face. Bill actually loved Leslie.

And never really loved her, Kitty Appleton, the woman who had given him four children and did everything he'd ever asked of her. She may be moving on but that revelation still hurt.

"Well then." Kitty took a deep, steadying breath. "I suppose you are going to have to have a baby with your wife."

Bill let out a long slow breath. "What will people think?"

"Who cares what they think?" She could see the irony in the words but in this case she truly believed the opinion of others shouldn't stop her ex-husband and his new wife from being happy.

"You aren't just saying this to make me look like an old fool are you?"

"Bill. Let's put us aside for a moment. You are married to Leslie. You two love each other." Those words were a little difficult to get out but she managed. "She wants to have baby with you. It's not so hard to understand when you think about the age gap. You aren't going to be around forever, Bill. Having a child will mean she won't be all alone when you're gone."

Her ex-husband studied his hands for a long moment. "I hadn't thought about it like that. I don't want Les to be alone when I'm gone."

"Good. It's settled." Kitty stood up. "Now go find her and share the good news. And send me an announcement when the bundle of joy arrives." She felt relieved in an odd way. She knew without a doubt that Bill was out of her life and moving on with Leslie. It may have taken her longer than it should have but she could see it now. And it was fine. Just fine.

Bill stood up as well. He was in awe of this sassy woman he had been married to for almost three decades and never knew existed. It bothered him only a little bit to admit he found that very attractive in her right now. "Kitty, you are an amazing woman."

As he walked to the door with his ex-wife ushering him along, he found himself not wanting to leave just yet. It had been almost two years since he'd set foot in his house. Well, okay her house. But still. There were a lot of memories here and most of them were pretty good.

Like that aroma that filled the house now. Kitty had something wonderful cooking he knew. She'd certainly been a wonderful wife in that regard. Bill always loved coming home at night to find a feast waiting for him at his table, his wife smiling demurely at one end of the table and his brood of four nestled in between. He'd always felt like a king when he came home to his little castle here in the wood.

Leslie was terrific and he did love her. But she didn't cook. Or make the little brick ranch they lived in feel homey. Not like this, he thought as he looked around the happy little living room. Leslie was better at other things and any man would be more than satisfied in that area. But still. He looked around the house again. This had been home for a long time. And Kitty was always there for him. She was dependable as the sun coming up in the morning. Dull maybe. But she never argued with him. Or defied him. Or turned him away when he wanted to assert his husbandly rights. His current wife was a much more difficult woman to manage, that was for sure.

Bill suddenly found himself in a dilemma.

Of course he loved Leslie. But walking out the door now would mean a venture into the unknown, a commitment to bringing a new life into the world when he should be looking at slowing down and enjoying retirement in a few more years. With Leslie it would be years of turmoil and change and tantrums and messy diapers. He crinkled his nose at the thought. He hadn't really changed diapers with the kids he already had, but as he recalled it didn't look pleasant at all. And he was pretty sure Leslie would make him change diapers with their child.

With Kitty things would be slow and steady. Easy. No crazy ups and downs. Just a comfortable existence with a good woman who knew his every whim and every desire. Their love life had never been the thrill ride he had with Leslie but certainly it was more than adequate. And at his age simple and predictable didn't sound as bad as it once did.

It sounded safe and rather nice actually.

Bill turned to face the woman he vowed to love and cherish. The years had been kind to Kitty, he realized. She really was still a very attractive woman. Not as pretty as Leslie but certainly he could look past that. And she'd lost weight too, which made her even more attractive in his eyes. She wasn't as voluptuous as his current wife but he could definitely work with what Kitty did have.

"Kitty. I think we should talk some more."

"I'm really tired. Maybe you should go find Leslie and talk with her. You two have a lot to discuss."

He reached out and took her hand. "But I want to tell you something."

Kitty didn't know what to make of his suddenly solicitous mood. There was a little gleam in his blue eyes that Kitty recognized but she couldn't fathom he was actually trying to put moves on her after what they had just discussed. That was absurd.

She gently pulled her hand away from his. "I think you better go." Kitty opened the front door for emphasis.

Bill thought her blue eyes looked very sexy when they were cloudy with confusion. He'd forgotten the exquisite color of them. He leaned forward and brushed a quick kiss on her cheek, deciding that for now he wouldn't push the issue. He had some things to consider anyway before making a rash decision like this. "Thank you Kitty." And he stepped past her into the chilly evening.

"You're welcome," she said softly before closing the door.

Chapter 5

Sunday morning Kitty went to church as usual carrying the capes in a plastic bag and sat with Charlie and Jenny and their families. Liza Jane arrived five minutes into the sermon, slipping noisily into the pew to make her way to Kitty's side. She plunked down and waved as the minister eyed her sternly over his glasses before continuing his remarks.

"You really ought to make an effort to be on time," Kitty scolded her friend in a whisper. "You *are* playing today during the offering." Liza Jane was a gifted pianist and had been coerced into using her vast talent most Sunday mornings.

Liza Jane shrugged out of her coat. "He's lucky I'm here at all. I was at the pub with Charlotte and Regina until almost one."

"Charlotte was there till one?" Kitty asked in amazement.

"We were playing peanut poker and she was winning. She wouldn't let us leave."

"Shhhh," Margie Bingham turned and shushed from the pew in front of them.

"You should have made her go home Liza. She's eighty-eight for goodness sake!" Kitty whispered in exasperation.

"I wanted to win some of those peanuts back."

Margie turned around once again and frowned fiercely at them.

Liza Jane made a face at the back of the woman's head but held her tongue for the rest of the sermon to Kitty's relief.

Outside on the church steps an hour later Jenny hugged Kitty good-bye before heading home for a rest with her husband in tow. Liza Jane invited Kitty to lunch with the girls once they were gone. "We're all meeting at Crabby's," she said, referring to the small seafood restaurant at the edge of town. It had the best lobster around and was popular with locals and tourists alike. "Are you coming?"

"I'm going to Charlie and Bridget's house. It's Sunday pot roast for the Appleton's."

"All right. We'll try not to have too much fun without you."

"I need to speak with Charlotte and then I'll send her along."

She spotted Charlotte speaking with the minister and waited for a lull in the conversation before making a beeline to the group. "Charlotte!" she called. "Reverend Moore."

The Reverend nodded in her direction and Charlotte turned, leaning on her cane. "I'm leaving now for Crabby's, don't worry."

"I know. I just talked with Liza Jane. I'm going to Charlie and Bridget's for lunch though."

Charlotte looked disappointed. "Oh, we'll miss you Kitty."

"Next time," Kitty promised. "Did you happen to take my bag by mistake from the rummage sale yesterday?"

"I did actually. I'm sorry for the mix-up."

"Can I stop by and get it this week? Or get it from you at book club Thursday night?"

"I don't have it any more."

"Where is it?"

"I gave the bag to Leslie."

"Leslie!" Kitty exclaimed in horror. "Why would you give my stuff to her?"

Charlotte shrugged. "When Leslie saw me going back to return them she offered to get it to you. So I gave her the bag."

Kitty felt slightly ill at the thought. "Why on earth would you do that?"

Charlotte peered at her sharply. "Kitty dear, these legs aren't what they used to be. I was exhausted from standing all morning at the bazaar. She offered to save me a trip back and I took it."

"It was a charitable act for sure," Reverend Moore offered. He was an older man, stooped from age and filled to capacity with wisdom that comes from reading the Word for so many decades. "And speaking of charitable acts, perhaps you could do one for me. Would you please speak to Liza Jane about being more prompt? The Lord appreciates her willingness to share the beautiful musical gift He has bestowed upon her but certainly He would enjoy it even more if Liza showed up in a more proper and timely manner."

"Of course Reverend. I will certainly remind her that timeliness is a blessing to all."

"Thank you Kitty. Now I must run. My dear wife is looking rather overwhelmed by Margie Bingham's flapping on about something as the lady is want to do. Would that her lips speak kindness as fervently as they do bitterness and we would all be the better for it." He nodded at Charlotte and waved to Kitty.

58

"Are you going to march over to Bill and Leslie's and demand your silver back?" Charlotte asked as soon as the Reverend was gone.

"No. I am not. I'll let her bring them to me."

Charlotte looked disappointed. "Are you sure? I'd go with you if you wanted me to."

Kitty patted her friend's arm. "That's all right. Go enjoy your lunch with the girls."

"All right. But if you need back up just call me. I feel somewhat responsible now for this dilemma you're in."

"Not to worry," Kitty said absently.

"All right then. I must be off. The girls are probably already ordering by now. Hopefully you'll come with us next week. Have a nice time with your family today."

"Thanks Charlotte. I will."

"We'll see you Thursday then at book club," the old woman called over her shoulder as she hobbled down the lane.

Kitty found her son and daughter-in-law speaking with some friends on the other side of the parking lot. Callie waved excitedly from her mother's hip while Sam raced over to throw himself into his grandmother's waiting arms and she caught him easily. Kitty gave him the bag and upon discovering his new cape insisted Kitty help him get it on at once. He then kissed Kitty loudly and she laughed. Charlie slung his arm around her shoulders as she joined the group in an affectionate welcome and kissed the top of her head. "Let's go eat. I'm starving."

Kitty chuckled. "You're always hungry Charlie." Her oldest son was as tall as his father, broad-shouldered and handsome enough to still turn heads with the young ladies. Unfortunately for them his heart belonged completely to his pretty young wife.

"You're right about that Mama Cat," Bridget said, using the affectionate nickname she'd given her mother-in-law years ago. She pulled her long blond hair out of her daughter's sticky hands. "He eats enough for three people."

Charlie reached over and plucked his daughter away from Bridget to give her a break. Callie put her hands on either side of his face and smooshed his cheeks up, giggling madly. "If your cooking wasn't so good I wouldn't eat so much," he told his wife, winking at her and completely un-phased by his daughter's antics. He merely turned to kiss each of her sticky hands quickly. "So quit jabber-jawing and let's go eat."

"So pushy," Bridget said but took her husband's free hand and smiled adoringly at him.

Kitty smiled behind Sam and felt her mood lighten. She may not have found true love in this lifetime but her son had. So had Jenny. And that was almost enough.

·

When Kitty got to the Rock Bottom Fire Station Monday evening it was overflowing with town support. She knew nearly every one of the residents squeezing inside for the famous chowder. Liza Jane was there with Lydia and they waved for her to join them. There was room for her if they squeezed over but she shook her head. Liza Jane was perplexed by her friend's refusal but shrugged it off as she watched Kitty lingering by the door.

Jeb arrived minutes later and spotted Kitty immediately. It was hard not to when she was just a few feet away. She was wearing a pink sweater and jeans and he thought she looked exactly the way a real woman should in them. When she saw him the dark blue eyes filled with relief. He smiled to reassure her the plan was still on and all was well. Their gaze locked as he made his way toward her. "Evening ma'am."

"Evening sheriff."

"I noticed you're here by yourself," he said as people milled around within earshot.

"Ayup."

"Perhaps you might join me? I hate to eat alone and still don't really know many people."

"I'd be very happy to join you." Kitty awkwardly led the way to the line and Jeb casually followed behind. He drew the eyes of many as he stood next to Kitty as they claimed their bowls of chowder and a pile of clam cakes before finding a recently vacated table.

Kitty watched Jeb demurely. "What should we talk about Sheriff?"

Jeb spread his napkin across his lap to protect his uniform. "Probably the usual things people talk about on a first date. So it looks convincing," he added.

"Right. Of course. That makes sense." She hadn't dated in thirty years. What should she start with?

Jeb could see her struggling for something to say and threw her a lifeline. "You mentioned you have kids too. Why don't we start with them?"

The conversation started awkwardly and eventually smoothed itself out. Once she saw Jeb was actually paying attention to what she said and even asked questions Kitty found herself relaxing enough to enjoy herself. Martha was right; he was easy to talk to. She really liked the sound of his deep voice. It wasn't loud or booming but there was authority in it when he spoke. The intensity in his eyes was less intimidating when she saw the engaging smile appear over something silly that came out of her mouth. He wasn't laughing at her though; Jeb wasn't like Bill. Her date was genuinely enjoying her company and it was flattering.

"Have you found a church home?" she asked him when they were down to the last clam cake.

He broke it in half and handed her a piece. "I've been attending Rock Bottom Methodist since I got here. When work permits."

"Some of my closest friends go there and you already know them. Lydia Myers, Regina Long, and Martha Stimple."

Jeb grinned. "I'm familiar with all of them. I have not gone out with Regina but she's dropped a few hints."

Kitty chuckled. "Regina's not usually subtle. And she wants to settle down."

"I'm way too old for her. I prefer the company of women my own age." His face actually turned red as he looked up in horror. "I didn't mean to offend you. You're younger than I am I'm sure. And if you aren't that's fine. I don't care. You look great for your age, whatever it is. Really great." His voice trailed off and he gave up trying to remove his size eleven foot from his mouth.

"It's okay. I understand what you meant."

"You're very kind Kitty."

They exchanged smiles and the conversation fell back into their mutual comfort zones of kids and work. Jeb proudly told her all about his son Jeff and about his duties in Augusta before transferring to Rock Bottom. Tables around them continued to empty and refill but Kitty and Jeb seemed not to notice.

"We should bump into each other again tomorrow," Jeb casually suggested.

"I'm helping Annie at the library in the morning until about two. I sometimes volunteer when her assistant is unavailable. Maybe you could come by then."

"I do have some books I was thinking about donating. I should stop by on my lunch hour and you could help me sort through them."

Kitty smiled. "I'd be happy to Sheriff."

When Jeb escorted her out on his arm in front of a significant portion of the Rock Bottom community Kitty felt all eyes in the room on her. She knew this was going to be the talk of the town tomorrow and that was fine with her. What better way to get things rolling than have rumors flying around about a possible relationship begun in the firehouse? It seemed like the perfect start to the perfect plan.

·

Kitty was the latest buzz around town the next morning. After the sheriff showed up at the library and visited with Kitty for nearly thirty minutes during his lunch hour speculation grew into full blown rumors. Liza was ecstatic and called her for details Tuesday evening. It was all Kitty could do to keep Liza calm and assure her that they had merely hit it off and were going to have an official date soon.

"When?" Liza demanded.

"Tomorrow night. He's coming over for dinner."

"Make comfort food. Men love that. And for goodness sake Kitty wear something besides that raggedy old blue tweed jacket!"

She spent Wednesday morning on the bluff overlooking the harbor painting boats below as they came and went and the afternoon planning the prefect evening with Jeb after a quick stop at the Bottom Boutique for something new to wear. Kitty thought she planned for every contingency as any practical woman would do. Plenty of food, a variety of music, no unmentionables hanging in the bathroom and expectations set at a minimum since this was really not a date at all.

The one thing she hadn't planned on was Bill on her doorstep just after six o'clock. "Is this a bad time?" he asked, noticing she was spruced up more than normal. He thought she looked pretty as a picture in a pale blue peasant blouse and khaki pants. The few pounds she'd lost were evident in the way those pants hugged her lovely assets, Bill decided with a gleam in his eye.

"Yes."

"I heard you're dating the sheriff."

"We're seeing each other," she acknowledged, both surprised and pleased to see a frown appear.

Bill clenched and unclenched his fists. "Is that really such a good idea?"

"I think it's none of your business."

"We're still a part of each other's lives, Kitty. We live in the same town, have a lot of the same friends and have four kids."

"We *aren't* a part of each other's lives any more Bill. *You* made that decision. I didn't. I never had a choice in the matter. But you've moved on with Leslie so please leave me alone." She never thought she'd speak those words out loud. Or actually mean them. In all her dreams of Bill standing on her doorstep it usually involved her throwing her arms around him and pleading for one more try at happiness. One more chance for her to try to make their marriage work. But she didn't have any impulse to throw her arms around him now and that in itself was surprising.

"Do you think it's possible to love two people at the same time?" he asked abruptly.

Kitty's attention was drawn to the brown marked SUV pulling up in front of her house. "What was that?" she asked absently while watching Jeb climb out. It was starting to rain and he didn't dally.

Bill turned and felt a slow, uncoiling anger in the pit of his stomach. Where was that coming from? he wondered. It didn't make sense to have these feelings surging forth out of nowhere. But he wanted to put his fist through the sheriff's face.

"I'm sorry Bill but you're going to have to leave."

Jeb came up the steps and Kitty welcomed him with a lovely smile that made her dark blue eyes sparkle. "Evening Sheriff."

"Evening Kitty." He wanted to expand on that but not in front of company. Jeb faced the man opposite him and waited to see if an introduction was forthcoming.

"We'll speak later," Kitty said quickly to her ex and pulled Jeb through the door before shutting it firmly in Bill's still stunned face.

Once inside Kitty took the sheriff's coat and hat and hung them in the front closet. Then she led him into the kitchen and encouraged him to take a seat at the small oak pedestal table tucked in the corner. Jeb instead stood by the counter and watched her move around the kitchen artlessly and savored the delicious smells that were toying with his senses. Whatever they were having it smelled divine. He watched as she took a bubbling pie out of the oven and set it on the stove.

Jeb cleared his throat discreetly. "That man that was just here. He your ex?"

Kitty nodded.

"He didn't look too happy about me being here."

Kitty's eyes met the deep brown eyes that were watching her with keen interest. "Bill is happily remarried to Leslie and now they are discussing having a baby. He has no business being upset with me if I want to date somebody."

"I see. How do you feel about the baby part?"

She shrugged. "I don't know. I suppose it doesn't really matter what I think."

"Sure it does. What was the first thing you felt when he told you? Anger? Hate? Jealousy?"

Kitty felt a tiny smile tug at her lips. "Honestly? I thought it was funny."

Jeb thought that was an excellent answer. "Why?"

"Because he barely got through the early years with our kids. Even now he doesn't spend time with his grandkids because they're messy and loud. I might actually like to see him doing the father thing at this age. I'm fairly sure Leslie will make him do half the work and Bill is not going to like that." She smiled at the thought of him changing dirty diapers and spit up.

"He never did half the work with you?"

"No. Bill was a good father once the kids were in elementary school and he could teach them to ride a bike and play baseball and fish. But for the first five years he loved them each from a distance."

Kitty took the food to the table and fixed them each a glass of Moxie. Jeb pulled out a chair for her and then they were sitting across the table looking at each other.

"You look very nice this evening," Jeb said. He thought she was about the prettiest lady he'd ever seen but didn't want to sound like a besotted idiot. So he played it safe and went with the tried and true.

"Thank you. But you don't have to say that. This isn't a real date. You're just here for the food, remember?" Kitty didn't mean for her tone to sound so peevish.

Jeb put his hand to his chest. "You wound me, madam. I came here for dinner with a lovely lady and plan on enjoying your company."

Kitty actually felt her cheeks pinken. "I'm sorry Sheriff. That was terrible of me. I guess I just feel cross because of Bill. He just upsets me." She automatically took his plate and heaped a large portion of chicken pot pie on it and handed the plate back. He accepted it and then she filled her own plate. Jeb took some warm bread and handed the basket to her before digging in.

"First of all you need to call me Jeb. 'Sheriff' sounds a bit formal for a date. Which this is. Secondly, you don't need to apologize for your feelings. The man upsets you and obviously for good reason. He's a jerk."

"Yes, I suppose he can be. But he's the father of my children and I should be more respectful."

Jeb decided changing the subject was in order. He didn't want to spend these few minutes he had with her discussing her ex-husband. "This is delicious. I haven't had anything this good since I moved here from Augusta."

"You mentioned you moved here partly to be closer to your son," Kitty recalled. "Have you visited him lately?"

Jeb nodded. "I saw Jeff and my daughter-in-law last month. I'm going to be a grandfather in the fall."

"That's wonderful Jeb."

They discussed the merits of grandparent-hood in the kitchen while outside torrential rain beat down on the roof. It was after eight before either thought to move.

"I'll clear the table and clean up if you want to retire to the living room," Kitty offered. "I can bring coffee and desert to you in a moment."

"I have a better idea," Jeb said, standing. "How about if you wash and I dry?"

"Oh," Kitty said. "That's nice of you but not necessary."

"Maybe I just like your company and don't want to go sit in the living room by myself."

Kitty felt her cheeks start to flush. The way he looked at her made her think he wasn't just being flirtatious or nice but quite serious. "Okay."

Jeb kept up a pleasant steam of conversation with Kitty while they worked side by side in the kitchen. By now Kitty had relaxed and he could see the change in her face and shoulders with thoughts of her ex-husband out of her mind. She had a soft shy smile and dimples that peeped out at him every now and then and each time they did he found himself wanting to keep them there.

When Jeb offered to get a fire going in the living room Kitty readily accepted. By the time she carried the tray of coffee and brownies in Jeb was settled on the couch with a roaring fire hissing and snapping in front of him. Miss Tulip was sitting in the chair across from him glaring unashamedly at the man in her space.

"Your cats don't seem to make friends easily," Jeb informed her. "The big multi-colored one stalked upstairs in a huff."

"That was my tortoiseshell, Petunia." Kitty accepted the help Jeb immediately offered by taking the tray from her and setting in on the coffee table. "The one glaring at you is Miss Tulip. I don't have a lot of company so they are a bit anti-social."

"Don't your kids and grandkids come over?"

Kitty sank down on to the sofa beside him, leaving a proper distance between them. "Sure. I even babysit a fair amount. But the girls hide upstairs. They aren't fond of children." She watched him as she sipped her coffee. "You don't like cats?"

"I like them just fine," he fibbed, uncomfortable under the glare of Miss Tulip. It was like she sensed his insincerity and chose that moment to stalk out of the room. "I'm more of a dog person though. Been thinking about getting one for company. Plus it'd be great to walk on the beach with a big sloppy dog by my side."

"Do you spend much time on the beach?"

"As much as I can. The house I rent overlooks Rockland Beach. It's what everyone calls the old Johnson house."

"I know where that is. I walk by it a lot," Kitty said, and Jeb quickly looked into the fire as she continued. "It's a great house. I've painted it in the foreground of some of my seascapes."

"I'd love to see some of them sometime."

"I'd be more than happy to show you my studio and my paintings any time."

Jeb didn't miss a beat. "How about Friday evening?"

Kitty nodded. "I'd like that."

Chapter 6

Book Club on Thursday evening was a nightmare. The girls wanted all the details on her recent dates and Kitty reluctantly shared a few morsels to keep them at bay. Liza Jane scolded her for withholding too much and Regina bemoaned not having a shot at the sheriff now. Martha and Lydia sat and listened, green with envy, while trying their best to be happy for Kitty. Annie resigned herself to remaining an old maid and Charlotte sent up a prayer of gratitude that finally, *finally*, there was some hope of romance for one of her girls.

Jeb arrived promptly at seven Friday evening with a small bouquet of flowers and an empty stomach. They had baked pork chops and easy conversation before going out to her studio. Jeb was impressed with the talent apparent in the many canvases spread out in a colorful mess around the small area. He was surprised by the lack of order out here when everything else about her person and her home and her life was so orderly. "Have you always wanted to be a painter?" he asked, studying a beautiful seascape with his own house in the distance.

"I suppose I have. I love it. I get lost in it."

"You're good."

"Thank you."

He looked at her quizzically. "You could go places with this kind of talent. It could open up a whole new world so to speak."

She spread her hands. "Where would I go? I've lived in Rock Bottom my whole life. This is home and I couldn't imagine myself living anywhere else."

"You're lucky."

"Lucky?" No one had ever said that to her before. Not about living her whole life in one tiny town anyway. "What do you mean?"

"You obviously have a sense of belonging. You probably know almost everyone in town, grew up with most of them and related to a lot of them. You have deep roots planted here that tie you to this place, and instead of feeling trapped, you love the safety and security it offers."

Kitty just stared at Jeb. "Very few people understand that. My son Charlie does. He gets it. But Bill never did. He wanted to travel and see the world and I think I held him back."

"He's free to leave now isn't he?"

"Yes."

"There you go," Jeb said, and turned back to the painting.

"Sometimes I think we weren't very compatible," she whispered, as if saying it out loud might bring down the wrath of God.

"You put a lot of years into your marriage. Nobody can accuse you of not trying, whether you were compatible or not."

She studied Jeb. "Were you and your wife?"

"Compatible? I suppose I thought so at the beginning. In the end she didn't want to be married to a cop. She's been happily remarried to an insurance adjuster for fifteen years. I was angry and resentful and honestly pretty horrid at first. But now we have a relatively amicable relationship."

"I can't imagine you being horrid to anyone. You're about the nicest man I've ever met," Kitty told him shyly.

Jeb studied a painting of the bluffs. He was pretty sure it was the view from the pub. "I didn't have Jesus then. Now I do. If there are changes in me they're because of Him."

"I never thought divorce would happen to me," Kitty admitted. "I thought we were solid. I thought we just had the normal ups and downs like everyone else. But I suppose in hindsight there were signs I should have seen, should have picked up on. Mostly I just feel so foolish for loving someone who never loved me."

"Diane tried to tell me in little ways from the beginning and I wouldn't listen. There's something to be said for getting older. You do learn from your mistakes. Now I proceed with a little more caution." Except maybe in this case, he thought wryly. "We can't be blamed for the foolishness of our hearts when we were younger. We love what we love and that's how it is."

Kitty nodded. "Yes. It is. But that's all in the past now isn't it?"

"For me it is."

"And for me too. Liza Jane says I wasted my life on Bill. Maybe she's right. I don't know. But I'm through living in the past. I really am ready to start over. I want to do something to celebrate." She racked her brain but for the life of her she couldn't come up with anything that fell into the 'new and exciting' category while still safely housed within her comfort zone.

Jeb pondered her words for a few moments. "Kitty, how do you feel about motorcycles?"

"They're dangerous and impractical, especially in this area. People who own them are foolish," she informed him sternly.

"Ayup," he agreed. "Would you want to go for a ride with me on mine?"

"Oh," was all she could think to say.

"I'm a very careful driver if that makes you feel any better."

"Where would we go?" she asked timidly.

"Not far. Tomorrow is the first day off I've had in three weeks and I plan on going hunting."

"Hunting?" Kitty was definitely not a fan of hunting.

"For books." He grimaced. "It's not a particularly masculine sport but I collect old books. And on my days off I get on big manly hog in my leather Harley Davidson jacket and drive around looking for Tennyson and Dickens in nearby towns." Jeb shrugged. "What do you think of that?"

"I'm a little shocked actually."

"At the motorcycle or the books?"

"Both. It's modern Renaissance man meets the Fonzi. Interesting."

"Interesting enough to throw caution to the wind and go with me?"

Kitty deliberated only a moment. After all, she was determined to try something new and exciting wasn't she? Here was the perfect opportunity. "Yes. I believe I would love to go."

"Perfect. I'll pick you up around eleven."

"Perfect," Kitty said, already quaking at the thought of riding on a motorcycle.

.

By the time eleven rolled around the next day Kitty wasn't sure the nerves were from anxiety or excitement. Although it wasn't as if this was a real date, she reminded herself. None of them were. They just needed to look like real dates. So maybe the butterflies in her stomach were all part of the show so to speak and would help make everything seem more authentic.

That's what she told herself anyway.

When the doorbell rang she checked herself one last time in the mirror and hurried to the door. Jeb was standing on her step, wearing jeans and a worn leather jacket over a rust colored shirt. Up until now she'd only ever seen him in his sheriff's uniform. He always came to her house directly from work looking so straight-laced and formal. Today he looked carefree and laid-back. His usual perfectly groomed hair was tousled and his smile was more relaxed. It occurred to Kitty that most women probably preferred men in uniform but in her case she was the polar opposite. Maybe it was the artist in her but she thought he looked ridiculously handsome standing there with a helmet in each hand looking casually GQ in a slightly rumpled shirt and black jeans.

Kitty realized she was pretend-dating a *very* attractive man.

"Hi," she said after staring for an inappropriately long time.

"Hi," Jeb said back, amused. "Do I look okay?"

When he smiled he had tiny laugh lines around his eyes that were more noticeable when he wasn't wearing that intimidating brown uniform. "Yes. You look good," she stammered, blushing.

"Thank you. And you look prettier today than you did yesterday if that's possible."

Kitty reminded herself that she was a level headed woman not prone to falling prey to flattery. "Thank you Sheriff. Are we ready?"

"Ayup." He offered her his arm and after a moment she took it.

He helped her get the helmet on just right and approved her wearing a leather jacket of her own. Then he had her climb on behind him and wrap her arms around his solid frame. The next thing she knew they were zipping down the lane into town and she was holding on to Jeb for dear life. She saw neighbors and friends and most all of them stopped to gape at the woman on the back of the sheriff's motorcycle. Kitty smiled bravely through the helmet and even dared a quick wave at Martha Stimple, who was walking down the lane with her reusable tote bulging with groceries. Martha smiled brightly and waved back as they zoomed by. Kitty glanced back over her shoulder and saw plump Martha making a beeline back into the market. She suspected everyone in town would know about her daring escapade before evening fell.

Jeb took them down the back roads to the small town of Butler Creek. It was several times the size of Rock Bottom but still fell well within the boundaries of a small town. He parked in the town square and assisted Kitty off the motorcycle, grinning as he took her helmet. "You look as white as my refrigerator. Was it that bad?"

Kitty felt a little queasy but overall she was exhilarated. She couldn't believe she'd just hopped on the back of a *hog* with a man she barely knew and left The Bottom. Granted they were only twenty minutes down the road, but still. This was huge for her. Monumental. And if she had to be completely honest it had been rather fun. Dangerous! Kitty hadn't done anything dangerous her entire life. Better late than never, she decided firmly. "I loved it," Kitty told Jeb tartly, reminding him of a school teacher informing him that his assignment was late. "Now let's go find some books for your collection."

"Yes ma'am."

There were plenty of shops to scour so they moved at a leisurely pace through the shops, checking in each store for literary treasure. Kitty found herself enjoying the hunt for hidden gems in the dozens of stores they explored. When she stumbled on to weathered and worn copies of the last two Hornblower books by C.S. Forester, she decided on a whim to buy them while Jeb was on the other side of the store. She paid for them and tucked them into her purse just as he came around the aisle.

"Did you find something?" she asked quickly.

He held up a book. "War and Peace. Don't know that I'll ever have time to read it but it would look great on my shelf."

She smiled. "Then you better get it."

Afterwards Jeb pointed her towards a Chinese restaurant and they settled into a booth. She was famished from all the walking and window shopping they'd done.

"You do like Chinese don't you?" Jeb suddenly asked as she perused the menu.

"I love Chinese. I can't remember the last time I had some though."

"Good. I guess so far I'm winning you over with my choice for a date."

Kitty put the menu down. "Jeb, this isn't a real date. You don't need to go to so much trouble."

He rubbed his chin thoughtfully. "Well now Ms. Appleton I would have to disagree. You and I may know it's not the real thing but to everyone else it needs to appear genuine. So I think a little effort is in order. And if we have a nice time together, well then so much the better."

The dimple he was starting to really become fond of peeped out at him. "If you insist. But nobody here really counts. It's just the folks at home we have to convince."

"Then consider this practice. We want to get it right for when we're back in The Bottom." When the waitress showed up at their table, he turned his attention to her. "Do we look like we're having a pleasant date?" he sternly asked the young woman, reminding Kitty of the more serious Sheriff-persona she was used to seeing.

The waitress nodded. "Yes, yes."

"Maybe I should hold the lady's hand though? What do you think about that? More romantic?" he inquired, and Kitty felt her cheeks flush.

Again the waitress nodded. "Yes, yes."

Jeb reached across the table and folded his large hands over her smaller ones. "There. That's better."

They ordered, Jeb in a steady voice and Kitty less so because she couldn't seem to forget the strong fingers covering her own hand. He asked her thoughtful questions and eventually his interest drew out the warm, bubbling personality hiding under her shy exterior. She laughed more easily, talked more readily with Jeb. She in turn interrogated him on police procedures and cases he had worked on, eager to learn firsthand from a man she saw as the most knowledgeable person in the field. He chuckled and answered her questions honestly and tried to steer the conversation towards the more unusual, almost humorous cases he had worked on. He didn't want to bring their cheerful mood down with all the doom and gloom he'd seen over the years. Instead he entertained her with some humorous characters he had encountered over the years. Kitty enjoyed listening to his smooth voice and the easy way he told a story.

Over tea Jeb pulled a small package out of his jacket pocket and slid it across the table to Kitty. She raised questioning eyes to him.

"Open it. It's just a little something I saw in one of the shops that made me think of you."

Kitty took the small bag and opened it, finding a small parcel wrapped in tissue paper. She unwrapped it quickly and found a finely detailed pewter paintbrush about four inches long with a chain dangling from the end. "A keychain! Oh Jeb it's wonderful!" She was so pleased with the small gift she could only smile at him like a silly teenage girl, her cheeks flushed with pleasure. How long had it been since someone had given her something just because?

Jeb could tell she was genuinely pleased with the small trinket. Her whole face lit up with happiness over the smallest gesture. He found that a very attractive quality in Kitty Appleton.

After attaching it to her own key ring she smiled smugly at him before reaching into her purse and pulling out a flat brown bag. She set it on the table and slid it over to him just as he done. He gave her the same quizzical look she gave him moments ago. "Open it. It's just a little something I saw in one of the shops that made me think of you," she repeated.

When he held the two Forester books in his hand he was amazed at her find. "Where did you get these? I love these books and have been searching for them for a while."

"I guess it was just meant for me to find them for you today," Kitty announced. "I'm sure they'll look perfect on your book shelf."

Jeb nodded in agreement. "Thank you Kitty. They will. And I was starting to think there wasn't anything sneaky about you but now I'm not so sure. Buying these behind my back was borderline devious." But he was smiling at her when he accused her and she returned the smile complete with dimples.

"Maybe I'm not all that predictable after all.

•

It was nearly six when Jeb dropped her at home. She thanked him for a wonderful time as she handed him back the helmet. Kitty noticed neighbors Mason and Myrtle talking with Regina animatedly two houses down while watching her and Jeb. It was clear they were the hot topic of conversation and it didn't bother her at all. She rather liked the idea of people talking about her and Jeb as if they were a real couple.

On a whim she leaned over and kissed Jeb on the cheek just as he was about to put his own helmet back on.

When she pulled back she wasn't sure who was more stunned: Jeb, their audience, or herself. Her eyes widened at her own behavior. She hadn't kissed a man other than her husband in years!

What had gotten into her?

"Well thank you Ms. Appleton," he said slowly. "That was a nice surprise."

"I better get inside," Kitty stammered and then she ran into the house like her tail was on fire.

Chapter 7

Monday night Liza Jane called and insisted Kitty meet the gang at the pub. She was hesitant to go and risk running into Bill and Leslie until Liza reminded her this would be the perfect opportunity to insist Leslie return the candlesticks. Her dates with Jeb had driven the candlesticks completely from her mind but when Liza Jane brought it up she concurred with Liza's assessment. It wouldn't hurt that she'd have the girls with her for moral support if it got ugly with Leslie. She pulled on her lightweight sweater coat and walked the short distance into town with some trepidation.

Lydia and Regina were already there with Liza. They were in a booth by the window laughing and eating cheesy fries when Kitty slid in next to her best friend. "It's about time you got here," Liza told her.

"Is Leslie here?" Kitty inquired, wanting to get the confrontation over before she lost her nerve.

"Nope. Apparently she left early."

"Shoot."

"Never mind that. We want to hear about your dates with the Sheriff."

"Saturday Kitty was on the back of Sheriff Carpenter's motorcycle!" Regina was pleased to inform everyone.

"And you didn't say a word at church yesterday!"

"Well Jeb was there so it would have been awkward." And thankfully Jeb had been a perfect gentleman yesterday by not bringing up the kiss and Kitty had appreciated that enormously.

"Spill now," Liza ordered.

Kitty told them about the jaunt up to Butler Creek and the fun afternoon they had. She left out the kiss but Regina thoughtfully brought it up and she wanted to sink into the seat cushions and disappear. Liza Jane hooted and Lydia grudgingly admitted that they sounded perfect for one another. Another round of Moxie was ordered and finally the subject moved on to something besides Jeb. Kitty breathed sigh of relief and helped herself to the remaining cheesy fries just as Annie came barreling in with her hair askew, her arms laden with papers and looking frazzled.

"Sorry I'm late," she huffed, plopping down at the table. "I had to stop at the printer and pick these up."

Liza Jane reached over and plucked one from the pile. "You paid for these?" She asked in surprise. "Why didn't you just run off a bunch for free at the library?"

"I have for the last couple batches but the printer at work died," Annie told her. She pushed the normally neat hair out of her face and glanced around the pub nervously. "I can't wait for a new one to come in. I have to get as many of these out as quickly as possible."

"I still think you're overreacting," Lydia insisted. "So Trescott makes a few improvements here. It's not the end of the world."

There was a commotion at the bar and they collectively turned their attention in that direction. There was a sparse group this evening seated around the counter and the men were laughing uproariously which carried in the nearly empty dining area. Maybe the flyers were working after all, Kitty decided.

She noticed that Leslie's ex-husband Randy seemed to be in the thick of the laughter. She had heard he frequented the pub but could never fully understand why. Kitty tried to avoid running into Bill or Leslie at all costs which meant bypassing the pub nowadays. Apparently Randy got on with his ex and Bill better than she did.

"There's another single one for you Regina," Liza purred. "He's closer to your age too."

"Randy is so full of himself it's all I can do to be in the same room as him," Regina groaned.

"Oh, we got another live one at nine o'clock," Lydia whispered dramatically, nodding towards the door. Sure enough, they all spotted Connor Abbott walk in. "He's just so serious all the time."

"Definitely a brooder," Liza Jane agreed.

"But so strong and masculine," Regina said dreamily. She thought Connor was just about the most delicious man on the planet but would cut out her own tongue before admitting that to him. Connor was tall and lanky with shaggy dark hair and eyes the color of the sea that always made her stomach do flip flops when he looked at her. "Don't you think he's handsome?"

"I don't know about handsome but I think he would be a good subject to sketch," Kitty said. "The hard planes of his face and his sharp eyes would be challenging to capture.'

Liza chuckled. "You've given the subject some thought have you?"

"Purely from an artistic perspective," Kitty assured her.

"You should sketch the sheriff," Liza Jane suggested. "If you can make even Bill look good in your drawings imagine what you could do with him as your subject."

"Whatever happened to all those charcoal drawings you did of Bill over the years?" Annie asked. "As I recall they were quite good."

"Bill took them. For Leslie. She liked them."

"Gees. She liked your husband and took him. She liked your drawings and took them. What else is she going to take from you?" Liza demanded hotly.

"My candlesticks," Kitty said automatically. "Honestly I forgot all about them until now." She blushed. "My brain hasn't been working lately I guess."

"Now she's got your grandmother's heirloom silver. When does it stop?" Regina asked. Leslie had been a few years ahead of her in school and Regina had never been a big fan. Leslie Abbott was a player. She always had been and always would be.

"I don't know. But I have a mind to go over there and demand them back right now."

"You should," Liza Jane insisted. "And we should go with you for moral support."

"Right on," Regina agreed. "Let's break down her door and demand Kitty's stuff back!"

"Amen!" Lydia cheered.

"You really think I should?"

"Yes!" Liza and Regina yelled in unison.

"I don't think it's a good idea at all," Annie said. She looked pale and Kitty thought maybe she wasn't feeling well all of a sudden.

"Maybe you should go home," Kitty suggested. "You've been working too hard again. You know you get run down easily."

"And miss the fun? Annie has to come. This could be the event of the year." Regina was fired up with indignation and she wanted justice for Kitty tonight. "It's bad enough Charlotte and Martha are going to miss out."

"All right. I suppose I can go," Annie agreed reluctantly.

"C'mon, ladies." Liza Jane slid out of her seat. "Hurry before Kitty changes her mind." She hurried to the bar and pushed through the throng of men. "Bob, we need the check quick. Kitty's on the warpath!"

"Our little Kitty is upset over something?" Clyde Richards slurred. He spun around in his seat and gazed with bloodshot eyes at their table. "Kitty, darling, what's the matter? Do you need us to go punch someone's lights out for ya?"

Kitty scooted out behind Liza. "No, Clyde. But thank you for the offer." It was moments like this she loved her little town even more. Even the town slush was willing to come to her aid. She'd known him nearly her entire life and couldn't help but forgive his weakness when he so earnestly wanted to help her in her moment of need.

"We're all going over to face Leslie," Lydia announced. "She has something that belongs to Kitty and she wants it back."

"I think you waited a bit too long to demand your husband back," Randy chuckled.

"Leslie has my candlesticks," Kitty informed everyone at the bar. She knew she was in mixed company when it came to loyalty around the bar. Kitty had been a part of the pub family for years since Bill owned half of it. But so had Leslie's family. She too had grown up here and knew the entire town. Everyone welcomed the new Mrs. Appleton but folks here were a sentimental lot and most still considered Kitty an important piece of the Bottom' Up history.

Edward Abbott reached out and tugged on Kitty's sleeve. "I can ask her if you'd like. Leslie always gives me my root beer when I ask. I bet she'll give you your candlesticks if I ask real nice for you."

Kitty smiled kindly at Edward. He was Henry's younger brother and simple-minded, having never matured mentally past that of a young child. Most of the town looked upon him fondly and with a watchful eye to keep him from harm's way. After all, Edward was a part of the Bottom's Up heritage too. He may not have been able to help run the pub his father built but he took great pride in cleaning the pub for the last fifty years. Edward even had a designated seat at the bar that he sat in every night till closing with his root beer and some type of puzzle to work on. Everyone knew Edward loved puzzles. "Thank you Edward. That's very sweet of you to offer but I'll talk to your niece myself.

"Okay. Do you know another word for forgive?" he asked, holding up his crossword. "Six letters."

"Pardon," Kitty suggested.

He studied the paper and then smiled. "That fits! Thanks Mrs. Appleton!"

"You're getting smarter every day Edward," Randy told the old man. "Pretty soon you'll be running this place."

"Bill and Leslie run the pub," he insisted, frowning at Randy. "I just clean it. Lots of words for clean: Dust. Brush. Disinfect. Scour. Wash. Mop. Vacuum. Should I keep going?"

"No," Liza interrupted. "We've got the picture Edward. And you do a super job too." She reached out and touched his shoulder. "You're the best cleaner in town."

"Thank you Miss Holbrook. You make dead people look good. Henry looked real nice when we put him in the casket." Edward turned back to his puzzle and ended the conversation just like that.

"Can we go already?" Regina was ready to move along.

"So you're just all going to march down there and demand Leslie hand over Kitty's candlesticks?" Randy laughed. "Have you met Leslie? Do you really think that's going to work?"

"What do you suggest we do?"

Randy shrugged. "I don't know. But I think this is the first night off she's had in a week. Probably shouldn't go over there tonight."

"We're going," Liza said stubbornly.

"Tell my sister I said hello," Connor said and Kitty noticed there wasn't much concern that a lynch party was headed his sister's way.

"You shouldn't walk over there alone," Bartender Bob said after listening in to the conversation.

"We aren't alone. There're five of us."

"I suppose I could go," Connor said without any enthusiasm.

"Or I could escort you there?" Randy asked with an alcohol-induced smile.

"It's not necessary," Regina insisted, her eyes locked on the tall, brooding fisherman staring back at her.

"But it would be the gentlemanly thing to do."

Connor snorted and Regina narrowed her eyes. "You know what? I'd love to have you walk with us Randy. And then maybe you can walk me home."

Connor frowned at Regina and she frowned right back. "Maybe I better go too," he finally said, finishing off his drink and slamming it on the counter.

"Whatever." She slipped her arm through Randy's and his smile was full of promises. That was fine with Regina. Randy was a good looking guy. He had a decent job designing and building office buildings and didn't back down when he wanted something. Right now she was what he wanted and that suited her just fine if it would get some reaction out of Connor Abbott. The big jerk.

"Let's everyone who's going move out," Liza Jane suggested before the momentum was lost.

Five women, one brooding fisherman and a slightly inebriated architect wound down the lane towards the Appleton house. A dark Humvee blew past them just as they reached the edge of town and Regina had to yank Randy out of the path of the on-coming vehicle to keep his drunk self from being run over. She read the driver the riot act even though he was well out of sight and the group resumed their trek albeit more carefully. It was a good twenty minute walk once they reached the edge of town and the conversation kept a steady pace with their feet as they made their way down the dirt road Bill and Leslie lived on. It was almost quarter till nine by the time they approached the desolate ranch house and Kitty started to question the wisdom of a confrontation. "Maybe we should go home."

"Nonsense," Liza Jane said. "The door is open. She's in there. Go."

Her support group stood in a semi-circle and nodded encouragement. Randy was grinning stupidly and Connor was trying to ignore everyone in general.

Kitty let out a huff. "Fine." She marched up and pounded on the storm door before she could change her mind.

After several moments she knocked again. And then a third time. When it became evident that no one was coming she put her nose to the glass and peered in. There was a lamp on in the living room in the corner. She could see the room was a mess. Newspapers and dirty glasses and plates littered the coffee table. There was a pile of laundry on a chair and a bag of groceries sitting on the floor.

Kitty tried the storm door and found it wasn't locked. She pulled it open and stuck her head inside. "Leslie? It's Kitty. Are you here?"

There was no answer so she started to step back and shut the door but Connor appeared, frowning. "She's got to be here," he said mostly to himself. "The door is open."

"She called me at the pub less than an hour ago," Randy said. "And I think she was in for the night."

"Her truck is still here," Liza pointed out.

"Maybe we shouldn't have come after all."

"While we're here let's check on her. My sister doesn't usually leave the door open like this."

"Leslie?" Randy yelled drunkenly from behind them.

"Shut up Randy," Connor snapped before pulling the storm door open. "Les? It's Connor."

There was no answer so he entered the house. Kitty hesitated, felling uncomfortable invading Bill's home. But curiosity got the best of her so she yanked the door open and followed Connor in. Randy stumbled awkwardly behind her and nearly crashed into her back.

Liza and company started to follow suit.

Connor saw them through the door and halted their progress. "Stop. No one else inside."

Kitty shrugged apologetically at her friends through the door and kept going.

She had never ventured into this part of Bill's life. Before it had been too painful. Now that she was moving on she found the opportunity to peek in and see what kind of life he chose over the neat, tidy one he had with her was too great to resist. Kitty headed down the hallway lined with laundry baskets of clothes waiting to be put away and heaps of everything from canned goods to dry cleaning to tennis rackets. Kitty paused with Randy nearly colliding into her. She hadn't known Bill played tennis. In the dining room she found more of the same and couldn't help but take note of all the little nuances that made up his new life. She poked her head in the bathroom and found it just as disorganized as the rest of the house and was quite satisfied that Bill had married a slob. She could hardly wait to see the kitchen.

They rounded the corner and found themselves in a very messy kitchen. There were piles of dishes waiting to be washed and food items that should have long been put away. The mail was tossed carelessly on the table and dry cleaning hung over a chair.

And Leslie's body was sprawled on the floor by the back door, motionless. Her eyes were staring unseeing at the baseboard across the small room. There was blood on the side of her pale face and a large silver candlestick was lying just a yard away with blood covering one end.

"Oh my precious God in heaven," Kitty whispered, feeling a wave of nausea and fear sweep over her entire body. She stood unmoving for several moments before her senses started working again. They were overwhelmed by the gruesome sight and the acrid smell of death.

"Leslie," Randy whispered in anguish from behind her. He started towards her but Connor grabbed his sleeve.

"No. We shouldn't touch anything," Connor said hoarsely.

Randy nodded, his eyes misty. "Of course. You're right. We need to call the police." He dared a quick glance at his ex-wife's lifeless body.

"We should go outside and make the call. Seeing her like this..." Connor trailed off.

In a daze Kitty stumbled through the house the way she came, anxious to be away from the scene she had just witnessed. She tumbled out the door to her waiting friends and their excited faces faded quickly when they saw the terror on her own. "What is it? What's wrong?" Liza Jane demanded.

"Leslie's dead," Kitty whispered in a strangled voice.

Chapter 8

One of the reasons Jeb came to Rock Bottom was to get away from big city crime. He'd seen his share of it as a Deputy Sheriff because it was all part of the job of course. But there came a point when one needed a change of scenery, a change of pace. The previous Sheriff here in Rock Bottom took ill and the county needed to appoint a temporary replacement until the next election. Jeb threw his name into the hat and trusted God would pave the way if it was meant to be. Nine months ago he'd packed up his old life in Augusta and moved to the tiny town where almost nothing ever happened. His coworkers thought he was crazy for moving out past the edge of civilization. He'd kill his career and possibly die of boredom all in one sweep living in a town where the biggest crime wave in the last ten years was a teenaged pickpocket who terrorized the summer tourists last year.

Standing in the Appleton's kitchen and looking down at Leslie's body made him realize that you could never get away from the evil that lurked in this world. It was everywhere. And it was up to him to protect the citizens of Rock Bottom. Tonight he had failed Leslie Appleton. He intended to do whatever it took to find whoever did this and was thankful he had experience to draw from. In a county like this the department was small and not used to dealing with this kind of heinous crime. His five deputies were young and smart but they lacked experience and Jeb knew he was going to be putting in a lot of time to get to the bottom of this murder, especially with one deputy on maternity leave and the other recovering from surgery.

The county medical examiner Harry Dutton was down on the floor, examining the body. His silver grey head was hunched over Leslie's form as he took notes. Jeb's deputies had already taken pictures of the body and crime scene. Now Harry was nearly done with his cursory evaluation. "What's the verdict Harry?"

"Blunt force trauma is the obvious conclusion. A single blow to the head. I'll know for sure after the autopsy." He indicated the bloody candlestick. "I'd say it's a safe bet that's your murder weapon. The indentations on the skull appear to match the pattern. Plus there's blood and hair on the bottom."

"Time of death?"

"Best guess is between five and eight. Again I'll know more after the autopsy." He stood up to his full height of just over six feet and faced the sheriff. "Any ideas about this?"

"You tell me. The wound looks pretty deep. That says intense rage to me."

"It is. It would take a significant amount of strength to do that much damage with one blow. You're thinking this is a crime of passion or rage which is a good indicator that the killer knew his victim."

Jeb nodded. "That's my gut instinct. I think it was very personal. Whoever did this knew her and was pretty angry with her. Plus there're no signs of forced entry. It would appear she let her assailant in."

"I'm sure you'll find plenty of suspects to choose from. She was a well-known woman in the community. Most loved her. Some really hated her."

"I would imagine so."

"I can tell you from the angle she was stuck the murderer was right-handed and more than likely a man based on amount of damage." Harry nodded as the body was loaded on to a gurney. "I should have something definitive for you by noon tomorrow."

"Good man. Thanks Harry."

Deputy Rob approached him. A strapping young man in his late twenties, he was Jeb's right hand man. "We found this crumpled up on the floor," he said, handing an evidence bag to the sheriff. Inside was a pamphlet with pictures of the Bottom's Up and a history of the place. There was also a list with what looked like hundreds of names on it. "Some kind of petition."

"Let's find out where this came from."

"Yes sir. Also, we've taken statements from the group that was here when we arrived. They all came together from the pub; their stories check out. Bill Appleton is already at the station. After he saw the body he was a mess. I thought it would be better to get him out of here."

"Fine. We'll start with Bill and the three who found the body. The rest can go home for now. Make sure they understand we may need to follow up tomorrow."

Rob nodded. "I'll take care of it."

•

Bill was in a daze. He arrived home from bowling to find the sheriff's vehicles and flashing lights in his driveway. The officers tried to stop him from getting through but he shoved past them into his house, calling for his wife. When he saw Leslie's lifeless body laying there it was like the whole world had ceased turning. Everything inside him just halted. He couldn't seem to think or feel anything. Just a numbing sensation everywhere.

Now he was in the sheriff's office and they were asking him questions, so many questions about Leslie and her family and their life together. His head was hurting and he was pretty sure he might be sick.

"All right Mr. Appleton. I need to know everything about this evening."

Bill swallowed audibly. "Leslie and I were both at the pub as usual until just before six. Out of the blue she told me she had something to take care of and rushed off."

"Where did she go?"

"She didn't say. She just said she'd see me at home later. That's it. Those were the last words my wife said to me." His voice quivered and he tried to keep the tears at bay.

"And you have no idea what it was about?"

"None."

"Okay. What about your movements this evening?"

"I left the pub around six-thirty. Went straight to the bowling alley. I was there the whole time with the guys. Got two turkeys," he said without thinking. "

"Then what?"

"We finished around nine-thirty and I headed home. That's when I saw all the vehicles and flashing lights." He mopped the moisture from his eyes. "Who did this? Was it a break-in? What was it?"

"I think your wife knew her attacker, Mr. Appleton. There was no sign of forced entry, and she was struck from behind, as though she had her back to him or her, maybe walking away. If she were scared or threatened she wouldn't have done that. Can you think of anyone who was angry with her?"

"So it's someone we know?" Bill asked, ignoring Jeb's question.

"Prossibly. Did your wife mention anyone in particular she was afraid of? Did she seem nervous lately?"

85

Bill shook his head. "No. Leslie wasn't afraid of anyone or anything."

"Is there anyone you can think of who had a grudge?"

"Just Kitty."

"You think your ex-wife had something to do with this?" Jeb tried to keep his voice neutral.

Bill shrugged. "She hasn't gotten over me leaving. She's still in love with me. I told her about Leslie wanting a baby. That could have been enough to make her snap."

"Uh-huh."

"Look I know you're seeing my wife - *ex-wife* - but the truth is she's a suspect."

"I get to decide who the suspects are, Mr. Appleton."

"But she made that big scene at the rummage sale." Bill went to great depths to make Kitty look desperate and shrewish. He didn't know why he did. Maybe because he wanted to go to Kitty for comfort now and that made him angry enough to lash out at her, blame her. "She could have hired someone to kill Leslie." A fresh wave of nausea hit and he felt tears burning his eyes.

"We'll look into it," Jeb said curtly. "I promise you we will find whoever did this to your wife." Whatever his personal feelings for the man, no one should have to suffer through this and he was determined to see justice done.

"Thank you sheriff," Bill said, and the tears started to come unbidden.

"I'm sorry for your loss Mr. Appleton. Can I have one of my men take you somewhere?"

"Home," Bill wept.

"I'm sorry but you can't go back to your house. It's a crime scene. You'll have to stay somewhere else. Do you have somewhere you can go?"

Bill quietly shook his head.

Jeb stood and walked to the door. As he stepped out he spoke softly to his deputy. "Let him stay there as long as he needs. Then see that he gets wherever he wants to go." He grabbed a cup of coffee and took the notes Rob had taken while talking with Kitty. Letting his deputy handle that query so there was no hint of impropriety at any level in this investigation was in everyone's best interest. Jeb skimmed through her statement as he walked into a small interrogation room. He sank into the chair opposite Randy Parker and surveyed the younger man. He looked like he was still in shock. "Tell me again what happened."

"I've told your deputy already. Why do I have to go through this again?"

"Humor me. Tell me about this evening."

Randy ran his hand through hair that was already a mess from the repeated gesture. "Fine. Leslie called me a little after six. I was en route home from Pebble Creek. Lionel told her from the beginning she could see the preliminary plans of the new pub when they were ready. I finished them and she wanted to see them. Actually she insisted. I got to her house a few minutes later. I showed her, we talked for a few minutes and then I left."

"Why did she want to see the plans exactly? If she's selling it to Trescott he can do whatever he wants to it."

"That's true. But Leslie really wanted to see what his vision was for her father's pub. We had every intention of keeping the integrity of the original design but with a few structural improvements and some modern amenities. It was the only way Bill would even consider selling and I think deep down Leslie felt the same way. She was pleased with what I came up with and thought Bill would be too. So everything was on track."

"And if she hadn't been? What difference would it have made? Would it have killed the sale?"

Randy shook his head adamantly. "No way. I would have worked twice as hard to please her, Bill and Trescott. This is an important job for the community and we all want it done right."

"All right. So what time did you leave Leslie's house?"

"Around six forty. The neighbor saw me. Mrs. Pritchet. She can verify the time. I went straight from there to the pub and stayed the whole evening until our group left around nine."

"It's a little strange you spend so much time at your ex-wife's place of business. And you were working with her on this deal. You were on friendly terms?"

"Yes of course we were on friendly terms. The past is the past. Les and I were fine. She'd moved on and I'm trying to with Regina if she'd give me the time of day." His smile was lopsided. "And there really isn't anywhere else to go in Rock Bottom to socialize. The Bottom's Up is it."

They touched on the conversation that led up to the unlikely group marching over to the Appleton home later in the evening. "We nearly got run over by a Humvee," Randy remembered. "Regina saved my life. It was cruising into town at about eighty miles an hour and she yanked me out of the way."

"Not too many people around here drive those."

"My boss does," Randy suddenly said and hiccupped. "Maybe it was him."

"I'll look into it. When you were inside the house, did you see or hear anything? Notice anything unusual?"

"Nothing Sheriff. Like I already said. Kitty Appleton, Connor and I went inside and we just stumbled on to the body." He shuddered. "I still can't believe Leslie is really dead."

"Why did you go in the house?"

"The door was open. It just seemed a little weird."

"Why?"

"Leslie never left doors open. She was always careful about that."

"You said Leslie called you? What time was that?"

"Er. I can check." He pulled out his cell phone and scrolled through it. "Six-fifty-five."

"Why did she call you if you just spoke earlier?"

"Oh. She had one more question about some of the details." He shrugged. "I don't even remember what it was exactly. But it was something to do with the finances. Leslie was all about the money," Randy said sadly. He met Jeb's eyes. "A lot of good it did her."

.

Connor Abbott was sitting quietly in holding room two staring at the cup of coffee in his hands.

"Sorry for the wait Mr. Abbott," Jeb said as he sank into the chair opposite his visitor.

"Call me Connor. My father was Mr. Abbott."

"I'm sorry about your sister. I promise we'll do everything we can to find whoever did this to her."

"Good."

"When was the last time you saw Leslie before tonight?"

"A few days ago. Saturday evening," he clarified.

"Where was that?"

"At the pub."

"You go there often?"

"Often enough."

"She seem okay to you?"

"Seemed fine. But looks can be deceiving."

Jeb thought that was an interesting statement. "Why do you say that?"

Connor shrugged. "Leslie was a hard person to really know. Her mind was almost...diabolical. She was always scheming and planning."

"That's quite an assessment. Diabolical."

"She didn't let things stand in her way and people's feelings were often hurt. She didn't care."

"It sounds like your sister was either loved or hated. No in between."

Connor nodded. "That would be an accurate assessment as well."

"Can you think of anyone offhand who had a grudge?"

"Charlie Appleton I suppose."

"Bill's son?" Jeb asked, flipping through the notes Rob had given him. "Why?"

"He didn't appreciate my sister selling his inheritance out from under him."

"Did they ever argue or get violent?"

"They had plenty of words. Charlie never liked Leslie after his father walked out on his mother for her and he'd shared his feelings with Leslie on multiple occasions. Can't say I honestly blame him. He has a pretty violent temper."

"And a pretty good motive. Tell me about Randy."

"He and Les had a bitter divorce when she left him for Bill, yet now they're almost friendly and working together." He looked away. "At least they were until tonight."

"Randy has been working rather closely with your sister. That seems odd."

Connor nodded. "Lionel Trescott has wanted the pub for a while. Randy is the architect he hired to do the renovation design. Dad would never consider selling and neither would Bill. When Leslie inherited it she saw dollar signs."

"Was Bill actually going to sell?"

"Heard he was considering it with Leslie pressuring him."

"So it's possible someone murdered her to stop the sale."

"Anything is possible."

"How did you feel about your sister selling the pub? Didn't you have any say in the matter?"

"Nope. It all went to Leslie."

At Jeb's questioning glance, he continued. "My father left me a Bible. A brand-new shiny red leather-bound Bible. And that's it. He left his half of the business – the business his father built from the ground up – to Leslie."

"That must have been a hard pill to swallow."

"Yeah. Well." Connor shrugged. "Not much I can do about it. I never wanted the pub anyway. Couldn't stand being cooped up all day." He shuddered. "I prefer the open sea."

"Still, he could have left you shares. Money. Something. But he left it all to her."

"If you're looking for a motive then you found one Sheriff," Connor said wryly.

"You certainly had a reason to hate your sister."

"And as you said earlier, so did a lot of people."

"What time did you get to the pub tonight Connor?"

"Just after eight."

"Where were you before that?"

"Around town. At the wharf for a while. Took a bottle of beer and a pack of smokes. Nobody saw me though." He shrugged. "Guess I'm a pretty good suspect."

Jeb stood up. "You can go now Mr. Abbott. But don't leave town."

Connor looked amused. "I wasn't planning on it."

.

Kitty was sitting in one of the burgundy chairs in the small lobby of the station sipping what the deputy assured her was coffee. It was hot and dark and bitter but tasted like day old sludge. Still, Kitty held the cup between her shaky hands and sipped the murky liquid.

She'd given her statement to Deputy Rob and answered questions for almost twenty minutes before he let her move out here. Kitty had seen Bill in Jeb's office then. She watched through a glass window for several moments as he sat quietly weeping. All she could

90

do was stand there on the other side of the glass and watch. As much as she wanted to keep her emotions in check they refused to yield. Her heart softened when she saw the pain her ex-husband was in. How could it not? She was married to him for twenty-seven years and he was the father of her four children. It would make her heartless if she didn't feel sorry for him. So she had watched with great compassion as he struggled with his grief before moving away to give him some privacy.

"When can I go home?" she asked Deputy Rob when he appeared moments later.

"You can go now, Ms. Appleton," Jeb said, coming up behind Rob. "I'll drop you off myself. It's late." It was in fact after eleven now.

"Oh that isn't necessary," Kitty said quickly. "I can see myself home."

"I'll drop you off," Jeb insisted and Kitty acquiesced.

In the car Kitty wasn't sure what to say. Was she allowed to speak with him freely about the case? Should she just remain silent about the whole thing? She peeked at Jeb as he drove. His face was set and he looked troubled. Kitty hated to think she was the cause of his upset. She didn't want him to get into any kind of trouble because of her and her foolish idea.

"Jeb I'm so sorry," she finally told him.

"For what? Did you kill Leslie?"

She flushed. "No of course not."

"Then you don't have anything to be sorry for."

"I feel like I do. I never meant to cause you any problems. If our relationship is going to cause any conflict-"

"It won't," he said flatly. "I'll admit it may not have been very convenient having you involved in discovering Leslie's body but we'll deal with the consequences if there are any."

"I wish I could be of more help."

"You just steer clear of Bill," Jeb said. "And let us do our job."

She hesitated a moment. "Is he okay?'

"In time he will be. Bill just stepped into a nightmare and he's in shock. And the next few days are going to get worse. He was able to answer some of our questions though, which was a big help. We'll find whoever did this. I promise." He cut his eyes to her. "How are you holding up? Finding a murder victim is never easy."

"I'm fine."

They arrived at her cottage within minutes. Jeb was already around the car by the time she got her door open and startled her. At her surprised face he smiled and Kitty momentarily forgot about everything happening in her life. He held out his arm for her to hold on to and the warmth of his smile went right to her heart.

The last time he dropped her off there had been an awkward kiss; awkward on her part anyway. They both knew it and neither wanted to bring it up now. Instead Jeb reached out to gently touch her cheek for a moment before saying good-night and walking away. Kitty stood on the front step and watched until the lights on his truck were out of sight.

After Jeb left Kitty fed her girls, who were complaining loudly at being alone so long. She stroked each of them as they ate the canned food she set out on the counter. It was comforting to be home. She wanted to forget the memory of Leslie lying dead on the floor but Kitty was quite sure that vivid image would be burned into her brain for the rest of her life.

It was well after midnight when the banging on the door woke her. She wrapped her faded blue cotton robe around herself and padded downstairs to see who was on her front step and what news the bearer might have. When she flung open the door she was shocked to see Bill standing in front of her, shoulders stooped and eyes misty with unshed tears. "Bill what are you doing here?"

"I can't go home," he said thickly. "The sheriff won't let me and even if they did I just couldn't go back inside. Not after what happened in there."

"I'm very sorry for you Bill," Kitty told him sincerely. "But you shouldn't be here."

"I have nowhere else to go."

"Charlie would let you stay with him under the circumstances. Or Jenny and Brad could put you up."

"I want to sleep in my own house."

At this Kitty bristled but dampened it down because of his obvious state of mind. "This isn't your home anymore. It's mine."

"Please Kitty. Let me in. I don't want to be alone. Don't turn me away."

Kitty tightened her grip on the door knob. "I'm not supposed to talk with you Bill. You have to find another place to stay. Try Jenny. Or the inn."

Bill stood rooted to the spot, staring her down and looking utterly pitiful.

"Fine. You can sleep in the guest room. Just for tonight." She stood aside to let him enter.

"We have a guest room now?"

"No *I* have a guest room. It's Jenny's old room."

Bill paused in the hallway. "I don't have any stuff. Do you still have any of my things?"

"No. You took everything that wasn't nailed down."

His reddened eyes searched hers. "What should I do?"

"Sleep in your underwear."

"But what about tomorrow? And the next day?"

"I'm sure you can get into the house to get some of your clothes. Or maybe they do it for you. I'm really not sure. We can ask Jeb tomorrow."

"Jeb, huh? So has your boyfriend stayed here before?" he lashed out suddenly from his own pain.

Kitty was angered and embarrassed by the question. "No. Not that it's any of your business. I'm going to bed. You know where your room is." And she hurried past him to escape to her own room.

Chapter 9

"I called as soon as I got here this morning."

Jeb was standing with Rob surveying the damage outside Randy Parker' office. The ground office Randy rented was on the back side of an old building in the middle of town. Small and practical with a minimalist interior as far as Jeb could see. The window in the back door had been smashed in and someone had proceeded to reach inside and unlock the door. Rob went in and surveyed the damage while Jeb merely poked his head into the trashed office and sneezed. The lingering smoke odor made Rob sneeze. "Sorry. Is there anything missing? Can you even tell in this mess?"

Randy nodded. "The plans for the new pub are gone and the model is smashed into pieces. I'm going to have to make a new one fast."

Rob and Jeb exchanged glances. It was obvious this wasn't a coincidence. Not after one of the owner's of the pub was murdered last night. "Nothing else?"

"Not a thing."

"Did you touch anything?"

"No. I took one look and called you. I've been waiting outside."

"Get forensics down here," Jeb told Rob as they stepped away from Randy. "Let's see if we catch a break here. I've got to go talk to Eileen Abbott. After this I want you and Bobby to talk to all the Appletons' neighbors. Maybe someone saw or heard something."

"Someone really had a problem with that pub being sold," Rob observed.

"It would appear that way," Jeb said cryptically as he left.

.

Jeb hated talking with the family of victims of such tragic deaths. It was the hardest part of the job and he would never get used to it as long as he was in law enforcement. He'd rather be out with Rob talking with the Appleton's neighbors to see if any had witnessed something. But here he was sitting in a little parlor with dark paneling and worn furniture with a woman who was trying her best to serve coffee and cake without falling apart.

"Sugar?" she asked, looking at him with reddened eyes.

"Yes, please."

He took the cup and waited for her to fix her own. Jeb didn't want the coffee. But he knew it helped the grief-stricken to have something trivial to do in moments like this. And the first step in finding the killer was finding out everything he could about the victim. "Mrs. Abbott, can you tell me about Leslie?"

"Of course," Mrs. Abbott said, setting the pot down on the coffee table. "My daughter was beautiful and ambitious and hard-working. She didn't back down when she wanted something. A lot of people found that a flaw in her character. I know she wasn't a particularly nice girl at times, Sheriff. But there was something about her that also drew people to her. And I loved her dearly."

"Bill said you and your husband took her in when she was little and raised her from a young age?"

Eileen Abbott nodded. "Her mother – my younger sister Margaret – died when Leslie was just a little thing. Barely two years old. Leslie's real father – Judge Leroy Burgess - was in the middle of a very important trial when it happened and felt he couldn't give a little girl the proper attention she needed to help her through the grieving process. He sent her to stay with us temporarily. But in the end she stayed here in The Bottom with Henry and Connor and me. Connor is my step-son by the way. He was five when Henry and I married. We were happy and complete when Leslie joined our family. And we *were* a family. I loved both Connor and Leslie as if they were my own, and they were brother and sister as far as anyone is concerned. The judge saw how well she was doing, how happy she was with a real family and decided she should stay with us. We never legally adopted her but we were her parents." Her eyes filled with tears. "I loved her as much as any mother could love a child."

"What was her relationship with her real father like?" He needed to get a complete picture of Leslie Appleton which included her past right up till the moment she died.

"He visited regularly of course when she was little. Sent her gifts. Always remembered her birthday," she said with a wistful smile. "Leslie adored seeing him when she was little. He was like a favorite uncle. I think there was a little resentment when she got older and we told her the truth." Mrs. Abbott met Jeb's eyes. "The judge is a hard man, Sheriff. He's always had trouble showing emotion, even when Margaret died. But he is a good man. Honest. Determined to make the world a better place. And he did the best he could for his only child."

"What about more recently? What was their relationship like as adults?"

"When Leslie went away to college she was able to spend time with the judge. Leslie always considered Henry her father but she and the judge did develop a closeness. I think it was hard for both of them to explore their feelings - Leslie was a lot like Leroy in many ways. But I know he loved her and she was fond of him. He'd always been a part of her life after all."

"Tell me about her first husband Randy."

"Oh." Eileen let out a soft sigh. "We were all so happy when she settled down. For a while we weren't sure where Leslie was going to end up. But Randy was good for her. He was several years younger but in some ways I think he was more mature than she was. He even gave up his business to move back here with Leslie when Henry took ill three years ago. We were so happy to have her back, even under the circumstances. With Henry dying we weren't sure what to do about the pub but Leslie jumped in and really helped Bill keep it going. And that's when Leslie set her sights on him I suppose. We were heartbroken when Leslie divorced Randy so she could be with Bill Appleton."

"You didn't approve of her marrying Bill?"

"How could I? She broke up a couple that had been a part of our lives for decades and caused so much pain. I was embarrassed to show my face for the longest time."

"When was the last time you saw her? And how did she seem?"

"I saw her Sunday afternoon. She always stopped by to check on me. She was on top of the world actually. It looked like they were going to be selling the pub and everything was going to work out the way she wanted."

"How did you feel about her selling your husband's pub?"

Eileen stared at the slim gold wedding band on her left hand. "I was sad. But it was hers to do with what she liked."

"Forgive me for saying this, but it seems odd that your late husband slighted you and his son and left the whole business to essentially his niece."

"Henry left me this wonderful little house free and clear and a comfortable life. Connor has his boat and his calling to the ocean. What did Leslie have? She was full of ambition and dreams and no direction to go in. Henry gave her a chance to take over his legacy to the town."

"And she was going to sell it to the highest bidder." Jeb shook his head.

Eileen shrugged. "Maybe. Maybe not. It was my conviction that Leslie would have realized in the end what the right thing to do was."

"You believe Leslie might have changed her mind?"

"I believe anything is possible Sheriff."

•

Tuesday morning Kitty got up and followed her morning ritual despite feeling tired and drained from the events of the previous evening. It seemed like the best way to get the whole ordeal out of her mind was to escape to her painting. She spent all morning in her studio trying not to think about what she had seen but it was always there in the back of her mind. It was nearly one when she put her brushes aside and hurried back to the house for a light lunch to settle her stomach. Bill was sitting at her kitchen table in the same rumpled clothes he had shown up in last night. She could tell he hadn't showered or combed his hair or done anything at all. He stared at her with bleak eyes.

"How are you feeling?" she asked kindly.

"I don't know. I don't know how I feel. Numb. But I ache everywhere. How is that possible?"

"I'm sorry for your loss Bill." It was awkward but it was the truth. "What are you going to do?"

"Do? What do you mean?"

"Where are you going to go? Have you thought about making arrangements? There's a lot to take care of."

"I guess I'll talk to Eileen," he mumbled.

"Okay." She sat down across from him. He really looked horrid. His eyes were red-rimmed, his face unshaven. Bill looked like a lost soul sitting in her kitchen. She hated to push him but he couldn't stay here. He needed to see that. "Where are you going to stay?"

"Here," he told her without really seeing her.

"You can't stay here. Last night was just a temporary fix. You need to pull yourself together Bill." Kitty tried to sound firm but failed miserably. Her voice was pleading and she hated it. With Bill she never had any kind of authority in any capacity and it was evident even now. She tried to get fired up like she had on Saturday but there were no smoldering embers left in her to fan into a raging flame. Right now she felt as lifeless as the burnt ashes still sitting in her fireplace.

Bill started weeping softly and Kitty groaned inwardly. Now what?

"They said it could be a while before I can go back to the house Kitty. Please can I come home?" he said, mopping his eyes.

She always thought deep down that seeing her ex-husband pleading to come back would be rewarding or empowering. It wasn't. It didn't make her heart happy at all seeing him like this. "Okay. All right. You can stay. But just for a few days. Until the Sheriff says you can go back to your own house."

He nodded, overwhelmed with relief. "Of course. But I don't have anything to wear. Could you go pick up my stuff for me?"

She shook her head. "No. You need to call the sheriff yourself."

"Please Kitty. I can't go back there. I can't be reminded of my beautiful Leslie lying there. I loved her so much. She was everything to me." He started weeping again and Kitty felt her stomach turn.

She wanted to kick him out then. Kitty suddenly wanted him to be alone and miserable and have to think about putting his life back together without the one he loved. The same way she did when he walked out. But the spurt of anger was eventually silenced by the compassionate heart that was alive and well in Kitty. As much as it irked her to do so she would do as he asked because it was the right thing to do. Because he was another human being in pain and Kitty could not, would not turn her back on that despite the pain he had inflicted on her. "All right Bill. I'll see what I can do."

Bill smiled a watery, heartfelt smile. "Thank you Kitty. You're always there for me."

•

After lunch Jeb headed over on foot to Trescott Developers. It was in an old brick firehouse that had been converted into a posh office building that lent a stately elegance to the town center. It also put it within walking distance of the station so he arrived within minutes.

Lionel Trescott was gracious, charming and owned half the county at the age of forty-five. He had a million-dollar haircut, sharp eyes and all the right answers.

"I was sorry to hear about Leslie Appleton," Lionel said gravely. "Lovely woman."

Jeb raised an eyebrow. "Really? You're the first one to say that."

Lionel chuckled. "I liked Leslie. She went after what she wanted. I can appreciate that quality better than most people."

"Because you're the same way. You wanted the pub and got it."

"More or less." He leaned back in his enormous leather chair and tapped the armrest. "It wasn't official yet but it would have been very soon."

"Why did you want the pub so bad? Rock Bottom seems like a rather inconsequential town."

"What you fail to see Sheriff is the potential. Developers are seizing land in this area and slapping up resort areas and condos all along the coast because the hard part is already done. People love the 'quaint little beachside communities' up here. They're established and have mass appeal. All we have to do is offer them a charming little place to eat and congregate and they will come in droves. It's money in the bank for my company as soon as the tourists discover what a gem my remodeled Bottom's Up Pub is. "

Jeb nodded towards the model on the credenza to his left. It didn't look that different from what was already standing on the bluff. "That's the new pub? The one that's going to make you a pot of money while exploiting the people who live here?"

"Yes, that's it. And I must say *exploiting* is a strong word. I rather see it as stimulating their economy by bringing in wealthy patrons to their little hick towns for a few months out of the year or longer in some cases. It's good for everyone."

"It wasn't so good for Leslie Appleton."

"What makes you so sure her death had anything to do with this pending sale? As you said she wasn't a popular person."

"Who do you think killed Leslie?"

Lionel drummed his finders on his massive cherry table. "I always say start close to home. Her husband's ex-wife would be the logical choice. I heard about her. Well, everyone has. One of those spineless, sad little women who never got over losing her husband." He feigned shock. "Oh, I believe I heard something about you being involved with the former Mrs. Appleton. That must make this investigation awkward."

Jeb wanted to lean across the desk and spit in the man's eye. "I'll look into that. Anything else?"

"Actually there is. There's a woman who has been trying to sabotage the deal the last couple weeks. She's been picketing my building and handing out these silly papers." He handed a colorful sheet to Jeb. "Trying to stop the Appleton's from selling. It was having a negligible effect really and I hardly think she's worth mentioning. But you did say anything."

Jeb skimmed the light blue paper. It was identical to the one at the murder scene except the color. "Do you know who it is leading this revolt?"

"I haven't bothered to look too deeply into it. She was more an annoyance than a threat. But I do know she works at the library."

"So as far as you could tell the deal was set and all was fine?"

Lionel nodded. "That's exactly what I'm saying. Therefore no motive here." He smiled easily again and his eyes indicated the door.

Jeb rose. "Thanks for your time." He opened the door and started to step through. "Just one more thing. Where were you Monday evening?"

"Check with my secretary on your way out. She can give you all the information you need."

"I'll do that."

•

As soon as he got back to the station he set Rob into checking Trescott's alibi. It was shaky at best. Apparently he'd been out of town over the weekend and flown into Portland at six. Forty-five minute drive plus time to get his luggage put him back into town around seven. He'd get the flights verified and have Ron confirm with his wife as well. If he was telling the truth it was certainly plausible that Lionel Trescott got back to Rock Bottom, whacked Leslie and gotten home at a reasonable time. But it didn't seem likely a man would come home from a long business trip and immediately go murder a business associate who was finally selling him the property he wanted.

Not likely. But still possible.

Jeb checked his voicemail and found there was a message to call Harry. He sank into his chair and called his chief M.E. "Tell me you have something," he said as soon as Harry answered.

"Well it's not the proverbial smoking gun, but it could be useful. I found several latent finger prints on the body. It may be nothing but it could be something. Sending them over for your boys to check out. It wasn't easy but I managed to get one good print and a partial."

"Harry, have I told you lately you're my favorite medical examiner?"

"No. But not many people do."

"I'll get Johnson on this. Thanks Harry."

"Just doing my job," Harry said before he hung up.

"Bobby!" Jeb yelled, and his youngest deputy appeared almost immediately.

"Yes sir?"

"The woman handing out the flyers works at the library. Find out who she is."

"Done," Rob interrupted from his desk. "Annie Goodwin. She's the librarian. I checked with the print shop in Pebble Creek and they made the flyers for her Monday. She picked them up Monday evening around six-fifteen."

"Good work.

"We also got the phone records in while you were gone. They confirmed Leslie's phone call to Randy at six-fifty. There was also another call to her home phone at six-twenty."

"From who?"

"Annie Goodwin."

"Let's go," Jeb said, standing back up. "Did we get anything from forensics yet?"

Rob pointed to the mess on Jeb's desk. "I put the folder with the report right there."

"Just tell me what it said."

"The candlestick was definitely the murder weapon as Dutton initially said. No prints though. Not a surprise."

"No of course not. Nothing ever goes that smoothly."

"There were traces of cigarette smoke on her clothes and green paint smudges on her fingertips. Everything is already at the lab to see if we can identify the brands."

"Good. In the mean time let's see a librarian about a motive."

Annie was sitting at the front desk area when Jeb and Rob walked into the Rock Bottom Library. It was quiet as death and not a soul in sight save the brown-haired woman watching and a small black dog who greeted them with much more enthusiasm than the woman at the desk. Jeb thought she paled considerably by the time they stood in front of her. "Annie Goodwin?" Jeb asked.

"Yes?"

"We're going to need to ask you some questions."

"About Leslie?"

"Yes. Specifically about those flyers you've been handing out and a petition. We found them at the murder scene."

Jeb thought he saw a spark of fear in her eyes as she stammered a reply. "Yes, I've been passing them out for a week now. All perfectly legal."

There was a pile of signs leaning against the back wall. The one in front was white with green lettering which he could read if he squinted just right: *Save the Pub! Fight Modernization!* "What did you hope to accomplish with the flyers and signs?" he asked nodding towards the stack of signs. "Did you expect it to stop the sale?"

Annie glared. "Public awareness is half the battle. If people saw in black and white what kind of historical significance that building has they might stand up and make a difference."

"Did it?"

"Possibly. We'll have to wait and see. Bill gets to decide the fate of the Bottom's Up now."

"You called Leslie Monday evening around six-twenty. Why?"

"I just wanted to try one last time to talk some sense into her. But she was in a mood and hung up on me."

"What did she say exactly?"

"Leslie was ranting about how 'he was going to be sorry.' That was all I got out of it, other than some curse words I won't repeat. Then she hung up."

"He? He who?"

Annie shrugged. "No idea."

Jeb wanted to reach across the counter and shake the woman. "And you didn't think that was relevant to the murder investigation? You didn't think to tell us this the other night?"

"No. Not really. How does it help? There's nothing definitive in the information I just provided you."

"We know it's a man she was angry with," Rob pointed out. "That's definitive."

"Is there anything else you want to share with us?" Jeb ground out.

Annie shook her head. "I don't think so Sheriff."

•

On his way back to the station there was a call patched through from Kitty. Bill wanted some things from the house and she wanted to know if that was possible. Normally Jeb would have had one of his other deputies take care of it but since he wanted to see how Kitty was he had Rob turn around and head over to the Appleton house.

Kitty shivered as she waited just inside the door while Jeb instructed Rob what could leave the house. After Rob left to fetch some meager possessions for Bill, Jeb turned his full attention on Kitty.

She looked stressed. Seeing something tragic often affected people harder than they ever would have expected. He'd encouraged Kitty to speak with someone about it to help her cope but she declined. He admired her gentle but firm spirit. She was determined to do the right thing no matter what it cost and the proof was her standing in this room now. It was very evident by her body language that she wanted to be anywhere but in this house. "How are you holding up?" Jeb asked her with genuine concern.

"I'm fine. Really. It was a shock more than anything. Bill is the one who is a mess of course."

"Where is he staying? With your son?" Jeb had assumed that was where Bill was and that Kitty was being considerate by pitching in and helping her family.

Kitty shook her head and couldn't meet his eyes. "He showed up on my doorstep last night. I let him stay in the guestroom."

For a couple of very different reasons this disturbed Jeb. First, he didn't like Bill being anywhere near Kitty. Second, her allowing Bill to stay at the home they shared together for more than two decades did not look good for her at all. If one was to start looking at motives, Kitty definitely had one even though he did not for a moment believe she had anything to do with the murder. But word around town was that she had been waiting and hoping for a reconciliation with her ex. It could certainly be misconstrued by anyone looking for a motive and make for some very unpleasant gossip. "That is not a good idea Kitty."

"I know. But he was so shattered I couldn't turn him away. He has nowhere to go."

"Send him to your son's house."

"Charlie and Bill don't really get along too well. Bill wasn't comfortable staying with them."

"But you're comfortable with him at your house?" Jeb had to ask.

"No," she said softly. "I am not. But it's the right thing to do."

Jeb studied her. She was nervous and fidgety. Her hands kept moving to her pockets, to her sides, to tucking an errant piece of hair behind an ear and then back to her pockets. "Why don't you wait outside? I'll bring the bag out to you when my deputy is through."

Kitty nodded jerkily. Being in the house was making her ill. She swore she could actually smell death in here and it was nauseating. No wonder Bill didn't want to come back inside.

Once Kitty left to wait outside Jeb headed to the back of the house in search of his deputy. He found his deputy filling a plastic bag with clothes he was checking over carefully. "Just the basics," Jeb told him.

"Yes Sir," the deputy nodded.

Jeb's phone rang and he answered it on the second ring. Harry was as good as his word. The autopsy confirmed his initial cause of death and also pinpointed the time of death to a smaller timeframe. "She was killed between six and eight," Harry said. "I'd guess closer to the earlier end."

"We're waiting on the phone records," Jeb told him. "If they confirm the call Randy Parker got then we can close the gap to between six-fifty and eight."

"Well then what do you need me for?" Harry quipped. "You already know everything I do."

"If you find anything else let me know."

"You're number one on my speed dial."

"Good to know," Jeb said.

Chapter 10

Kitty returned to her house and tugged the heavy suitcase from the Volvo. As she approached her front step she noticed Miss Tulip sitting forlornly on the front step waiting for her. Kitty let go of the suitcase and hurried to Miss Tulip, scooping her up and hugging her close. "What are you doing outside?" Miss Tulip didn't answer but seemed relieved to have been rescued based on the mad purring that ensued.

She stormed into her house and released Miss Tulip once the door was firmly closed behind her. Bill was sitting on the sofa watching TV in his underwear and eating a bowl of cereal out of her mother's China rose pattern serving bowl. "Bill!"

He continued watching the TV until a commercial freed his attention long enough to notice Kitty. "You're back. Where's my stuff?"

Kitty went over and turned off the TV. "Why was Miss Tulip outside?"

Bill blinked. "Who?"

Kitty pointed to her large black and white cat, now perched on the credenza by the door. "My cat. Did you let her out?"

"I put them out because I hate cats. You know that."

"Them! You mean Petunia is still outside too?" Kitty asked in horror. Her cats weren't used to being outside. They were declawed and defenseless, especially around here. There was a wide range of wild life in this area and small cats and dogs often fell prey if owners were careless with their pets. "Bill you had no right to do that! Get dressed and come help me look for her!"

"I'm not going out looking for a cat."

"Yes. You are."

Bill was once again aghast at Kitty's tone. She never used to speak to him in this manner. Now she was yanking the bowl out of his hands and looking quite perturbed. "And this is my mother's china! You don't eat cereal out of it sitting on the couch looking like a bum. Now go get some pants on. I'll get a flashlight. It's going to be dark before long." He watched her hurry out of the living room with his supper.

"Just a dumb ole cat," he grumped as he heaved himself up. "I just lost my wife and she's more upset about losing a cat than a person in our community." He glared at Miss Tulip when he got in front of her. "You and your friend just ruined my evening, thank you very much." He swiped at her to send her flying off the furniture but Miss Tulip hissed and swatted him back.

"You little devil!" he croaked at her.

"Bill! Stop messing with my cat!"

"Fine." He stomped up the stairs muttering under his breath.

Miss Tulip turned her eyes to her human companion. There was a silent plea in them. "We'll find Petunia," Kitty said, stroking the glossy coat. "And then Bill needs to find other accommodations."

•

They searched for an hour in every direction but couldn't find her. By the time they got back to the house Kitty was tired and miserable and in tears. Bill was almost no help at all in the search. He complained incessantly about the inconvenience and her lack of sympathy for what he was going through. Kitty understood his grief and of course sympathized but she had seen this as a chance for him to get out of his slump, if only for a few minutes. She suspected he had been sitting all day in the house grieving and thought a little time outside in the cool air might help clear his head some small bit. That and she was rather angry at him for being so insensitive as to let her feline baby outside and expected he should help retrieve that which he lost.

But they returned empty handed. Bill was without remorse and sank back down on her sofa, reaching for the remote. "Could you get me something to drink Kitty? Maybe something to settle my stomach. Ginger Ale or something like that would be perfect."

"I don't have any."

Bill turned that baleful expression on her. "Maybe you could get me some at the market when you go get my stuff."

"Your stuff? You mean the suitcase that's still sitting on my front lawn?"

He nodded. "I'm pretty wiped out. Could you get it?"

Kitty's shoulders slumped. Her anger was gone and she wanted to sit and cry. Bill didn't understand how fond of her cats she was and how much Petunia's loss meant. She was upset too.

But his loss was so much more than hers, she scolded herself. Surely she was being petty. Resigned to the fact that she had lost a beloved cat and gained a grieving ex-husband she went back outside and dragged the heavy suitcase inside. She continued until she was upstairs in the guest room and had it opened up on the bed. Without thinking she pulled out his shirts and hung them in the closet. She put his underwear and socks in the dresser, socks on the left and underwear on the right the way he always liked and arranged by color, light to dark.

She stared at his clothes. What on earth was she doing? He wasn't supposed to be here in her house. He left her. Why was she folding his underwear for him?

Because it was the right thing to do, she reminded herself. It's what God would want her to do. Bill was the father of her four children and a huge part of who she was. She couldn't turn her back on him because he had made a mistake years ago.

Kitty went back downstairs and fixed Bill a glass of water and dropped an antacid in it. She knew it always soothed his stomach when he was stressed. He accepted it with a smile and drank it down quickly. He let out a loud belch and then reddened. "Sorry Kitty. But I do feel better. You always could make me feel better."

"Good." She paused and took a fortifying breath. She had to be strong to do this. It's what the good Lord wanted her to do, she was sure of it. "Bill, you may stay here as long as you need to. I shouldn't have been so cross with you earlier. I know you're suffering a terrible loss right now and I need to be a little more compassionate."

Her words took him by surprise. "Thank you Kitty. I do appreciate how uncomfortable this must be for you and I am grateful. If I were in your shoes I don't know if I could do what you are doing."

Bill had never uttered his appreciation in the entire time they were married, or empathized with her in any situation. "Thank you for saying that Bill." She hesitated only because she was still upset about Petunia but in the end she did what was expected of her. "If you'd like I'll go fix us something to eat. You must be starving since I took your cereal away from you."

For the first time Bill saw what a gem he had tossed aside in a careless moment. "That would be very nice."

Rob leaned in the doorway of Jeb's office. "We finished talking with all the guys Bill was bowling with last night. Plus the crew that worked at the bowling alley last night. There's a gap in his alibi."

"How long?"

"About twenty minutes. Several of the lanes went down and quite a few folks were left hanging till they got them fixed. People were milling around talking, getting food, taking smoke breaks. No one remembers for sure where Bill went. He could have slipped home, killed Leslie and been back in time. It's eight minutes from the bowling alley to the house. I timed it," Rob ended triumphantly.

"It'd be cutting it close but feasible," Jeb mused.

"Should we bring him in again?"

"Not until we have something solid." As much as he'd like to see Bill hauled away in handcuffs he had a hard time believing Bill's grief had been anything but genuine. Jeb still intended to look into every last aspect of the man's life before moving on to the next suspect. But it made him supremely uncomfortable knowing the best suspect they had for the murder was staying under Kitty's roof.

•

After supper Kitty put away the food and cleaned the dishes as usual. What was unusual about the evening was that Bill was in her living room watching TV like he had for most of the years they were married. It was odd really. She'd gotten used to the quiet, the solitude over the last year. Now having him here seemed strange. Dinner had been not quite awkward but certainly less than comfortable. Somewhere in the middle. They had talked about the kids and mutual acquaintances and avoided speaking of Leslie. It was for the best for both of them and Kitty was relieved to not have to watch him fall apart yet again at the mention of her name.

Around seven the doorbell rang and Kitty tossed the dish cloth she had been drying dishes with on the counter and hurried to see who was at her door. By the time she got to it Bill was already there letting a very surprised Liza Jane in.

"Liza! I wasn't expecting you."

"Yes. I see that," she said, eyeing Bill suspiciously. "What's he doing here?"

"Kitty is very graciously putting me up for a couple days."

"Isn't that very hospitable of Kitty?" Liza Jane grabbed Kitty by the arm and dragged her down the hall to the kitchen. Once they were out of earshot Liza set the bottle of Moxie she carried on the counter and faced her friend squarely. "What are you doing letting that man within ten feet of this house?"

Kitty shrugged. "He had nowhere else to go."

"That's not true. You have four kids. He could have crashed with one of them if he asked. This is ridiculous. He shouldn't be here!"

"Is it really so bad to want to help him? We *were* married for twenty-seven years."

"I don't care if you were married for fifty! He's a mess. He just lost his wife and now he's running back to you for sympathy and support. This is not a good idea Kitty."

"I don't think that's it," Kitty argued weakly. "He's just lonely and sad. I know how that feels."

"Yes you do. Because he's the one who made you feel that way!"

"It's just for a few days. Until his house is cleared by the police."

"Umm hmm," Liza Jane said. She went to the cupboard and pulled out glasses. "I hope you have cheesecake."

"I always have cheesecake," Kitty assured her friend. She got out the plates and dessert and then they settled in at the table she had just cleared.

"Kitty I am really worried about this situation," Liza Jane told her friend. "You know I love you and only want the best for you. And I don't think Bill being here is the best for you."

"It's just temporary, I promise."

Liza Jane wasn't sure she believed Kitty but decided she'd hounded her enough on the subject. "How are you holding up? I know seeing dead people can be traumatic for some."

"It was unpleasant and I really don't want to talk about it Liza. I know to you it's just part of everyday life. I can't be so cavalier about seeing death."

"It takes some getting used to. And of course when I get them it's in another context. You saw a crime scene so I would imagine there's more to process," Liza Jane said as she ate. "I can understand how that can mess with you."

"I think the whole image is permanently imprinted on to my brain. I don't want to see it but I can see everything. Like a photograph." Kitty shook herself. "Other than that I'm doing all right. I hope Jeb can find whoever did this quickly."

"How is Jeb doing?" Liza asked casually.

Kitty blushed. "Jeb is fine."

"He is that. You two make an adorable couple if you don't mind me saying." She reached across the table and touched her best friend's arm. "I am so happy that you found someone as special as Jeb. You deserve someone who appreciates you sweetie."

"We've only been out handful of times. Don't go planning our wedding."

"Wedding? Who's getting married?" Bill wanted to know. He was suddenly standing in the doorway with that sad, blank expression again.

"No one," Kitty assured him.

"But Kitty and the Sheriff sure would make a nice couple, don't you think so Bill? He's so handsome and looks great in that uniform.".

Bill frowned and Kitty pleaded with her eyes for Liza to stop speaking nonsense. "Would you like some cheesecake Bill? There's plenty. I don't know what I was thinking not offering you any."

"Okay. That would be nice." It occurred to him to make an effort to be nice so he added, "Thank you."

"Here. Sit" Liza ordered as she pushed a chair out with her foot.

"All right. If you don't mind." He slid into the chair he had always sat in at dinner and felt oddly comforted.

"Doesn't matter if I mind or not. This is Kitty's house and you're her guest. For a very short time," Liza added and glared meaningfully at Bill.

Bill avoided the pointed stare and watched Kitty as she approached with his plate. She really was pretty, he thought sadly. Not as pretty as Leslie had been. But nice to look at, especially when she was taking care of him. He missed being taken care of.

They ate in silence for several moments, each lost in their own thoughts. It was of course Liza who finally broke the quiet. "So Bill do you have any idea who might have whacked Leslie?"

Kitty's fork clattered against her plate. "Liza! Must we keep bringing this up?" She thought it was terribly inconsiderate to bring up his recently murdered wife in conversation so casually.

"I'm sure he's been over it with the sheriff. I was just curious," Liza Jane said defensively.

Bill shook his head. "The only person who would really have a grudge is Kitty." He looked dolefully at his ex-wife. "But she wouldn't hurt Leslie." He might be confused about a lot of things but he knew that now.

Kitty smiled weakly at Bill. His faith in her dimmed some of the anger over Petunia. "Of course I wouldn't."

"What about work? Was anything going on at the pub?"

"Nothing unusual. No squabble with employees. No irritated customers. Just the usual stuff. Everybody loved Leslie." His eyes reddened and he wiped them with the napkin Kitty immediately handed him. "She was so full of life and amazing at so many things."

"She certainly was," Kitty agreed because it was the polite thing to say.

"Well I'll admit I'm worried about the whole thing. Nothing like this ever happened here in Rock Bottom," Liza said as she pushed her plate away. "What kind of world is it coming to when we aren't even safe here?"

"I don't know," Bill said quietly. "But I do know my life just got a whole lot lonelier without someone to share it with."

"I'm sure Sheriff Carpenter will find whoever did this horrible thing," Kitty assured Bill for lack of anything else to say, and Liza worried at the tentative smiles the two exchanged.

•

Tuesday evening Jeb got to his house just after eight. He didn't consider it *home*. It was a place to rest his head but it didn't have any of the qualities he associated with home. The rooms were comfortable enough and the location was prime. A little work had turned the former summer cottage into a tolerable year-round abode for a single man who was hardly here anyway. But it lacked heart and Jeb didn't know how to go about giving it one. So he generally avoided the issue by going outside on his little stretch of beach for solace.

Tonight his brain wanted to continue working on the case but he'd been working for thirty-six hours straight and his body was demanding rest. He found something in a box at the back of the freezer and microwaved it for five minutes. It tasted like cardboard with bland brown gravy but he finished it and showered. Since he was still wound up from the case he decided a quick walk on the beach would help get his mind off the case so he could come home and crash for eight hours. He knew he needed sleep if he was going to be of any use to anyone but it was hard to shut down with his so much to occupy his mind.

Jeb half hoped he'd run into Kitty but that was unlikely since he purposely headed away from town to avoid any other late night walkers. He walked a mile down the beach until he couldn't go any further without endangering himself. The sand stopped and turned rocky up ahead, eventually forming a jutting, jagged coast of nearly impassible rocks. In the daytime it was possible to climb the slippery reef if necessary but at night it would be suicidal. So he stopped and watched by moonlight as the water thrashed angrily against the rocks and then withdrew, over and over again. The repetitive motion kept his attention and the sloshing, swooshing sound of the water calmed the anxious flow of energy that had been surging through him ever since they found Leslie Appleton dead.

By the time he returned home he felt calm enough to settle in for the night. Jeb read his Bible for only a few minutes before sliding into bed and seeking the sleep he desperately needed. Laying there waiting for sleep to come he thought about the time he'd spent with Kitty over the last week. She was so much more than he ever expected. He enjoyed talking with her, seeing her face light up, listening to her soft laugh, sharing stories about their work and children. They may have started meeting under a pretense but he felt like the tender feelings he harbored were mutual, at least to some degree. His brain was starting to catch up with what his heart had been telling him since they first started spending time together: falling in love with Kitty Appleton was just about the easiest thing in the world to do. It was clear to Jeb that Kitty was a blessing to everyone she knew and he had no intention of walking away the way her husband had. His last waking thought as he drifted to sleep was the way her dark blues eyes lit up when he walked in the room.

Chapter 11

Wednesday morning Jeb sent Rob and another deputy digging into every nook and cranny of Bill's life. He wanted to know where Bill was every minute of every day for the last three months and all his finances checked thoroughly with an emphasis on a possible insurance policy or large withdrawals recently made. Jeb went to the bowling alley and spoke again with the manager to get his own read on the situation and found nothing more or less than Rob had. He checked the local businesses and gas station to see if anyone remembered seeing Bill's car go by at any point in the early evening but came up empty.

He knew Kitty was an early riser so he swung by her place on the way back. She answered the door looking tired but unthreatened and unharmed. He felt foolish for worrying but the idea of Bill hurting Leslie and then turning on Kitty was gnawing at him. "Is Bill around?" he asked after a moment of losing himself in her mesmerizing blue eyes.

Kitty shook her head. "He's not come down yet. I don't think he slept well. I heard him tossing and turning and crying most of the night."

Jeb frowned. "I'll need to speak with him again soon. I'll try back later today or tomorrow." He started to go but turned back, hating to leave. "If you need me don't hesitate to call. For anything. Promise me."

"I will," she promised sweetly and waited until he had backed out and waved one last time before shutting the door.

•

Judge Leroy Burgess was not used to waiting. He expected people to be where they were supposed to be when they were supposed to be there and defer to his authority. Sitting here in this tiny town at the bottom of nowhere with Leslie's dead body close by was bad enough, but the people here were treating him like he was just another person in mourning. An anybody instead of a Somebody.

Leroy took a sip of lukewarm coffee. It was surreal sitting here at the Rock Bottom sheriff's station knowing his daughter's body was laying on a cold slab in the morgue not far from here. They never had a normal father-daughter relationship and that was his choice. He gave his only child away because he recognized his inability to give a little girl the emotional support she would need throughout her life. Heartless to some but in his mind he made the most pragmatic decision he could to ensure his offspring was loved and nurtured properly. Isn't that was parents were supposed to do? Didn't that show the world how much he actually loved Leslie?

Because he had loved her.

That was why he was here now. What had happened to his only child? Who could have murdered her in her own house? And why? And most importantly, what was the Sheriff doing about it? Leroy would not waste time on worthless emotions. His daughter was dead and tears would not bring her back. All he could do was find the answers to these questions and make sure whoever did this was brought to justice. It was all he had to offer her now.

When the sheriff finally arrived Judge Burgess was short on patience and long on letting such insubordination be reprimanded in full view of the station – such as it was with the one deputy and an older woman helping with dispatch and paperwork. He waited until the sheriff was in front of him before he finally rose to his feet slowly with an air of importance and anticipation as he reached his full stature of five foot nine. Judge Burgess had learned decades ago how to look down on a man taller than himself and he used this skill now on the tall man before him.

Jeb met the judge's cold displeasure with unaffected politeness and his usual professional demeanor. "Judge Burgess. I apologize for the wait. My condolences to you. I was very sorry to have to inform you of your daughter's death. We intend to find out exactly what happened."

The judge was unmoved by his words. "As do I. And I will do whatever it takes Sheriff. Including stepping on your toes or all over your investigation as I see fit. I have a lot of friends in Maine and intend to take whatever action is necessary to see that this investigation is handled properly."

Jeb nodded. "It will be." He didn't appreciate the man coming into his office with guns blazing and ugly threats but he could understand a man acting foolishly in the face of his only child's death. Jeb was willing to give him the benefit of the doubt for now that he was simply acting out of grief.

"Do you have any leads?" the judge demanded. "Any indication as to who did this?"

Jeb didn't particularly like discussing his open investigation with anyone outside the office, even a judge. "We have some things we're looking into," he finally said. "Perhaps you can help with a couple of them."

Judge Burgess nodded slightly. "That is why I'm here."

"Let's step into my office." Once they were both seated Jeb decided to get right to the point. The judge clearly preferred it that way. "When was the last time you talked with your daughter?"

"We spoke briefly last week. She mentioned coming for a visit soon."

"Did you see her often?"

"Not really. I'm a busy man."

And a heartless one, Jeb thought to himself but kept any sentiment out of his own voice. "When was the last time you actually saw her?"

The judge thought for a moment. "New Year's Day. Leslie and Bill came up. We had a relatively pleasant visit."

"Relatively pleasant?"

"I'm not a fan of her husband. Bill. I don't like a man who walks out on his wife for a younger woman. I believed it was only a matter of time until he cheated on Leslie. Once a cheater, always a cheater in my experience."

"Perhaps." That tended to be his own view on the matter but Jeb also believed in redemption and forgiveness but that seemed pointless to bring up in this matter. "Did they seem to get along all right? Any discord or underlying tension in your opinion?"

Judge Burgess straightened. "Why? Did he kill her? Was it Bill?"

"I'm just asking the question. Did you sense anything wrong between them?"

"My daughter appeared happy. Bill as always acted very fondly towards Leslie. It is my perception that their marriage was as solid as it could be, considering."

"Considering what?"

"Considering he was a cheat. We already established that. Keep up Sheriff." Judge Burgess feared he was dealing with a complete incompetent at this point. "Now. Was it Bill who found the body?"

"No."

"Who then?"

When Jeb told him Judge Burgess' eyebrows furrowed together. "The ex-wife? What was she doing there?"

"I'd appreciate it if you let me ask the rest of the questions, Judge."

"Why was she there? And Randy? Is it common for their ex's to wander into their house? Do those two have alibis for the time of the murder? Maybe they were in on it together."

Jeb ignored the outburst. "Tell me about Randy."

The Judge frowned his displeasure. "I didn't care for him much more than Appleton but at least he showed some promise. Smooth with the ladies. Says all the right things. He and Leslie actually seemed well suited to each other. They were both ambitious. Big plans, big dreams. I was surprised when Leslie told me she was leaving him for that over-the-hill business partner of hers."

"How did Randy get along with your daughter after the divorce?"

"She did mention that he fought it in the beginning. Determined to win her back and all that. In the end he gave in because it was the right thing to do. Sometimes love means walking away."

"You think he still loved her even after she left him for Bill?"

The Judge nodded slowly. "Yes. I think he did. Which is why I find it hard to believe he would hurt her."

"Did you know Leslie wanted to sell the pub?"

"Yes. She mentioned it. Leslie wanted to move away and start over somewhere new with Bill."

"Tell me about Connor and Henry. Why did he snub his own son in his will? By all accounts they got on fair enough."

"Henry was a good man. Honest and hardworking. The pub was a source of great pride to him. Connor is also a hardworking, decent man. But his interest was always in the sea. Used to drive Henry crazy. He wanted his son to have his head for business, but Connor preferred a lonely life out on the water away from people. I suppose Henry left it to Les because she was a lot like him. And she grew up working in the pub. It was a logical choice."

"How did Leslie and Connor get along? Did she mention anything to you that indicated he was angry or upset about being left out of the inheritance?"

Leroy shook his head. "No. I think they got on as any siblings would. And they absolutely considered themselves siblings even though legally they weren't. They had disagreements. She knew her brother didn't approve of a lot of her actions but she was more amused by his concern than anything. Leslie had a brazen outlook on life. She wasn't afraid to dare fate and oftentimes that got her into trouble. Connor often bailed her out, as I did on occasion. She was never grateful. Just ready to try something new." He shook his head. "I can't see Connor hurting her no matter how much he may have disapproved. Because I felt exactly the same way."

That may have been the case but Jeb still had to wonder if Connor had finally had enough, especially with a sizable profit looming in the distance that should have been at least partly his. It was a pretty strong motive.

"What about Bill?" the Judge demanded. "Does he check out?"

"We're looking into it. That's all I can tell you at the moment."

"What about forensics? Have you heard anything?"

Jeb shook his head. "We won't hear anything for days, maybe a week. The lab is backed up as it is and we're at the bottom of the list."

"A week? The case will be cold by then." Leroy didn't like the idea of his daughter's killer wandering around for a moment longer than necessary.

"No sir. We'll stay on top of it."

Judge Burgess pulled out his cell phone. "I'll make a call."

"That's not necessary."

But the man didn't listen to Jeb and a few moments later he hung up. "You'll have the results tomorrow."

Jeb nodded. He didn't as a rule like circumventing the system and cutting in line. On the other hand, this would be a tremendous help. "Thank you."

"Whatever I can do to help."

"I appreciate that sir. But from now on let us handle this case. In the meantime maybe you should speak with Bill. I think he could use some help making the arrangements."

Judge Burgess didn't like being put off. "I am not going to back off from this Sheriff. I intend to get answers."

"And I understand that sir. Right now I don't have the answers you want but I will if you give me the space to do my job."

The judge stood. "Fine. But I am here to stay until this case is resolved. And if I think for a moment you are botching this investigation I have every means of bringing the wrath of the entire state down on your head."

"Understood," Jeb said quietly and watched the judge stalk out of his office.

•

Just after lunch Jeb banged on the Appleton's door. It was a big old rambling house on a quiet side street right in town. There was an iron fence around the property and a squeaky gate at the front of the walkway. With a lot of work it could be a nice home for a young family.

Bridget opened the door and peered out at him. She was a pretty little thing with large green eyes and long blond hair in a ponytail. In Jeb's opinion she didn't look old enough to be out of high school but he knew she was at least in her mid-twenties based on the history Kitty had shared with him. She had a toddler on her hip and another child peeking out from behind her. "Sheriff?"

"Mrs. Appleton, I need to ask you and your husband some questions."

Bridget frowned. "Charlie isn't home and I don't know if I should talk to you alone."

"It will only take a few minutes. I can do it here and make it as painless as possible or we can go over to the station and then it will be a little more unpleasant." He looked down at the two young children.

"Is that a real gun?" the little boy asked, pointing to his holster.

"Yes."

"Are you going to arrest Mommy?" the boy pressed, looking very concerned.

"No," Jeb assured him. "I just need to talk to her."

"Fine." Bridget let him in and led him into the living room where she set the little girl down. "Let me put a movie on so these two will be distracted while we talk." She quickly did and then led him into the hallway and remained in the doorway where she could see her children but keep the conversation away from small ears. "What do you want to know?"

"Your husband didn't get along with his stepmother."

"Neither did I. That doesn't mean we killed her."

"Charlie was upset his father was contemplating selling because of Leslie pushing him to do so."

Bridget nodded slowly. "That's true. Charlie was upset that the family business would be run by a stranger. He had every right to be upset and told them both how he felt. But he certainly wouldn't murder anyone."

"Where were both of you Monday night?"

"I was here with the kids. You can ask my neighbor Martha Stimple. She came over to give me some brownies for the kids and ended up staying for almost an hour. She's a sweet lady but she loves to talk."

"Ahh Martha. I know her. What about Charlie?"

"Charlie was working."

"Where?"

"Helping one of his friends with something." She waved her hands. "I don't remember which one."

"Where can I find your husband today?"

"Down at the docks or out on the water. Hard to say."

"You used to work at the pub. What was your impression of Bill and Leslie's marriage?"

Bridget snorted. "Those two were disgusting and they deserved each other. Bill was always a flirt. That's just how he was; Kitty knew it and accepted it. We all did. I was already a part of the Appleton family when Leslie started coming on to Bill. And I never really thought Bill would actually give into the flirtations honestly. I thought he and Kitty had a pretty solid, albeit one-sided, marriage."

"What do you mean by that?"

"Kitty did everything for him and he never really...saw her, you know what I mean?" Bridget asked, her finely arched brow drawn as she considered her words carefully. "Kitty was the perfect wife and mother but it was like she did it all in vain because she was almost invisible. And it wasn't enough for him. I know people always say there're two sides to everything but to me it just seemed like Bill took everything she had to offer all the years they were married and then threw her away when Leslie offered herself up."

"And everyone knew about Bill and Leslie but Kitty."

Bridget slumped against the wall. "You don't know what it's like to be in that position. To know and not want to know. I never saw anything definite because they tried to be discreet but everyone suspected the truth. I didn't want to be the one to tell Kitty. None of us did I guess. And Charlie tried to talk his father into doing the right thing but Bill just played dumb. He's the most selfish person on the planet.

"You don't care for your father-in-law."

"I manage to be polite. I recognize that my children need a grandfather but he doesn't seem all that interested in them. And Charlie of course has a hard time with the whole thing. He is very protective of his mother now after what Bill did to her." She shook her head sadly.

"Your husband has a temper."

Bridget's head shot up. "He stands up when no one else will."

Jeb put his hat back on and tipped it slightly. "Thank you for all your help. Good day, Mrs. Appleton."

Chapter 12

Charlie was at the docks working on a boat when Jeb found him shortly after one. Crouched down and focused on his work, Charlie ignored Jeb as he slowly followed the curved lines of the letters *Shore Leave* in dark green paint.

"I'd like to speak with you about your stepmother's murder."

"Fine." Charlie kept painting.

"Where were you on Monday evening between six and eight?"

"Here."

"Your wife said you were helping a friend. Was he here too?"

Charlie's hand stilled and he looked up at Jeb. "You talked to Bridge? What did you say? Did you upset her?" he demanded.

"No. I merely asked her some routine questions. Just like I'm asking you. She has an alibi. I already talked with Martha Stimple. I just need to know if anyone can verify you were here."

The younger man finally stood. He was a little bit taller than Jeb and bulked up with muscles, probably from hard work out here as opposed to benching pressing at a gym. Jeb guessed he was as tough as he looked. "I was here working on this very boat. No one can vouch for me."

Jeb surveyed the boat Charlie had been working on. "You do this stuff fairly often?"

Charlie nodded. "I do odd jobs like this aside from the regular job."

"Groundfishing is a tough industry to survive on. Nothing wrong with supplementing your income."

"I'll do whatever I have to for my family."

"Why don't you give me your friend's name and I'll talk to him myself. Maybe he came back to check on you and you didn't realize it."

Charlie's face hardened. "Is this really necessary? I didn't kill Leslie."

"Son you have a pretty strong motive with your father possibly selling off what should be your inheritance. Everyone I talked to says you have a temper and that you didn't get along with your stepmother. I'd be remiss in my job if I didn't check your alibi."

The deep blue eyes that reminded Jeb of Kitty stared off over the water. "I suppose I am a pretty good suspect."

"So what's your friend's name?"

"Connor Abbott." Charlie flashed Jeb a lop-sided smile. "You see sheriff? Neither one of us can vouch for the other. And we had the exact same motive. So which of us do you believe whacked Leslie?"

Jeb didn't like the turn the conversation was taking. He had hoped that he could easily verify Charlie Appleton's alibi and breathe a sigh of relief. The last thing he wanted to do was investigate the son of the woman he was seeing for murder. "This isn't a game Charlie. I intend to get to the bottom of this wherever it leads me."

"So you dating my mother isn't going to help me, huh?"

"No, it isn't."

"What exactly are your intentions towards my mother Sheriff?"

Under other circumstances he'd be amused by Charlie's question. "To not hurt her the way your father did." Jeb turned and started up the pier. "Don't leave town Charlie," he called over his shoulder.

.

Kitty ran through the pounding rain from her studio to the house Wednesday afternoon. She'd been out there most of the day and was ready to call it quits. The temperature suddenly plummeted down into the low forties and with the cold rain slicing through the county Kitty was anxious to settle in for the evening. There was still plenty of wood by the fireplace and she thought it would be a good evening to sit by a crackling fire while listening to the rain pelt the roof.

She hung her jacket in the small mud room off the kitchen and went looking for Bill, expecting to find him in the front of the TV. To her surprise Petunia was sitting on the credenza in the foyer, her eyes slit and her tail flitting back and forth.

"Petunia!" Kitty scooped up the bedraggled cat and hugged her tightly. "How did you get here?" she asked. Petunia grudgingly began purring and acknowledged that she too was happy to be home.

Bill came scuffling in wiping his face with a towel. Kitty raised her eyes to his, feeling happy and charitable enough to give him a warm greeting. "Hello, Bill." His clothes were damp and wrinkled and he looked rather put out.

"I found her," he said as a combined greeting and explanation. "Took me an hour out in the rain but I finally got her."

"Thank you. You have no idea what a relief it is to have her back." Kitty released her fluffy baby to the floor and Petunia stalked past Bill, giving him a withering look just in case he had any doubts about her feelings towards him.

"She's not very grateful," he grumbled.

"Well I am and because of that I am going to make your favorite supper." Kitty started towards the kitchen her mood lighter than it had been in the last three days when a thought struck her. She stopped and turned back halfway down the hallway. "Baked clams and linguine is still your favorite, right?"

Bill nodded, his mouth watering at the thought.

Kitty smiled. "I thought so." And she hustled into the kitchen to start the celebratory dinner.

By six o'clock she had a wonderful dinner laid out on the kitchen table. It was nice to have someone to cook for this evening. Even Bill. A tiny voice in her head pointed out that Jeb's company would be the preferred choice but she did her best to ignore it. Kitty certainly enjoyed the time she got to spend with Jeb but she had to remind herself it was simply a pretense. While Bill wasn't perfect at least their feelings – whatever they may be – were real and Kitty cold draw on that. He was a huge part of her life for a long time and there would always be a connection with him because of that. The fact that he was here now was proof enough.

Bill was now seated at the table and sitting very still. His hands were in his lap and he waited quietly while Kitty finally seated herself. She couldn't remember him ever waiting for her to join him before. He always dug in while she was rushing around trying to make sure everything was perfect. Kitty watched as Bill took a napkin and carefully laid it on his lap before meeting her own curious blue ones. "Everything looks wonderful, Kitty. As usual."

Kitty was more than surprised by his words but hid it well as she reached over to fix her plate. Bill immediately grabbed the spoon and her plate from her. "Let me," he said gruffly.

"Thank you." She took the filled plate he handed back to her.

"How was your day painting?" he asked suddenly, heaping his own plate with food.

"It was fine. Just fine." That part of her day was quite normal. This part was what was throwing her at the moment. "And how was your day?"

"I spoke with the judge today. He and Eileen have helped quite a bit with the...arrangements." He swallowed audibly but kept his eyes on his plate. Kitty was sure she saw moisture in them that he quickly tried to blink away. "Her funeral will be Monday morning. Eileen is going to..to...help pick out stuff for her to wear. The judge wants her buried near Margaret and I think that's a nice idea. Eileen agreed Leslie would like that a lot."

"I'm sure she would," Kitty said consolingly.

"I won't be able to get back into the house for some time according to your boy...according to Sheriff Carpenter," he continued. "I realize I can't stay here forever, but I don't think I can start looking for another place to stay until after the funeral." He looked at her helplessly.

There wasn't anything else she could say with the sympathy for his situation ruling her heart over common sense. "You're welcome to stay here until you find another place, Bill."

His eyes were so sincere she was lost in them for a moment. "Thank you, Kitty. You have no idea what that means to me."

•

Kitty was sewing in her craft room when the doorbell rang. When she opened the door she was both surprised and pleased to see Jeb standing on her doorstep, hat in hand. "Good evening Sheriff. What can I do for you this evening?"

The words sounded formal coming out of her mouth but the smile she gave him was so sweet and sincere Jeb momentarily blanked out. He actually missed not seeing her the last couple days and wished this was a social call. He'd love to sit and talk with her. He'd really like to steal another kiss but that would be unwise. Jeb cleared his throat. "I need to speak with Bill."

"Oh." She should have realized that he was here on official business. Kitty shouldn't have been disappointed but she was. She did her best to hide it. "Please come in."

"Thank you." He stepped past her and she closed the door.

"I'll just run upstairs and tell him you're here."

Kitty returned moments later with an apologetic smile. "He's in the shower right now. If you don't mind waiting I'll fix you some coffee if you'd like."

"That would be nice." A few moments with her was all he needed right now. She had a soothing presence and in the midst of the chaos he felt drawn to her. And his stomach rumbled at the thought of getting something, anything, sent its way since he'd been too busy to think about food.

"Have you eaten?" she asked softly.

"Rob brought in dinner from the cafe but I didn't have time to eat it." It sat on his desk and by the time he got to it the congealed grease and fat had eroded his appetite on the spot. Now he could smell some lingering aroma of something he was quite certain had been wonderful, and the hunger pains returned full force.

"It doesn't sound like you got to eat it," Kitty said kindly.

"I'm fine."

She raised an eyebrow and indicated he should follow her. He did and wound up in the kitchen watching her dig through the refrigerator. "I'm warming you a plate. We had plenty leftover."

"That's not necessary."

"You need to eat. Sit."

He sat down at the table properly chastised and waited while Kitty warmed a plate in the microwave for him. When it beeped she took a steaming plate of something divine and set it in front of him. He looked up at her and was pleased to see the smile was back in place and the dimples were peeping out. "I expect you to clean that plate if you want dessert."

"Yes ma'am," he agreed.

It didn't take him long to polish off the whole plate of clams and pasta. He was so full and so happy the idea of going back to work now didn't seem half bad. Sure it was cold and still pouring out, but his stomach was filled to the gill with the best meal he'd had all week and that pretty much countered any other negatives at the moment.

When she set a steaming cup of coffee and a piece of cheesecake in front of him, he seriously started rethinking the benefits of bachelorhood. There weren't that many to begin with anyway. "That's a lot of cheesecake."

"Bill said he didn't want any and I want it gone before I eat it all myself." Kitty sat across from him with a piece of dessert half the size of his and a cup of black coffee. "How is the case going?" she asked softly, unsure if she should bring it up.

"We've had a few leads. Nothing definitive yet, but we'll get there."

"I know you will." She hesitated. "I talked with Bridget a little while ago."

"She okay?"

Kitty nodded. "She was upset about the talk you had with both her and Charlie. I know you were just doing your job. But Charlie and Bridget have nothing to hide. They had nothing to do with Leslie's death."

Jeb cleared his throat. "Kitty in a murder investigation I have to ask unpleasant questions of everyone involved. It's part of the process. It doesn't necessarily mean I think your son murdered his stepmother but I have to go wherever the case takes me. There can't be any bias particularly under these circumstances."

"Well I'm his mother so I am biased. I know my son. He may kill to protect his family if they were threatened like most people would but he wouldn't do it in cold blood."

"Then we have nothing to worry about, right? The facts will clear him if that's the case. Now. How are you holding up with Bill still here?"

Kitty hated that Jeb thought her son might actually be capable of such an act. It was her natural instinct to protect and defend her child from such an accusation. But wisdom slowly tempered the irrational, emotional reaction and she took a moment to see it from Jeb's side. He didn't know her Charlie. He didn't know the man her son was and so she needed to trust him to do his job just as he needed her to not overreact. The truth would come out in the end. "We're both making an effort to be polite and mindful of each other. I'll admit it's a bit disconcerting at times having him back in the house after being alone for nearly two years."

"Is my being here adding to the discomfort?"

Kitty shook her head. "No. Not at all. I enjoy your company very much." That was still the truth despite the topics they were covering tonight.

Jeb relaxed at her words. "Good."

They were enjoying the coffee she made when Bill entered the room a little while later. Upon seeing the sheriff sitting at the table with Kitty his face hardened. "Evening Sheriff," he said stiffly.

"Mr. Appleton." Jeb nodded a greeting. "I have a few questions for you if you're up to it."

"Suppose so." He pulled out a chair and settled into it, noticing the dessert and coffee. "Any of that left?" he asked Kitty hopefully.

"That was the end of it. I'm sorry, Bill."

"You took my dessert?" he accused the man across from him.

"Didn't think you wanted it anymore," Jeb said evenly.

"Maybe I was saving it for later. A man can't change his mind?"

"I suppose he can."

Kitty despaired over the sudden upset in the room. "Bill, I'll fix you something else instead. How about if I make you some chocolate cake? I know you love that." She started to get up but Jeb instinctively reached for her hand.

"Please just sit. You've done enough. For both of us." His eyes caught Bill's and held them, a soft warning in them to let it be. He did not like Kitty jumping through hoops for this man.

Kitty sank back down and looked from Jeb to Bill, hoping things would smooth themselves out but not entirely confident they would. She jumped back up. "I'll just get you some coffee then." And she hurried to fix Bill a cup, cream and two sugars, just the way he liked.

Jeb tried to ignore the way Kitty looked when she was concentrating on fixing the coffee just right. Her deep blue eyes were focused on the task and her mouth was parted slightly. Even her eyebrows were arched perfectly while she stirred and tapped the spoon on the rim. When she was done, she plastered that pleasant smile on her face that he was pretty sure hid a myriad of emotions at any given time. She placed the cup in front of Bill and sat back down next to her ex-husband. Ever the obedient and devoted wife. "Kitty, you might want to leave the room while I talk to your ex-husband."

"She can stay. I don't mind," Bill insisted gruffly and Kitty smiled shyly at him.

Jeb sighed.

"Mr. Appleton forensics found paint on your wife's hands and clothes. Do you have any idea where she might have come into contact with paint? Was she working on something at the pub or home?"

"No. Leslie didn't paint." He shot a curious glance toward Kitty. "She didn't come here did she?"

Kitty shook her head. "Not during the day. And if she came in the evening I was at the pub so I wouldn't know for sure."

"Can you think of anywhere she might have been where she would have been exposed to paint?"

"No, I really can't sheriff. I can't think at all actually."

"Did you know Randy was at your house that evening to show Leslie some drawings of the proposed renovations?"

Bill gaped. "Randy was there? In our house? Was it him?" he demanded. "Did he kill her?"

Jeb held up his hands to try to calm the man down. "I'm not saying anything of the kind. I just wanted to know if you knew he was meeting Leslie."

"No. But it doesn't surprise me. He still wanted her. And why wouldn't he? How could you get over losing a woman like Leslie? I certainly won't be able to. She was the love of my life," he said heavily, oblivious to the effect his words had on the woman sitting next to him.

Kitty got up abruptly. "I should let you two talk alone." And she scooted out of sight.

But not before Jeb saw the wounded look in her brilliant blue eyes.

He really wanted to throttle Bill Appleton.

Instead, he asked, "How did you perceive Leslie's relationship with the Abbotts?"

"They all adored her and vice-versa. Henry, Eileen. Edward. Even Connor got on well with her despite the fact that he was cut out of the will."

"Edward. Who is Edward?" He hadn't heard mention of any other Abbotts up until now.

"Leslie's uncle. Henry's younger brother. He's a regular at the pub. Everyone knows Edward."

"Did he have any ill feelings about the pub being sold?"

"Edward doesn't have ill feelings at all. He doesn't know anything about this," Bill assured him.

"I think I'd like to talk to him anyway."

"It'll be complete waste of time. There are plenty of other people out there with a motive you should be talking to."

"Actually I'm talking to the very person with best motive in town. You're going to be a very wealthy man from the life insurance policy and the sale of the pub."

"I didn't kill my wife. I was bowling. Check at the bowling alley!" Bill grumped.

"We already did and you were missing for about twenty minutes. Do you care to explain that?"

Bill paled. "I stepped out for a few but I don't think I was gone for twenty minutes."

"Seems you were. Without an alibi..." Jeb let his voice trail off.

"I didn't kill Leslie I swear. I loved her."

"Where were you Bill?"

Bill rubbed his temple for several long moments, weighing his options. Finally he spoke. "I was with one of the cashiers."

"And what exactly were you doing?" But he knew. Heaven help him he already knew.

"We were just messing around a bit. A little flirting and a little laughing, that's all."

Jeb let out a long slow breath. This guy was truly a piece of work. "She'll vouch for you?"

Bill nodded. "Her name is Sandy. She'll tell you we were having a bit of fun."

"'Having a bit of fun', is that what you call it nowadays?" Jeb bit out.

"It was just a little harmless flirting," Bill said defensively. "Not cheating. I know it sounds bad but nothing actually happened I swear. I wouldn't do that to Leslie. I suppose you're going to run and tell Kitty now and exaggerate the details to make me look bad." Bill wasn't thrilled about Kitty finding out about his slight indiscretion. Not when he was making some serious progress with her. He knew she'd blow it all out of proportion. If she threw him out he didn't know where he'd go.

Jeb stared at his folded hands. "I'm not going to say a word to Kitty. It would only hurt her more to find out how despicable you are." Jeb raised his eyes to the cold blue ones watching him. "Tell me the truth. This is a pattern for you isn't it? You were probably unfaithful to Kitty your whole marriage weren't you?"

"Not the whole marriage," Bill insisted. "But sometimes in a stagnant marriage a man needs a little more than what he's getting at home. That's why I found Leslie and in the process fell in love with her. Surely you must know what I'm talking about. It doesn't mean I didn't care about Kitty. But I loved Leslie and never cheated on her. If she ever found out about me flirting with other women she'd either laugh it off or we'd have a shouting match that ended in the bedroom. That's just how we are. I mean...were." He blinked and looked away.

Jeb stood up, unable to stay at the same table with Bill Appleton a moment longer. "A man doesn't go looking for affection away from home. He treasures a good wife and honors her. That's what makes him a real man. Evening Mr. Appleton."

·

Kitty sat in her old rocking chair staring out the window into the dark, wet night. She watched the raindrops drizzle down the glass as the rain pummeled the world outside. *She* felt pummeled on the inside. The words her ex uttered still had the power to hurt her and that baffled her. She didn't love him anymore, she was pretty sure of that. So why then did it break her heart when he said things like that about Leslie? Because he had never said that about her, never felt that way about her in all their years together? Which begged the question, what did they have for all those years? A loveless marriage? Kitty hadn't thought so at all. While her marriage had never been perfect, she'd always thought at least it was a normal one, with ups and downs like everyone else. But maybe that was not that case. Maybe Liza Jane was right and she had thrown her life away on a man who had never, not for a single moment, actually loved her.

That thought made her want to crawl in her bed and pull the covers over her head for the rest of her dreary, dull, predicable, empty life.

Because apparently she was completely unlovable.

There was a knock at the door and the sheriff's tall figure appeared a moment later. He stood there awkwardly, rolling the rim of his hat through his fingers as he studied her. "Are you all right, Kitty?"

Even a near stranger could pick up on her emotions better than the man she was married to for most of her life. Obviously Sheriff Carpenter had seen how upset she was by Bill's words, and while his concern was appreciated, it also embarrassed her having him witness her humiliation first hand. "I'm fine," she assured him.

It was written all over her face how *not* fine she was. Bill's words had cut her deeply. He didn't understand exactly why she was so upset if she was over him as she stated. If she really knew what kind of man Bill was she'd probably be better off. But it wasn't his place to say anything, not yet anyway, and he knew it would only hurt her more if he told her the truth right now. It didn't make sense to him, but then again Jeb had never claimed to understand women one iota. Frankly, he'd rather be hunting down a wanted criminal than try to figure out a woman's feelings.

But here he was, standing in the doorway like an idiot, feeling all kinds of stupid and worried over the wounded heart of a woman he barely knew but already cared about deeply. "You don't look fine. Or sound fine."

"I'm simply tired. I think I should head on up to bed now. Are you through speaking with Bill?"

"Yes."

"Then I'll see you out, Sheriff."

He searched the sad blue eyes for a moment before nodding. She stepped past him and Jeb was forced to follow her to the front door. He bid her good night and drove off into the dark stormy evening with those blue eyes heavy on his heart.

Chapter 13

Kitty came home Thursday afternoon from grocery shopping only to find a strange man sitting in her kitchen. She stopped short in the doorway and tried not to panic. He was an older man, well dressed, and had an intimidating, intense gaze that was focused directly at her. As if she were the intruder.

"You must be Kitty," the man finally said dispassionately. "I'm Judge Leroy Burgess. Leslie's father. We met briefly years ago I believe."

"Oh. I remember now." Relief swept through her. "I am so very sorry for your loss Judge Burgess." She set her reusable totes down and went over to shake the man's hand because it seemed the right thing to do. No other words like *"she was a lovely person"* or *"she'll be greatly missed"* would come forth so Kitty stared mutely at him as he accepted the small gesture for what it was.

"I was here speaking with Bill about some arrangements. He stepped out for a moment and assured me it would be fine to wait here."

"Yes of course."

"If not I can wait at my hotel."

"It's fine," she assured the man. "Let me fix you some coffee or tea."

"Tea would be splendid, thank you."

She boiled water in her electric pot and pulled a cup out of the cupboard. "I have Earl Grey or regular if you prefer."

"Earl Grey."

She set the steaming cup in front of him moments later. "Are you hungry Judge? I have some cake that goes very nicely with a cup of tea in the afternoon."

"If it isn't too much trouble."

Kitty sliced a piece of her spiced apple cake and set that plate in front of him as well. "There you are. I'm sure Bill will be along any minute."

"I appreciate your kindness considering you must not have had very kind feelings towards my daughter."

"I...I...wouldn't wish this on anyone regardless."

"Still this must be a relief for you," he said, his eyebrows drawn together as he studied the woman before him. He'd met her once or twice over the last thirty years but didn't remember her well at all. Leslie had painted a picture of a clinging, unpleasant woman, shrewish and jaded enough to drive her henpecked husband into Leslie's waiting arms. The Kitty Appleton in front of him didn't strike him as shrewish or unkind.

He realized sadly that it would not have been the first time his daughter lied in order to justify her behavior. Still, this woman before him could simply be a very good actress.

"A relief?" Kitty asked. "Whatever do you mean?"

"Now that my daughter is out of the way I suppose you have a good chance of winning your husband back." He gestured generically around. "He's already moved back into your little love nest."

"Oh no. No, you have it all wrong." She sat down across from the Judge. "Bill is only staying here until he can move back home. Or find another place. This is completely temporary, I assure you."

"I see."

"Bill has never been alone. I don't think he knows how to be really. Him staying here isn't a reflection of his feelings for me or lack of them for your daughter. I can honestly say that Bill loved Leslie more than he ever loved me. And I have no desire to be second best again. I lived that way for a very long time and didn't see it. Now I do." She stood up and went to her bags sitting on the floor. "I'm sorry to sound bitter. Your daughter and I may not have been friends but I never, ever would have wished for something like this to happen to her."

"Thank you for your honesty and level-headedness in this time. It's a refreshing change." He frowned in pure displeasure at the memory of his son-in-law just moments earlier. "Bill is like a driveling idiot at times. Every time we try to make any decisions regarding the funeral he starts crying. Eileen is no better. Between the two of them I wondered if we were ever going to get anything settled."

"Is that why you're here?" Kitty asked as she closed the refrigerator door. "To plan the funeral?"

"Most of it has finally been arranged now that the body has officially been released. There are only a few loose ends to tie up."

"I see." Tying up loose ends didn't seem the proper words to describe this situation. Kitty decided either he was a very cold man or he hid his grief very well. "So where is Bill?"

"He said he needed to take a walk to clear his head. I told him I would wait here."

"It's very nice of you and Eileen to assist him with the arrangements. I suppose I could have offered but I didn't think it was my place."

"No it wasn't."

His brusque manner didn't deter her from her next words. "Would you like to stay for supper Judge?"

"I couldn't possibly."

"Are you sure? I don't want you to be alone."

"I've been taking supper with Eileen the past few evenings. Most of the time is spent discussing Leslie." He stirred his tea. "Her company is preferable to Bill's."

"I see."

"I'll just wait to speak with him and then be on my way."

"I'm sure Eileen is enjoying the company. I know she's been lonely since Henry died."

"Yes and now with Leslie gone it will be even harder for her. She still has Connor of course."

"I don't know him that well but I know he's a hard worker."

"A lot like Leslie." She politely listened to the judge reminisce about his visits with his daughter, which he remembered because each was associated to a particular case he was hearing at the time. He seemed to recall the details of the trials more vividly than time spent with his only child, Kitty thought sadly as she prepared the scrod for dinner. She supposed that some men weren't equipped to deal with their feelings of loss and this was the best way he could do that.

Kitty was actually relieved when Bill wondered in a short time later. He smiled weakly at her and asked how her day had been. She assured him it was a fine day and set a mug of Moxie down in front of him. As the conversation swung back around to final arrangements, Kitty decided to escape to her craft room until supper was ready. She was almost through the doorway when Bill called her back.

"Kitty, I realize this is really a lot to ask, but the Judge and I were wondering if perhaps we could have people come here after the funeral? The sheriff still hasn't cleared our house yet and I wouldn't feel comfortable anywhere else. Eileen offered but it's really too much for her."

The fact that this would make *her* uncomfortable didn't seem to factor into the equation. She wanted desperately to deny the request, but with two sad pair of eyes waiting for an answer she found she didn't have the heart to say no. "Of course."

"Would it be too much trouble to prepare some light refreshments?" Bill persisted. "I would appreciate it very much."

"I'd be happy too," Kitty managed to get out in a reasonably sincere voice.

"Thank you very much Kitty," the Judge said with quiet dignity. "I am humbled by your willingness to do this for my daughter after the pain Leslie caused you."

She nodded and fled the room before they asked any more of her.

.

Supper was more of the same sad small talk with Bill. By the time it was over and she had all the dishes washed Kitty was good and ready to escape to her Book Club meeting. She hung her dish towel on the hook to dry and then headed upstairs to freshen up. Back downstairs she breezed by Bill with only a quick good-bye as he sat mutely watching TV, lost in a show she wasn't entirely sure he was even aware of based on the glazed over eyes.

Kitty happily settled into her favorite spot on the sofa next to Liza and felt better than she had all evening. When the book club ladies steered the conversation towards the recent death, Kitty couldn't bare another word about the dearly departed Leslie. "No more! We can talk about anything you want but I do not want to hear that woman's name mentioned for the rest of the hour!" she insisted.

"But it's the talk of the town," Lydia said. "Nothing like this has ever happened before. We have to discuss it."

"Why?" Kitty demanded.

"Because frankly I'm scared," Lydia admitted. "If someone can sneak into Leslie's house then who's to say they won't sneak into mine? I don't have a husband to protect me."

"Get a dog," Charlotte advised.

"Sleep with your cell phone under your pillow," Regina suggested.

"What if something happens?" Lydia pressed. "Like what if I'm kidnapped and held against my will but can't let on because he's holding a knife to my throat so I can't actually say I've been kidnapped but I need to let you know?" Lydia knew she let both her fear and her wild imagination run away but sometimes she just had nothing else to do with her time but worry.

"Good grief," Liza Jane moaned.

"That's when you should have a duress phrase or word. You know, something prearranged to say that only the person on the other end of the phone will recognize and knows that you're in trouble. It has to be a word you don't say all the time but can be worked into a conversation," Annie explained.

"I want one of those," Lydia said quickly. "We should all have one, just in case."

"That's not a bad idea," Charlotte agreed. "I'll start. Mine shall be *it's only money*." Charlotte was most the frugal woman in town and proudly claimed that title. Such a statement would send those who knew her into a panicked frenzy thinking that she was suffering from a stroke or losing her marbles. "That was easy. Next?"

"Me!" Martha volunteered eagerly. "Mine will be *check on the cat*. I don't have a cat. See? Isn't that clever? You'll all know I'm in trouble then," Martha beamed.

"Excellent Martha," Annie praised her. "Lydia?"

Lydia chewed her lip. "Gosh this is hard. How about *orange*? I hate the color and the fruit. So if I say I want anything to do with orange you'll know I'm in deep trouble."

Annie nodded. "Liza?"

"*Where are all the men?*"

"You ask that regularly. Pick something else."

Liza frowned. "Fine. I'll go with *cadaver*."

"You can work that into a conversation?" Annie asked doubtfully.

"Piece of cake. I left a cadaver on ice until tomorrow. See? It pays to work with corpses."

"You really are obsessed with death," Regina decided. "I'll go with *I object.* I can't wait until I can use that phrase in the line of work."

"You are power hungry," Liza Jane observed dryly.

"Still better than working with dead people."

Liza frowned and Annie quickly pushed forward. "Kitty?"

"Well I bake a lot so I think I'll do something with that. How about *I burned the cookies*?"

"Great. Mine will be *my book is overdue*," Annie said primly.

"As if that would ever happen," Regina snorted.

Annie eyed her. "Which is precisely why it's an excellent panic phrase. And by the way, you have two overdue books I'll expect back tomorrow."

Regina frowned and Martha giggled.

"Feel better now Lydia?" Charlotte asked. "Just yell out your phrase and the cavalry shall come running."

"Much better. Thank you ladies. I know I'm being silly."

"You're not. It was an excellent idea. Now let's get back to the book."

"That plot isn't nearly as interesting as what's going on here at The Bottom," Martha pointed out. "Murder and mayhem right here in our little town! It's so exciting!" Lydia grimaced and Martha relented. "Fine. Let's talk about the book."

"We could talk about the sheriff and Kitty," Liza suggested nonchalantly.

"Or Bill and Kitty," Lydia said slyly. "How is it having him back in your life?"

"You aren't shacking up with him are you?" Charlotte demanded and Kitty flushed bright red.

"No Charlotte. He's in the guest room."

Charlotte patted her knee. "Good girl."

"Stay strong girl. Unless you want to take him back?"

"She definitely doesn't need Bill back."

"Kitty could play the sheriff and Bill against each other in a desperate attempt for one of them to boldly declare their undying love," Lydia gushed, her eyes staring off dreamily.

Liza Jane rolled her eyes. "Kitty has only been seeing the sheriff for a short time. And Bill should be permanently pulled off the shelves. No woman in The Bottom should want any part of him."

"It has been odd having Bill stay at the house," Kitty admitted. "When he first left I just wanted him back no matter what. Now I'm feeling a bit unsure of myself. I know he's treated me poorly and I still get angry with him. But I have to admit there are times I like having him back home. I feel safe at night. It's nice having the company at dinner time, aside from tonight. There's a comfortable familiarity that we still share. I know he's always been a selfish person but I do see him trying to make an effort for me. That's more than he ever did in all the time we were married."

"I think I pointed out the 'selfish' character flaw thirty years ago when you started dating him," Liza Jane informed her. "But you wouldn't listen. You were so in love with him you couldn't see straight."

"Bill is a handsome man," Lydia said. "Any woman could be turned his way."

"I still think the sheriff is better looking," Martha chirped happily. "There's just something about him. I think you should pick him."

"I'm not picking either. Bill and I are divorced. And the sheriff and I have only just started dating. It's not serious yet." How could she tell them that the sheriff wasn't actually an option since it wasn't a real relationship? That at this point in her life, if Bill actually did come crawling back he might be the only chance she had at having someone to grow old with?

"Yet?" Charlotte perked up. "Did you say yet? Does that mean you at least have a shot at hooking that one?"

"There have been multiple dates so far. That's more than any other woman," Regina declared. "I think Kitty is the winner ladies."

"Well done!" Lydia clapped. "Perhaps you could give the rest of us some pointers."

Kitty decided this was only a slight improvement in topics. After all, her dating status was really a scam and she hated deceiving her friends. She certainly didn't want to go on about how she had bagged the sheriff when that really couldn't be further from the truth.

"What did you use on him?" Regina wanted to know. "Apparently I need all the help I can get."

"That's silly," Kitty scolded. "You are absolutely beautiful Regina. Plus you're smart, funny, and have a loving heart. Any man would be lucky to have you in his life."

Regina rolled her eyes.

"Randy seems quite taken with you," Liza Jane said. "We all saw that the other night."

"I didn't think he was ever going to get over Leslie," Annie reminisced. "He was pretty glum when Leslie left him for Bill."

"What was it about that woman that made men so loony?" Lydia sulked. "She wasn't that pretty. Or nice."

"We shouldn't speak ill of the dead. But she really was a two-bit floozy," Charlotte pronounced.

"Charlotte!" Kitty scolded.

"I'm eighty-eight. I can call it as I see it."

"We all knew how Leslie could be," Liza said discreetly.

"I can't say I'm particularly glad she's dead. But there are only so many available men here in The Bottom and she seemed to have a way with them," Lydia said.

"Less competition now," Regina agreed.

"She was harmless. She already had a husband," Martha pointed out.

"Whom she stole from Kitty! What's to say that she wouldn't have gone after some other poor suspecting fool when she was tired of him?"

"You know," Lydia said thoughtfully, "there are an awful lot of us who are better off with Leslie Appleton dead."

·

Bartender Bob pointed out Edward Abbott on the stool farthest from the door. Edward Abbott was in his sixties, with neat grey hair and dressed casually in a button down shirt and corduroy pants. He had thick soled shoes on and was sipping something with a straw while concentrating on a book in front of him. Jeb approached and waited for the older man to notice him.

Bartender Bob was suddenly concerned with cleaning this end of the bar and Jeb frowned at him. The man, heavyset and fiftyish, merely continued to wipe down glasses and didn't budge.

"Mr. Abbott?" Jeb finally said to the older gentlemen completely involved in what looked like a crossword puzzle. "I need to talk to you."

There was no answer, no evidence the man even heard him. "Mr. Abbott?"

Jeb leaned on the bar and peered at the man and felt a little testy. Before he could say anything else the bartender spoke. "Eddy the sheriff wants to talk to you."

Edward looked up at Bartender Bob and then turned slightly to face Jeb. His eyes widened at the sight of a man in uniform sitting next to him. "What'd I do?"

"Nothing Mr. Abbott. I'm sorry for your loss but I do need to ask you some questions about your niece."

Edward considered this for a moment and then smiled. "Leslie. Smart. Funny. Pushy. Loyal."

"Right." Jeb sat down. "When was the last time you saw her?"

Edward tapped out his fingers on the counter. "Monday night. Five nights ago. Right over there. You want a root beer?"

"No thank you." Jeb studied the man. Either he'd had a few too many or there was something not quite right with Edward Abbott. Based on Bartender Bob hovering over them he decided on the latter and proceeded gingerly. "Did you talk with Leslie?"

"Of course."

"Do you remember when you talked? Was it early in the day or closer to when she left?"

"Right before. That's why she left. Because of what I found out."

"You told her something and that's when she decided to leave the Bottom's Up?" Jeb asked, feeling like finally he was on the brink of getting somewhere.

"Yes."

"What was it?"

Edward swiveled in his chair and stared straight ahead. "Can't tell you. Sorry Sheriff."

Jeb's interest was piqued and his patience was still holding true, so he turned to face forward as well. "I think I'll have that root beer," he told the bartender. The man hesitated but Jeb held his hand up in a conciliatory gesture, an acknowledgment of Edward's limitations. Bartender Bob left to fetch the drink but cast worried glances over his shoulder as he shuffled off.

"Edward, it would really help me a lot if you could tell me what you and your niece talked about that night."

Edward shook his head slowly. "Secret."

Jeb took off his badge and placed it carefully on the counter. He could see Edward watching out of the corner of his eye as he slowly slid it down the counter to stop right next to the puzzle book. Edward couldn't resist glancing at it. "You know what that is don't you Eddy?" Jeb decided the buddy approach was going to be his best bet and used the name Bartender Bob used earlier.

"Yes. Your badge."

"That means I'm one of the good guys. I'm trying to find whoever hurt Leslie and I think you know something that could help me a lot. Don't you want to help us catch the bad guy?"

Edward reached out and touched the badge with a single finger. "Yes."

"Then I need to know what Leslie said to you."

"I promised. A promise is a promise. A bond. An oath. Pact. Pledge. Word of honor."

"All right Eddy. You're right. A promise is a promise." Jeb was frustrated but determined to win this...this...whatever this was. "A man is only as good as his word. And you are obviously a very loyal and trustworthy fellow."

"I am."

"Do you work here Edward?"

"I clean the pub. And other places in town too. Lots of offices. I'm the best cleaner in Rock Bottom. Everyone says so."

"I believe you. Leslie and Bill must have thought so to let you work here at the pub."

"My father made this place," Edward said proudly. He pointed to a picture over the bar. "That's him. That's Dad. And that's Henry." He pointed to the photo next to the first. There was a strong family resemblance between all three men. "You only get your picture up there after you die. Someday I'll be up there," he said wistfully. "Leslie gets to go first though."

Jeb looked meaningfully around the pub. "This place must be very special to you."

"This is home."

"How did you feel about Leslie and Bill selling it?"

"I don't want to talk anymore. Can I go back to my puzzle now?" Edward slanted his eyes to his book. "I'm almost done. I need a seven letter word for sad that starts with 'f'."

"Forlorn."

"That fits. Thanks, Sheriff."

Bartender Bob interrupted with the root beer. "Here you are sheriff. Edward, why don't you go get started on the bathrooms?"

Edward looked at his watch. "It's not nine yet. I don't clean those until nine o'clock."

"Just this once Eddy."

Grudgingly the older man left to see to his duties. The bartender faced Jeb. "He means well Sheriff. But he won't crack no matter what you say or do."

"He may have some of the answers we're looking for."

Bartender Bob shrugged. "I think you're going to have to get them somewhere else. Eddy is stubborn as a mule when he wants to be."

Jeb considered Edward's puzzle. Maybe there was another way to go about it, he mused as he drank his root beer. But not tonight. He'd wait a day to come back and then figure out what answers were locked away in Edward Abbott's head.

•

After the book club meeting the small group of women stood on the library steps. They waited patiently for Annie to lock the library for the evening while Arnold danced excitedly in anticipation of a walk. It was just after eight and the ladies decided to continue their discussion over coffee and desert at the cafe per Martha's suggestion.

Kitty was on board with the idea simply because it meant she didn't have to go home and listen to Bill talk about beloved Leslie. Or watch him fall apart for the hundredth time at the mere mention of her name.

A black patrol SUV pulled up in front of the ladies as they stood huddled on the bottom step. Kitty was surprised and pleased to see Jeb step out of the vehicle. He ambled over to her, nodding at the other women in greeting but his eyes were fixed on the petite auburn haired lady. "Evening Kitty."

"Hello Sheriff."

"How are you feeling this evening?" he asked cautiously.

Her heart was feeling less bruised after some time with her friends. Now seeing such sweet concern on Jeb's face wiped away the last of the self-pity and resentment from the previous evening. "I have to say I'm feeling quite well."

Jeb felt lighter than he had all day when he saw the genuine smile and the dimples peep out at him. He'd worried about her since he left last night but now that he saw with his own eyes she was better he relaxed. He smiled easily at her. "No need to be so formal in front of your friends. They all know we're seeing each other."

The ladies smiled and suppressed chuckles as Kitty shot them a look that clearly suggested they hush up. "Of course. You're right. How has your day been Jeb?" she asked quickly.

"To be honest, this is the highlight right now. We're chasing down some leads but nothing yet." He addressed the women as they watched with anxious eyes. "We'll find whoever did this."

"I have no doubt," Liza Jane purred, eyeing him like a piece of Godiva chocolate. "You seem like a very capable sheriff."

"Thank you." Jeb turned back to Kitty. "Will you be attending Leslie's funeral?"

Kitty nodded. "It would be in poor taste not to. Plus Bill and the Judge have coerced me into having visitation at my house afterwards. It's Monday morning at eleven."

"I'd like to take you. It might help to have me by your side." Jeb didn't mean it to sound arrogant. He simply wanted to be there if she needed him.

"I'd like that very much. Thank you, Jeb."

He nodded and started to head back to his SUV but then remembered the other reason he stopped in front of the library when he saw Kitty standing with her friends. Ever since he left her last night she'd been on his mind. He'd worried about her of course. And he'd determined that he needed to step things up a notch if he was going to win her over. Because Jeb was pretty sure that was exactly what he needed to do. "There was one other thing."

"Yes?"

He walked back over to her and because she was still on the bottom step she was almost eye to eye with his tall frame. Almost, but not quite. He smiled down at her. "Ever since you kissed me last weekend I've been thinking about this." And then he gently pulled her face forward and kissed her softly with six pairs of female eyes locked on with avid interest.

Jeb pulled away after a few moments because he didn't want to be indecent or out of line. But he did want to make his intentions known to Kitty and this seemed like the perfect place to start. In public for anyone and everyone to bear witness to whether it set tongues wagging or not. Jeb didn't care. It seemed to him that a romantic kiss was called for so that was what he delivered.

Kitty hadn't realized she'd grabbed hold of Jeb's uniform to steady herself until he pulled back. It wasn't because of the awkward position she was in standing on the bottom step. The absolute truth was that his kiss made her knees weak and her mind turn to mush and she would have surely fallen over if she didn't hold on to him for support.

Had Bill ever been able to do that with just a kiss? she asked herself dreamily as Jeb winked and got back in his truck. It roared to life and a moment later they watched the fading taillights disappear down Main Street.

Kitty finally turned and found her friends staring at her in awe.

"Oh my goodness," Liza Jane breathed. "If that wasn't the most romantic kiss I've ever seen in my life!"

"I think I felt it from here," Lydia swooned, fanning hers cheeks.

"I didn't know there were still men alive that could be so romantic," Annie admitted.

"When is that going to happen to *me*?" Regina wailed. "What do I have to do to find a husband who can kiss like that?"

"My darling, there aren't many of those around these days," Charlotte told her with some regret. "That one there is a keeper."

"I told you he was a dreamboat," Martha sighed happily.

Chapter 14

Kitty sort of floated through the evening while her friends gabbed about her love life and the murder and eventually to what to order off the menu. Having Jeb make such a bold and public display of his affection was something totally new and unexpected. She had never even considered asking such a thing of him as part of their agreement. Obviously he felt compelled to step up their façade and while it had been absolutely dreamy it also left her totally confused.

She had *really* enjoyed being kissed by him *a lot*.

Her husband of nearly three decades had never been terribly affectionate in public. Holding hands wasn't something he was comfortable with and kissing was something reserved only as a prelude to other things in the privacy of their own home. He would have never committed such a brash act with people watching. Not with her anyway.

Kitty thought back to the times she saw Bill and Leslie together around The Bottom, which was often in a town as small as this. Bill hadn't completely changed his ways but there had been little things about him that were different. She'd seen him hold Leslie's hand, even seen them share a kiss at the pub. Maybe it just mattered who you were with, she mused. Maybe being with the right one could change a person's heart and mind and attitude.

Kitty wondered if maybe her own heart and mind and attitude needed some changing.

When she got home she stuck her head in the living room only long enough to say good-night to Bill before zipping up to her room and enjoying the evening's success. The plan was starting to work and she was thrilled. Already the girls were looking at her in a whole new light. And getting to spend time with Jeb was turning out to be so much more than she thought possible.

Kitty sat at her dressing table and stared at herself in the mirror. Was it really possible to develop feelings for someone so quickly? She'd only been out with the man a handful of times yet it seemed like more than that. It felt like they'd known each other forever. He was a Christian and kept his relationship with God as a priority in his life. When she was with Jeb she felt lifted up and at peace with him, with herself, with God. The question was did he have any real feelings for her at all or were they merely all part of the plan?"

And what about Bill? Here he was back in her life and she couldn't help but wonder if there was a purpose in that which she was still ignorant of. Kitty could not easily discount twenty-eight years and four children from the equation. There may have been some rough times but there had also been many happy memories made as well.

Her hairbrush was sitting on the table and she picked it up automatically. Kitty brushed her hair while her thoughts drifted back to Jeb. Her heart was not supposed to get caught up in this arrangement but she feared it was being dragged into the mix despite dire warnings from her brain. Especially with her ex-husband back in her life. How had things gotten so complicated so quickly?

•

Friday morning Judge Burgess was waiting in Jeb's office when he got there. Again. He'd been here yesterday at nine AM sharp wanting an update as well. Rob shot his boss an apologetic look but said nothing. Jeb took a moment to get some coffee before settling into his office. Only then did he acknowledge the older man waiting impatiently on the other side of the desk. "Morning Judge."

"Do we have any new leads?" the Judge cut right to the chase. He wasn't here to exchange pleasantries. He wanted to know if an arrest was imminent.

"A few," Jeb hedged.

"It's been four days Sheriff. We ought to know something by now. Have a person of interest at the least. But I don't see anything significant happening."

Jeb sipped his coffee and leaned back in his chair. "We're making progress. It takes time to talk to everyone and wait on the lab results even when we have connections. It's not like in the movies. It's a long process."

The judge frowned his most intimidating frown. This was unacceptable in his eyes. "I expected more from you Sheriff."

"As I've said we have some leads and we're working round the clock. Eventually we'll catch the break we need if we're diligent and follow procedure." Jeb met the older man's eyes and waited.

"I don't see you bringing anyone in, singling anyone out, figuring out the motive. Nothing. It's like you're still at square one. I intend to get answers and if that involves going over your head I will. I told you that from the beginning."

"You do what you need to Judge Burgess. Right now I have a murder to solve. If you could shut the door on the way out I'd appreciate it."

Rob stuck his head in the office. "We got a hit on the prints."

The judge responded before Jeb could. "Spit it out. Whose prints were they? Who killed my daughter?"

"It was Annie Goodwin," Rob said before Jeb could stop him.

"All right. Go make an arrest," Judge Burgess ordered as he turned to face Jeb.

Jeb looked pointedly around the man standing in front of his desk. "Go get her and bring her to my office. I'll talk to her here."

"Yes sir."

•

When her son and daughter-in-law dropped off Callie and Sam Friday morning Charlie questioned the wisdom of letting Bill stay at the house. He was quite upset about the arrangement but Kitty assured him it was temporary. Bill wasn't up yet and she didn't need a confrontation in her kitchen so she ushered them out the front door with forced cheer and a quick wave.

She turned her attention to her grandchildren now settling into the living room with the toys they usually played with when they were here. Kitty had mixed feelings about the visit today. She was hopeful that having the grandchildren around might pull Bill out of his grief for even a little while. But since he hadn't made an effort to spend time with them in the past she wasn't sure that was possible. Hope and worry warred within her all morning. They moved out to the studio and she got them set up with their own little easels and plenty of paint to keep them busy and away from Bill a little longer.

By eleven-thirty both kids were hungry so she set aside their personalized aprons and paints and they traipsed back into the house. Bill was sitting at the table reading the newspaper looking glum. When he saw Sam and Callie, glum turned to annoyed.

"What are they doing here?"

"I always watch them on Fridays for Bridget. Sometimes other days too. She spends Friday with her grandmother at the nursing home in Port Bell. Charlie went with her today." She went to the fridge and took out two juice boxes and then fixed two peanut butter and jelly sandwiches. Kitty helped them get settled at the table, Callie in a booster seat and Sam on his knees staring at Bill while he chewed his sandwich. He was wearing the cape she'd made him and a hat that was too big for his head.

Bill shook his paper out and resumed reading. Sam chewed loudly and watched, intent on annoying his target.

"Must you be so noisy?" Bill demanded.

Sam nodded and chomped like a cow.

"Good grief. Kitty, do something."

"Sam love, don't chew with your mouth open."

"But it's fun," he insisted.

"It is, isn't it? But your grandpa doesn't like it so let's not do that right now."

"Okay. I'll save it for mommy and daddy."

Kitty couldn't help but smile. "I don't think they'll like it either."

"They will," Sam said with authority. "Mommy and daddy are fun."

"Parents aren't supposed to be fun," Bill grumbled. "They're supposed to be firm and make their children mind basic manners."

"Charlie and Bridget are wonderful parents," Kitty immediately defended her son. "Look how happy and well-adjusted Sam and Callie are."

"Hmmph."

"If you got to know Sam you'd see what a great little boy he is," Kitty continued, winking at her little guy. "He's smart and funny and loves to run really fast up and down the beach."

"I run faster than everybody," Sam told Bill, daring him to argue that fact.

"Me, too!" Callie squealed, squishing her sandwich and holding some out for Bill.

He grimaced and attempted once again to read the paper.

"Do you like to run?" Sam asked his grandfather.

"No."

"I do. Do you like to paint?"

"No."

"I do. Do you like Superman?"

"No."

"I do. Do you like to fish?"

"No. Yes." Bill peeked around the paper. "Do you?"

"Yes. Daddy takes me. He's the best fisherman in the *entire* world!"

"Me, too!" Callie echoed her favorite phrase.

Bill considered the boy across from him. He did look a lot like Charlie did at that age. Fair-haired, fair skinned and blue eyes full of curiosity. "What's the biggest fish you ever caught?"

Sam held his hands as far apart as he could. "It was this big." He nearly toppled out of his seat but caught himself in time. "What about you?"

Bill set his paper down and spread his arms out as far as they could go. "Mine was like this."

"Not uh," Sam said in awe.

"Yep. Got a picture somewhere."

Sam looked to his beloved grandmother for confirmation of this information.

"It's true Sam. Your grandpa used to love to fish. He took your dad and Uncle Teddy all the time."

"Wow," Sam breathed. "You may be better than my dad."

Bill felt a little crack in the armor around his heart. "Your dad was a natural. Still is I'd imagine."

"Well maybe you can take me fishing sometime?" Sam asked, wondering if this grandpa of his might be some kind of fishing superhero.

"Me, too!" Callie said, throwing her sandwich in excitement.

Bill slowly wiped peanut butter off his face with a napkin Kitty thoughtfully handed him. "Maybe."

Kitty watched in awe as Sam and Bill engaged in a tentative conversation that ping ponged between fishing, Spiderman, getting a dog and the merits of a real job versus collecting indefinitely from the tooth fairy. She occupied herself with keeping Callie happy while they played silly games with their hands and shared what was left of some cookies she baked the day before all the while listening to Bill and Sam converse.

"Gramma can we go to the beach?" Sam wanted to know.

"Of course." The weather was mild enough and a couple hours on the beach would tucker them out for a nice long nap when they returned.

"Can we bring him?" Sam asked, indicating with his thumb the grandfather he was starting to like.

Kitty looked to Bill for an answer, who shrugged nonchalantly. "I suppose I could go. Some fresh air might to do me some good."

"All right. Let's clean up and find some light jackets. It still gets cool by the water." She pretended like it was perfectly normal for her and Bill to take the kids to the beach. But inside voices were secretly screeching like cheerleaders at a pep rally.

They had a marvelous time. Sam raced ahead of them and then darted back as fast as his four-year-old legs would take him only to repeat the process. Callie walked between Kitty and Bill, each chubby little hand grasping one of theirs. Occasionally they swung her forward and back as they went and she whooped with delight. Kitty wanted to whoop with delight to at this amazing transformation in Bill. It was obvious that he was a little unsure how to approach Callie at all but bless his heart he was trying. He even held his granddaughter while Kitty tied the little pink sneakers so she wouldn't have to bend down. She watched surreptitiously as Callie planted a kiss on Bill's face and giggled. It made her heart soar when, after a moment, Bill smiled a wobbly smile back at her. "She's kind of cute," he said in awe. The blond ringlets and dark blue eyes passed down from Kitty were striking on such a little person, he decided proudly.

"Yes," Kitty agreed happily but kept her eyes on the shoe-tying.

"Maybe we should do this again tomorrow," Bill suggested quietly as they trekked up the sandy dune towards the Volvo more than an hour later. Sam was holding on to Bill's hand and trudging along on tired little legs but he didn't complain as long as he had his grandfather to help him along.

"If you'd like to we certainly can."

Bill hesitantly smiled down at the little boy watching him with adoration – just like his own boys used to look at him. "I think I would."

•

It was after lunch before Rob finally found Annie and had her sitting in a chair looking jumpy as a long-tailed cat in a room full of rocking chairs. Her hands were locked together on her lap and her eyes were enormous.

"You weren't entirely truthful with us Annie," Jeb said quietly, deciding to ease into the interrogation slowly and gently. Sometimes that was the best way.

Annie burst into tears.

Like most men tears made him uncomfortable. Jeb shifted in his chair, trying to look unmoved and uncaring and wishing he had a hankie for the distressed woman. "I didn't kill anyone," she managed to get out between snorts and snobs.

"Okay. Let's talk about that night. What happened? We know you were at the Appleton house. We found your fingerprints on Leslie and the colored flyer on the floor was one of the flyers you had just picked up in Port Bell that very evening."

Annie stopped sniffing and swiped the tears away. "You can really get finger prints off a body? I thought that was only on TV?"

"It's difficult and time-consuming but possible. We know you were there," he reiterated. "Tell me everything that happened."

"I called Leslie after work to see if I could try to talk to her one last time. Appeal to her sense of family and honor. Apparently she doesn't have one though because she hung up on me. I decided on my way back from the printer to stop at their house and try to talk to her in person. Show her the flyer and make her see how awful it would be if Trescott got hold of the Bottom's Up."

"What time did you get there?"

"It was about quarter past seven. I banged on the storm door but there was no answer. Her truck was there so I knew she had to be inside. I just sort of walked in," she admitted sheepishly. "When I saw her lying on the floor I dropped everything. The flyers went all over and in my hurry to pick them up and get out I must have missed one."

"But you didn't just leave. You touched her at some point."

"I started to run," Annie admitted. "But I realized that whoever did it was probably long gone. The house was as still as death." She shuddered. "I went over to see if there was a chance she was still alive. I checked for a pulse but there was none. Leslie was dead. I know I should have called nine-one-one but there was no point. I ran."

Jeb strummed his fingers on the table. "You didn't see or hear anything?"

"No."

"If you got there just after seven and she was already dead, we can narrow the time frame of death considerably. She called her ex-husband just before seven. That means you could have scared the killer away when you were banging on the door."

"Oh my," Annie breathed. "I didn't think...I mean I just assumed...I thought she'd been dead a while."

"Why?"

"She seemed to have already started cooling."

"If she'd been dead for twenty minutes she would have."

"Well all I know is that I didn't kill her." She looked Jeb squarely in the eye. "Do you believe me?"

There was the question of the day. Here was a woman with a clear motive, admitting to being at the murder scene and had even touched the body and left evidence of being there. There was an excellent chance of getting a conviction with the circumstantial evidence they had already. "I wish you had been upfront from the beginning Miss Goodwin."

"I was scared."

"I believe you were. I'll be honest with you. It doesn't look good."

After fifteen more minutes of questioning Jeb was satisfied that Annie had told him all she knew. He slipped out of the office to call Harry for a second opinion on something that had occurred to him.

Harry answered immediately. "What can I do for you, Sheriff?"

"I need more information about the prints you found on Leslie."

"Did you get a match yet?"

"We did. The local librarian. She says she was checking for a pulse. Is that possible?"

"The prints we took off were on the victim's wrist so that's entirely plausible," Harry told him and Jeb felt a sense of relief. "Of course, if she grabbed the victim from behind, to yank her back in order to swing the candlestick down, that would be plausible too."

The sense of relief vanished. "That doesn't help me either way Harry."

"If I were grabbing someone in a life or death situation I'd probably use my entire hand to ensure maximum force. Checking for a pulse only requires one or two fingers. There were exactly two prints left on the body. It doesn't necessarily negate the one but it does support the other."

"So it would seem."

"She'd also have to be pretty strong and over five foot-ten based on the angle of the blow. Unless the victim was already down on the floor which is unlikely."

"Thanks Harry." Jeb hung up, feeling slightly more inclined to believe Annie's story. She was a tall woman, maybe five nine at the most; close to Leslie Appleton's height. It would have been awkward for her to swing the candlestick down at the angle required with so little difference in their height. Unless the woman was wearing heels. Jeb went back in the room and looked at Annie's shoes. "You wear those to work most of the time? Or do you sometimes wear heels?"

Annie shook her head. "I'm up and down all day. I couldn't wear heels. My feet would swell up like two big sausages."

"Sheriff!" The Judges' bark carried across the main area in the station. "A word please."

"Fine."

Jeb led the judge into one of the interrogation rooms and closed the door after the older man entered. He already had a pretty good idea where this conversation was going. "What is it Judge?"

"That woman killed my daughter. Are you going to arrest her?"

"We're holding her for the moment. I'm not convinced she did it."

"What more do you need?" Leroy blustered. "A written confession. She had motive, means and opportunity. You have DNA evidence. Arrest the woman already!"

"Judge, you aren't thinking rationally. We need to make sure everything adds up and right now it doesn't."

"The only thing that doesn't add up is how you became Sheriff! The suspect is guilty."

"She is not guilty until she's proven guilty in a court of law. That's your jurisdiction. This is mine. Don't tell me how to do my job and I won't tell you how to do yours."

Leroy scrutinized the sheriff from under tightly drawn brows. "You're making a mistake. Is that woman worth risking your career?"

Jeb was trying to cut the man some slack since his daughter was just murdered. But now his patience was starting to wear thin. "I will not be pressured into making an arrest until I am sure we have the right person." To make his point he opened the door and leaned out. "Rob! Take Miss Goodwin home!"

He turned and faced the sour faced judge. "I'll let you know when we make an arrest. Now please get out of my station and let us do our job."

•

After supper, Kitty invited Bill to join her on one of her evening walks to the beach.

"We already went once today," he said from the couch. As soon as the kids left Bill was lost in his grief again.

"I just thought it would be nice. We can go in the opposite direction this time. Away from town."

"I think I'll stay here this time. I'm not up to leaving the house again."

"All right. If you're sure. I won't be long." Kitty ducked out and took the shortcut across the Mason's field and around the center of town to the long expansive beach front that she enjoyed walking in the evenings. Between the moonlight and the lights from the pub and the dozen or so homes along the coast there was enough light to see with the aid of a flashlight. She meandered along for nearly twenty minutes before she saw a figure walking her way. Kitty felt a momentary rush of panic when she realized how alone she was out here. Instinctively she put her hand in her pocket and felt for the small can of mace she always carried. Grasping it tightly she resumed her walk and kept her eyes on the figure coming towards her. She tried not to think about the fact that there was a murderer still on the loose but images of Leslie's dead body danced through her mind.

The figure waved a hand in greeting. "Kitty! It's me, Jeb!"

She relaxed her grip on the mace and hurried towards him. "I'm glad it's you. I was worried for a moment."

"You shouldn't be out walking alone at night," he chastised her gently. Inside he was delighted to have bumped into her and pretty certain that subconsciously that was why he chose this route to walk.

"If I hadn't I wouldn't have run into you," Kitty told him, smiling absurdly because she was so delighted to see him. She turned and fell into step beside him so he wouldn't see the silly grin on her face.

"How about if I walk you home?"

154

"How about if you walk me to the cafe and we can have a cup of coffee? You can tell me about your day," Kitty suggested, trying to squelch down the hope of spending a few stolen moments with this man.

The stress of the day started melting away for Jeb. "That sounds even better."

•

Jeb didn't have to be in until noon Saturday and appreciated the extra hours to catch up on some sleep after the hours he'd put in at the station all week. Most of the time he felt pretty good but when the stress of a murder investigation started weighing down he felt every one of his fifty-two years. He showered and sipped his coffee in the kitchen, staring out the window at the waves just a hundred yards away.

He also noticed people on the beach, which wasn't unusual this time of year on the weekends. Locals walked it all the time when the weather was nice and today promised to be a heat wave in the sixties, bringing folks out in droves. He didn't normally pay too much attention to who was out there but this group of people caught his attention. With his mug still in his hand he stepped outside and stood on the edge of his deck watching.

Jeb would recognize Kitty anywhere now that he knew her, even with old eyes at a distance. Her auburn hair stood out to him. It was obvious who she was with as well: Bill and their grandkids. Laughter and shrieks pierced the air and Kitty ran from the little boy who was determined to show her something in his hand as he chased after her. Bill was down on the ground with the little girl looking at something intently. Before long Kitty and the boy joined them and then they were all huddled together, laughing and pointing and having a wonderful time.

Jeb felt a sharp pang right to his heart and turned away. He went back inside and set his cup in the sink, looking one last time through the window at the happy scene unfolding on his beach. Maybe it was nothing. Maybe it was just a way for Kitty to help Bill through the sadness that had been consuming him all week. That was understandable. There was no shame in finding joy in those little stolen moments even in the midst of tragedy. It didn't mean they were back together. It didn't mean that the fragile feelings developing between Kitty and himself were no longer valid. He just had to trust that God would sort it all out the way it was supposed to be sorted.

•

"He's coming!" Bill yelled, bounding down the stairs and into the kitchen.

"Who?" Kitty asked. She was stirring the gravy on the stove and checking the potatoes.

"Teddy! He'll be here tonight and he's staying for a week."

"Oh Bill! That's wonderful! I'm so glad he'll be able to come for the funeral," she said sincerely. "I know it's important to you that all the kids are here." Teddy was always Bill's favorite and he hadn't done a very good job of hiding it. She didn't think he intentionally slighted the other three; Bill simply wasn't perceptive enough to know when he was favoring Teddy over the others because they were so alike and had similar interests.

She phoned Teddy last Wednesday to make sure he'd be able to come back for the funeral to support his father and he hadn't been very receptive to her call. Now that she knew her youngest son would be home for even a couple days her mood brightened considerably. She hadn't seen him in over a year because his work kept him so busy that he hadn't been able to visit or have visitors. He'd been home for a very brief visit last spring when Jenny and Brad got married and had stayed at the local inn.

"Of course my boy is going to come home for his step-mother's funeral," Bill said. "He adored Leslie."

"Oh? I didn't think Teddy was particularly close to her. I thought he only saw her at the wedding really."

"Plus all the times we went and visited him."

"Visit? When did you visit Teddy?"

"Les and I were up there just a few weeks ago. We went at least once a month. We all went out to eat and sometimes caught a show." Bill shook himself. "I can't believe we won't be able to do those things together anymore."

"I see." Kitty turned the burner off and moved to drain the potatoes. This was news to her. She had no idea Bill had been seeing so much of Teddy when his job was so demanding. "I'm surprised he had time for you with his work schedule."

Bill guffawed. "Schedule. Right. When you're the manager you can make your own hours."

"Manager?" Kitty spun around. "Teddy's a manager? Where?"

"Don't you ever talk to your own son? He's been managing a club for the last six months. The owner was impressed with him and promoted him faster than anyone's ever worked there before. Teddy is the youngest to make manager," Bill said proudly.

Kitty walked to the table on autopilot with plates and silverware. Why hadn't her son told her this? She tried to call him at least once a month because he insisted that was all he ever had time for. Surely he could have mentioned his big promotion in one of those phone calls. It hurt her to know that he had kept this news from her and yet he told Bill and Leslie. And apparently he had time to spend with them regularly yet he couldn't spare her more than five minutes each month on a rushed phone call.

Most likely she was just being petty. Surely there was a good reason for him not mentioning his promotion and the visits. Maybe he wanted to surprise her in person with the news.

When Teddy arrived two hours later Kitty couldn't believe the young man standing in her living room was her son. He'd changed so much since she last saw him. His frame had filled out so much his shoulders were as wide and full as Bill's. The light brown hair the exact shade as his father's was shaggy and curling at the back of his neck. Charlie had always been the bigger, more muscular of the two but now Teddy looked like he was catching up and possibly surpassing his brother.

"Teddy!" she finally said after soaking in everything. She went to him and squeezed him tightly.   He responded with a light hug and awkward pat on her back. "Hey mom," he said without much enthusiasm.

"Thank you for coming. I know your dad is glad to have you here," she said, pulling back but still holding on to his hands. "And I'm just so happy you're home!"

"There's nothing to be happy about right now," Teddy said, pulling away from her. "Poor Leslie is dead. This has got to be hard on Dad. I hope you aren't this incessantly cheerful around him all day, acting like nothing is wrong."

"Of course not! I only meant it's nice to see you. It's been so long."

"Son!" Bill exclaimed, following the noise down the stairs. He bounded down to the entryway and wrapped his son in a bear hug. "It's good you're here," he said gruffly.

"Of course Dad. You know I'd do anything for you and Les."

"She was a good woman," Bill said, his arm still slung around Teddy's shoulder.

"The best," Teddy said with feeling.

"Come in and sit down," Bill encouraged, taking his son's bag and handing it to Kitty. "Your mom will see to all that. She's a wonder at that stuff."

Kitty watched as they wandered over to the couch and sat down. She felt snubbed but didn't want to upset Teddy after he just drove for three hours. She supposed the least she could do was take his bag up for him so she did. When she returned a few minutes later she joined them on the couch.

"You must be hungry and thirsty after the drive. Your mother made a wonderful pot roast. You want her to heat some up for you?"

"I'm fine. I ate before I left."

"What about a drink?"

"What have you got?"

Bill looked to Kitty for the answer. "I've got Moxie," she told Teddy. "I know how much you love that."

Teddy blanched. "I think I'll pass. You have anything stronger?"

"No, I'm sorry."

Teddy sighed in disappointment. "Leslie always had a nice supply of liquor in that antique buffet, didn't she dad?"

"That she did," Bill agreed, leaning back against the couch and relaxing completely for the first time in days. His favored child was returned home and now he had someone to truly share the grief with, someone who understood it because Teddy had loved Leslie too.

"How did you know Leslie kept liquor in an antique buffet?" Kitty asked suddenly. As far as she knew he hadn't been to Bill and Leslie's house. He hadn't been home in over a year.

"Because he visits often enough to know," Bill said, clapping his son on the shoulder. "This guy couldn't stay away."

"When did you visit your father?" Kitty asked her son in bewilderment.

"Thanksgiving. Christmas. Last month."

"You were here for Thanksgiving? And Christmas?" Kitty asked, feeling like a knife just went through her heart. "Why didn't you come by? Everyone else was here. Your brother and sisters didn't even know you were in town."

"Charlie did. He saw me."

"Charlie knew?" Kitty was dumbfounded.

"Yes," Teddy said irritably. He sounded just like Bill when he had gotten tired of speaking with her about something. "He saw me at the gas station just outside town."

"Why didn't he say anything?"

"Probably because he didn't want to mention the black sheep of the family had returned," Teddy grunted. "Wouldn't want to ruin a perfectly good holiday by mentioning me."

"But I don't understand," Kitty tried again.

"I came to spend Christmas with Dad and Leslie, not you and the happy homemakers," he bit out. "All you do is fuss over everyone and everything. Like now. It drives a man crazy. No wonder Dad left you."

Kitty felt a pain so sharp and so deep it left her momentarily unable to speak. Or breathe. Or do anything but stare at the young man in front of her.

"Now Teddy you don't need to speak so harshly to your mother," Bill said, patting his son's knee. "She was a good enough wife to me for many years and a fine mother to the four of you."

Teddy rubbed his brow. "Yeah I know."

Bill looked at Kitty. "He's going through a hard time right now. Don't make a big deal out of what he said."

"Not make a big deal?" Kitty repeated. "He's been here all of five minutes and I find out he's lied to me, ignored me, and looked down at me for a very long time apparently. I think I deserve an explanation and an apology," she said quietly.

"Sorry," Teddy shot back.

"You ought to be," Kitty continued, feeling a small spark ignite. "I've done everything for you. All of you. At least Charlie and Jenny appreciate how I've always been there for them. And Becca too. But you. What have I ever done to deserve this?"

"This is why I don't come here," Teddy said, turning to Bill. "I never hear the end of it. And you know it's only going to get worse when she finds out."

"You're going to have to tell her," Bill said. "Maybe it's a bit of good news. I know Leslie was excited for you."

"Tell me what?" Kitty demanded. "What was Leslie excited about?"

"Emily's pregnant."

"Who is Emily?"

"My girlfriend."

"Oh my." Kitty sat back. Her head was swimming and she felt a flood of emotions overwhelm her at the news. She wanted Teddy to find someone and settle down. She had hoped and prayed he'd find a good mate, a nice Christian girl with a clear head and a pure heart. She didn't want to make snap judgments about Emily but her heart felt heavy. "What are you going to do?"

Teddy shrugged. "Maybe get married. Emily isn't sure yet."

"Did you ask her?"

"We've talked about it but haven't made a decision."

"I see."

"We might just want to live together first."

"Oh Teddy, that doesn't sound right."

"This isn't the fifties," Teddy snapped. "We don't have to get married to have a life together."

"Teddy, I don't think living together is the right thing to do. You know how we feel about that."

"Dad is okay with it. Not that it matters. It's our decision."

Kitty gaped at Bill. "You told him it's okay to live together?"

Bill shrugged. "Sure. Maybe if we had tried the living together thing first..." He stopped, his face suddenly turning red. "Well. I just don't see that's it's such a bad option. They're young. They need to figure things out."

Kitty stood up, her heart hammering. "You wish we had lived together first as a trial run? Is that what you were going to say? Then you wouldn't have wasted twenty-seven years on me?"

"Calm down Kitty. You're getting all worked up. And I just can't deal with anymore right now. With Leslie's funeral coming up I'd rather focus on something happy, just for a little while. Is that so bad?" Bill asked her, giving her the doleful eyes again. "This has been a really hard week for me, and having Teddy here is just what I need."

Kitty was aghast. She wanted to hold her tongue; normally it came so easily to hold back. But the two of them sitting here on her couch and treating her so shabbily just galled her enough to speak her mind. "Your son just dropped a bomb on me. And I know it's his life and he can do as he pleases. He's twenty-four years old. But that doesn't mean we need to give him foolish council when he needs guidance Bill. For goodness sake." She tried to regain her composure but it was slipping away from her. "The pregnancy isn't even the most upsetting news. The fact that our son has been sneaking into town and avoiding the rest of the family is what hurts the most. Why Teddy? Why would you do that?"

"Because I didn't want to deal with this," he spat. "You're so close-minded it makes me crazy. At least Dad doesn't judge. He and Leslie were cool about the kid and Emily. I should have known you'd go all religious fanatic on me about how I'm sinning and going to burn in hell." He cursed. "I should have gone to a hotel."

Kitty tried to sooth his temper even though hers was frayed just as much. "I'm not judging you Teddy. It's just-"

"Oh yes you are! And I'm not good enough. Not like perfect Charlie and Jenny. At least Becca is smart enough to stay away so she can just avoid all this crap."

She tried to blink the tears away. Every word out of his mouth pained her more than the last. "I love you Teddy. But you've got to grow up. You're going to be a father. Emily needs you."

"You don't know anything about the situation. Gees I need a drink." He turned to Bill. "Let's go to the pub."

Bill paled. "I can't Teddy. I haven't been there since...before."

"Everyone there knows you and knows you loved Les. Let's go down there and have a drink for her. Let's celebrate life instead of sitting here listening to this."

"I don't know son."

Teddy stood. "Well I for one am going to go down there and toast her. She'd get a kick out of it. We'll have everyone raise a glass to her."

Bill wanted to go, to do that for Leslie. But the idea of going there seemed wrong. It was a happy place. He couldn't take a moment out of his grief to be happy about Leslie's life could he? Should he? He'd felt guilty enough about having a respite on the beach with Kitty and the grandkids. It had helped to stop thinking about his dead wife for a few hours but now he needed to resume grieving again.

Life was suddenly so difficult.

"Come on Dad. Let's honor her."

"I don't know Teddy."

"You know how much she loved life and just…sparkled. Leslie was all about life and grabbing it by the horns. She's hate to see you sitting here wasting away."

"I guess maybe she'd appreciate the gesture," Bill finally admitted. "All right. But just one drink to her memory."

"Great. One drink. I guess that's better than no drink. Let's go." Teddy helped his father up and they started towards the door. "Don't wait up," he called over his shoulder and then the door slammed shut.

Kitty stood rooted to the spot. She was fighting not to fall apart, not to give into the tears and overwhelming pain. Where had all the anger in Teddy come from? Had she been such a horrible mother to have scarred him somehow? How else could his words be explained away if not for her own failure? Slowly she sank into a wing chair and stared at the blank TV screen. Visions of Teddy as a little boy played through her mind as if they were on the screen. So many memories of her precocious little boy filled her heart. Kitty wanted to help that little boy, help the hurt angry man he was today. The only way she knew to do that was to pray so she dropped further to her knees and let the tears fall as she cried out to God. There was so much to pray about. How had she not seen how damaged her relationship with her son was? What had caused it? And what could she do to fix it? She bowed her head and sat that way for a long time.

Chapter 15

When Bill and Teddy arrived at the pub it was just after seven. The tables were full and there was a somber aura in the room as people talked in hushed tones. As Bill entered the establishment the whispered tones silenced completely and all eyes settled on him.

Bill walked over to the bar and met the eyes of friends and neighbors he'd known for decades. Some had snubbed him when he left Kitty, others had long since forgotten that transgression. Now they all offered silent sympathy as they shook his hand or laid a hand on his back. He was overcome with emotion by the feeling of affection he felt in this place. He ordered a beer and took it firmly in hand. He held it up and faced the room. "To Leslie."

"To Leslie!" the voices followed around the room. They started as quiet echoes and grew to boisterous cheers.

Bill felt his own spirits lift temporarily and turned to the barkeep. "Bob, a round on the house! For Leslie!" Another cheer from the patrons and he found the hollow ache in his heart was temporarily appeased. Being here made him feel closer to his wife. Deep down she had loved this place. He had wondered oftentimes if she truly wanted to sell it or if she had seriously realized what giving up the pub meant.

"Dad, you did a good thing," Teddy said, clapping his father on the back. "Les would love it. She wasn't one to sit around and wallow. And she wouldn't want you to, either."

"No. It just seems too soon, though."

"Monday we'll mourn her death. Tonight let's celebrate her life."

Connor approached them then and Bill worried his brother-in-law would be angry with him for this celebration of sorts. Instead Connor offered his hand. "My sister would have appreciated the gesture."

Bill clasped the younger man's hand. "Thank you." He noticed Charlie sitting opposite them, frowning in his general direction. He waved to his son to come over but Charlie ignored him.

"Charlie is a mama's boy," Teddy said, sipping another beer. "Always has been, always will be."

"Your brother is a good guy," Connor said quietly.

"He had no use for Leslie. Why is he even here?"

"Probably trying to get the latest update on this place. Rumors are swarming about whether or not Bill is going to sell." Connor raised a brow in question at the one mentioned.

"Ahh. Big brother is worried about his inheritance," Teddy chuckled dryly.

Connor chuckled without humor. "And you aren't?"

Teddy shrugged. "I'm sure they'll be plenty of money when the folks die now that Dad has the insurance policy and the money from the sale, if he decides to sell. I figure either way I'm good. If Dad doesn't sell, I will when I get my share of this place."

Bill nodded. "And it's yours to do with what you want. An inheritance should be a blessing, not a burden."

"See? Just being pragmatic. Unlike Big Brother over there who's chomping at the bit about losing this place no doubt."

"He grew up here, worked by your father's side in addition to his own job until my sister upset the apple cart. I think he has a right to be angry," Connor said.

"Charlie had issues with me leaving his mother for Les," Bill admitted, staring across the bar at his oldest son. Charlie was leaning against the counter, glaring in their direction and still nursing the same drink he'd had when they got there. "But I don't think he'd do anything crazy."

"Your son has always had a temper," Randy threw in from down the counter. "Everyone knew he hated Leslie. Is it such a stretch to think he finally had enough?"

"What are you doing here Parker?" Teddy wanted to know. "Celebrating her death?"

"Just because Leslie and I got divorced doesn't mean I wished her any harm," he snapped. "You're an idiot Teddy."

"Come over here and say that to my face."

Bill put a hand on his youngest son's chest to restrain him. "No. No fighting tonight. We're just here to share a good time and good memories."

Teddy relaxed. "Fine."

Lionel Trescott emerged from the shadowy depths. "Evening gentlemen. I thought I'd stop by and offer my condolences."

"That's what the funeral is for," Connor growled. "If you're here to talk business you can get out right now."

Lionel smiled. "No need to get unpleasant. I just thought since you were all here I'd come over and tell you how sorry I was to hear about dear Leslie."

"Thank you," Bill mumbled.

"She was a visionary," Lionel continued. "She wanted to see her family's business live on and be more than they ever thought it would be. That's why she was selling it. She believed I could take her father's dream to the next level."

"This pub was my family's dream too," Bill said slowly. "And neither my father nor Henry or his father wanted to sell. I was only going to sign the papers because it was what Leslie wanted."

"She'd surely still want you to."

"You don't have an ounce of decency do you?" Connor demanded of Lionel. "My sister isn't even in the ground yet and you're sniffing around here trying to manipulate Bill into selling."

"Your sister is gone but the deal is still intact if Bill wants it to be. I only thought I'd let him know that I'm honor-bound to see the vision through to the end. Just as Randy is." Lionel nodded at that one who was listening with interest. "It might be hard for Bill to return here without her. Sometimes it's best to get a clean fresh start."

While Lionel's timing and approach were less than considerate Bill saw the wisdom in his words. It would be hard being back here without his wife by his side. She had come in here like a whirlwind three years ago to take over for Henry when that one was bedridden and dying. Bill hadn't seen her in more than a decade when she left Rock Bottom for college but when she walked through the door he felt like he was alive for the first time in years. He never meant to fall in love with her but being pursued by a young attractive woman was hard for any man to resist. Now the place felt less alive without her vibrant presence to fill the space. "I'll have to think about it Lionel. I just don't know right now."

Lionel reached out and put a sympathetic hand on Bill's shoulder. "I understand. Just know I'm here for you. When you're ready to talk let me know."

"Let's have another round for Leslie," Randy said suddenly. "She'd hate all this morbid talk. Let's lighten up the mood for her."

At Bill's nod Bartender Bob brought them all another round. Charlie watched from a distance in disgust while Connor did the same face to face but he still intended to down the gin the bartender handed him. Lionel lifted his glass and Randy made the toast. "To Leslie!"

Bill lifted his glass and wondered how he was going to get through the rest of his life.

∙

An hour later he was still sitting in the bar, having a drink and pretending to celebrate Leslie's life with everyone else. Blending in was essential to playing the part. He had to grieve along with everyone else, look as upset about Leslie's death as the rest of the community. Of course he hadn't really meant to kill her but now that he had he wasn't sorry she was dead. With her out of the picture all would progress smoothly and things would be as they should.

There was only one person who could possibly figure out his mistake. And if she did figure it out, well, he'd just kill her too. They always said curiosity killed the cat, he thought smugly. And little Kitty better watch herself.

∙

At eight o'clock Kitty was tired of staring at the four walls. She didn't know if she was anxious to see Teddy and Bill again or dreading it. She wanted to unload all the hurt and pain she was carrying and find out what she could do to ease his. It was eating at her and making her crazy. Maybe she just needed to get out for a little while. Walking by the water always helped her to think so on a whim she grabbed a light jacket and slipped out of the house.

The night air was cool and felt delicious on her face. The salt in the air was heavy tonight as the light wind came in off the ocean. She cut down the path that took her directly to her beloved water's edge and avoided going through town. Solace was what she sought and that had always been found walking along the coastline, whether along the sandy beaches or the near the jagged rocky edge didn't matter. Tonight she chose the comfort of the beach. Kitty took her shoes off and let the sand slide between her toes.

There was a chill in the air but she didn't care. The cold water rolled in to play with her toes and then slid away. It was soothing and familiar and she kept walking along, guided by the moonlight and her knowledge of the land that she had walked since she was old enough to stand.

She had brought her own kids here so many times they were too numerous to count. How many times had Teddy run up and down this very stretch, laughing in delight? Or splashed his sisters with the cold water just to make them squeal? The memories played through her mind with each step she took. So many wonderful moments spent with each of her children that had helped nurture the close relationships she had with all of her children. Except Teddy.

His behavior deeply concerned her. Now that she was here and her mind was clear, she realized that her own hurt feelings were irrelevant. He was trying to get his life on track but he was going about it in the wrong way. She knew he needed to get his relationship with God right before anything else and she wasn't sure how to help him see that. At the moment nothing she said was going to be well-received by her son.

The tiny house up ahead was the Johnson's cottage. The one that Jeb was renting. It sat just a stone's throw from the beach and had a spectacular view of the best cove in the area. Kitty stopped in front of it and stared. Had she meant to come here? Had her heart led to this place? Or was it just a coincidence that she ended up at Jeb's home?

The longer she stared at the house dimly lit by the moon the more she could make out of it. And she noticed a man in the distance sitting on a weathered log watching her. She took a step backwards.

"Don't leave," Jeb called softly.

"I didn't mean to come. I was just out walking."

"I'm glad you're here. Come on up and sit next to me."

There was no reason to leave. She had nothing to hurry back to except an empty house. Or possibly an uncomfortable silence with her ex-husband and son. Neither was what she needed. So she made her way through the darkness and dropped down beside Jeb.

"You're troubled."

"How can you tell?" Kitty gazed up at the moon. "There's not enough light."

"I can tell by the way you were walking down the beach. Slowly. Heavily. Like you had the weight of the world on your shoulders."

"You could see all that from this far away?"

"I'm old but not that old. I can see just fine."

"Teddy is home."

"Isn't that a good thing?"

She shook her head. "No. He's angry at me. He's lied to me. He was here at Christmas and didn't visit me or his brother and sisters. And now he just dropped another bomb on me." Kitty took a deep breath. "His girlfriend is pregnant and they aren't sure what they want to do about it."

"I see."

"It's his life and his decision. I understand that. But as a parent I can't help but want to make him see what a mess he's making of his life. He doesn't have a relationship with the Lord and I know that's where he needs to start. But nothing I say matters."

Jeb reached out and took her hand, squeezing it gently. "Maybe words aren't the answer."

She turned slightly sideways without breaking the warm contact of his hand wrapped around hers. "What do you mean?"

"I mean sometimes telling them what to do isn't enough. You need to show them by example what the right decision is. Let God shine through you when you're around him. Maybe that's what he needs more than advice and lectures."

"I don't know," she said, feeling dejected. "I don't think God is shining through me at all these days. I suddenly feel like a complete failure."

Jeb reached out and touched her face. "I see Jesus every time I look at you. You're kind and generous and the most forgiving person I've ever met in my life."

His words soothed the ache in her heart. "Thank you Jeb. You are a good man." She shivered as a sudden chill chased up her spine.

He felt the movement. "How about if I start a fire?"

"Oh no, you don't need to go to so much trouble."

"No trouble. The wood is right over there. I was going to start one when I came out but it's lonely sitting by a fire by yourself. Much better to have someone to share it with."

It only took a few minutes for him to set the wood and get a small fire crackling. He was a pro at fanning the piles of driftwood he kept out here into a small circle of warmth. They sat side by side, warming their hands and listening to the pop and snap of the fire.

"This is nice," Kitty finally said, mesmerized by the flames. "Thank you."

"You're welcome."

"We sometimes did this when the kids were little. Not often. But when we did it was always such fun."

"I'm surprised you didn't do this more. You seem to love the beach. I've seen you walking along it dozens of times since I've been here."

"You remember seeing me?"

"Of course. You are hard not to notice."

"I wouldn't think so," she laughed lightly.

Jeb turned so he could look into her eyes. She sure was pretty by the firelight. "You are a very beautiful woman, Ms. Appleton. Just because your husband is too blind to see it doesn't mean the rest of the world is." He could see she was uncomfortable with the compliment so he turned his gaze back to the fire. "Speaking of Bill, is he going to be staying with you after the funeral?"

"I don't know how long he's going to be with me," she admitted.

"Do you want him to stay?"

"Of course not. But he needs me," she said without thinking.

I need you, Jeb thought. But it was too soon to feel that way much less speak the words out loud. They barely knew each other but he found himself feeling things he hadn't thought possible. He poked at the fire with a stick and watched the tiny sparks shoot upward. "Has it occurred to you that maybe you and Bill have some unresolved issues?"

"How could we? He walked out on me. I don't think there's any question about how he feels about me."

"But how do you really feel about him, Kitty? You said you were over him before. But you were married for a very long time and now he's just been dropped back into your life. If he wanted to try to come back to you, would you have him?"

This was the question quietly nagging at her mind and her heart. Bill seemed to have settled back into her life, finding comfort in the familiarity she offered. She didn't think he loved her; she had no illusions about that. But Kitty knew he needed her. The question was for how long? And if he did want to try again wasn't she obligated to do just that? Her vows to God were sacred to her and she still wanted to honor them. But the thought of being with someone who didn't love her made her heart ache. "I don't know Jeb. And it hasn't come up so I don't think it's even an issue."

But deep down she did. Because she knew Bill better than anyone else in the world. And one thing she knew with certainty was that Bill wouldn't like being alone.

"Well it would certainly add drama to your plan wouldn't it? Two men vying for your affections. Any woman would love being in that position."

"I'm not *any woman*. I don't want to hurt you. Or Bill for that matter."

"Don't worry about me. This is all just a pretense, remember?" he said softly. "I'm just a willing pawn in this game."

"Jeb, please don't say that. You're more than that. You're..."

"I'm what?"

"My friend."

"Good. Friends. Great." He poked the fire harder. He felt like he was sixteen and the girl he had a crush on just told him she didn't *like* him that way but they could still be friends.

"I could use a friend right now."

"You have all your girlfriends. Liza Jane. The mouthy one."

Kitty smiled. "She is my best friend in the world. But she can't be objective about this."

"Why not?"

"Liza never really liked Bill. I don't know why. She doesn't want me anywhere near him."

"And you think I can be objective?"

"Yes. I do. You don't have a motive in any of this."

He nearly laughed out loud. "Right. Of course. No ulterior motives here."

"I respect your opinion and your integrity Jeb. I know if I ask you a question you will give me an honest answer."

"Yes," he sighed. "I will."

She smiled at him and he saw those darn dimples appear. "Don't make it sound so horrible. Honesty is a virtue. You are a good and decent man Jeb Carpenter. And a fine sheriff by the way. You seem like you were born to be a cop."

Jeb nodded. "I suppose I was. My father was a cop. My older brother is a cop. You know my son is. I guess it's in our blood."

"You have an innate need to help people."

"I suppose."

"Which is why you agreed to help me with my incredibly silly plan."

Maybe that was a part of it. The other part wasn't so honorable. "I guess you have me all figured out, Ms. Appleton."

"You don't need to be so formal now. You're off-duty. Call me Kitty."

"I suppose I'm just trying to be on my best behavior."

She leaned closer to the fire to warm her hands and chase away the chill that was coming in off the water. "Just be yourself Jeb. I am when I'm around you. It's actually a nice change."

"You're cold. Scoot over." She did and he wrapped his arm around her, snuggling her into his side. She relaxed against him and he decided he liked the way she fit just right beside him. "What did you mean by that? 'It's a nice change?' Are you not yourself around others?"

"I guess I feel like everyone expects so much of me. I've tried to be the perfect wife, mother, friend, neighbor. I volunteer for everything and bake for every fundraiser there is in this town. I organize, plan, donate, and coordinate every time someone needs something. But no one really sees *me*. With you I don't have to be anything except me. Because there isn't anything real at stake."

"I see."

"It was actually meant as a compliment."

"I know."

They sat in silence for a long time, each lost in their own thoughts. As the fire started to dwindle Jeb squeezed her shoulder lightly. "I should see you home."

"Not necessary." She stood and stretched, feeling more at peace than she had thought possible after the words exchanged earlier with her son. Jeb had such a calming effect.

"There is a murderer on the loose. I'd feel better walking you home."

Kitty dug into her pocket and held up a small can. "I have mace. I'm fine."

"Good girl. But I'm still walking you home. I'd feel better."

"Then I accept your offer."

He kicked sand on the dying fire. "Let me grab a flashlight."

It was just after ten when they got back to the house. Bill was waiting anxiously at the door and frowned when he saw Kitty and Jeb approaching. "Where have you been Kitty?" he demanded when they were almost to the front steps.

"I went for a walk," she said, trying to soothe him with her tone.

"Well we got back and had no idea where you were."

"I'm sorry I worried you."

"There's a lot to be done for the funeral. We have to plan everything and you've got all the food to prepare and the house to clean. I can't believe you just took off on a whim like that without thinking of anybody else."

"Bill, you don't need to speak to Kitty like that."

"You ought to be out looking for whoever killed my wife instead of fooling around with my ex! Wait until the Judge finds out about this. You're too busy snoodling Kitty to do your job!"

Jeb raised an eyebrow. "I can only guess what 'snoodling' refers to and I don't appreciate the implication even if it is none of your business."

"We were just talking," Kitty quickly assured Bill. She didn't appreciate his tone but he was probably right. It was inconsiderate of her to have run off without leaving a note at least. "I had to get out of the house for a while after the way Teddy behaved."

"Teddy is just a boy. He was upset. There's a lot on his mind right now."

"He's twenty-four years old Bill. You can't treat him like a child. For goodness sake he's going to be a father!"

"This isn't about Teddy. It's about Leslie. Monday needs to be perfect for her. And you said you'd help me with that. You promised Kitty."

"And I will," Kitty bit out sharply. "I'm always there for you. I always have been."

"I think I better go," Jeb said. If he stayed any longer he was going to haul Bill down to the station on some trumped-up charges just because he found the man repulsive. "Are you going to be okay Kitty?"

She turned to face him and smiled tremulously for him. "Of course I will be. Thank you for listening, Jeb. I appreciate you being there for me."

"Is mom back?" Teddy's frame loomed in the doorway. He saw Kitty and his face looked grim. "It's about time. Dad was worried."

"I'm here and all is well," she assured her son.

Teddy sized up Jeb. "So is this your new boyfriend?"

"Yes," Kitty said boldly. "It is. Sheriff Jeb Carpenter. Do you have a problem with that?"

"I'm guessing it wouldn't matter even if I did."

"That is not fair Teddy."

"You need to show your mother a little more respect," Jeb said quietly.

"Isn't it time for you to leave? My mother has a lot to do and my father is upset enough. He doesn't need you two in his face making things worse."

"Maybe it would be better if you just left," Kitty said softly. "Their behavior is abhorrent and I hate for you to have to endure it a moment longer."

"It's fine." Jeb leaned forward and kissed her forehead lightly. "I'll see you tomorrow at church."

•

After church Kitty reluctantly declined having lunch with Jeb because she felt honor-bound to return home to Bill and Teddy. They were anxious about the funeral tomorrow and she felt it was her place to be with them. There was also heaps of food to make and Martha agreed to come over for the afternoon to assist. Together they prepared enough food for half the town. They had three crock pots going and the fridge packed with trays of goodies before Martha finally left around four. Liza stopped by and dropped off a bag full of disposable plates and silverware and Kitty thanked her for the practical contribution. She still had cookies in the oven and some homemade bread cooling on racks while frosting a cake. Liza Jane plunked down at the kitchen table and cut vegetables for a tray all the time watching Kitty exhaust herself for her ex-husband.

"Why did you agree to do this?" she finally asked as Kitty leaned against the counter to catch her breath. "You're killing yourself for that man."

"I'm fine," Kitty said tiredly. "I just need five minutes and then I've got to vacuum and clean the bathrooms. I forgot how messy they get having men in the house."

Liza shook her head.

Bill poked his head in the kitchen. "Teddy and I are going for a drive. He thought it might do me some good to get out of the house for a while."

"Why aren't you helping Kitty?" Liza demanded. "She's doing all this for you! The least you could do is help with cleaning up or something."

Bill managed a pitiful pout. "I'm pretty tired Liza. It's been a long, emotional week. I really don't think I can be any good to Kitty right now. We'll be back in a couple hours," he added to Kitty. "Don't worry about fixing us supper. Since you didn't fix us any lunch we're going to grab something while we're out."

Kitty waved good-bye tiredly. "I should go clean while they're gone," she said absently and disappeared into the living room.

"Men," Liza Jane spat, nearly slicing her finger off in the process.

·

Monday morning Kitty was rushing around trying to make sure all the food was ready and the house was in tip-top shape. She expected most of the town to file through at some point today after the funeral and she really did want everything to be perfect. The last thing she needed in her life were tongues wagging about how she had failed to make Leslie's reception less than stellar for Bill and the rest of the family. To her surprise Charlotte arrived at ten and insisted on staying to take care of setting out the food. "You go on. I don't feel much like making small talk over that dreadful woman," she explained. "I'd rather be here knowing I'm being helpful rather than sitting there being a hypocrite."

"You are an angel," Kitty told her, hugging the frail older woman.

"Not even close," Charlotte assured her. "But Jesus already knows that and He loves me anyway."

Jeb was prompt and Kitty was relieved to see him. It would make the whole experience a little easier having him at her side. They arrived at the funeral home in plenty of time and found seats next to Jenny, Brad and Becca, who had come back to The Bottom last night and stayed with Jenny. Kitty hugged her youngest child and took comfort in having them around her, especially when Charlie and Bridget arrived and sat behind them. Charlie didn't look pleased to be there but Kitty was glad he made the effort to be here for his father despite the discord between them.

Kitty was pleased that they all seemed openly receptive to Jeb being at her side. Jenny smiled and warmly shook his hand and her husband followed suit. Becca spoke to him briefly while they waited and seemed to enjoy the conversation.

Liza Jane and Lydia slid in beside Becca. "Oh good, we're not late!" Liza said. "I didn't want to miss a thing."

"You work here, how could you be late?" Becca asked. She had long strawberry blond hair, an enviable figure, her mother's sweet nature and a blend of Kitty and Bill's facial features. Becca was the peacemaker of the family and avoided taking sides in the divorce.

"You'd be surprised," Lydia said. "She's late for everything."

Liza Jane frowned. "Work is why I was almost late. I had to adjust her shawl for optimal effect." Liza was fastidious about her work and wanted every one of her customers to look their absolute best. Even Leslie Appleton. It was a matter of personal pride. She winked at Kitty. "You'll thank me later."

"Oh no," Kitty said, mostly to herself. She leaned over Becca's lap. "Liza Jane, what did you do?"

Liza Jane pretended to be offended. "Do? I didn't do anything. Now hush. The service is about to start."

By the time it was over Kitty was good and ready to be out of there. But first they had to do the customary final viewing. Kitty got in line and allowed herself to be pushed along to the front with Liza Jane and Lydia in front of her, Jeb beside her, and three of her four children right behind. Teddy was with Bill and the Judge and hadn't even made an effort to speak with either her or his siblings. As upsetting as that situation was this was neither the time nor place to address it so she continued walking the somber walk up to the casket. As they neared it she noticed there was a lot of whispering going on as people walked away. Kitty frowned and shot a glance at the back of Liza's curly head.

She finally got to the casket and stood looking down as Leslie. It was a terrible sight to behold in any situation but Liza always wanted her to admire her work. So she felt the need to say something positive despite the circumstances.

"You did her expression up real nice," she told her best friend sincerely. "You caught Leslie's pout perfectly."

Lydia pushed her way between them and took in the view. "Where are her double-D's?" she asked after a moment.

Kitty hadn't noticed anything wrong in that area until Lydia pointed it out. She looked at that part of Leslie which had previously been covered in a pretty purple shawl that went quite nicely with the sparkly purple dress Eileen had picked out for her. Leslie had always been a full-figured lady in that department. Now it appeared her hefty goods had dwindled down to humble offerings. It was quite evident by the way the v-neck sagged into a rumpled pile of almost nothingness. "Liza Jane! What did you do?" Kitty whispered furiously at her best friend.

"I won the bet," she said simply.

"What bet?" Kitty asked incredulously.

"Remember when we saw her at the beach with Bill right after they got married and we were trying to decide if she had implants? I said she did and you said she was just genetically lucky and blossomed late in life, which was possible since we hadn't seen her since she left for college as a skinny straggly teenager. We bet ten dollars." Liza shrugged. "You owe me ten dollars."

Kitty stared in horror at the deflated chest. "I can't believe you stole Leslie's implants."

"Technically I didn't. I simply asked Harry not to put them back in after the autopsy because sometimes there are problems and I didn't want anything bursting while I was readying the body."

"Is that true?" Lydia asked before Jeb could because he was dying to ask the same question.

"No of course not. But it sounded plausible and he was willing to humor me without asking questions."

Becca leaned around them and considered her step-mother's new look. "I don't think she'll miss them if that helps."

Liza Jane smiled triumphantly and Lydia groaned.

Kitty shook her head. The line was getting backed up and people were starting to point. "We better move on before anyone comes over and makes a scene."

But it was too late. Bill was stomping over to see what the hold-up was. "What is going on here ladies? We have a schedule to keep with the hearse and the gravesite and what happened to Leslie?" he ended in disbelief as he stared at his wife's chest.

"What do you mean?" Lydia asked nonchalantly.

"Her boobs. They're gone!"

"They must have gotten lost in the shuffle at the morgue," Liza Jane said quickly. "Sometimes things shift during transport. Especially implants."

Bill blinked in surprise. "I didn't know that."

176

"Yes. Well." Kitty took his arm. "Let's get you back over to the line so you can thank people properly." She gently urged him back in the direction from which he came. He turned back a couple times, clearly befuddled by Leslie's change in appearance.

"Let's get back to the house," Kitty suggested as soon as she was free of Bill.

"All right. Now that the fun is over," Liza Jane agreed.

"There is nothing fun about funerals," Lydia chastised. "Even for Leslie."

"You all have a very dreary outlook on death for Christians," Liza complained as they made their way out under the scrutiny of nearly half the town. "Caring for the dead is no different than caring for the living," she continued. "You have to treat them with respect and dignity. And there's no shame in sharing a laugh at a funeral. It lightens the mood. The dearly departed would surely appreciate it."

"I can't believe you did that," Kitty told her as they finally arrived outside on the church steps.

"It's part of your birthday present. Just keep that in mind when you get the other half of it, which will be considerably smaller and less symbolic."

"You certainly do liven things up," Jeb commented. He was sticking close to Kitty and her friends and finding the whole experience enlightening. He rather liked Liza Jane now that she wasn't chasing after him and could appreciate her quirky sense of humor. "Now I know why Kitty has kept you around for so long."

"And you had a chance at all this," Liza said with a grin. "But for some reason you prefer this classy, sweet friend of mine. Go figure."

Kitty blushed while Jeb smiled and reached for her hand. "There's no accounting for taste I guess," he said, winking at her.

As soon as the brief gravesite service was complete Jeb took Kitty home to prepare for those people who would come to pay further respects to Bill. He considered leaving but when Kitty asked him to stay he couldn't resist the softly spoken request. Liza Jane and Charlotte were there to assist Kitty so he tried to stay out of the way and mingle with the guests. It was going off without a hitch thanks to her friends pitching in. Around one Martha had to leave so Jeb grabbed a platter and made the rounds, making small talk as he went.

"I can't believe your boyfriend the sheriff is out there playing waiter for you," Liza whispered to her best friend. "He must be crazy about you."

"Or just crazy," Kitty responded. She was thinking Jeb must be plain crazy to have signed up for all this just for some home cooked meals and a little company.

"Umm hmmm." Liza Jane smiled knowingly before grabbing a tray of deserts and returning to the packed living room.

Chapter 16

Bill disappeared upstairs after everyone left in need of a rest and left Kitty to deal with the clean up aided by Liza Jane. Kitty flat out refused to let Jeb help even though he offered and insisted he relax. Jeb wasn't anxious to leave so he wandered out to the studio to look at her paintings again. He marveled at the talent she had. It was amazing how Kitty managed to capture the beauty of the sea with each brushstroke. It was truly her gift from God and she was using it to its full potential now. He liked how she added scripture in the corners of most of them. As he stood lost in the art he head the door open behind him. He assumed it was Kitty and turned to greet her with a ready smile.

Jeb was more than surprised to find Rob standing in the doorway. The smile fell away. "Rob? What's happened?"

"We got the lab results back on the signs Annie Goodwin had for her little picket line. The paint is a perfect match to what was on Leslie Appleton's fingers."

Jeb swore softly and immediately repented. "Find her and bring her in. I'll meet you at the station."

"Yes sir."

.

Jeb thought he could say a quick good-bye without arousing suspicion but unfortunately for him Kitty had already seen Rob arrive. When Jeb slipped into the kitchen to tell Kitty he had to leave she cornered him while Liza Jane was in the living room.

"What happened?" she demanded in a whisper.

"I really can't tell you right now."

"But something has happened hasn't it? Do you know who killed Leslie?"

"It would appear we may have a good idea who did it," he admitted without meeting her eyes.

"Who?"

Jeb kissed her forehead. "I've got to go. Just know that I'm doing everything I can to make sure we get the right person."

Kitty wouldn't be put off. She had a sinking feeling in her stomach. "It's someone we all know isn't it? Please Jeb. Tell me. I don't want to find out on the six o'clock news."

Her pleading eyes and the gentle hand on his arm undid him. "It looks like Annie Goodwin may have done it after all. Keep it under your hat for now."

Kitty was horrified. She pulled back. "I've known Annie for decades. She wouldn't hurt anyone. She's odd and obsessed with her ideas of preserving the past but she's always been against any kind of violence."

"I'm sorry," Jeb told her sincerely. "I don't like it either." He started for the door. "Remember what I said about telling anyone else please."

He was already outside when she flew after him, stopping in the doorway. "Jeb!"

He turned. "Yes?"

"Do you believe she did it? Does your gut say she's the one?" Kitty wanted to know.

Jeb hesitated. "No."

"Then you'll keep looking?"

"Leslie's father has called the Mayor, the town council, the Governor. They're calling my office daily wanting an update. I don't know how long I can hold off making an arrest now that we have physical and circumstantial evidence piling up. But I am going to do everything I can to make sure justice is done."

After Jeb was gone Kitty remained in the doorway still watching where his taillights had been only moments before. With some resolve she spoke quietly. "So am I."

.

An hour later an emergency meeting of the Rock Bottom Mystery Book Club was in progress. "Why exactly are we here?" Lydia asked after they were all settled. "And where is Annie?"

"Annie is very likely going to be charged with murder."

The collective gasps filled the room. "Why?"

"Jeb is being pressured to make an arrest and the evidence is piling up against Annie."

"They can't make him do that," Charlotte said indignantly. "He's an elected official and doesn't answer to them. He answers to us the people!"

"It's all politics," Regina griped.

"They can make his life miserable," Kitty explained. "He's trying to buy time before officially booking her and transferring her out. They are still looking into other avenues but that Judge Burgess is making it difficult for him."

"Can we do anything for her?" Martha wanted to know.

"I had an idea," Kitty began uneasily. "I thought maybe we could sort of become unofficial deputies and poke around."

"Poke around? In a murder investigation?" Lydia demanded. "Are you crazy? What do we know about solving a murder?"

"We've read hundreds of mystery novels. Surely we can learn from those."

Martha fidgeted. "I was thinking of just bringing her some chicken soup or homemade cookies, not getting involved in a police investigation."

Lydia agreed with Martha. She wasn't a big risk taker either. "We aren't detectives Kitty. We wouldn't know the first thing about solving a murder!"

"If we don't do something Annie is going to be charged with murder. Once that happens they stop looking for other suspects. Do we want to let Annie down?" Kitty asked her friends.

"No of course we don't. But how can we help?"

"I think we all have special gifts and talents we could use," Kitty said slowly. "I think between the six of us we could figure this out."

"I'm guess I'm willing to try for Annie. We've been friends for a long time. But I don't know what my special gift is. I don't think I really have one."

"Of course you do," Liza Jane told Martha, determined to support her best friend's plan. "You have worked at the Bottom Dollar Market for twenty-one years. You know everyone. And they talk to you. Tell you all sorts of interesting little tidbits."

"I suppose."

"Well I know for a fact people love to tell you their life stories," Regina added. "Standing in your line takes forever because they always want to chat with you about the latest goings-on. It's frustrating when you just run in for milk and bread, I can tell you that."

"Sorry," Martha said. "I've been pushing for that express lane for years but no luck yet."

"Maybe if you just limit your chats to one subject per person that would help," Regina suggested.

"I suppose I could try."

"The point is," Kitty interrupted, "Liza Jane is right. The whole town talks to you. You could pump people for information and they wouldn't even know it."

Martha perked up, her blue eyes twinkling. "I get to pump people! Oh this is so exciting!"

"What about me?" Regina leaned forward. "What's my gift?"

"You're the pretty one," Lydia answered before Kitty could. "Everyone knows that."

Regina looked around and then slumped back in her seat. "Why am I always the *pretty one*? Why can't I be the *smart one* or the *funny one* for a change? Labels are hurtful."

"Really? You're going to complain about that? You have men swarming around you who will do anything you ask. You could have any man you want in this town!"

"Not *any* man," she grumbled. "Just *most* men."

"Well I would love to trade places with you just for one day. Oh to have your problems!" Lydia threw her hands up in disgust.

"Beauty is wasted on youth," Charlotte said wisely.

"And wisdom is wasted on the old," Regina mumbled.

"Perhaps you can use your feminine wiles on Connor and Randy since they both have motives," Martha suggested brightly. "And they both seem to like you."

"You think Connor likes me?"

"Of course. He's a man," Lydia snipped.

"Martha's right. Maybe you could talk with the both of them and just see what you find out about the evening Leslie died."

"*Fine*. I'll use my stunning good looks to get a confession. That's apparently what the *pretty one* does."

"Moving on," Liza Jane said quickly before another round on that subject started, "What about me? How can I help?"

"You," Kitty said thoughtfully, "have a very special talent that no other person in this room has."

"What's that?" Liza asked enthusiastically. Surely it was something terrific, like her unwavering nerve or her super sassy comebacks. Or maybe it was her keen insight into other people's minds.

"You work with dead people."

"Oh." *What a letdown,* Liza Jane thought. "Well, if you're hoping Leslie can tell me who whacked her you're out of luck. I'm not the Corpse Whisperer you know."

"No. But you saw the body. You may have noticed something. And if you didn't maybe you could ask Harry for a look at the autopsy report. Make up some reason to see it."

"Use my ex-husband for my own agenda?" Liza Jane asked out loud. She definitely liked the sound of that. Not that Harry wasn't a terrific guy. He was and they had an amicable relationship. But it just tickled her fancy to try to wheedle information out of him. It was a challenge and Liza Jane never walked away from a challenge. "No problem."

"What about me?" Lydia wanted to know. "What's my part?"

"Working in the Realtor's office you have access to property values and sales," Kitty said thoughtfully. "Can you look into the Bottom's Up? Find out what it appraised for, if anyone else was interested in it, that kind of thing? Maybe everyone's missed something obvious about the pub."

"You mean like maybe it's sitting on some natural resource worth millions that would make someone kill for?"

"Something like that."

Lydia glowed. "Absolutely. I'll get everything you could possibly want on it."

"I suppose that just leaves me," Charlotte said tiredly. "And I suppose my gift is my vast knowledge on life and all its mysteries."

"You certainly have the most experience of all of us," Regina pointed out.

Charlotte nodded. "I do have a lot of life experience. And perhaps somewhere in the deep recesses of my mind are the answers you need to solve this murder. Which incidentally is on my bucket list."

"You have a bucket list?" Lydia asked in surprise. She didn't even have a bucket list and she was only forty-one. "What kinds of things are on it?"

"Oh the usual. Bungi jumping, sky diving, running a marathon. Maybe hold public office. I'd like to give back to the community before I become one of Liza Jane's customers."

"I think the ship has sailed for you on most of those. But maybe you could run for something in the next election. I'd probably vote for you," Regina offered, feeling charitable at the moment. She loved the old woman; she really did. But sometimes Charlotte was a bit old-school and Regina had to bite her tongue. That in itself showed how fond she was of the elderly lady because Regina rarely held her tongue.

"Hogwash. You're a *liberal*. Everyone knows you are. You don't agree with any of my traditional views."

"That's not true. I'm a moderate conservative."

"Same thing," Charlotte said tartly.

Regina snorted and Lydia covered a laugh with a cough.

"Can we not turn this into a political debate?" Liza Jane asked "The last time we did Charlotte nearly had a heart attack. The paramedics even scolded us for upsetting her."

"Poppycock," Charlotte argued. "It was just a little indigestion because Lydia proposed socialized medicine was a viable alternative."

"It is," Lydia insisted hotly. She didn't care if she was the only bleeding-heart liberal in the group. "The facts support it. Why can't you admit you're wrong on this? There are people out there who need the health care our system is trying to-"

"Don't upset an old woman," Charlotte interrupted quickly, quickly feigning illness and looking pathetic. Obviously a soft touch was called for now. She preferred her more acerbic nature but she had to use what the good Lord gave her.

"Oh dear, now look what you've done. Charlotte dear, are you okay?" Martha fussed.

"She looks pale," Liza observed.

"We shouldn't upset her," Kitty fretted.

"She started it," Lydia insisted.

"Stop already. This is why I prefer working with dead people."

Kitty patted Liza's shoulder while she turned the conversation back to the subject at hand. "We should probably focus on the people who had the strongest motive. Like Lionel Trescott. Randy. And I suppose Connor."

"And Bill. Don't forget Bill," Liza added.

"But Bill has an alibi."

"I think if we're going to shake one tree we may as well shake them all and see what falls out. You never know what he might be hiding."

"He did have an affair with Leslie for months without you knowing about it," Martha pointed out. "Who knows what else he may be capable of?"

Kitty frowned but nodded. She didn't believe for a moment that Bill killed Leslie but if they wanted to poke into his affairs then she really couldn't stop them. "Fine. We check everyone's alibis and poke into Leslie's life. We have a pulse on the goings-on here in The Bottom that Jeb just doesn't have access to since he's still considered an outsider. There's got to be something out there that will prove Annie didn't do it and we're going to find it."

"Are we absolutely sure she didn't?" Regina asked hesitantly. "We all know how passionate she is about her old buildings."

"Annie wouldn't kill anyone. She's much too practical for that," Charlotte insisted. She refused to believe one of her girls was a cold-blooded murderer.

"I agree," Martha said cheerfully. "Annie is all about passive resistance rather than aggression. She'd much rather use her brains than brawn to defeat her opposition. I saw that on TV somewhere and I think it really suits our Annie."

"Way to go Martha," Regina said. "You really know people."

"People are my life. Well, people and groceries. You can tell a lot about a person by what they buy."

"I buy chocolate," Liza Jane said. "Lots of chocolate and hardly anything healthy. What does that say about me?"

"That you're going to die fat and happy," Charlotte snapped. "Now back to business! What's the plan Kitty dear?"

"She already said what it was. We go talk to everybody and get the dirt on anyone who had a grudge against Leslie. Weren't you paying attention?" Liza Jane asked in exasperation.

"I may have dozed off for a few moments. Sometimes that happens."

"We'll do our best," Lydia promised Kitty. "While I'm out doing all this detective work tomorrow though I'm going to stop by Leticia's and get a manicure."

"Oh I think Mom's offering a special too," Regina quickly said, looking at her own cuticles. "Maybe I'll go with you."

Lydia squealed with delight.

"Well don't forget to stop by the market. I'll be there until six."

The conversation nose-dived into all the errands they could run while they were out solving the murder and the possibility of meeting up for supper once they unveiled the real killer. "It shouldn't take us too long if we all do our part," Regina pronounced and everyone concurred as Kitty watched in awe. "So what say we all meet at the cafe at six tomorrow night to celebrate?"

"Tomorrow is all you can eat spaghetti night," Lydia said, crunching up her nose. "Too many carbs. How about we just meet here with a pizza? Kitty you can bring desert."

"That's healthier than pasta?"

"No but if I'm going to eat all those calories I'd rather get them from gobs of mozzarella cheese and pepperoni swimming in grease," Lydia admitted.

"I'm in. But make it seven," Regina added.

The rest agreed that after a full day of sleuthing pizza would be the perfect finale. Kitty wasn't entirely convinced they would accomplish the feat of catching a cold-blooded killer by supper time but she could admit that the pizza sounded pretty good. "Seven it is."

Chapter 17

Lydia arrived at work the next morning early so she could check the files before Margie got in at nine. She threw her lunch in the fridge and tossed her heavy sweater on the chair before making a beeline to Margie's office. Margie kept certain files in her own personal file cabinet and the ones on the Bottom's Up apparently fell into that category. Lydia knew because she'd asked about it months ago out of sheer curiosity and Margie had flat out refused to divulge any information about the property. At the time Lydia thought she was just being high-handed and snooty. Now Lydia wondered if there was more to it than that.

She rifled through the cabinet, checking behind her every few seconds. Margie would have a fit if she saw someone pawing through her stuff. Lydia could feel her heart racing and her palms were sweaty as she scanned through all the papers. She spotted Trescott Developers in the back and on impulse snatched it out of the mess of manila envelopes shoved in the top drawer. Still keeping one eye on the door, Lydia flipped through it, reading as fast as she could. When she heard a car door slam outside the office she quickly jammed the file back in the drawer, slammed it shut and ran out of the office, nearly forgetting to shut the door behind her. She parked herself in her seat just as Margie burst in and stopped mid-step.

"You're here bright and early," the older woman said to Lydia suspiciously. "You're never early."

"I wanted to get a jump on today's work," Lydia said quickly.

Margie flicked her eyes to the blank computer screen. "Shouldn't you turn on your computer to do that?"

"Oh," Lydia said, frowning. "Right. I forgot to do that."

Margie stomped past, wondering how Lydia managed to get through a day without misplacing her own brain. "I'm not paying you overtime, just so you know."

"That's fine," Lydia called after Margie. "I'll get the coffee going."

Margie stuck her head back out and eyed Lydia. "Why does my office smell like your perfume?"

Lydia thought as fast as she could, which wasn't very fast at all. But it finally came to her. "I was bringing you your mail."

"At nine in the morning?"

"I was trying to be efficient."

"Fine. Where is it?"

"Where's what?"

"The mail!"

"It hasn't come yet."

Margie gritted her teeth. "It's a good thing customers like you Lydia because some days I surely don't." And she slammed the door shut.

Lydia made a face at the door. "You think I'm an airhead but I'll show you Margie Bingham! I may have just solved a murder!"

•

Liza Jane didn't waste timing calling Harry on Monday evening. She could hear the surprise in his voice but he covered it well and agreed to meet with her for lunch at Crabby's the next day. After hanging up the phone Liza went through her closet and tried on exactly twenty-three outfits before deciding on the right one. She wanted to look absolutely delicious but completely respectable. It was a very difficult task for a woman who didn't normally give a flying fig about what people thought. But this was Harry and that made all the difference.

Precisely at noon on Tuesday she marched into the restaurant and met her ex-husband with an easy smile and a breezy attitude, as though they did this all the time and it was of no consequence. He was still tall and handsome as ever, with strong features and a head full of silvery grey hair that Liza thought made him look even more distinguished than before. She decided it complimented his blue-grey eyes quite nicely and that age had made Harry even more attractive if that was even possible.

Harry leaned over and gave her an obligatory quick kiss on the cheek. "You're actually on time."

"I always was for you," Liza said with a quick grin. There was no reason to make coy conversation in her opinion. They had known each other forever, been through the highest of highs and lowest of lows.

With that kind of history Liza believed one could just cut through all the inane talk that usually preceded the meat of the conversation and get to whatever needed saying. Once they were settled in their seats she spoke bluntly. "How are you doing without Lynn?"

Harry shrugged. "It's not been easy. Watching your wife get sicker each day and then finally having to say good-bye...well, you have to dig deep for the strength most days. But God has been gracious through it all."

Liza studied the eyes that still haunted her dreams. "You seem to be getting back to your old self, Harry. I'm glad. I only ever wanted you to be happy and I'm sorry that you had to go through this."

"Thanks Liza. That means a lot." They ordered drinks and after the waitress left his attention was once again on the pretty blond woman across from him. "So what did you want to talk to me about?"

"Leslie Appleton."

"What about her?"

"We're looking into her murder."

Her eyes dared him to question the wisdom behind the words. But Harry knew better. He wasn't even surprised. Nothing Liza said or did ever surprised him. He knew to expect the unexpected with her, even after all these years. It was one of the many things that he had fallen head-over-heels in love with thirty plus years ago when they were still in high school. "What do you need to know?"

"Everything. Anything. Annie Goodwin is going to be arrested for her murder and we have to come up with an alternative suspect quickly."

"Maybe she did it."

Liza shook her head adamantly. "Absolutely not. She says she didn't and I believe her. So I'll do whatever I can to help."

Harry felt an odd sensation creeping into the vicinity of his heart. He always admired her fierce loyalty and devotion to those she cared about. It saddened him that she hadn't had that same fierce love for him all those years ago.

Stop it, he ordered himself. *We were just kids. We were too young. Don't think about the past.*

Harry took a sip of his club soda. He'd had a good marriage with Lynn. He loved her and they had a nice life together. He'd been faithful from the moment they met and he would have remained so until the day he died. But he never forgot the first girl he ever loved and married and imagined spending his life with. Those vows had meant something to him even though he was barely a man when he said them. It still pained him to know that what could have been absolutely wonderful and special and beyond compare escaped him because of pride and stupidity and a complete lack of trust in the Lord.

Now he was sitting across from Liza and he realized the embers of the love he had for her were still there, still buried deep inside of him. He supposed he had always known that was true. And upon reflection maybe Lynn did too. But they had been happy nevertheless. His genuine affection for his second wife had dimmed the flame of first love but not completely doused it. And with a little encouragement he was sure his heart could fan the flame into the full, rich love that God had intended it to be.

But this wasn't the time for such matters. Liza had something on her mind and she wasn't going to be deterred by some fanciful idea about everlasting love.

Harry sighed. "I don't suppose there's any harm in telling you what I know. Unless of course it was you who murdered Leslie?"

"I deal with dead bodies all day long. I don't need to add to my workload."

Harry smiled and Liza felt the butterflies fluttering madly. "I know." And then he filled her in on everything he could.

.

After lunch Kitty decided to go see Lionel Trescott. She had the perfect cover and walked boldly into his office with her portfolio under her arm and false bravado in check. His secretary insisted he was too busy to see her but Kitty was just as insistent about waiting so she plopped down on a plush mint green settee and settled in for the duration. Frowning, the secretary discreetly made a call and just ten minutes later Kitty was ushered into the office. It was well-appointed with plush furniture, a massive desk and enough smoke residue to indicate Lionel enjoyed a fine smoke despite the air purifier humming in the corner.

"Kitty Appleton. How nice of you to drop by," Lionel said as he stood.

His outstretched hand and friendly smile bespoke a long and enduring friendship when in truth Kitty barely knew the man. But she strolled to him and grasped his hand, returning the friendly smile. "Mr. Trescott."

"Lionel, please. Have seat. What can I do for you Mrs. Appleton?"

"It's Ms. Appleton actually. But you already knew that. I wanted to talk to you about using some of my artwork in the newly renovated Bottom's Up pub."

Lionel leaned back in his chair. "I see."

"I thought maybe it would be a nice mix of the old and the new. A sense of nostalgia immersed with the new look. I could do some of the pub itself, of the views from the bluff it sits on. I could even do a painting from a snapshot of the Bottom's Up Bill has that his grandfather took shortly after it opened seventy-five years ago."

"It's certainly an interesting concept." He studied her thoughtfully. "As a matter of fact I have another project I was considering using your paintings in so this is rather fortuitous that you stopped by today. It's a rather large undertaking. And lucrative. I think you'd be very pleased at the numbers I have in mind."

"I'd love to hear about it."

Lionel told her about the hotel they were planning on putting up the following summer up the coast. "We don't have a lock on the property yet but it's nearly a done deal," he explained. "And I'd love to have your artwork displayed throughout the lobby and the suites. It's going to be what I like to call *Rustic Nautical.* Your seascapes would capture the essence of what we're trying to achieve. And I know people would love seeing the work of a local artist displayed, especially one as prominent as you."

Kitty blushed. "I don't know if *prominent* is the right word."

"Of course it is. Word has gotten out about you Kitty Appleton. You're on the threshold of greatness."

His flattery made her uneasy. She glanced around the room while he continued prattling on about the merits of her talent and his upscale vacation getaway being a perfect match. The room was large and plush, with opulent furniture and expensive details. There was a fancy sideboard to her right with a large scaled model of what she presumed was the hotel he was speaking about. It looked quite impressive even from where she was sitting.

"Is that the project you're referring to?" she asked when there was a break in the conversation.

"Yes. Yes it is."

Kitty rose and glided over to inspect it. It was beautifully designed, with lots of modern angles and windows everywhere, no doubt to enjoy the oceanside view. The attention to detail was surprising too. In the front tiny detailed trees and hedges had been added around the perimeter and the circular driveway. On the backside was a sweeping deck with tiny people lounging around in chairs and leaning against the railing, presumably overlooking the water. Kitty bent down so she could see the people, who were merely an inch tall but still looked like they were having a wonderful time. "This is amazing," Kitty said in awe.

"Randy Parker is quite talented. He's another one destined to go places."

"Randy did this? The design is amazing."

"That's why I pay him the big bucks," Lionel laughed. "But let's get back to the merging of two empires. Your art with my real estate."

Kitty decided she'd learned all she could today. "I think perhaps I'll let my agent handle the details of this arrangement. I can leave my portfolio with you for a few days if you'd like and just let her know what you decide. Her card is in the case."

"If that's how you'd like to handle it that's fine with me."

Kitty smiled politely and took his offered hand. "Thank you for your time Mr. Trescott. I'll see myself out."

•

Martha Stimple was sure she could get the scoop on the murder at the Bottom Dollar. Here along the aisles was an assortment of idle talk that varied as much as the daily deliveries did. The trick was sorting through it and finding the tastiest morsels amidst the drivel, much like shopping for the best bargains in the store.

When Randy Parker came through her line she felt a rush of adrenaline. Finally something exciting might happen! She smoothed her apron and put on her best Bottom Dollar smile as he dropped his items in front of her. Strawberry wine, cigarettes, steak, salad. "You cooking for someone special?" she asked him with what she hoped was her usual enthusiasm.

"Maybe. Haven't asked her yet but I'm feeling lucky."

"It wouldn't happen to be Regina?"

Randy grinned. "Could be."

Martha nodded. "She needs a nice young man in her life. And you've had a tough time since Leslie left you. Maybe it's about time you two went out."

"That's what I've been telling her."

Martha scanned the wine. "I was sorry to hear about Leslie. I remember you two were crazy about each other when you were younger."

"That was a long time ago. Things changed. We both moved on."

"It must have been hard on you, seeing them together all the time and so happy. Leslie and Bill, I mean."

"Sure it was hard at first. But like I said, you move on."

"Still it must have been horrid finding her body like that," she said in a whisper. "Just ghastly. I don't know how you and Kitty and Connor sleep at night. If I walked into a house and found a body..." Martha shivered. "It's just awful."

Yeah." Randy looked solemn for a moment, his eyes downcast and his hands at his side. "Unfortunately my ex-wife wasn't a very nice person. I suppose it was only a matter of time until something ugly happened. Especially with her selling the pub. Lot of people weren't happy about it."

"What about you? Were you happy about it?" Martha asked.

Randy shrugged. "Didn't really matter to me either way."

.

Regina was sitting at the bar sipping a soda. For all her toughness she was really a sissy, she realized. Alcohol was one of the few things she couldn't handle and it galled her quite a bit that one drink and she was under the table. It was just one of the many things she learned about herself in college. So it was with shameful wisdom that she avoided alcohol completely and stuck with the good friend she had in Coke.

Randy sauntered up to her with a cigarette dangling out of one side of his mouth. He ordered a beer and turned to her. "Hey girl. What's going on?"

"Not much." She nodded at the offending curl of smoke. "I thought you quit."

"I did. But I'm having a relapse. It's temporary." He took it out and blew a steady whoosh of smoke away from her. "If I promise to stop right now will you have dinner with me? You'd be doing me a favor, adding years to my life."

She shook her head of copper curls. "Sorry. You're trouble Randy. And I don't need that in my life right now."

"It's just dinner Regina."

"And you'd be expecting to have breakfast with me in the morning, wouldn't you?" she asked bluntly.

"That's certainly an option."

"Not for me. I'm not that kind of girl, despite what many seem to think."

He frowned. "There's nothing wrong with having a good time. Lighten up."

Regina turned back to her drink. "I'm not gonna get all preachy and stuff but let's just say that I don't believe sleeping around is God's plan for any of us. So I'm waiting for the right one."

"If you're hoping there's a marriage proposal in this crowd you might want to reconsider that plan." He took the beer Bob the bartender set down in front of him and indicated the folks sparsely populating the room. "Slim pickins. And marriage is overrated anyway. Trust me."

"You and Leslie ended pretty badly, huh?"

"At first. But it got better. We even managed a sort of psudeo-friendship. I suppose I can see now that I'm just not husband material. So Leslie really did me a favor walking out."

"Well I'm not giving up on the dream." Regina shot a discreet glance at Connor sitting across from them.

Randy saw where her eyes darted and his mouth hardened. "Really? Him? You could do better than that. He works on a boat all day and smells like dead fish." He'd never really cared for his brother-in-law. The man had an edge to him. He was closed off and somber and Randy couldn't imagine the man knew what fun was if it came up and bit him in the behind.

"I could do worse," she said, facing him directly.

Randy called her an unpleasant name before grabbing his beer and skulking off to a booth where Regina noticed he was quick to start hitting on the waitress. She rolled her eyes and turned back to her drink.

194

She nearly fell off her stool when she found Connor leaning on the counter next to her. "You okay?" he asked, serious as ever.

"Why wouldn't I be?" Regina asked, trying to put some attitude into it. She was kind of flustered so she wasn't sure if she actually pulled it off.

Connor nodded towards Randy. "Looked like he was giving you a hard time."

Regina waved his words away. "I can handle Randy. He's all talk."

"Maybe. Maybe not."

Since the opportunity presented itself she decided to broach the subject of murder with Connor. It had absolutely nothing to do with keeping him close by so she could talk with him and smell his cologne. He probably doused it on to cover the fish smell. That didn't bother her. If you didn't like the smells associated with living on the coast than it was probably best not to be living there as far as Regina was concerned. The strong odors of saltwater and hard work mingled with the spicy aftershave was very appealing to her.

But that was neither here nor there. She had a task to complete. "I'm sorry about your sister. It's just a tragedy something like this happened at The Bottom."

He nodded. "Thanks for that. I realize she wasn't very popular."

Regina wasn't one to hold back punches. "No she wasn't. Leslie was a piece of work. But she didn't deserve what she got."

She thought she saw a softening in his eyes. But she could have imagined it. "I heard the police have the librarian in custody. Upset about the Bottom's Up being sold to Trescott."

Regina nodded. "I heard that too. Do you believe she did it?"

Connor shrugged. "Doesn't matter what I think, does it?"

"Sure it does."

"I think there are other people with a better reason."

"Like who?"

"Bill for one. He gets a truckload of money from the insurance and the sale of this place. Seems like a good motive to me."

"I agree. But what about his alibi?"

"A bunch of old good old boys he's known forever. That's handy." He took a swig of whatever he was drinking. "And then there's Randy."

"You can't possibly think he did it. He was here the whole time."

"I just know I don't like the guy."

195

"That doesn't make him a murderer. Why would he kill Leslie?"

"Because he still loved her."

"That doesn't make sense."

Connor shrugged. "You asked my opinion."

"Well I can think of some other people with a lot better motive and no alibi."

"Like me?" he asked, meeting her eyes without flinching.

Regina swallowed. "You did get the short end of the stick when your father died. That's a humdinger of a motive."

Connor reached out and traced a finger down her cheek. Regina didn't know whether to bolt or swoon. He'd never touched her before. Ever. She felt goose bumps chase up and down her whole body when he spoke softly. "I suppose it is. I don't have a lot of tolerance for people who get in my way."

"Did Leslie get in your way?" she whispered, her eyes locked with his.

He leaned forward till his mouth was just inches from her ear. "Keep poking around and you'll find out."

.

Charlotte had been at the pub since four. She was quite certain that vital information pertaining to the case could be obtained here if she was patient enough. It was now just after six. Other than Regina and Connor having what looked to be a very interesting conversation at the bar minutes ago nothing of interest had transpired. In fact, Charlotte was so bored she had agreed to play cards with Edward Abbott.

"Gin!" Edward said excitedly for the third time.

Charlotte frowned and peered closely at the cards he laid down. "Are you cheating Eddy?"

"No I am not," Edward said indignantly. "I do not cheat!"

"Then you are exceedingly lucky."

"Blessed. Charmed. Fortuitous."

"Yes Eddy." She watched him shuffle and deal like a pro. Charlotte picked up the cards he dealt her. "You're here all the time, Eddy. Did you ever notice anything strange with Leslie? Was there anyone she didn't get along with?"

"Lots of people. She was plucky."

Charlotte smiled. "Yes, you're right. She was. But was there anything just before she died that was unusual? Anything at all? Think Eddy."

"Well there was the secret she told me."

"What secret?" Charlotte demanded.

"I can't tell you either. The sheriff wanted to know too. But I promised Leslie I wouldn't say a word."

"Oh dear," Charlotte said softly. Looking at Edward's determined face she knew he wasn't going to crack. But maybe she could get it out of him with a little finessing. There was always more than one way to skin a cat. Charlotte had taught middle school for thirty years. She knew how to handle stubborn and hard-headed. "Well I suppose if you promised then you really can't say."

Eddy's shoulders relaxed. "That's right."

Charlotte discarded a five of hearts. "Of course, if we made a game out of it and I were to guess then you could tell me if I was right. Technically that wouldn't be confiding in me. You like to figure out puzzles, too. I know you understand how exciting it is to finally solve a difficult one."

"I love puzzles. But I don't think I should say anything."

"That's not very sporting of you Edward," Charlotte scolded as she picked up the ten of spades. "I mean you just dangled a mystery of sorts in front of me. It's only fair I should get a crack at it."

Edward balked. He was a tough nut to crack. But Charlotte dearly wanted to know what the big secret was. She changed tactics.

"I probably won't guess it anyway. I'm not particularly clever after all. I just thought since you like games and I like games...well, it was just an idea. It would have kept us busy here for quite a while. But I suppose you'd rather go sit on your stool by yourself than keep a lonely old woman company." Charlotte did her best to look shriveled up and pathetic.

"That's not true."

"Oh it is. I'm a senile old thing that nobody wants to talk to." Charlotte discreetly stomped her cane on her big toe and tears sprang to her eyes, making for a very convincing effect.

Soft-hearted Edward didn't have a chance. "I'll stay here and talk with you Miss Charlotte."

"Really?" Charlotte perked up. "And you'll let me try to guess the big secret? Maybe even give me clues if I get stumped?"

"All right. But only two," Edward decided. "And only if you *really* need them."

"Oh I have a feeling I'm really going to need them," Charlotte promised. "As I said, I'm not very clever at all."

Chapter 18

Tuesday evening they gathered in the familiar back room of the library to compare notes. Each was anxious to share what they had learned, and all were convinced their own information was the most important piece of the puzzle. The pizza boxes were open and wonderful greasy-cholesterol filled smells were filling the room

"Who gets to start?" Martha bubbled, putting off taking her first bite of pizza in case she got the honor. "I think I should get to start. Can I please?"

"Does it really matter Martha?" Lydia asked in exasperation.

"No, I don't suppose it does. But I'm very sure what I have to say is vitally important to cracking the case wide open."

"Just let her go first," Regina said. "It's not worth risking her health since her head might explode if she doesn't get it out soon."

"Go ahead Martha," Kitty said kindly.

"Thank you. Okay here's what I found out." She paused for a dramatic moment. "Randy never got over Leslie."

They waited for her to continue but there was nothing else following so Regina decided some coaxing might be in order. "And?"

"And what? That's it. That's the news. He's been flirting with you Regina just to save face." She nodded. "I'm quite sure about that. He bought a cheap bottle of wine for you. But last week when he was going to talk to Leslie about the deal I remember distinctly that he bought the fancy strawberry wine she liked so much."

"What does that prove?" Liza Jane asked and then answered herself. "Nothing."

"Except that he was still trying to sweet talk her with good wine," Lydia added.

Martha shook her head. "He was hung up on Leslie. I'm telling you. That's his motive. Unrequited love. Leslie was going to sell the pub, move away and never be seen again here in The Bottom. He couldn't bare for that to happen."

"That's stupid," Regina insisted. She may not be interested in Randy but she couldn't accept the idea that he had just been using her to get back at Leslie somehow. "Plus he was in the pub when she died."

"I think maybe he had an accomplice," Martha mused. "I just haven't figured that part out yet. Maybe one of you did."

Regina cleared her throat and fidgeted. "Connor Abbott was acting weird. Weirder than usual. Is it possible that he and Randy were working together?"

"That's preposterous," Charlotte insisted. "Connor wouldn't kill his own sister."

"He didn't get to the pub until well after eight," Lydia pointed out. "He could have been involved."

"They don't even like each other. I can't imagine they planned something like this together. Maybe Connor did it on his own," Liza added.

"He's bitter about being cut out of his father's will," Regina said quietly. "He tries to act like it doesn't bother him. But it does. A lot."

"Hmmm," said Charlotte thoughtfully. Maybe she was wrong about Connor Abbott after all.

"What else did we find out?" Kitty asked. "Lydia, did you find out anything?"

"I did. It's very exciting to. You wouldn't believe how nervous I was getting this information. I nearly got caught by Margie and you know how cranky she can be."

"Worse than Charlotte," Regina agreed.

Charlotte gave Regina a sour look but kept quiet.

"Anyway, I didn't see a whole lot about the pub itself. But I did peek in the Trescott Development file and found something very interesting." Lydia paused for a grand effect. "He's bought up two properties on either side of the Bottom's Up."

"So?" Regina asked.

"Well I think that's very important. Why would he need those properties?"

"Extra parking for when the new pub turns into a gold mine."

"That's an awful lot of parking."

"It's peculiar," Charlotte agreed. "And it makes one wonder if maybe Annie wasn't right all along."

"Which makes her motive even stronger."

A sad quietness filled the room as they all considered that fact. Not one of them believed that Annie had really committed the heinous crime. But all could admit it didn't look good for her.

"Well I have the biggest news of all," Liza Jane finally broke the silence. "It's big!"

"What is it?" Martha asked excitedly.

"Is it about Bill?" Lydia inquired. She remembered Liza's fervent hope was for Bill to be the guilty party.

"No, I didn't find out anything on him unfortunately."

"Then what?"

Liza preened. "Harry told me he found evidence of cigarette smoke on Leslie's clothes."

"Leslie didn't smoke. She even banned it in the pub because it irritated her allergies."

"I know. Which is why this is important. Her final moments were spent with a smoker."

"Connor smokes," Regina said softly.

"So does Randy," Martha added. "I just sold him a pack."

"Trescott is a smoker," Kitty said slowly. "He had one of those air purifiers going but it still smelled like smoke. Plus there was a half-filled ashtray on his desk."

"Well then we know it's got to be one of them," Lydia said happily.

"Yeah but which one? And why?"

"I might be able to help with that," Charlotte pronounced. "I believe I hold the key to the entire puzzle thanks to Edward Abbott."

"Then spit it out," Liza insisted, certain that her news could not be trumped.

Charlotte scooted to the edge of her seat and looked around in anticipation. "Edward Abbott had a secret. And I got it out of him. Not even your sheriff could get him to talk."

"Really? What is it?" Kitty asked for the whole group.

"Leslie was *not* going to sell the Bottom's Up."

The response from her girls was just as she expected as they gasped in surprise and interjected denials and disbelief.

"Are you certain?" Kitty asked. "Are you sure Edward knew what he was saying?"

"His brain isn't working at full capacity." Liza Jane was fond of the dear man as most residents were but it was also a known fact that

Edward had the mental faculties of a nine-year-old. Anything he said had to be taken with a grain of salt.

"Of course he knew what he was talking about. He was perfectly lucid, and so was I," she added at the end in case any one of them started to question her own mental capacity.

"If Leslie changed her mind about selling then what does that mean?" Lydia inquired. She knew it must mean something but she sometimes had a hard time figuring these sorts of things out. She *never* guessed who the murderer was in any of the mysteries they read.

"It changes everything," Kitty decided.

"But apparently no one even knew she changed her mind except Edward," Liza Jane argued.

"And the killer," Kitty added. She stood and paced back and forth. Her mind was trying to sort through everything they had learned and work it into the facts they already had. It was a giant puzzle, and they had most of the pieces now. The trouble was making them all fit together. "I know we're getting closer to the truth. But we aren't quite there yet. We're missing something."

"What? What are we missing?" Regina was getting exasperated with the whole playing detective thing. It clearly wasn't working.

"Whenever the detective on a TV show or in a book gets stumped they go back to the scene of the crime and discover something that was previously overlooked," Martha chimed in. "Maybe we should try that."

"We can't get back into Leslie and Bill's house. It's sealed off with all that cool yellow crime scene tape," Liza pointed out.

"The crime scene," Kitty mused. "Maybe if Jeb let me look at the crime scene pictures I might notice something."

"Like what?"

Kitty slumped back down in her chair. "I have no idea."

"I doubt your boyfriend is just going to let you look at photos from a murder investigation anyway," Charlotte said.

"Well I for one have a phenomenal idea," Liza announced proudly. All eyes turned to her. She smiled widely, quite pleased with herself for coming up with the notion. "Kitty, you need to sketch out the crime scene."

"Excuse me?"

"The crime scene. Draw it. Or paint it. Whichever. You have an artist's eye. You see things and capture them on paper better than anyone I know. Maybe if you go home and relax in your studio with pen and paper and just start drawing what you saw something might come to you."

"But if I draw the crime scene I'd have to draw Leslie's body. That would be morbid and just plain creepy."

Liza Jane rolled her eyes. "What is it with you people and death? It's not as ugly and depraved as you all think. What's left behind is just the empty shell of a person. It's not morbid or sad. It's a memorial to a life lived. So just draw a person sleeping peacefully on the floor. Or if you can't do that draw a stick figure."

"I don't do stick figures," Kitty said automatically.

"Then draw an abstract interpretation for all I care," Liza snipped. "But do it!"

"I think it's a good idea actually," Regina said. "It could help you see things more clearly. But I do think drawing dead people is totally creepy. I'd go with the stick figure."

"Well I for one have no desire to see you draw the crime scene from your ex-husband's wife's murder," Lydia said, standing up. "And if we're through then I need to get home."

The rest of the women followed suit and then it was just Kitty left in the library with Charlotte as she hobbled along to the door. "Charlotte, you're the most logical of us. What do you think about the whole thing?"

"I think," Charlotte said gravely, "that perhaps Leslie was trying to do the right thing after all. And someone didn't like it."

Chapter 19

On Wednesday Kitty offered to watch Sam and Callie for Bridget and Charlie. It was their anniversary and Kitty was adamant they should get to spend some time together. So just after eleven Kitty was waving off her son and daughter-in-law with her two grandbabies at her side on the step. Once inside, Sam sought out his new favorite person, finding Bill watching TV with Teddy. He climbed on the couch and snuggled himself between the two men.

"Can we go to the beach?" he asked, tugging on Bill's arm.

"Ask you grandmother."

"Can we grandma?"

Kitty had settled into the chair by the fireplace and was watching Callie go through a box of Jenny and Becca's old toys she'd dug out. "Not today sweetheart. It's a little chilly I think. Plus Callie seems to have a bit of a cold." She grabbed a tissue and wiped the mess from around Callie's little nose.

Teddy grimaced. "Gah, kids are messy."

"You might want to get used to it since you're going to have one soon."

"Not my job to clean up after the kid. That'll be Emily's job."

Kitty froze. It dawned on her as she saw the two men sitting side by side on the couch how alike they were. Not just in looks but in thoughts and actions. It broke her heart to think that Teddy was going to be the same unsupportive and self-serving partner that Bill had always been. "Teddy being a parent means stepping up and doing what needs to be done. Don't you want to be a hands-on father to your child?"

"Sure. I'll teach him to ride a bike and help him with his homework," her son answered, taking a swig of Moxie. "Those are important things. Those are *dad* things."

"My dad taught me to fish," Sam announced.

"That's terrific kid."

"He's the best."

"Yeah," Teddy signed. "I've heard that all my life."

"Your brother is a wonderful father," Kitty said gently. "And you can be too. I know you can."

"Everyone parents a little differently," Bill said because a commercial was on and he might as well participate in the conversation for a few moments. "Teddy will be more like me. Once they're old enough to do stuff he'll be terrific." He patted his son's knee for emphasis.

"Thank Dad."

"My dad does stuff with us all the time. He even plays with Callie and her dumb dolls."

Teddy stood. "I don't think I can stand hearing anymore about the great and mighty Charlie. I'm going to the pub. You want to come dad?"

Bill shook his head. "I think I'll just stay here." He glanced at his grandson watching with adoring eyes. "Maybe Sam and I can go out in the backyard for a little while. If your grandmother says it's okay." He looked to Kitty for permission.

Kitty was floored. "All right. Just for a bit. If Sam looks cold though come back inside."

Sam puffed out his little chest. "I'm tough grandma. I'll be okay."

Teddy grabbed his coat and stormed out the door. All this family time was making him nuts. He needed a drink fast.

·

Since a cold front had moved in to stay for a few days Kitty remained indoors all of Wednesday afternoon with the kids. They made cookies and Bill sampled them, exclaiming with vigor how good they turned out much to Callie's delight. Jeb stopped by to see how she was doing and only visited for a few minutes. He was polite and professional while he was there and no more. Kitty attributed the aloofness to being on duty and having Bill and Teddy staring daggers at him. She felt an unrealistic void in the vicinity of her heart when he left with just a nod to her in the kitchen. How strange that she had become so fond of his affectionate nature so quickly even though she knew it was just a façade. It gave her something to worry over throughout the day in the few moments she wasn't busy with the children.

Both Bill and Teddy made themselves scarce when Charlie and Bridget arrived late in the evening to pick up their children. Kitty wanted to get the boys together to talk but feared what the outcome might be. They had been so close growing up. Fiercely so. She didn't understand exactly why they had grown so far apart. She wanted to intervene on their behalf but a voice in her head held her back, insisting this was neither the time nor the place. So she waved off the young family before returning to the living room to spend an evening walking on eggshells around the two men currently planted in her life.

Thursday morning brought more cool temperatures and rain. Kitty sipped her coffee and thought about what Liza Jane had suggested the other day. It was morbid. And weird. But the more she thought about it while Petunia and Miss Tulip kept her company at the table, the more the idea started to make sense. Sometimes her artist eye enabled her to perceive things differently, to notice little details that most people would just glean over. It was from decades of trying to see things so clearly in order to accurately capture whatever she happened to be painting down to the most miniscule feature.

She put away her dishes and walked to her studio with determination and dread. Kitty turned up the heat and set a medium canvas on her easel. She got out her favorite paints and laid everything out precisely as she always did before a project. There was a routine she followed to help her slip into her artist skin and let the world fall away. When that happened all she saw was the vision in her head, or the scene spread out before her that she wished to capture. Either way she had to organize herself, her tools, and then her mind. Once everything was in place, she could allow herself to start feeling the art around her, spreading colors around the canvas in a careful rhythm that would play out a lovely aria when she was done.

The first step was a rough charcoal sketch. Kitty liked to outline the main points and boundaries when she painted buildings or interiors. It helped her get the depth and perception more accurate. Not that that was essential in this particular instance but breaking the habit now would inhibit the flow so she worked slowly and methodically sketching any details she could remember from that night. Occasionally she paused and closed her eyes to focus on the image burned into her memory.

She worked that way till lunch and joined Bill in the kitchen for some soup and sandwiches. Teddy was down at the pub and Kitty was relieved to not have to face him right now. It seemed everything she said was wrong and everything he said was hurtful.

"What are you working on out in your shed?"

Bill's voice interrupted her thoughts.

"Nothing really," she hedged. "Sometimes I just paint to paint. You know, to de-stress. It's therapeutic for me."

"Huh," he grunted. "Maybe I should try it. I need some sort of therapy. Do you think you could give me some lessons?"

"All right. But not today."

"Why not today? You said you were just painting for fun."

"Bill, you ought to be thinking about the future. Have you thought about what you're going to do?"

The blue eyes looked lost all over again. "No. I can't go back to the house."

"What about work? Maybe you should think about getting back to the pub."

Bill shook his head. "Too soon Kitty. I can't go back there. Everywhere I look I see her."

Kitty frowned. "You can't sit here and wallow Bill. You've got to get out of the house. Out of my house. Perhaps you should decide if you even want to go back to your house or find something new."

He dropped the spoon and sat back in his chair, his appetite gone. "I don't want to live in that house anymore. I just couldn't."

Kitty nodded. "I understand. So maybe we should call Lydia and see if she can find a rental for you. I know she'd be happy to help."

"You're kicking me out again?" he asked, gazing dolefully at her.

The front door opened and they heard footsteps coming down the hallway.

"I just think that maybe sitting here in self-pity isn't helping you. Finding a new place to stay is a difficult first step, but putting it off won't make it less painful. Maybe Teddy can help you since he's staying for a couple more days."

"Help with what?" Teddy asked, entering the kitchen. He spied the soup on the stove and headed over to the cupboard, finding a bowl and helping himself to the beef stew.

"Your mom is kicking me out."

"I'm not. But I think you need to start looking for another place to live."

Teddy's face was taut, his eyes brittle. "How can you bring this up just days after he buried his wife? He needs time."

207

"Time for what? To heal? Yes, I agree," Kitty said, trying not to feel like the enemy in her own home. "But he can't do it here. We're divorced Teddy."

"But this was his house for almost thirty years."

Kitty felt a tiny spark ignite. "His house? No. It was *our* house. Now it's mine. He got the business, I got my grandmother's cottage. You didn't see me camping out in his place of business after the divorce when I was having a difficult time adjusting."

"You sure can talk about forgiveness and being a good Christian but I don't see that in you. All I see is pettiness and bitterness," Teddy accused. "You want Dad to suffer as much as possible."

"I don't know about that," Bill said without much conviction.

"I don't want your father to suffer," Kitty denied. "I've never wished that. But he walked out on me for another woman after cheating with her for almost a year. I've opened my home up to him for this past week because it was the right thing to do. But he's got to move on just as I did."

"Men don't leave their wives without a reason," Teddy shot back. "Obviously you were failing in some area. I don't know which one, but I do know that Leslie made him very happy for the last two years. Everyone who knows him saw it. I don't recall him ever being that happy when he was with you."

Kitty stared at her son. His words were cruel but they were the truth. She thought she was the only one who saw it. But apparently it was evident to the entire world. "You're right," she said with quiet dignity. "I never made your father that happy. But I was always faithful and devoted to him. Even now, after he humiliated me and hurt me I've opened my doors up and let him stay with me because no one else would have him. I do believe it was the Christian thing to do. And now the best thing I can do for your father is make him stand on his own and face his new future the same way I had to. Hiding here or trying to escape back to his old life isn't the answer. He needs to move forward. And it's not here."

Sitting there in the kitchen surrounded by the safe and the comfortable, Bill couldn't help but think Kitty was right about a lot things. She was a smart lady. And kind and generous and forgiving. He could see that now. He could see a lot of things more clearly now. Love really was a fickle beast. He had loved Leslie desperately and completely, but he had built a life with Kitty from scratch and she had been exactly what she said: Faithful and devoted. Those were fine qualities in a wife and it occurred to him that perhaps what they had could somehow be recaptured. Because there was one thing Bill knew for certain: he didn't want to be alone.

Bill cleared his throat. "How do you know?"

"How do I know what?"

"How do you know that the answer isn't here? My future, my life?"

Kitty swallowed. "What are you saying Bill?"

"I'm not sure. But don't we both deserve to find out?"

"Well," Teddy said unhappily. "You might get Dad back after all this. Wouldn't that be something for you?"

"Yes," Kitty said softly, standing and clearing her plate and cup. "Wouldn't that be something."

•

She returned to the little studio and locked the door behind her. The last thing she needed was Bill or Teddy bursting in on her project. Lunch had unsettled her. What was Bill thinking? He couldn't really be considering reconciliation. That was insane. Leslie's funeral was barely behind them. It would be insensitive and just plain wrong to take him back under these circumstances. Wouldn't it? Especially since she didn't love him anymore. Not really. Sure there were moments when she felt her heart soften towards him but that wasn't the same thing. Was it? She didn't think so. But maybe love at this point in her life was different than the love once felt in her youth. Maybe loving her ex-husband was her duty and God would call her on that.

Kitty wasn't sure how she felt about that and since she didn't want to contemplate it any further she took the energy whirling around inside and funneled it into her painting. It took several hours of painstaking attention to detail the fleeting memories flashing through her mind but at last she set the paintbrush down. She had captured everything she could remember about the scene and now she wanted to sit back and just look at it.

After staring at it for ten minutes and not having any luck she decided the only way to see if there was anything in her painting to help Annie would be to compare it to actual photos of the crime scene. She unlocked the door and then carefully took the still wet canvas down.

209

Kitty carried it out and set against the side of the Volvo while she dashed into the house to get her purse. Bill was in the living room looking at photo albums and looked up at her hurried motions. "Kitty, what are you running around for? Why don't you sit with me and look at these pictures?" He was having a nice walk down memory lane, memories that didn't include Leslie and that was exactly what he wanted. To not think about her for just a little while.

"Can't!" she yelled over her shoulder. "Going into town!"

She nearly plowed into Teddy as he came walking down the stairs. "What's the hurry?" he demanded.

"Got to see the sheriff!"

Teddy followed her outside to her dismay. She tried to get the hatchback open quickly and slide the painting in but he caught sight of the painting and wanted to know what it was. He grabbed it from her and stared in horror at the picture. "You painted the murder scene? Is that's Leslie's body?"

"Teddy, put that back in the car."

"What is wrong with you? This is sick."

She tried to yank it from him but only managed in smearing some of the paint. "Teddy stop. This is really important. It might help figure out who killed Leslie."

"I heard they had someone in custody."

"Annie Goodwin did not kill anybody."

"So dating a cop makes you a cop now, is that it? Aren't you a wonder."

Kitty sighed. "Teddy. We need to sit down and talk when I get back. Right now I've got to see Jeb."

He slammed the hatch closed. "Then you better hurry."

It was just after four when she burst into the sheriff's office. "Is Jeb in?" she demanded of Rob.

"Nope. Should be back in an hour."

"Is there any way I could see a photo of the crime scene?"

This time Rob frowned. "I don't think that would be appropriate Ms. Appleton."

Kitty held up the canvas. "Look. I just painted everything I remember from that night. Maybe if we compare the painting to the photos something might pop out at us."

"Ms. Appleton the photos show us everything we need to know." He nodded unenthusiastically towards the canvas. "A painting isn't going to help."

"But sometimes I see things differently than other people. If I could just compare the picture to the painting…"

"They aren't pretty. I know the Sheriff would not want you to see them."

"Don't worry about my sensibilities."

"Sorry Ms. Appleton."

Kitty's shoulders slumped. She really acted so foolhardy sometimes. Here she was running down to the station with a painting because she thought somehow she might have seen something that everyone else – all the trained professionals – hadn't. She was such a goose sometimes. Bill was right. "I'm sorry Deputy. Sometimes I just don't know what gets into me."

The eyes that studied her softened. "It's all right. I know you're just trying to help."

She picked the canvas up and gave it one last sweeping glance. "I thought I was on to something."

"You certainly captured all the details. It's amazing actually."

Kitty pointed. "The pattern on the tablecloth. The label on the wine. Even the brand allergy medicine she took for her allergies to the cigarette smoke she was around earlier that evening."

"She must have gone through a lot of that stuff working in a pub," Rob snickered.

Kitty glanced up at him. "The pub is non-smoking. Leslie banned it when she took over for Henry. She even had the walls and floors cleaned at the time. I remember that distinctly."

Rob frowned. This was all news to him. "But her clothes…" he said, half to himself.

"I know. They had trace cigarette smoke on them. Obviously the killer smoked."

"How did you know about that?" Rob demanded. He was quite sure the Sheriff would not have told her that information.

Kitty handed the painting to him feeling pleased with herself. "I have my sources. I may know something else too. Please just show that to Jeb. It might help."

"Ms. Appleton if you know something you need to tell me."

"I'd rather speak with Jeb. And tell him Edward Appleton cracked." And she skedaddled before he arrested her for withholding information.

Chapter 20

At the Bottom's Up there was a celebration going on. Food and drink were flowing in abundance and the mood was celebratory. It was no longer the somber remembrance from the night before, but instead a boisterous spirit filled the room. There was laughter and talk as people shared their favorite 'Leslie' story and Bill felt surrounded once again by warmth and affection. He waved to Connor and even lifted a beer to Randy, who returned the gesture with a grin and bellow, "To Leslie!" They air clinked their glasses from across the bar and downed the amber liquid. Lionel Trescott approached him at the bar and Bill offered him a tentative smile. He didn't want to talk business this evening and hoped the man was here only in a celebratory capacity.

"This is great," Lionel said, leaning against the bar and nodding around at the packed room. "Very festive. Death has a way of bringing people together in the oddest ways sometimes."

Ayup," Bill said, taking another swallow of beer.

"I can see why she loved this place. I think it's important that we keep the same feeling when I take over. If I take over. I know you haven't decided." He smiled. "But I want you to know what I envision. I want to upgrade and improve this place, bring in live entertainment, make it more than just a local hangout. This place could be a pot of gold once tourists hear what a little gem we have here. But I would absolutely want to keep the same atmosphere that's always been true of the Bottom's Up. In memory of Leslie and Henry."

"That sounds good," Bill admitted. "Leslie used to talk about expanding and having local artists come in and play on weekends."

"See? She and I were in tune. We had the same dream."

Bill stared down at his glass. Had he emptied it already? "Look Lionel, I know you want this place. But I haven't had time to think about anything. We'll talk in a week or two, all right?"

Lionel reached out and patted Bill on the shoulder. "Of course Bill. We can talk later. You enjoy your evening."

Across the room Connor shook his head in disgust as he watched Trescott leave. He didn't like the man and it galled him that his sister had actually planned to sell the family legacy to him before her death. Maybe Bill would reconsider and keep the place now.

"Hey Connor."

He turned and saw Regina slide on to the bar stool vacated only seconds ago. She was wearing a fringed leather coat and tight red jeans. Her abundant hair was pulled back off her face into a big pile of copper curls at the back of her head and her chocolate brown eyes were watching him with a mixture of interest and fear. "Regina."

"Surprised to see you here."

"Why? It's for my sister." He nodded towards the smiling picture of his sister hanging above the bar. "Who wouldn't want to celebrate that?"

"You." She ordered a Coke and he refrained from smiling at her choice of beverage.

"What's that supposed to mean exactly?"

"It means that where there are happy people you usually ain't," she clarified.

Connor shrugged. "I made an exception tonight."

She sipped the coke Bob the bartender brought her. "Why? Is it out of guilt?"

"Why would I feel guilty?"

"I don't know."

He pivoted on his stool so he could face her full length. "You got something to say then say it. You never were one to hold back."

Regina pivoted so she faced him as well. "Fine. Did you kill Leslie because you were jealous over this place?"

He stared at her so hard she was afraid something was going to start shooting out of his eyes. Then he smiled slowly. "Anyone but you say that and I'd be offended."

"You're not offended by me?"

"Honey you could say just about anything you wanted to when you're looking at me like that."

Regina glared at him now. "What you mean? How am I looking at you?"

"Like you don't know if I'm the man of your dreams or the monster in your nightmares. And you're not sure it matters either."

She didn't know if she was more upset by the fact that he knew she was attracted to him or afraid of him. It didn't really matter though. She was angry enough for both reasons. Mostly she was angry at herself but she'd die before she admitted that. "You're full of yourself Connor Abbott."

"And yet you want me."

Regina threw her drink in his face before common sense dictated otherwise. Then she slid off her stool and surveyed the damage. "You're a miserable man Connor. I don't know if it's because you made yourself that way or someone else did it for you. Now I know why you spend so much time on that blasted boat of yours." Then she turned on her heel and disappeared into the crowd.

"That one's gonna be a handful for whoever ends up with her," Pete Wilson said from the stool on the other side. "You can just tell. But I kind of envy him, whoever he is."

"Yea," said Connor as he wiped his face and neck with the napkins that Bartender Bob had brought over. "I only know it won't be me."

"Just as well," another customer named John said. "I heard she's an uptight little twit. Thinks she's too good for the likes of us."

"Maybe's she's just got principles," Pete shot back.

"Maybe I ought to just find out what her problem is. Thinks her little black self is too good for me," John grumbled drunkenly. "I'll just show her one of these days."

Connor was off his seat so fast no one saw him move. He had John by the back of the neck with his head slammed down on the bar. "Say that again and I'll hurt you. *Touch* her and I'll kill you. Got it?"

"Sure Connor," John mumbled against the gleaming mahogany countertop. "I got it."

"Good." Connor released him and resumed wiping his beer off his shirt.

∙

Randy saw Regina throw a drink in Connor's face and was quite amused. Noting the time he decided he'd stayed long enough as well. He made his way around Connor and over to Bill, Teddy and Lionel. "This was a nice tribute."

"Ayup."

"Look Bill, I know we've never been on the best of terms but I am sorry. She was a good woman. She may have chosen someone over me but I think we put that behind us and moved past it. I'll miss her."

Connor snorted from three seats down but Randy ignored it.

Bill nodded. "Ayup. She said about the same. She didn't have any bad feelings toward you Randy. That's why she was able to work with you on this deal. She was actually proud of you."

"Really?"

Bill nodded. He held out his hand and Randy tentatively shook it. "I better get home. I got a busy week ahead of me. Another deal with a new office building in Port Bell. I've got to go to the office and work on the plans before my presentation."

"Sounds important," Lionel said affably. "Who will you be working with on this one?"

"Blakely & Garrett. They want 'contemporary beachside'. Tell me what that is please?" Randy laughed. "Because I'm not exactly sure."

"You'll get it. You're good," Lionel said lightly. "You did a great design on the pub."

"Thanks."

"Well if you can do the 'contemporary', Kitty could help you with the 'beachside'. Her paintings are always in demand you know," Bill said proudly. "They'd look great in any building you design."

"That's a terrific idea Bill. Thanks."

Lionel held up his drink in a silent toast. "Great minds think alike. I spoke with Kitty about the very same thing."

"Mom has expanded her portfolio so make sure you specify what you want," Teddy told the three men curtly. "She's into murder and mayhem now."

"What are you talking about?"

"She painted the crime scene. Every detail. It was really disturbing. And she was taking it to the police because she was convinced it was going to solve the murder." He took a swig of his drink. "Someone needs to do something about her."

"That is bizarre," Trescott said, waving the Bartender away. "I suppose we all have our quirks though, don't we? I better be off as well."

When it was just father and son again Teddy faced his father. "You aren't seriously thinking about getting back with mom are you?"

Bill shrugged. "I can think of worse things that could happen. She's a good person, a partner you can depend on. That's important son." He twirled his drink before asking the next question. "Is Emily still thinking about marrying you?"

Teddy shrugged. "I guess so. We haven't talked much this weekend. I'm just not sure what I want anymore."

"Marriage is a big commitment son. Make sure you're ready for it before you jump into it."

"I could say the same to you," Teddy responded, and they drank their beers lost in their own thoughts.

•

Kitty was on the phone with Liza Jane as she bent over to check the double chocolate chip cookies in the oven. "The cookies aren't quite done. But I'll be there. Promise," she said, standing up.

"Well you better because I think I've come up with some new ideas," she said excitedly. "I'll go over my plan with the girls and we can do some more snooping."

"All right. As long as it's not too dangerous. It occurred to me that all our poking around might make the killer mad. Even if we're coming up empty if has to be making the person uncomfortable with us asking questions."

"That's the beauty of it. Eventually we'll ask the right person the right question. But I think we need to keep at it. I'm going to call Harry and set up another meeting."

Kitty wanted to know what else Harry could possibly contribute since she was certain Liza had picked his brain clean the last time they met. Of course it dawned on her that the case might not be the only reason Liza Jane wanted to meet with her ex-husband. "Liza, is there something going on between you and Harry?"

"Kitty, really. Don't be a goose. We're just friends."

There was tone in Liza's voice that Kitty knew well. She sometimes thought they knew each other better than themselves. "Just be careful."

Liza groaned. "Just hurry up and get to the book club meeting."

"I might be a few minutes late but I'll be there."

They hung up and Kitty checked the cookies again. She shouldn't have gone back out to the studio. It was too easy to lose track of time when she was painting. Now she was going to be late and the first batch of cookies were slightly burned to boot. She looked at the well done batch cooling on counter and snatched one. Nibbling on it while she watched the clock she decided they were still quite passable.

The doorbell rang and she hurried to get it, intending to shoo them so she didn't burn this batch as well.

Connor Abbott stood on her step. "Ms. Appleton."

"Connor. This is a surprise. What can I do for you?"

"I heard about the painting you did."

Kitty felt her cheeks flush with color. "Oh Connor. I'm sorry if it upsets you. I was trying to help Jeb-Sheriff Carpenter. It wasn't meant to be disrespectful."

"Can I come in?" he asked, glancing back at the road.

"I was actually on my way out."

"It'll only take a moment."

Here was a pickle. Concerned citizen or vicious killer? Kitty waned back and forth but curiosity won out. "All right." She opened the door and let him in, glancing down the lane as he had. "Let me just call Liza again and tell her I've been delayed." Kitty yanked out her cell phone and let Liza know who was on her doorstep. "If you don't hear from me in ten minutes send in the reinforcements," she whispered before hanging up and following Connor into the living room.

•

Regina stood on the pub steps and watched Connor disappear into the night. Why did she let him get to her? It irked her beyond measure that he was the only man in Rock Bottom worth his salt and he didn't seem even remotely interested in her. He barely knew she was alive. He'd never fall for her. There would be no romantic gesture or declaration that he cared for her even a smidge. Her pride screamed at her to forget about him and take a chance with Randy, if only to let Connor see what he was missing out on. But her stupid, confused heart wouldn't listen to reason. It was quite possible she had feelings for a murderer.

What was wrong with her?

She turned and nearly bumped into Randy.

"Oh hey! Regina, I wanted to apologize for being a jerk earlier," he said quickly. "The last couple weeks I've been under a lot of stress to get this deal done for Trescott. I guess I was just blowing off steam and I shouldn't have."

"Forget about it," she told him. "I have."

"Okay." He smiled. "We still friends?"

Regina figured that in this town she probably shouldn't turn away any overtures of friendship and maybe even something more. She wasn't ready to start anything tonight though. "Sure Randy. I've got to go. Book club meeting."

"That sounds rather boring actually."

"They used to be until we all decided to play detective. Kitty is determined to solve this murder. It's like her new mission in life." She glanced back down the lane where Connor had been moments ago. "I suppose we're making some progress. But Kitty is the one with all the ideas." She realized that technically Randy was still a suspect and she probably shouldn't have run off at the mouth like that. Curse Connor for distracting her! "I better be off."

She hurried down the steps and noticed a man in the shadows smoking a cigarette. "Hi Mr. Trescott."

"Evening." He blew out a ring of smoke and waited until she was out of sight before he stepped from the shadows.

•

Connor was standing by the fireplace and Kitty sat on the edge of her sofa, waiting for him to speak. He wasn't a particularly friendly man but she had known Eileen and Henry all her life. They were good people and she attributed that same characteristic to their son, deserved or not until he proved otherwise.

Still, he was hard to read and she wasn't sure exactly why he was here wanting to talk about the painting at this hour.

"Bill and Teddy are talking about you at The Bottom's up. About a painting of the murder and how you think you might know something."

Kitty felt a little pang of fear at the intense look on his face. "It was just a hunch. I could be totally wrong."

The frown deepened on his weather-hardened face. "Ms. Appleton, I know what you and your friends are up to. Regina isn't any more subtle than Mrs. Stimple or old Mrs. Perry. You're all poking your noses into this and I'm afraid someone is going to get hurt."

She didn't even try to deny it. "We only want to help."

"My sister is dead. I'd hate to see another person hurt or worse." His mind flew to Regina. He had tried to scare her off, warn her away from this silly investigation to keep her safe. Even now she wasn't sure if he had killed his sister, and her fear of him was good. It would keep her at bay and hopefully deter her from getting into a dangerous situation. Short of following the women around to protect them that was the best he could come up with. "Please. For your own safety let the sheriff do his job."

"We are. The girls and I are just helping him do a little legwork."

Connor ran his hand through his hair. Why were women so stubborn? "There's a killer out there. If any of you get too close who knows what could happen."

"Not to worry, Connor. We're fine." Kitty smiled reassuringly at him, feeling safe. She was quite certain if he were the murderer he would have killed her by now. "I promise. Would you like something to drink? Or eat?" She remembered the cookies. "Oh! The cookies!" Kitty jumped up and ran to salvage them. "Oh dear I hope they aren't ruined!"

"I'll see myself out, Ms. Appleton," Connor called after her. "Please think about what I said!"

"I will!"

•

Liza checked her watch for the third time. "Kitty should be here soon. She said Connor already left and she was leaving immediately. I can't wait to hear what he said to her."

"Can't we start without her?" Lydia complained

"Hush," Charlotte said. "We're waiting for Martha anyway."

"Connor probably confessed," Regina sulked. "He all but admitted it in the pub."

"Really?" Lydia wanted to know. "Tell us everything."

Regina reluctantly gave them detailed accounts of her recent encounters with Connor Abbott. "So it's him. It has to be."

"Well Kitty sounded all right after he left so maybe he isn't involved."

"She probably convinced him to turn himself in."

"Why didn't you tell us all this before?"

"I don't know."

"I wish I'd been there when you threw a drink at him," Charlotte said. "I've always wanted to see that in person. It's on my bucket list as a matter of fact."

Martha toddled in with a tote on one arm and Arnold in the other. "Sorry I'm late. I had to go get this little guy since I'm watching him for Annie. I hated leaving him alone at the house another moment."

"You got anything good in there?" Lydia asked. "I'm starving and Kitty isn't here with the snacks."

"I did pick up a few things," Martha said brightly. "Help yourselves."

Lydia and Regina dug through the tote and pulled out a bag of candy bars and some dog treats. Regina handed Arnold a treat and took a chocolate bar to cheer herself.

"I'm waiting for whatever Kitty is bringing," Charlotte announced. "She always brings something delicious."

"I'll call her again if she isn't here in exactly three minutes," Liza Jane said, eyeing the candy with interest.

.

The cookies were burned but she was taking them anyway. They were all stacked neatly in a Tupperware container and she was heading out. It was already a few minutes after seven and the girls would be wondering where she was. She'd have to drive this evening if there was hope of getting there at this point. As she slipped a lightweight coat on there was another knock at the door.

She pulled it open and was surprised at who stood on her step. "I'm so sorry but I don't have time to talk right now. I'm on my way out. Can we talk another time?"

"This will just take a moment," he said, stepping into the house.

Frowning, Kitty closed the door and followed her guest back into the living room, realizing her cell phone was in the kitchen.

.

Jeb got back from Fairfield around six-thirty and wanted nothing more than to go home and not think about criminals for the rest of the evening. But out of habit and dedication he stopped at the station to check on a few things that had been bothering him all day.

Rob of course was still there. His dedication was admirable and Jeb appreciated his fervor in trying to solve the case. "Anything new?" he asked while hanging his hat on the rack.

"As a matter of fact your lady friend dropped that off." Rob nodded towards the far wall and Jeb turned to see what it was that Kitty had ventured here for. "What in the world..." He went over and gawked up close. "Is that the crime scene?" He looked to his deputy for confirmation of the unbelievable.

"Ayup." Rob came to his side. "She's got an eye for detail, you got to give her that."

"I'll say. Get me the photos forensics took."

Rob already had them in his hand and passed them to the sheriff. "Seems she remembered just about everything."

Jeb compared the photos against the painting. "I see that." He propped everything up on Rob's desk and the two of them stood there gawking at the side-by-side comparison. "Something isn't quite right." He pointed. "Look at that."

"The cell phone?"

"It's in the crime scene photos just a foot from the victim's hand. But in Kitty's painting," he pointed to the other side, "nothing."

"Maybe she just forgot it."

"She managed to remember the tiniest detail down to a stain on the carpet and the brand of medicine on that tiny bottle but she forgot the phone? I don't think so."

"That reminds me. Your lady friend knew about the cigarette smoke on Leslie's clothes." He filled the sheriff in on the brief conversation he had with Kitty, including her parting remark about Edward Abbott.

"So what we can conclude from that would be that the last person she saw – the killer – was probably a smoker. Or at the very least she met in a room that reeked of cigarette smoke."

"Randy's office stank," Rob remembered.

"So did Trescott's office."

"Shall we go to their offices?"

Jeb shook his head. "They're closed by now. I have a better idea."

The women of the book club were surprised when Jeb walked in right at seven. "Evening sheriff," Liza said with a bright smile. "Kitty isn't here yet. I just talked to her a couple minutes ago. She should be here shortly."

"This isn't a social visit. I need to know what Edward Abbott knows."

All eyes went to Charlotte, so Jeb naturally swung his attention to the elderly woman sitting forlornly by herself. "It's Charlotte isn't it?"

"Yes," she said meekly, resorting to her old and pathetic routine. "I don't really know what I can tell you though. I just had a brief conversation with him the other night. I don't even know if I remember what he said come to think of it."

"Cut the act. Kitty told me you're the most shrewd, astute person she knows and how you use your age to your advantage. I don't have time to humor you the way she does."

Charlotte narrowed her eyes. "Fine. Edward told me that Leslie changed her mind. She was not going to sell the pub."

"You sure?"

"Really sheriff. You just accused me of being shrewd and astute and then you turn around and question my comprehension of a very simple matter."

"My apologies. Was there anything else he told you?"

Charlotte shifted uncomfortably and darted a glance at the girls. Regina was watching with those eagle eyes of hers.

"She knows something!" Regina accused. "You old goat, you were holding out on us!"

"Not exactly," Charlotte denied. "It's just that Edward knows more than he was telling. I had the distinct impression there was more to the story. But I couldn't get it out of him. I had already used up my clues."

"Your clues?"

"It's not important. I just didn't want the girls to know I had failed at my task," she said sadly. Charlotte discreetly pinched herself and blinked back tears. "Their respect means more to me than anything."

"Would you quit doing that!" Regina nearly yelled. "You are SO faking that pitiful old lady act. We all know you're a tough old bird."

Charlotte stomped her cane. "Fine! I wanted to one-up Liza Jane but I knew if I didn't have the whole story it wouldn't be as impressive. There. Are you happy now?" she said, glaring.

Liza Jane rolled her eyes at Jeb. "The living are so dramatic. This is why I prefer to work with dead people."

Jeb ignored her. "Did anybody else know that Leslie wasn't going to sell the pub?"

Charlotte shrugged. "Only Eddie has the answer to that question."

•

They found Edward on his stool in the corner again. He had a root beer float and a puzzle book in front of him. "Eddy, we need to talk," Jeb said, leaning against the counter.

Edward flicked his eyes from Jeb to Rob. "We already talked. I'm not telling you my secret."

"I already know your secret," Jeb said easily. "Leslie wasn't going to sell the Bottom's Up. Everyone knows Eddy."

Edward's jaw dropped. "But she said it was a secret. And she made me promise not to tell anyone where she was going."

Jeb snapped his fingers like he just remembered something. "That's right! She was going to see him, wasn't she Eddy? The one who made her so mad."

"I told her not to. She wouldn't listen. I should have never told her about..." his voice trailed off.

"Who was it she was going to see Eddy?"

Edward pursed his lips and remained silent.

Jeb drummed his fingers on the counter, trying to stay calm but wanting desperately to rip the information he needed right out of the old man. But he had to do this the hard way. "Eddy you said you clean several offices around town, right?"

The older man nodded.

"You clean for Trescott Development don't you? And Randy Parker?"

"Ayup."

"The reason that Leslie went tearing out of here the night she was murdered was because of something you told her. Something you saw. What did you see Eddy? And where did you see it?"

"It was so pretty I had to touch it. All the little people and the little cars. It was like a giant toy," Edward explained. "I didn't mean to break it."

Jeb knew exactly what Edward was referring to. "The model in Trescott's office? The new pub? That's what you broke isn't it Eddy?"

"Sort of. It wasn't what it was supposed to be. Even I knew that. But I didn't mean to break it!" he yelled after Jeb and Rob started toward the door.

"Randy just left a few minutes ago. So did Trescott. He usually goes out and smokes his cigar out there," Bartender Bob offered helpfully, having listened in to the whole conversation.

Jeb didn't mind. "Thanks!" he called over his shoulder as they hustled out the door.

They backtracked outside and found his very recognizable Humvee in the parking lot. "He's still around," Jeb said, searching the darkened lot. He thought he heard voices and started in the direction they seemed to be coming from. He kept his hand on his holster as he made his way toward the unlit area behind the building. The voices were louder and he could tell it was a man and a woman.

What he stumbled on appalled him. Lionel Trescott was in a very compromising position with young Beth from the cafe. She gasped when she saw the Sheriff and tried to extricate herself from underneath the man on top of her.

Trescott hastened to adjust his clothing. "It's not what it looks like," he tried.

"It's exactly what it looks like. She's just a kid," Jeb said in disgust. "Close your fly and let's go. I'm bringing you in."

"But sheriff you can't. She's eighteen now and it's legal."

Jeb looked to the young woman who didn't look old enough to be out of high school. She nodded, but her face burned brightly with humiliation. It galled him that Trescott could get away with this behavior but there wasn't much he could do.

"Stay away from this guy. He's a pig. Go home to your parents. Wait for a nice guy your own age and get married before you do this again." He jerked his head to the side. "Go."

"Yes sir," she whispered and darted past them without a backwards glance.

Lionel glared at Jeb. "You had no business running her off like."

"I could still get you for indecent exposure."

"We're behind a building in the dark. Who are we going to offend?" he demanded.

"Doesn't matter. But I may overlook that charge and go with murder."

"What are you talking about?"

"Leslie Appleton."

"I told you I was driving back from Portland."

"We have reason to believe she was murdered around seven. Your wife said you didn't get home until eight-thirty yet your flight arrived at six. Plenty of time to get here and kill Leslie. Plus I have several witnesses who were nearly run off the road by a Humvee around eight-twenty. You're the only one in the county who owns one."

"Why would I kill Leslie?"

"It seems Leslie may have changed her mind about selling the pub to you."

Lionel frowned. "You are a persistent man Sheriff. But I do have an alibi."

Jeb frowned. "What is it?"

"I was with Beth. We were in my office from about six-fifty until quarter past eight when I had to get home. You can ask her. I was trying to avoid this coming out on account of my wife Sheriff."

Jeb didn't like that alibi at all. The girl might lie for him if she were infatuated with the older, worldly Lionel Trescott. But there were too many other things that pointed to Trescott to not pursue this. "What about the scale model in your office? What kind of paint is on it?"

"Paint? How should I know? I didn't make it."

The truth dawned on Jeb. "Randy Parker did."

"Yes. It's what I pay him for. He does a remarkable job too. You saw the one in my office."

"It didn't strike me as all that impressive. Looked a lot like the pub looks now."

"You should see the one he just completed for me. A five star resort with all the luxuries. Quite impressive. The real thing will be even more so once we get the project underway."

"And where will this five star resort be going?"

"Port Bell."

"Really? Because I checked while I was there and you don't own any commercial property there." Jeb waited out the other man, determined to get answers if it took him all night. "You have however very discreetly bought up quite a few properties here in Rock Bottom."

"Well I haven't acquired the property in Port Bell yet. We have to find the perfect place that overlooks the water."

"Kind of like the bluff the pub sits on here in Rock Bottom," Jeb mused.

Lionel straightened his tie and avoided eye contact. "Right. Just like that."

The seconds ticked by and Jeb waited for just the right moment strike. When Lionel checked his watch for the second time, he made his move. "There wasn't going to be a new pub was there? That fancy resort model is what you planned all along to put up in its place. I'm right aren't I?"

Lionel smiled charmingly. "Okay, okay. But this is just between you and me," he said confidentially. "I had Randy make two designs. One for a new pub and one for the Rock Bottom Seaside Resort."

"Two models?"

"A fake one to appease the Appletons and the real one of our actual resort. I was going to flatten this place," Lionel explained, looking around to make sure no one could hear.

"You were conning Leslie Appleton."

"That's a strong word. No, I was giving her what she wanted: a whole pile of money and in return I promised to keep her father's sad little dream alive. I was helping her get what she wanted without the guilt. Once I owned it there would have been some permit problems or wiring concerns. Maybe a fire. Anyway, it would have been too much to deal with and better for me to just knock it all down and start over. You see?" Lionel spread his hands. "Everyone would have won that way."

"Did Leslie find out?"

"How could she have? I didn't tell her and Randy certainly wouldn't have told her. I had the model of the remodeled pub at my office and he kept the Rock Bottom Resort model under lock and key at his office. Of course she never went to his office so I don't see how she could have found out."

"Her Uncle Edward cleaned Randy's office."

"The stupid one?"

"He's not stupid," Jeb ground out. "I think he saw the resort model." Jeb remembered how upset he was over breaking it. "He saw

226

the fancy model with all the bells and whistles a kid could ask for and had to look at it, touch it. But he broke it and went to Leslie because he was upset. He must have told her the name of it and she would have at the very least been curious. From what we know of Leslie she probably would have assumed the worst and gone over in a huff to see if what Edward saw was what she feared."

"She must have seen what we really intended to put up," Lionel said in astonishment.

Jeb nodded. "I think she busted in through the back door to get inside for a look. And when she did-"

"If she did she would have gone ballistic."

Which would explain the mess in the office and the paint on her hands if she flew into a rage and smashed the miniature pub design.

"If Leslie decided not to sell the pub then what would happen to you and Randy?"

"I have my hands in a lot of cookie jars, so to speak. I'm quite solvent. But young Mr. Parker was counting on this to put his mark on the world. He was hoping it would open up a whole new world for him. There would have been a lot of money, a lot of exposure, more jobs, maybe even a chain out of this deal."

"Losing all that could push a man to do something drastic."

Lionel shrugged. "Possibly. But Randy has a pretty solid alibi. It's a good theory but there must be someone else in all this you're overlooking. Try the brother. Connor. He's an angry soul."

"I'd still like to talk to Randy. Have you seen him this evening?" They were finally getting somewhere. They were on the brink now. He just had a couple more questions for Randy.

"He was here earlier but he left just before I did. We were talking with Bill and Teddy Appleton about his wife's painting of the murder scene. He seemed quite interested in her art work." Lionel's phone rang and he instinctively reached for his left front inside pocket. "Oh wait. That's my personal phone." He changed course and pulled one out of his hip holster. He paused before answering it. "Are we done? Can I take this?"

"Sure." Far be it for him to stand in the way of business, Jeb thought irritably. The man was so in demand he needed two cell phones.

And like a murky picture slowly coming into focus Jeb realized what could have been, what probably was the answer. The cell phone was the key to the whole thing.

It explained it all.

Jeb turned and ran back to the parking lot where Rob was speaking into his radio. "We just got funny call," he said when he saw Jeb come tearing across the lot.

"Never mind that! Get in the car!" Jeb hollered, yanking the door open and hoping it wasn't too late.

Chapter 21

Randy was pacing back and forth, his face a mask of fury. Kitty sat on the couch watching, afraid to speak and afraid not to. The longer the quiet remained, it seemed the more agitated he became in his own thoughts.

Finally she spoke. "Randy I think you ought to talk to someone. Maybe Sheriff Carpenter can help you."

"I think you've done enough talking for both of us," he snapped, running both of his hands through his hair. "Why did you and your friends have to get involved? Why? Bunch of old busybodies, that's what you are."

Kitty knew the truth now. It was hard not to. "Why did you kill Leslie?" she asked softly.

"She laughed at me. She LAUGHED at me!" Randy yelled, and then laughed eerily. "Well look who's laughing last. Not her!"

"Tell me what happened," Kitty coaxed.

"Sure. I'll tell you because you understood the pain she caused. Edward saw the model in my office that Monday evening and broke it. Apparently he went back to the pub in a dither and told Leslie hoping she could fix it but when Edward told her the name he saw on the placard she realized what was going on. She broke into my office and saw what we were really going to build on her father's property. The Rock Bottom Seaside Resort, five stars across the board. Would have been beautiful. But she freaked when she saw it. Smashed it to pieces and left. The only good thing about that was that I was able to play off the break-in and make it look like someone was trying to sabotage the deal."

"Anyway, when I got to my office – which was literally just minutes after she left - I realized Les somehow had found out the truth so I went to her house to explain that I did it for us. For her and I. That the money she got from the sale and all the money I made from working with Lionel would be enough for us to start over somewhere. I told her I still loved her and forgave her for her stupid fling with Bill." He stopped pacing and faced Kitty directly. "That's when she laughed."

"I'm sure that must have been hard for you."

"She told me she loved Bill. That they were happy and going to have a baby. That her whole life was coming together because of him. She actually preferred that tired excuse for a man over me." He shook his head. "I didn't understand. I still don't. But she said she never really loved me. I tried to show her how much I loved her, wanted her, needed her. But she told me to get out and if I came near her again Bill would take care of me. She said that the deal was off and the pub was staying in the family. Her family. Leslie told me she didn't even want me to stay in Rock Bottom because she couldn't stand the sight of me anymore."

He looked at his hands. "I couldn't bear seeing her with him. Happy. Having a family with him. And watching my life crumble into a million pieces. I just grabbed the candlestick and hit her. It was so strange, seeing her lie there with her eyes just staring straight ahead and not seeing anything. Not happy anymore." Randy shook himself. "I knew at once what I had to do."

"You took her phone."

He smiled now. "Yes. I thought it was brilliant really. I sat in the pub, reached into my jacket and speed dialed my own cell phone. Everyone believed it was her calling. The phone records confirmed it and it gave me alibi. I was going to slip it back in the house before Bill got back from bowling but you ladies altered the plan a bit. After we discovered the body and you rushed out to call for help, it only took me seconds to wipe the phone clean and press it into her hand so it had her prints on it. Then I kicked it away. No one noticed it. Connor certainly didn't. But you did." He narrowed his eyes. "What am I going to do about you?"

"I don't know," Kitty stammered. "But surely someone else will figure it out too. Jeb certainly will. And what about Edward? He must have suspected something? Were you going to kill him too?"

"Edward was never a problem; I know how to manipulate him. And with no one to testify about the phone not being there when we first got to the scene the Sheriff has nothing. No physical evidence at all. I probably could have let this ride out and nothing would come of it but I felt like you were a loose end that just needed tying up, especially with you and your friends poking around. I figure we don't really need another murder though because that would be too suspicious."

Kitty breathed a sigh of relief.

"But everyone knows you walk a lot at night along the beach or the bluffs. No one would think much of an accident. Finding your battered body on the rocks would be tragic but certainly understandable."

"Oh dear," Kitty said out loud. Her heart was racing and she feared she might be ill. *Pull yourself together,* she firmly ordered herself.

Her phone rang from the kitchen and she jumped.

"Don't answer that."

"But I have to. It's Liza. The girls are waiting for me and if I don't show up soon they'll be banging down the door." That wasn't true at all but she said anything that might encourage him to let her answer the phone.

Randy reached over and grabbed the fireplace poker, "Answer it. One wrong word and your head is going to be split open all over this lovely rug. I have nothing to lose."

Kitty nodded and hurried into the kitchen with Randy stalking her. "Hello?"

"Where are you?" Liza demanded.

"I got delayed."

"By what? Goodness Kitty you're the one who insisted we all get together to hash over this murder one more time. And I think I may have come up with a new theory."

"Me too," Kitty said, eyeing Randy as he swung the poker ominously back and forth in front of her.

"Then what's the hold up?"

"I burned the cookies," Kitty said automatically. Then a surge of hope swelled up inside her trembling body. Her panic phrase! Surely Liza remembered. "*I burned the cookies!*" she said hysterically.

"For goodness sake calm down. We'll eat them burned or not when you get here. Just hurry up."

"But I *burned the cookies* Liza," Kitty said, wanting to sob.

"Good grief. You're being a bit melodramatic."

"I'm not *bluffing*. They are burned and I don't want to *walk* all the way down there with burned cookies! It's so bleak walking over there along the *bluff*. With the burned cookies."

"Just hurry up already!" Then Liza Jane hung up.

Kitty set the phone down on the counter slowly and realized she was in deep trouble.

•

Rob screeched to a stop in front of the library and Jeb jumped out before it had stopped moving. He took the steps two at a time and stormed in the library expecting Randy to be there trying to drag Kitty away from her little book club meeting and all the women in a fright. Instead the front was quiet and he could hear laughter and women's voices from the back room. He breathed a sigh of relief as he hurried to them.

His relief was short lived when he didn't see Kitty sitting with the other women. "Where's Kitty?" he demanded.

"I just talked to her," Liza Jane laughed. "She's at home in a tither because she burned the cookies."

"She takes her cooking very seriously," Regina explained to him. "It's a bit prideful of her but I suppose it's only fair. She's the best cook in the county."

"Do you remember that blackberry cobbler she made last year for the fourth of July?" Lydia asked the group. "It was heavenly. I still wake up thinking about that pie. We need to have her make it again soon."

"Definitely," Martha greed. "Yummy!"

"Have any of you seen Randy this evening?"

"I did. He was walking down the lane earlier. Like out towards Kitty's house."

Jeb paled and turned to tear back outside but collided into Rob's tall frame. "Rob! Move! Kitty's in trouble!"

"What's going on?" Regina demanded. "Is Kitty in trouble? Was it Randy all along?"

"Don't panic. Kitty's fine. I just talked to her," Liza reminded him. "Screaming about burnt cookies but otherwise fine."

"Wasn't that her panic phrase?" Martha suddenly asked.

"Oh yeah!" Regina gasped. "It was!"

"We were only supposed to use it in life or death situations," Lydia whispered, paling at the thought of someone she knew and cared about meeting the same fate as Leslie Appleton.

"Oh my," Martha breathed. "Our Kitty is in trouble!"

"Call for back up!" Jeb roared into Rob's ear, and shoved past him, nearly knocking them both over in the process.

"Stop dillydallying and go rescue her!" Charlotte barked and thumped her came for good measure.

They were walking along the bluff north of the pub. The temperature had dropped and the cold wind blowing in off the ocean cut through Kitty's thin jacket and whipped her hair around. Randy was prodding her with the poker and she wished desperately that she had grabbed the jacket with the mace in the pocket instead of the one with her keys. A lot of good the mace was doing hanging on the peg by the back door.

"You won't get away with this!" she yelled into the wind. Either he didn't hear her or chose not to reply, only prodded her along with the poker. She tried to break away once but he caught her easily and shoved her back along the path to the bluff and her very unpleasant end.

·

The women sat on pins and needles for five minutes, alternately praying and talking nervously to each other as they silently pondered what was happening to their dear friend. Liza Jane fretted and nearly burst into tears as the rest of the women tried to console her. "I should have known Kitty was in trouble," Liza wailed. "I'm her best friend. We practically read each other's minds!"

"It's not really your fault," Martha said consolingly. "I mean, maybe a tiny bit for not recognizing her duress words but still. Not entirely your fault at all."

"She was blabbering and I didn't see it. What if those were the last words I ever hear from her?"

"How long has it been since they left?"

"Almost six minutes."

"Well it only takes three minutes to drive to Kitty's house from here," Lydia pointed out. "Surely they've rescued her by now."

"Let's call," Lydia urged. "Call Kitty's house. At least we'll know one way or another."

Liza grabbed her cell phone and dialed. "It's ringing," she told the ladies watching with bated breath.

"Hello!"

The sheriff's sharp bark nearly broke her eardrum "Sheriff what's going on?"

"She's not here! It looks like there was a struggle. What did she say to you Liza Jane? Did she say anything at all?"

Liza Jane broke down then as the ugly truth hit her like a physical blow. Her best friend was surely dead. "No," she said between sobs. "She was just blabbering. About the cookies. That she wasn't bluffing. That's what she yelled at me. And that she didn't want to walk down here with them. That's all. Nothing else. Just the stupid burned cookies" She sobbed softly. "We would have eaten them anyway." She hung up the phone because she was too distressed to speak.

"Since when does Kitty not want to walk anywhere?" Martha whispered to the group so as not to take away from Liza Jane's discussion. "She walks everywhere."

"That's true," Lydia agreed, wiping her eyes. "Kitty loves to walk on the beach or along the bluffs in the evening. I've seen her thousands of times."

"And Kitty doesn't bluff either. Because she never does anything to bluff about."

"That was an odd choice of words," Regina thought out loud. "Why would she say something like that?"

"It's a code," Charlotte announced. "Kitty was trying to tell us something."

"A code? Really?" Lydia asked. "For what?"

"It seems pretty obvious. They were going to go for a walk along the bluffs," Martha said happily. "It's not an ideal night for a walk but still probably a lovely view."

Liza dropped the phone in absolute horror. "Oh my gosh! I think Martha is right. Randy is taking her up to the bluffs."

"He's going to shove her over the edge," Charlotte explained matter–of–factly in case they hadn't gotten that far in their thinking. She wasn't always sure they could follow a simple line of logic, these girls. But she did love them despite that. "It's what I'd do if I was him."

"We've got to save her!" Liza Jane cried, leaping to her feet and the others didn't hesitate a moment. Four desperate, distraught women charged out of the library determined to save their friend and one elderly lady followed behind wielding a cane and the good common sense to call the Sheriff for back-up.

"This looks like a good spot," Randy yelled into the wind, and Kitty shrunk away from the edge only to find her shoulders grasped firmly from behind. "Any last words Ms. Appleton?"

"You don't have to do this!" she cried into the howling wind.

"I kind of do!" he yelled in her ear. "Self-preservation you see."

Kitty was consumed by fear. Everything inside was freezing up. Except her heart. Her heart was pounding madly and she feared it was going to explode right inside her chest before her feet ever left the ground. Maybe that would be better, she thought irrationally. To die of fright here at the top rather than meeting the horrid death that awaited her down at the bottom. She peeked over the edge and even in the black of night she could make out the angry waves crashing and smashing the rocks below. It would be grizzly and painful, she thought. It would be horrible for her kids to hear about such a death when Jeb delivered the news.

A picture of his face flashed through her mind. She wanted to see it one more time. Or a hundred more times. Maybe even every day for the rest of her life if she somehow lived through this.

And in that instant she decided Jeb and her kids and Liza Jane and her book club friends were all worth fighting for. Whatever happened, she was not going to make it easy for Randy to snuff out her life like it was nothing, like she was unimportant.

Kitty dug her heels in and pushed back against the hands that held her, trying to ease away from the edge if only a few inches.

Randy laughed. "You don't have a chance, Ms. Appleton. I'm so much more than you. Taller. Stronger. Fitter." He leaned closer to her ear and though he yelled it was like a sinister whisper. "You can't win. Just like Leslie couldn't either."

She didn't have any real weapons; she lacked strength and skill. But she remembered some of the defensive moves she learned at the community center years ago and the words they drilled into her mind: Use whatever you had on you. Fight! Desperately she searched her pockets and her right hand closed around the paint brush key chain Jeb got her. As fast as she could she yanked it out of her pocket and thrust it into the vicinity of his face still looming by her ear.

His scream of pain nearly shattered her eardrum but it didn't matter; the hands that had been holding her shoulders in a vice-like grip released her and she didn't dally. Kitty spun and shoved hard at him while he was clutching at his face with both hands, screeching a string of curses at her. Survival instincts sent her feet into overdrive and she ran blindly away from the edge, away from the man stumbling after her all the while yelling horrible things at her fleeing figure. Kitty focused on moving her feet as fast as possible over the uneven terrain without falling. It was damp and she was on a slope which made it even more difficult in the pitch black but she couldn't slow down with Randy stumbling after her on his long legs. He was already catching up with her and Kitty couldn't keep the scream inside any longer. It came out in a piercing shriek and repeated itself as she scrambled across the uneven ground towards town.

Kitty thought she heard a noise, a voice ahead and she felt a surge of hope. "Help!" she screamed. "Help me!"

"Over here! She's over here!"

The screeching voice in the dark was distorted from fear but Kitty would recognize it anywhere. "Liza!" she screamed. "Liza! Help!"

"We're coming!"

And then they appeared in the shadows racing to her aid. Four angry women flanked her in the distance, shadowy figures charging forth fearlessly even as Randy was upon her again. He grabbed for her and caught her shoulder, knocking her off-balance and sending them both tumbling to the ground in a mess of feet and arms. Kitty struck out at him, trying to wriggle away but his arm shot out again and caught her leg. He pulled her back towards him and she could feel the blood pounding in her ears as she struggled to get away. "Help!" she screamed, kicking furiously.

"Let her go!" Liza Jane yelled, hurtling herself into the fray.

And then Lydia was there, yanking at Randy for all she was worth in an effort to dislodge his grip. Regina jumped into the fight, kicking Randy repeatedly and fervently hoping she was breaking bones somewhere. Martha stood hovering in indecision, wanting to help but frightened of even moving. She screamed as she sidestepped the wrestling figures and then thwacked Randy with her purse when his head popped into sight. Seeing it was effective she did so each time he came into view and punctuated each hit with a scream of victory as he struggled to get the upper hand over the women. Charlotte finally arrived, huffing and puffing from the extreme effort of climbing the embankment. She surveyed the scene and logic prevailed even in the midst of chaos. With the last bit of strength she raised her cane as high as she could and brought it down forcefully. The solid *thud* could be heard even above the wind as it made precise contact with Randy's skull.

He quit struggling and fell limp among the tangle of women.

"Jerk," Regina muttered, kicking him one last time. "Don't be messing with my friends!"

Charlotte nodded in satisfaction as the girls extricated themselves and helped Kitty up. "I've never been fond of him," she said tartly, looking down at his still form. "He's a Democrat you know."

"So am I," Lydia said, brushing herself off. "That doesn't mean I should be knocked over the head though."

Charlotte chose not to answer that but instead turned to Kitty. "Are you all right dear?"

Kitty nodded shakily. "I think so. You girls saved my life!"

"We're just glad everyone is okay," Lydia told her, sinking back down on Randy's form. She suddenly felt drained and he was the only thing to sit on comfortably.

"Thank the good Lord we found you in time!" Martha said, dabbing at her eyes. How she would have dearly missed Kitty and all those wonderful baked goods she always brought to book club!

Liza hugged her fiercely. "You nearly gave me a heart attack Kitten! I thought I lost you, you goose!"

Sirens blared in the distance and then Jeb was there. It may not have been proper procedure to grab the victim in a fierce hug but he did anyway. His heart was thundering in his chest and he was sure she could feel it as he held her close. "I'm sorry," he whispered to her. "I'm so sorry I wasn't here for you."

Kitty pulled back and smiled up at him shakily. "You did save me." She held up the keychain. "Right in his eye. It was enough to break free from him until the cavalry arrived."

"I should have been here," he insisted, touching her hair and her face.

"You're here now. And I'm fine. My girls saved the day! God is good!"

"Yes. He is." Jeb pulled Kitty close again and didn't care about the smirks and grins from the five women watching him.

Rob was on his radio and had more deputies there in minutes. The paramedics arrived and checked over the women but other than some bruises everyone appeared fine. Randy was taken into custody and he groaned as he was led away, one eye covered in gauze. "I've lost an eye and I think they broke some ribs," he moaned. "I'm pressing assault charges."

"Go ahead and try!" Regina called after him. "I know every lawyer in the county. See what happens to you then!" Adrenaline was still coursing through her and she was feeling pretty sassy. And happy. Not only was Kitty safe but Connor was innocent!

Not that she had ever really doubted him.

Jeb coughed lightly. "It's all right ladies. I don't think that's going to be a problem." He was more than confident the traces of cigarette smoke on Leslie's clothes would match Randy's brand, just as the paint would match the ones he used for his model. With Kitty's testimony about the phone and the ladies' testimony about this assault he felt pretty sure Randy would be going to prison for a very long time.

"Can we leave now Sheriff?" Charlotte asked tiredly. "I'm rather worn out and I would imagine the rest of the girls are too."

His eyes found Kitty one more time. He didn't want her to go but he had work to do. "Of course. One of my deputies will see you home."

One by one Jeb watched the women disappear down the dark hill into town and he was left to face his own feelings at nearly losing the woman he had somehow fallen in love with in a very short amount of time.

Chapter 22

Kitty was actually grateful that Bill and Teddy were just down the hall from her that night when she finally settled into her own bed hours later. Miss Tulip and Petunia snuggled closer than usual, as if they sensed the unease Kitty still felt when she thought of how close her life had come to ending tonight. It was all so surreal now as she thought back on it, like a living nightmare that she kept replaying in her head and wished that she could push from her mind. She took her Bible and read for a little while, finding some comfort in the scriptures and knowing that the Lord had indeed been her fortress and shield tonight.

Both Bill and Teddy had been solicitous when she was returned home and they heard what had happened. Teddy actually made her a cup of tea while Bill sat with her. She shared with him what had happened and he was overwhelmed at the news that Randy had indeed killed Leslie. There was so much to absorb as they sat side by side on the couch just barely touching. Each was very much aware of what could have happened and what a miracle it was that Kitty had survived. Bill reached out and took her hand and squeezed it gently.

When Kitty finally decided to go to bed Bill assured her he was right down the hall if she was frightened. "We'll both leave our doors open and you just call if you need anything," he told her with the most honest display of concern she'd seen in him since he arrived.

"Thank you Bill."

He stood awkwardly by her doorway, clearly uncertain about leaving her alone after such a harrowing ordeal. "I'm glad you're all right Kitty," Bill said gruffly before kissing her softly on the cheek. "I really and truly am."

Now she was snuggled deep under the covers, safe and secure. Since sleep refused to visit she was forced to think, which was really something she didn't want to do. But as she recalled the scary moments she lived through this evening and considered the alternate ending, she felt so blessed to be alive and well. It also gave her a breath-taking perspective on life and all its facets. There was so much to do, so much she hadn't experienced yet, and so much that God had put in front of her to do yet. She needed to start living the life He intended for her instead of hiding from it.

Kitty lay in bed for a long while thinking about Jeb and Bill and wondering what part either might play in her life. It seemed to her that God put certain people in your path for a reason and she couldn't help but wonder if it was all for the culmination of this evening's events or if there was a greater purpose still to come. Jeb was such a sweet wonderful man and her feeling's had long since passed friendship. If she spent a lifetime getting to know him it didn't seem like enough. But there was a history with Bill she couldn't easily ignore even though she very much wanted to and the fact that he had changed even a small amount was truly miraculous. Tonight he had been caring and even considerate of her feelings and the sweet familiarity of the man she'd loved for so long doting on her was like a balm to her soul. How long had she craved attention like that from her husband and if he was truly willing to make an effort for her than could she turn him away? Of course he was still crass and unappreciative and selfish most of the time but that was how Bill was and she'd endured his imperfections for decades as he had endured hers. Wasn't that what it was supposed to be about? Didn't the vows they took still bind their hearts together even after all the pain?

Kitty fell asleep praying for an answer to that question.

.

The next morning Rock Bottom was buzzing from one end to the other as its residents awoke to news of the events from the previous evening. After the initial shock wore off there was a lot of nodding and knowing looks exchanged. The locals had suspected Randy from the beginning after all, they told whoever asked. There was a little bit of crazy in him, they claimed. Everyone always knew it deep down.

Kitty was hailed a hero in town. Word got out how she had tackled Randy on the bluff and held him down until help arrived in the form of the book club women, who had also figured out the identity of the murderer due to their highly evolved deductive reasoning developed from years of immersion in the great mystery classics. Books save lives, the town realized, and resolved to start reading more. Annie was more euphoric at the promise of donations and readers pouring into her library than she had been at being released from jail. Regina swore off men completely when she realized a certain fisherman was still uninterested in her despite the danger she had faced. Resigned to being alone for the rest of her life she adopted a mutt from the pound who became absolutely devoted to her within minutes. Martha's line became the only one anybody wanted to go through in order to get the most up-to-date news in Rock Bottom and Lydia finally got to see Margie Bingham at a loss for words over her part in saving the day. Liza was just glad that her dearest friend in the world wasn't going to be her newest customer, while Charlotte secretly started planning her platform for elections in the coming fall.

•

Teddy helped Bill move into an apartment in town that weekend. He didn't speak much to Kitty the time he was there and only informed her that he'd be staying with his father in the new place that evening before returning to Bar Harbor the following morning. Kitty tried to get him to talk but he simply ignored her pleas and went about helping Bill.

Jeb stopped by each evening to check on her and she appreciated his concern. He hadn't belittled her attempts to help with the case or become enraged at her prying into things that didn't concern her but he had gently chastised her for placing herself in danger. His genuine concern for her well-being and caring nature spoke to her heart and she could clearly see that her behavior had really not been practical at all. She promised not to interfere in his police work again and he thanked her for her understanding. Then he winked and promised he'd consult with her if he ever needed her help again.

Over the next several weeks the visits and outings together continued. They attended church and went for drives on Jeb's motorcycle as spring finally appeared to be settling for good. Jeb was the highlight of any day she got to see him even though it was silly since it was still just a façade. Kitty had a hard time keeping her heart in check when they seemed so compatible in every way. They enjoyed so many of the same things and never lacked for conversation. Their time together seemed bittersweet to Kitty with all the concerns she had swirling around inside and there were moments she wished she could just get Bill out of her system completely.

That was difficult since Bill stopped by regularly too. Kitty was always patient and sympathetic to his grief and went out of her way to make time for him even when it wasn't convenient. There was something between them that she wasn't sure was real or imagined but she believed Bill was back in her life for a reason. Their behavior never wavered from improper and she still felt like her heart was with another man. But it was imperative she find out what God had in mind for her and so she continued building a bridge with her ex-husband.

Jeb wasn't thrilled about that situation. He feared the tender feelings his heart held in abundance for Kitty were going to be his undoing if she suddenly chose to go back to Bill. But he guarded these secret feelings deep inside because he wasn't supposed to have them in the first place. Jeb often found himself wavering from utter joy and contentment when he was with her to a foul disposition when he realized it could, and most likely would, all come to a crushing end soon when she decided she'd achieved what she set out to.

Rob noticed the mood swings in his boss and took a chance on mentioning them one day when Jeb seemed especially troubled. "Are things going okay with your lady friend?" he asked tentatively when they were alone at the station.

"Ayup," Jeb answered automatically. "Why?"

"You just seem moody."

Jeb eyed him across his desk. "Moody?"

Rob flushed. "Well, yeah."

"Everything is fine."

"You two serious then?"

"Rob, this is none of your business and highly inappropriate."

"It just seems like when you're with her you're really happy," Rob plunged on. "And that maybe you two were going to, you know, end up together."

Jeb frowned. "It's complicated."

"Do you love her?"

"What?" Jeb hedged, feeling cornered.

"Yes or no. Do you love the woman?"

"Rob-"

"Yes or no."

There was a definite glare in Jeb's eyes as he stared down his deputy. "Yes."

"Then tell the woman and get on with your lives. There hasn't been a wedding in town in a while. I bet we could throw something together lickety-split."

"Rob, you're young and enthusiastic and I appreciate those qualities in you. Which is why I am not going to fire you for this conversation. Now drop it."

"Fine. I was hoping to bring Regina to the wedding if you got married since we'd probably both be in the wedding party and all. Plus I look good in a suit. But since you aren't going to do me any favors I guess I'll just ask her out to the movies or something."

"Good luck with that," Jeb shot back, thinking that the pretty Regina would make mincemeat out of his young deputy.

"At least I'm willing to take a chance," Rob said, standing up and grabbing his hat. "I'm going to go ask her."

"Right now?"

"Yes. What have I got to lose?"

"Everything. Your pride. Your heart. Your dignity."

Rob adjusted his hat and sauntered past the sheriff. "At least I'll have made the effort to win the woman of my dreams."

Jeb watched him leave and sat in stony silence as he considered his own life. After several minutes weighing all the possible outcomes, he slowly stood up and went around the desk to fetch his hat off the rack by the door.

•

Bill was sitting at her table again and Kitty couldn't get rid of him. It was like he had some burden to get off his chest and she wished he would just get on with it. Perhaps he just needed a little encouraging, Kitty decided. "Bill, I've known you since we were six years old. I know when you have something on your mind. You always told me when you were good and ready. But I don't have the time to wait on you anymore so please just say what you want to say."

Bill cleared his throat. "Kitty, I never really said thank you for all that you did for me. Those days right after Leslie died were hard. Real hard. And you had no reason to take me in but you did. That says a lot about the kind of woman you are."

His sincerity touched her more than the actual words. "You're welcome."

"And then for you to risk your life to find out who killed Leslie. Well, you are amazing Kitty. I see that now. I guess I didn't for the longest time. I didn't see how much you loved me, loved our family. That's really everything isn't it?"

"Not everything," Kitty said softly. "But it is important."

"We had a good life and I messed up. I didn't mean to you know. I didn't mean to fall out of love with you and in love with Leslie. It just happened. When you meet the one you're supposed to be with it just all becomes so clear." He shook himself. "I'm not saying what I mean to. I loved Leslie. But I did love you to. In my own way. We spent decades together and it would be impossible not to have feelings for you." He was never good at sharing his feelings with Kitty for some reason. It was easier with Leslie. She *got* him. And maybe because of that he was able to tell her how he felt about her so easily. But Les was gone and he had to move on. Moving on with Kitty was his best option for a simple and content life. It would be easy to slide back into the old role and far better to have Kitty than no one at all. All he had to do was make her see that deep down he was her best option as well.

"Bill." Kitty set her cup down. "Why exactly are we doing this now? Is it because you need closure or my forgiveness? Because if that's it then know I've moved past the hurt and anger and forgive you." And she realized she meant it. She understood about what he said when you met the one you were supposed to be with.

Because she had those same wondrous feelings for Jeb.

"I'm saying it because I realize where we both are in life. At a crossroads. And we have this opportunity to try again."

"Try again?"

"Yes. I know it's what you wanted right after I left you. I realize you've been seeing the sheriff and may have some feelings for him but we have a history together and that should trump anything you feel for him."

"It should?"

"We could get married again. We could start over. Be better this time around. I'll try to not be gone so much so we can spend more time together. I know I was always away too much before."

Kitty was overwhelmed. "I see."

"Of course we'd both have to make some compromises. I would go church with you if you want," he conceded, knowing that religion was important to her. He was sure if he threw in sitting in church for an hour each week she'd see what an effort he was willing to make. "And if you could be a little more *affectionate* then I would certainly be happier at home this time around."

There might have been some growth in the man but most times Bill was still very much Bill. "I don't know what to think. It's so sudden." The thoughts had been flitting through her mind for weeks but now that the moment was here she felt panicked and unsure.

Bill was bemused at her lack of excitement at his offer. "Kitty, you understand what I'm offering don't you? I want to marry you. Try again. Till death do us part and all that. You said our vows were sacred. Don't' you owe it to us to do the right thing and honor God? Isn't this what He would want?" Bill was sure God was going to be his ace-in-the hole here. Kitty was real big on God. And truth be told he was willing to give it a shot if it helped with the empty ache in his heart.

Kitty felt like her emotions were running rampant. "I don't know what to think Bill."

"You know I've changed. You've seen it."

"I know you have Bill. You seem to listen more. You're a little more considerate certainly. And the fact that you've taken an interest in Sam and Callie is the most wonderful gift you could give me."

Bill nodded, feeling victory at hand. "I could do better. I'd really try this time. I threw away twenty-eight years of our past. Don't throw away twenty-eight years of a possible future."

Kitty hesitated. "Give me some time to figure all this out."

"All right. I'll come by tomorrow and see how you feel then."

"No Bill. I'll call you when I'm ready to talk. Please give me some space to think."

He was surprised but nodded in agreement. She watched him leave and then bowed her head to pray. It was the only thing her heart and mind could agree on doing at the moment.

·

Jeb knocked on her door several times before she answered. His smile disappeared when he saw her anguished face. "Kitty, what's the matter? What happened?"

"Bill was here," she said, waving distractedly. "Everything is a mess." She turned and walked back into the house and he assumed he was to follow since she left the door open.

He followed her into the kitchen and watched her fix them each a soda on autopilot. She went to the pot simmering on the stove and ladled out two bowls of beef stew which she set down on the table. He sat, watching as she moved listlessly to fetch silverware and napkins. She was completely out of sorts.

"Kitty, honey, what is it? What's wrong?" He reached across the table when she finally sat and took her hand in his, squeezing it reassuringly.

"Bill wants us to get re-married. Try again. Just like that."

Jeb felt like he was on a roller coaster ride and his stomach just bottomed out. "Married? Is that what you want?"

"I don't know what I want," she half yelled, half cried. "How am I supposed to know what to do now?"

"It's pretty simple. Do you love him?"

"It's not that simple."

"It is. Do you love him? Yes or no."

She rubbed her brow. "I don't think so."

"You don't think so," he repeated. "Love is pretty cut and dry. Take me for example. I just rushed over here because I realized that this stupid game we've been playing is wreaking havoc on my life. I care about you Kitty. No. That's not what I came here to say." Jeb took a deep breath. "I love you Kitty. I know it's fast. I know it's crazy. But there it is. I thought that maybe you felt that way too." He couldn't hold on to the anger when he felt defeated now. He should have never gone along with the pretense of caring when he knew his heart could end up broken. But it was too late now. Jeb let out a long slow breath. "I should have known you really were just pretending the whole time. It's what you wanted from the start."

"No Jeb. That isn't the case. I care for you. So much," she croaked. "But I don't know what to do."

"Make a decision," he demanded irrationally.

"I'm not sure what the right one is anymore. I can't help but wonder if maybe Bill was brought back into my life for a reason."

She was torn up inside over this; he could see it if he looked through his own pain. "I'm sorry Kitty. You just hit me with this and I don't know what I'm supposed to do with it either. I only know how I feel about you and I don't want to see you suffering. What can I do to help?"

She let the tears come. "Will you pray with me?"

"Yes."

They held each other's hands and bowed their heads.

•

Kitty didn't sleep at all that night. She felt like she was being torn in two and even reading the Bible didn't seem to help. Praying with Jeb was bittersweet. She loved that he was willing to do that with her and honestly seek God's wisdom in this matter. Having a partner to pray with was a blessing she never had and yearned for but if God didn't want her with Jeb then it was a special bonding that she wouldn't be able to share with him again.

Since she felt lost and completely unsure what to do she decided to seek out Reverend Moore. She had known him since she was a girl and trusted him with her heart in this matter. He was in his office and ushered her in immediately when he saw the state she was in.

"Sit Kitty, and tell me what it is that has you so troubled."

She poured out the whole story, even explaining the nature of her relationship with Jeb and what it had progressed into. "It was all so clear when Jeb and I started seeing each other and the rules were in place. But then I started to care for him. And now Bill is back in my life and he seems different. He's changed," she admitted. "Not a lot. But some. The very fact that he's even willing to take those first few steps is astonishing to me. I prayed so hard and for so long that we would be reconciled. I didn't care about my pride or what he did. I just wanted my husband back."

"Do you believe Bill loves you the way a husband is supposed to love his wife?" he asked candidly.

"No," Kitty answered softly. "But he might learn to."

"Love isn't supposed to hurt," Reverend Moore spoke kindly. "And loving Bill before hurt you."

"Yes," Kitty sniffled, dabbing at her eyes with a tissue.

"How do you truly feel about Bill? Be honest with yourself Kitty."

"I do care about him. How could I not? When I think about the vows we made and broke it breaks my heart all over again. I never wanted that. He came home and told me he was leaving me for a woman he'd been having an affair with for ten months and no amount of begging would change that. He wouldn't listen, wouldn't consider counseling. But now that he's apologized and wants to try again I feel like it's the right thing to do. It doesn't even really matter how it's come about."

"I remember what you went through when he left," Reverend Moore sympathized. "It was a painful time for you."

"I meant the words 'till death do us part' when I said them in front of you and God all those years ago," Kitty said earnestly. "Divorce was not something I wanted and if it's God's plan is for me to go back to him then I will."

"Kitty, divorce isn't something that God wants for any of us. When Bill walked out on you he walked out on God too. Bill broke two hearts that day. But he made a choice and there wasn't anything that you or I could do to change it. That path led him further away from God. Now he's come back to you repenting and asking forgiveness. That's a fine step for him to take. But has Bill done the same with God? Is he trying to make it right with the Lord?"

"He offered to go to church with me."

"But has he confessed to God and asked forgiveness?"

"I don't think so." She hesitated to speak out loud her thoughts on the subject but now was the time for complete honesty. "It seems like he's only interested in religion to appease me."

"That is not the foundation of a successful, happy marriage Kitty. You already know that. It has to be based on Biblical principles, rooted in everything Jesus taught and blessed wholly by God. What Bill is offering you appears to be none of those things." He sat back in his chair. "I understand and respect that you want to honor your wedding vows. However, the Bible clearly teaches that we are not to be unequally yoked. It will put a heavy burden on you that you aren't designed to carry. And God doesn't give us these rules arbitrarily or to make our lives more difficult. He made them because He loves us and wants the best for us. They're to help guide us to make the right decisions when we face these tough choices. God is love and forgiveness Kitty but He expects obedience from His children."

"I suppose," Kitty said, her voice cracking, "that I still seek His forgiveness for my marriage failing. I know it's silly but it's true."

"Kitty child, God sees all the years and tears you put into that marriage. He heard the prayers you sent up to save it. *He doesn't blame you for Bill's actions*. He isn't angry with you. He loves you and I believe all He really wants is for you to trust Him with this. Your relationship with Him is ever so much more important than anything else. It is true that He will always want to see marriages reconciled; but I know that there are times and circumstances that He deems it acceptable to take a different path. A path that He opens up. If God himself has a new path chosen for you, there's no reason to look back at the road previously travelled. It means He has found another way to prosper and grow you."

"Then what I really need to do is to stop looking back and start looking forward. I need to trust God to show me where to go," Kitty said softly. She didn't need to make this decision alone. All she had to do was keep her eyes on Him. He would never take her somewhere she shouldn't be.

"You are not obligated in God's eyes to take your ex-husband back. In fact, it would be a contradiction of the scriptures since you are saved and he doesn't seem to be. But if Bill *is* saved and you feel led to take this journey with him seeking God first in all you do then this could be the brand new life He has waiting for you. I can't tell you which path to take Kitty. You need to seek God's will and trust He will answer you in his own time. And the best place to do that is down on your knees."

Kitty nodded. "I will."

Reverend Moore smiled kindly at the woman in front of him. "God has been holding your heart in His hand child the whole time. Continue to trust him with it and He will never lead you astray."

Chapter 23

Kitty spent a considerable amount of time praying over the next few days. She prayed while she cooked and cleaned and she prayed when she went for long walks along the beach. There was also a lot of time spent reading her Bible in the afternoons when the wind suddenly kicked up and brought with it torrential rains and one last cold spell before spring showed signs of staying for a while.

She didn't know how long it would take her to figure out what to do or how long it even should. Did God expect her to know immediately the right course of action or was it something that would slowly take root in her heart and bloom into reality over weeks or even months? She fretted over this until she decided to trust that God would give her peace and wisdom to discern when His timing was in place in this matter.

Sunday morning Kitty sat in church with Liza Jane and her children. Things were slowly getting back to normal, although it seemed people looked at her a bit differently now. As if they were actually seeing her for the first time. They nodded and spoke to her after the service like she was Somebody.

Kitty Appleton was no longer invisible.

Bill was sitting on her front steps when she came walking down the lane. Kitty opened the gate and shut it behind her slowly, trying to gauge her reaction to him. There was some apprehension but mostly there was relief to finally face her future. She trusted God would give her the right words now that she needed them.

He stood when she stopped just a few feet from him. "I know you said to wait for your call but I couldn't wait any longer."

Kitty studied the man before her. He was tall and strong and still very handsome. She understood why Leslie had been drawn to him, just as she had been a lifetime ago. But when she looked at him she saw past all the things that had appealed to her younger, naive self and saw the things that had troubled their marriage for years. His selfish nature. His lack of respect for her and the neglect in taking a role of leadership as a husband and father. And most importantly his lack of faith in Jesus Christ throughout their marriage. She simply couldn't live with those things in her life again. She didn't have to. "Bill, has your heart changed?"

"Changed? Of course it's changed. I told you I had feelings for you again. Or still. Either way I want to start over with you."

"I mean towards God. Do you know Jesus?"

"Not personally," he grumped. "But who does?"

"I do."

"Is this about going to church again? Because I already said I'm willing to go."

"It's more than that Bill."

"What do you mean?"

Kitty felt a lump in her throat. "You have to make amends to God before we could ever consider being together again. That's how a relationship works best."

"I see. I get what you want. You want me to get down on my knees and pray for forgiveness for my sins. Some kind of punishment for humiliating you right? Fine. I suppose I deserve that. But then that's it. We move forward. Agreed?"

She reached out to stop him from bending down. "Bill, stop. You don't understand. Don't do this for me. You can only do it for yourself."

"Kitty." He straightened up and frowned down at her, upset that she was making this more difficult than it ought to be. "I know I've made mistakes. I apologized and I meant it. You said you forgave me. Let's stop this nonsense and do what we're supposed to. You accepted me before like this so I don't think you have any reason to get all high and mighty just because you suddenly found religion."

"I've always had God in my life. I thought you did too when we got married. But if you ever did you slowly turned from Him, from me. I tried to keep the marriage going by myself but it was so hard Bill. It was exhausting and painful and I just don't have the strength in me to do that again. If I ever get married again I want a partner who believes the same thing I do and who will put their whole heart into it and in God. Can you promise me that?"

Bill considered her words. "I'm offering you all I can Kitty. Isn't that good enough?"

All along Kitty was willing to go back to this man who had hurt her and betrayed her if that was what God wanted. If Bill's heart had been reconciled to God. But his heart was still like stone and Kitty knew now without any doubt or fear or guilt that she did not have to go back to her ex-husband. God was setting her free. "Then no Bill, I can't marry you. I can't go back to what we were before."

The color actually drained from his face. Bill had been so sure the groveling he'd done would be enough. Apparently it wasn't. He was both resentful and strangely attracted to this strong side of Kitty. Maybe he needed to make more of an effort to win back this woman he kept seeing new and exciting things in. "If I pray then can I come back?"

"Oh Bill. You don't want to come back. You're just terrified of being alone."

"That's the stupidest thing I've ever heard. I could have any woman I want in town. You should feel lucky I chose to come home to you."

She spread her hand towards the road. "Then go pick one. Because I am no longer an option."

"You're a goose, you know that?" he said, wanting to hurt her now. Cursed woman. What right did she have to turn him away? He crawled back to her and offered her everything! "You're almost fifty and starting to wilt, Kitty. I see things are already starting to go. You really think you can do better than me?"

"Yes. I do." Being alone the rest of her life would be better than being with this man, she decided, squaring her shoulders. It may have taken a long time to understand it but now that she was on the other side of the fire she could see that God had walked her through this ordeal and made her stronger for it. Refined her and loved her through the whole process unlike the husband who had vowed to always cherish her. Whatever the future brought He would always be by her side. She didn't need or deserve a husband like Bill. No one did.

"The sheriff?!" Bill laughed. "He's nothing. I'm taller, smarter, stronger, better looking. I make more money than he does and I'm pretty sure I'm better at a lot of things." He narrowed his eyes. "You lied to me about sleeping with him, didn't you?"

"Get out," she ordered him softly. "Get out of my yard and my life. I don't love you anymore. If you should happen to come to your senses and realize there's more to life than *you*, you might start trying to repair the relationships with the three children you've been neglecting. But I'm done. All I have left for you are my prayers and my pity."

"But Kitty!" he exclaimed, feeling like the rug was just pulled out from under him. "What am I supposed to do now?"

"You wanted a life without me and God," Kitty said softly. "Now you have one." And she walked into her house, shutting the door firmly behind her.

∙

Bill closed the gate slowly and stood there gazing at her front door, his hand gripping the post. He stood that way for a long time, hoping Kitty would change her mind and come running after him. But she didn't come after him. She meant what she said.

He looked down the lane towards an empty life waiting for him in town and back at the door where he had hoped to find love and comfort. Despite his efforts he had failed miserably and now he was going to pay the price. Never in his life had Bill felt so utterly lost and alone. He was literally at Rock Bottom.

Bill raised his eyes to the sky, wondering who or what exactly was up there. Maybe Kitty was on to something after all. He had never really taken God or church seriously. It was just someplace he had to go on Sundays growing up. Now he wondered if maybe, possibly he had missed out on something. "Are you there?" Bill called softly and waited.

When no easy answer came he turned and started down the lane. "Nonsense," Bill muttered to himself. He'd go to the pub and have a drink instead. Yes, that's what he'd do. A drink would ease the pain. And there would be people to talk to and sympathy to be had. Bill Appleton didn't need God at all. He realized he'd be just fine as long as he could get rid of the dull ache in his heart with a few drinks.

∙

"You did it again!" Liza threw up her hands in exasperation. "You told off Bill and I missed it!"

They were sitting on Kitty's porch steps Sunday evening watching the sun makes its descent over Rock Bottom. There was a little chill in the air but they were Mainers and barely felt it.

"Sorry Liza. It didn't feel like a victory. Not really." Kitty still felt like she had done the right thing. But she was sad for Bill, for his inability to recognize the need for God in his own life and how it was affecting their children. Grown or not they needed a relationship with their father.

"Well what about Jeb? Have you talked with him yet?"

Kitty shook her head. "No. He went to Portland to visit his son for a few days. I only found that out when I went to see him at the station and Rob told me. Jeb didn't even tell me himself."

"You did put him off while you were thinking things through. Maybe he thought it would help you if he was out of the picture for a little while."

"Or maybe he changed his mind completely."

"All you have to do is wait till he gets back and then go talk to the man. I'm sure it will all work out. You deserve a good man in your life and I approve of Jeb Carpenter," Liza Jane told her. "You can tell he's a Godly man and will treat you right. He's nothing like Bill."

"You haven't liked Bill for years but you would never say why. Can you tell me now?"

Liza Jane took Kitty's hand and squeezed. "I never wanted to hurt you. That's why I didn't tell you."

"I think I need to know."

Liza Jane contemplated the sunset. "Bill tried to get me in bed once. It was right after you had Teddy. He said you weren't able to take care of him and he rather liked the idea of 'keeping it in the family' so to speak. I wanted to tell you but he begged me not to and promised it would never happen again. What a fool I was to believe him. I feel like I betrayed you."

"Oh Liza." Kitty hugged her best friend. "You goose."

"Do you forgive me? I should have told you back then but I didn't want to hurt you," Liza said quietly. "You had three beautiful children and seemed so happy. And he assured me he would never do it again. Who was I to ruin your happy world with one momentary indiscretion on his part?" She shook her head. "I should have seen what kind of a man he was right away but by the time I did I felt like it was too late. And the whole Leslie thing should have set off bells. I had my suspicions but never actually saw them together. I should have gone with my gut and confronted him. I'm so sorry Kitten for not having your back," she ended brokenly, resorting to her pet name for her best friend.

"I understand why you didn't tell me. I wish you had. But I do understand. I've forgiven myself and Bill. How can I not forgive you?" It didn't matter what had happened with Bill. Not anymore. The past was officially in the past.

"You are too forgiving for your own good," Liza scolded. But she gave Kitty a teary smile.

"We both have made some pretty dumb decisions over the years Liza. I'm not going to judge either of us."

"What dumb decision did I make?"

"Divorcing Harry."

"Really? You think that was dumb? Why didn't you tell me back then?"

"Because I was trying to be supportive. That's what friends do. But the love you two shared was so special. I wish you two could have worked things out back then."

"Me too," Liza whispered. "But that was a lifetime ago. You can't ever go back, can you?" she asked wistfully.

"Why can't you?" Kitty asked thoughtfully. "Why can't you try again?"

Liza Jane didn't admit that her heart had been wondering the same thing.

•

Monday evening Jeb was sitting on the driftwood bench overlooking the beach that he called his backyard. There was still enough light to easily see her making her way down the beach towards him and he felt a spurt of joy even though it was foolish. For days he'd tried to convince his heart it was folly to love a woman that wasn't meant to be his but it wouldn't listen. He had to trust that God was in control and whichever way it worked out was for the best.

He should have retreated inside but that was cowardly so he held his ground and watched her slow approach. Jeb realized she was going as slowly as possible, as if she too were dreading the conversation that was about to take place. His heart sank further and he tried to look impassive as she came upon him.

"Hi Jeb," she said in the soft easy voice he realized he could never tire of hearing.

"Kitty," he said, nodding an informal greeting.

"I didn't know you were back."

"Just got back an hour ago."

"I see." She put her hands in her pockets and looked down the beach, trying to figure out how to proceed.

The wind ruffled her hair and Jeb wanted to smooth it back. "How are you doing?"

His voice was polite and devoid of emotion. She wanted to retreat but neither her feet nor her heart would budge until she got an answer. "I'm fine."

"Good."

Kitty took a deep breath. All the times she had stood by and watched life pass her by were over. She was determined not to live that way anymore. Not after seeing how precious life was. "I lied. I'm not fine."

"What's the matter?"

"I miss you. I know we haven't known each other long but something happened after I met you. I changed. I like who I am when I'm with you. I'm happy. I'm secure. You make me feel special Jeb. And I've fallen in love with you. I'm tired of being boring, predictable Kitty all the time. Most of the time she's okay but sometimes I want to shake things up and take risks. And I think you're the best one I could ever take."

She stood there trying so hard to look strong and brave and really all he could see was how vulnerable she was deep down inside. He stood up, wary of the hope she was giving him. "What about Bill?"

Kitty smiled tremulously. "Bill is completely out of my heart. You are the only one there."

"You're sure?"

"Absolutely one hundred percent sure."

Jeb stared over her shoulder at the miles of ocean. "Then I suppose there's only one thing to do since I've fallen in love with you." His eyes found Kitty. "I am officially done playing the part of your fake love interest. I want a more permanent role with full billing. But there's one thing you have to promise me."

"What?" Kitty asked, blinking back the tears of joy that were threatening to ruin the moment.

"You said before that when you're around me you can be yourself because there wasn't anything real at stake. Now that there is I don't want that to change. I want to keep getting to know the real you and vice-versa. We say what we really think about everything and disagree over where to eat and you tell me when I'm being a great big jerk. We pray about it and let God lead it where it goes." Jeb already knew exactly where *he* wanted it to go. He'd known since the first time he saw her on the beach she was the one for him and each moment spent with her since then only confirmed that. "Deal?"

Kitty offered him her hand and a lovely smile, complete with dimples. "Deal."

Jeb ignored her hand and instead pulled her to him to seal the deal with a proper kiss.

Epilogue

Jeb proposed on the Fourth of July at the town picnic under the fireworks. He wasn't the most romantic guy in the world but he did recognize the need to make an effort. And apparently he did fine because Kitty threw herself into his arms and told him *'yes!'* at least a dozen times as he tried to slip the ring on her finger.

They decided on an October wedding, simple and with minimal planning since it was only months away. The fall foliage would be a perfect backdrop on their wedding day and they could be happily settled into the cottage together before winter hit. Kitty was deliriously happy with the turn of events her life had taken and couldn't believe that God was blessing her with such a wonderful husband. She felt like they knew everything there was to know about each other and yet each day Jeb surprised her. They'd been counseled by Reverend Moore and everything had fallen into place as though the Lord had orchestrated it all from the very beginning. Kitty loved Jeb with her whole heart, she loved the pattern their life together was forming and she loved knowing that their marriage would be a marriage of three with God at the center of it.

Bill surprised them both and offered the Bottom's Up for the reception since he decided keeping it in the family was more important than any offer from Lionel Trescott. He seemed to be making an effort to be happy for Kitty and she was deeply appreciative. When the wedding day arrived the ceremony was perfect and afterwards the pub was filled to capacity with friends and family to wish them well on their new life together. It was close to perfection in Kitty's eyes. The only blemish on the day was Teddy's absence but she refused to let her errant son ruin the day. It was his choice not to be there and she couldn't change his mind. Her parents were there as well as Jeb's son Jeff with his wife and their new daughter along with Kitty's other three children and their families. They were all embracing this new chapter in Jeb and Kitty's lives and that was enough.

When it was time to leave the reception, Jeb fully expected to find Kitty's Volvo outside the church, packed with the few bags she had assured him that she could make do with. He honestly didn't care if she brought one bag or twenty as long as he finally got to be alone with his wonderful new wife. She grabbed his hand and pulled him out the front door of the Bottom's Up with their closest friends and family waving them off.

Jeb stepped outside into the gorgeous autumn afternoon and stopped, gawking at what was in front of him.

His Harley Davidson was parked directly in front of the door with his bag on it and next to it was another motorcycle. With Kitty's bag on it. He turned to his new wife with a bemused expression.

She was grinning like the Cheshire cat. "I wanted to surprise you. I thought I needed my own hog now that I'm married to a Harley Davidson man."

"You can drive that?" Jeb asked because it was the only thing that came to mind.

"I can. I took the course and have my motorcycle endorsement. Would you like to see my license Sheriff Carpenter?" Kitty was smiling up at with him with shining blue eyes and he felt humbled and blessed knowing she would be at his side for the rest of his days on this earth. She was stunningly beautiful to him both inside and out.

"There are a lot of things I'd like to see Mrs. Carpenter," he said just loud enough for her to hear as he pulled her close for a quick kiss. He was grinning rakishly and she flushed in surprise and pleasure. "And I suppose we could start with that."

The End

Dear Reader,

I hope you enjoyed this visit to Rock Bottom with Kitty and Jeb. I always enjoy stories about second chances and believe age doesn't matter when it comes to true love. It was fully my intention to make this a single stand-alone title when I began this story but as I started to get to know the characters I realized that some of them were demanding their own story! While I need to focus once again on The Sweet Life series, I foresee another visit to Rock Bottom in the distant future. I can't stand loose ends and Regina and Liza are most definitely loose ends! So I can safely say that there will be another title involving the Rock Bottom Mystery Book Club ladies and their quest for love. I also want to know if Charlotte ends up in public office and if Kitty and Jeb are still living in wedded bliss...well of course they are but I still want to see them anyway. In the meantime, keep reading and keep dreaming!

Blessings,

KLB